THE PLEASURE OF A KISS

She glanced up at him as he looked down at her. Before she had always been fascinated by his eyes, but now she noticed how well-shaped his lips were. His bottom lip was slightly larger than his top lip, but not so much that he appeared as if he was pouting.

What she really wanted to know was how his lips would feel on her lips. If only she could bring herself to stand on tiptoes and press her mouth to his. But even she was not that bold. There were some things that she must leave to him.

She felt herself move closer to him, and his arm went around her waist. Then his head bent, and his lips touched hers as if they were a feather brushing gently.

Henrietta placed her hand on his jacket and slid them over his shoulders and around his neck. Fotherby pulled her closer, tilted his head, and deepened the kiss. Frissons of pleasure speared through her body, and she pressed closer . . .

Books by Ella Quinn

The Marriage Game
THE SEDUCTION OF LADY PHOEBE
THE SECRET LIFE OF MISS ANNA MARSH
THE TEMPTATION OF LADY SERENA
DESIRING LADY CARO
ENTICING MISS EUGENIE VILLARET
A KISS FOR LADY MARY
LADY BERESFORD'S LOVER
MISS FEATHERTON'S CHRISTMAS PRINCE
THE MARQUIS SHE'S BEEN WAITING FOR

The Worthingtons
THREE WEEKS TO WED
WHEN A MARQUIS CHOOSES A BRIDE
IT STARTED WITH A KISS
THE MARQUIS AND I
YOU NEVER FORGET YOUR FIRST EARL
BELIEVE IN ME

The Lords of London
THE MOST ELIGIBLE LORD IN LONDON
THE MOST ELIGIBLE VISCOUNT IN LONDON
THE MOST ELIGIBLE BRIDE IN LONDON

Novellas
MADELEINE'S CHRISTMAS WISH
THE SECOND TIME AROUND
I'LL ALWAYS LOVE YOU

Published by Kensington Publishing Corp.

The Most
ELIGIBLE
BRIDE
in
LONDON

ELLA
QUINN

ZEBRA BOOKS
KENSINGTON PUBLISHING CORP.
www.kensingtonbooks.com

First Printing: March 2022
ISBN-13: 978-1-4201-4971-5
ISBN-13: 978-1-4201-4972-2 (eBook)

10 9 8 7 6 5 4 3 2 1

Printed in the United States of America

CHAPTER ONE

Ouse Tower, Bedfordshire
March 1819

Padraig, Nathanael, Viscount Fotherby's Irish Wolfhound, opened one eye and closed it again when the knock came on the study door. Nate glanced up from the planting scheme he'd been reviewing. "Yes, Hulatt, what is it?"

"Mr. Beamish, the runner you hired, wishes to speak with you. He says it's urgent." The tenor of the butler's voice clearly indicated he disapproved of the visitor. What Hulatt had against the man, Nate didn't know.

But why Beamish had come all the way here . . . unless . . . "I'll see him."

"As you wish, my lord." The door shut behind Hulatt.

They'd had false starts before, but if Beamish had indeed found the girl, it would all have been worth it.

Several moments later the door opened again and the runner was shown in. The man was about average height, with straight, medium-brown hair and eyes to match. Someone that no one would particularly notice. He'd been recommended as the best at finding people gone missing, but this had taken much longer than any of them thought it would.

He stood in front of Nate's desk. "Please have a seat. I take it that you are certain this time."

"Yes, my lord. She is at a workhouse under her own name. There's no mistake." The man folded his lips under. "There is also a babe."

Nate leaned back in his chair. "I cannot say that is surprising. Which workhouse is she in?"

"That's more good news. She went to Whitechapel. It ain't as bad as some others. Still, I'd fetch her soon if that's what you're intending on doing."

Beamish was right. Whitechapel wasn't nearly as bad as St Giles or Seven Dials, nor was it the best of neighborhoods. Nate glanced at the clock. It was already past four in the afternoon. "I take it you plan to spend the night."

"Yes, my lord. I have a room at the inn at Ouse Run. I took the mail coach as soon as I confirmed it was her."

"Is she in good health?" That would determine how soon they could bring her home. If she'd agree to come.

"She's skinny." Beamish didn't beat around the bush. "And she won't put on any flesh there."

"Thank you. Mr. Odell might wish to speak with you after I tell him we've found her." Odell's eldest son was to have married Miss Bywater, but he died before the ceremony could take place. Then she had disappeared. When her parents refused to discuss her, he'd come to Nate asking for assistance in finding her.

"I'll keep an eye out for him." The runner stood. "I hired a carriage in Bedford and plan on catching the mail back to London."

"I might be able to provide your transportation. It won't be as fast."

"Thank you, my lord, but I need to get back as soon as possible." The man bowed. "Let me know if I can be of further assistance."

"I will. Thank you."

Hulatt, hovering in the corridor, saw Mr. Beamish out, then returned to the study. "I took the liberty of sending for Mr. Odell."

"Thank you. It appears that I'll be going to Town to-morrow. Please let the coachman know." Nate glanced around the room that had at first been his prison, but for a few years now was his refuge. The trim, shelves, and cabinets were all dark, almost black, ash. A year after he had been sent back to the country, he'd had the blue walls covered with cream-colored silk, with curtains to match. It had given the study a lighter feel.

He rose from the chair. "Do you know if my mother is here?"

"She is in her parlor, my lord."

Nate nodded. "Thank you." Once his butler left, he opened the door to his secretary's office. "I'm traveling to Town in the morning. Please have anything I need to work on ready to go, and make arrangements for all the correspondence to be sent to Fotherby House. You will follow me as soon as you are ready. Bring Padraig as well."

"As you wish, my lord." If Chetwin was surprised, he didn't show it. Then again, one of the reasons Nate had hired him when he'd had to retire the old secretary was his unflappable nature and good sense.

He closed the door. He didn't wish to go to the metrop-olis at all, but needs must. Miss Bywater must be dealt with, and it was time he retook his place in the Lords and in Polite Society. In addition to that, he was approaching his twenty-ninth birthday, and it was past time he found a wife. That decision would make his mother happy, but he dreaded returning to the bosom of the *ton*.

He took his time tracing the familiar way to the hall and up the stairs to his mother's parlor. Before knocking on the door, he took a breath. Once he had committed to this plan of action, she wouldn't let him reverse course. Nor did he need to. Among his duties and responsibilities was marrying and filling his nursery.

"Come." His mother placed her open book on her lap, glanced at him, and smiled. "What a pleasant surprise. I did not expect to see you until dinner."

He stepped forward and bussed the cheek she offered. "We have found Miss Bywater. I depart for Town tomorrow." Her sharp turquoise eyes, eyes the same color as his, searched his face. "I shall remain for the Season."

She nodded in approval. "I am glad you are finally ready. Four years is long enough."

"It is, but you and I both know it was necessary." Remembering himself then and looking at himself now, Nate was amazed at how much he'd changed. How much he had needed to change. "When will you leave?"

"In a few days." She put her book on the small, round cherry table next to her chaise. "I shall plan several entertainments this Season. Possibly even a ball."

Surmising that this was for his benefit, Nate inclined his head. "Very well. I'll take the traveling coach, but will send it back for you."

"Thank you. I might want to purchase my own coach this Season." It was clear she hoped he'd marry.

"We have plenty of time to discuss that later. I should go back downstairs. I expect Mr. Odell to arrive shortly."

"I shall see you at dinner."

"Until then."

He reached his study shortly before his butler came to announce Odell. The older man appeared to be on tenterhooks, but one could hardly blame him. When Nate waved Odell to take a seat, he took the same chair the runner had occupied. "I take it we're sure it's her?"

"Yes. She is at the Whitechapel workhouse under her own name." Hulatt brought a tea tray and Nate poured. "We should depart early tomorrow morning. I have horses posted along the Great North Road to London." He handed a cup to Mr. Odell. "The runner said she was very thin. I propose we bring my older traveling coach so that you can ride back in that."

"No need, my lord. We have our own coach. If you'll permit me to travel with you, my coach can follow with my wife."

Nate smiled to himself. The man was a gentleman farmer, thus not gentry, and would not allow himself to be any more beholden to Nate than he had to. "If that will suit you better. There is one other thing." Mr. Odell glanced up. "There is a child. I do not know the state of its health."

Odell's lips pressed together. "I can't say I'm surprised. If the good Lord hadn't taken my son so soon, they would've been wed before he died. We'll take them both and be glad for it. The babe is the only thing left of my boy."

"Meet me here at sunrise." The faster they reached London, the safer Miss Bywater would be.

The man rose with more energy than he'd had when he'd come in. "That I will."

Nate came out from behind his desk and offered his hand, which Mr. Odell took and shook heartily. "I'm glad we found her."

"And we're more than glad for your help." Although

Odell didn't smile, his eyes held a spark of hope. "Good country air and food will see them both right."

"Will you tell Bywater?" The families had been cordial at one time.

"I can't think of a good reason why I should." Odell's jaw jutted out belligerently. "In fact, if Emily will let me, I'll adopt her. Change her name to Odell. Her and the child both. That's what my son would have wanted."

"Yes. I'm convinced you are correct." From attempting to persuade the local vicar to marry the couple even though the last banns had not been read to obtaining a special license, which they had been denied due to their status, the family had tried everything to see the couple wed before John Odell died. "Until tomorrow."

"Thank you again, my lord."

Nate saw him to the front door. A light rain had begun to fall, and he hoped it wouldn't go on for long. "Give your wife my greetings, and hurry home before you become too wet."

"I'll do that." Odell waved his arm. "No need to worry about me. I'll be fine."

Nate watched his neighbor leave the room. Offering to find the girl had been only one of his steps to redemption, and he was glad he'd done it. He did not even want to imagine what Miss Bywater's life and that of her child would be like if they had not been found.

The next morning dawned cold but clear. That in itself was a blessing insomuch as it meant the roads wouldn't be mired in mud. Padraig followed Nate to the door. "I'm sorry, boy, but you can't come this time." He rubbed the wiry fur on the dog's head. "I'll see you in a few days." Mr.

and Mrs. Odell were waiting for him when Nate stepped outside. "I would have been happy to offer you tea."

"Don't I know it, my lord," Mrs. Odell, a plump, good-hearted woman said. "But we've broken our fast, and I packed a flask of tea. You two get on your way, and I'll follow. I don't know how far behind you I'll be, us not having bloodstock like yours, but if you tell me where to meet you, I'll be there as soon as I can be."

She'd most likely fall a good distance behind them. But the carriage appeared to be well sprung, and if the horses weren't matched bays, they were still sweet-goers. "Go to Fotherby House on Grosvenor Street. We'll meet you there." Nate wished he could offer a change of cattle at the posting inns, but because only his mother had been making the journey, he wasn't sure there was more than one team at each stop. "Let's be off." He bowed to Mrs. Odell. "If you allow, I'll arrange for your changes when we stop. It will be faster that way."

"Now that I'll accept." Her green eyes sparkled with happiness. "The sooner we get there and fetch our girl and the babe, the happier I'll be."

He said a brief prayer that both the woman and the child were in good health and able to make the trip home. It was only then that a thought occurred to him. "I'm an idiot. I must send my coach back for my mother. There is no reason you should take yours when you can ride back in mine."

Mrs. Odell shook her head. "Thank you for the offer. But if Emily or the child are doing poorly, we might have to take a few days more to return."

"It was just a thought." It was frustrating to want to do more and not be allowed to.

"And a good one." Mrs. Odell smiled. "I'll say farewell now. Have a good journey."

"You too." He climbed into his traveling carriage.

Mr. Odell kissed his wife and joined Nate. They followed the Odell coach out of the drive to the main road, but quickly overtook it.

The sun was still up, but low in the sky when they approached the workhouse that afternoon. They'd made good time to the metropolis, stopping only for changes. Nate had had his cook pack sufficient food in a large basket so they didn't have to waste time halting to eat.

"I'll tell you, my lord, I never could abide London. It's the smell." Odell watched out the window as they pulled up in front of the long brick building.

Well, this wasn't the most salubrious area of Town. Still, the degradation of Whitechapel surprised Nate. And he was certain most people wouldn't want to be walking around here at night.

The coach door opened and a footman let the steps down. "Do you want me to come in with you? Just until they allow you to see her? I have no idea what the protocol is."

The older man frowned. "That might be a good idea. I suppose they won't deny a peer much of anything."

"No, I believe you are correct." As sad a state of affairs that was, at least Nate would be able to speed things along. "As soon as you're with her, I'll come back out here and wait."

Odell inclined his head. "Thank you."

The soot-covered building stretched down the street in both directions, with one arched entrance in the middle. Men, women, and children were held in a queue waiting to be admitted to the single entrance. There was a time when Nate would not have thought anything of walking straight in ahead of everyone else, but the last four years had humbled him. Still, he was a peer of the realm and had some rights. He slid a look at his companion. Dressed in his good wool jacket and breeches, Odell would still no doubt be made to wait in a queue.

Taking his cane, Nate descended from the coach. "Go to the door and announce me."

"Yes, my lord." The footman hurried away to do as he was bid while Nate waited for Mr. Odell. "Stay beside me, if you will."

Odell stared at the long queue. "I begin to think it's a good thing you're with me, my lord."

Nate allowed himself a small grin. "We peers are good for something every now and again."

The other man flushed. "My lord, you know I meant no—"

"I am not at all insulted. Come, let's find your daughter." He strode up the steps and reached the door as it opened. A man attempted to stop Mr. Odell, but Nate waved him away. "It is on his business we are here."

By the time they entered the hall, his footman was speaking with a thin, stern-looking woman whose mobcap almost covered all the steel-gray curls at her forehead. "Here is his lordship now." His footman bowed. "My lord, this is Mrs. Rankin."

Nate handed the woman his card. "I am Fotherby. My companion, Mr. Odell, is here to take Miss Bywater and her child home." Mrs. Rankin, a hatchet-faced woman of middle years, frowned. "We have been searching for her since she left and were only yesterday apprised of her location. Mrs. Odell is waiting at my home for her."

"If you will wait in here"—she opened the door to a small, plainly furnished parlor—"I shall fetch her, my lord."

A young maid brought in a meager tea tray and set it

down on the only table in the room. Nate went over and poured, adding sugar and thin, bluish milk to the cups.

Odell took his cup. "If all they have is this, no wonder my girl is too thin."

Several minutes later the door opened, and Emily Bywater entered the room. Nate had seen her once or twice before John died. London had not been kind to her. Her once-golden hair was dull and her complexion almost ashen.

"Emily." Odell didn't wait to be greeted before enveloping her in his arms. "We've been looking for you for an age. Mrs. Odell is here, or will be soon. We're taking you back home with us where you and the babe belong."

"I can't. My father—"

"We won't have anything to do with him unless you want to." He stepped back. "John would have wanted you with us."

Tears streamed down Emily's face, but she nodded her head as she made an attempt to wipe her face.

Nate had stayed by the door and now slipped out, leaving the pair alone. Unsurprisingly, Mrs. Rankin was still in the hall. "Please have the child brought down. My footman will collect Miss Bywater's belongings."

Once his footman and the servant had gone, Nate stepped out into the growing gloom as a black town coach passed. As he glanced back at the door to the building two feelings competed within him. A sense of satisfaction that he'd been able to help the Odells and frustration that he could not help more people. Yet, perhaps he could do more. There must be many charities that would accept his assistance.

CHAPTER TWO

Merton House, Grosvenor Square, Mayfair, London

"Miss, what should we do?" the messenger, a young boy named Toby they had hired for messages and odd jobs, asked Miss Henrietta Stern.

"Where is Mrs. Perriman?" She and her sister, Dotty, Marchioness of Merton, had assisted in the rescue of many children and infants during the time Henrietta had been in Town for her first Season. However, due to her sister's pregnancy, they had asked Mrs. Perriman, the widow and daughter of army officers, who ran their charity, the Phoenix House, to perform the rescues. Normally Henrietta would not have hesitated, but she had never gone alone before.

"She's out on another call, and I don't know when she'll be back." The lad bounced from one foot to the other, clearly distraught. "The boy who brought the message said the baby's mam died and the babe was poorly."

There was only one thing to do. "I shall go." Henrietta had read the short, barely literate note stating the sender had a baby they were willing to sell. "We'll need to have a wet nurse brought here."

"Miss Henrietta." Parkin, her brother-in-law's butler's eyes rounded. "Neither her ladyship nor his lordship would approve."

"It's not as if I am going to St Giles or worse. It is still light and will be for the next hour. If we do not rescue this child now, it may die." The butler's stern countenance did not change. "I'll take Cullen with me." He was the largest of all Merton's tall footmen. Henrietta suspected the man had been a soldier at one time, as many of the footmen were. "I shall be perfectly safe." She would also take the Manton pistol that had been made for her.

"You will need a groom as well," the butler said.

Henrietta stifled a sigh of relief. Parkin was not happy about this, but he would not stop her. "Yes, of course. Thank you."

By the time she had changed into a sturdy, dark-blue wool serge gown she'd had made by the modiste at home, donned a plain bonnet, tucked her pistol in the pocket she'd had sewn into her mantle, and taken the coins needed from the strongbox kept for the purpose, the unmarked town coach was waiting in the street. "The address is just down from the Whitechapel workhouse. We must hurry. I do wish to be there and gone before it is dark."

"Yes, miss." The footman, now dressed in regular clothing, closed the coach door behind her, and the coach dipped as he climbed on the back.

The journey would take about a half hour, and the sun was already lower in the sky than she would have liked. Still, the chance to save another child was worth the risk, and she had three servants with her. Granted, two would remain with the coach. Still, Cullen would be enough to keep her safe.

A large traveling coach almost blocked the street, but they slid past the vehicle and pulled up on the other side of the road. It was still light enough, but the sun was sinking by the minute. The narrow street and tall buildings did not help.

The coachman opened the hatch in the roof. "The street we want is just ahead on the left."

The footman opened the door and helped her out. "I'll stay a bit behind you just in case they're up to no good."

"Thank you." That was always a risk. It did not happen often, and never in Whitechapel. But once in a while, the person purporting to have a child to sell decided he would be better served by having a lady to ransom. That was when she and her sister began carrying pistols every time they went on a rescue. The footman would remain just far enough back that no one would be able to attack her from behind.

Although it wasn't always or even mostly men selling the children. Many times women, unable or unwilling to care for a baby, gave them up, but never without payment. The worst cases were when Henrietta could smell the gin on the poor babe's breath. There was always a fight to get the child healthy again.

She touched the outside of the pocket, feeling the pistol, and carried the reticule with the coins in her other hand. Normally, she was excited to be picking up a child, but today the back of her neck prickled and made her more alert. Why were these exchanges always in narrow streets or alleys? "I'm ready."

Henrietta started off down the street, not striding quickly, but walking cautiously, taking care to be aware of her surroundings. The daily queue going into the workhouse had dwindled, and the rest of the street was almost empty of people. For a second she almost turned back, but a child was at risk, and she had to help it. Still, she refused to shake off her sense of foreboding. The worst thing she could do was ignore any feelings of danger.

She turned the corner into a street so narrow the houses on each side almost met in the middle. Two men were a few doors down, standing on the pavement. Dressed in worn jackets and breeches, neither man was above-average height, and both of them had dark-blond hair. They looked to be in their thirties, but could have been younger. One of them held a bundle in the shape of a swaddled babe.

Not glancing back, Henrietta continued forward until she was about six feet from them, just out of arm's reach. She made sure to use the type of accent from where she lived in the country. "I've come from the charity house to collect the baby."

"Let's see the bit," the man holding the baby said. The bundle in his arm didn't move at all.

"It's in here." She lifted the sack for them to see it. "Let me see the child and you shall have it."

"I think we might just take you instead of the money." The other man leered at her.

Henrietta slipped her hand into her pocket and wrapped her fingers around the pistol butt. "I think not. I came for a babe. If that is what you have with you."

The man tossed the bundle up and down, and there was a weak cry. "It's a lullaby cheat all right."

They wanted her to panic. No, they were attempting to make her panic *and* reach out for the infant. "The child for the money. That's the only deal on offer." It was almost full dark now. "And it had best be immediately."

The man with the infant stopped tossing it, but the other man reached out toward her.

"Miss, behind you!" Cullen snapped, and she heard a scuffle.

Henrietta put her back against a building and whipped out her pistol, drawing back the hammer as she did, and pointed it at the man approaching her. "I gave you a choice."

"Here, take it." The man holding the babe tossed it in her direction as the other man lunged at her.

She shot the man reaching for her, then tried to catch the child, but someone else was ahead of her.

"I've got it," a man said.

She heard the satisfying sound of bones crunching. He couldn't be Cullen, but who was he? The blackguard who'd tried to grab her was on the ground holding his stomach, crying. His accomplice had fled. When she turned, Cullen had knocked out a third criminal. Finally, Henrietta glanced at the gentleman—for he had not been disguising his voice—who held the babe and caught her breath. Even in the dim light, he was magnificent. He was taller than average. His legs were encased in pantaloons that appeared to have been sewn on him, and highly shined boots. His broad chest and shoulders were covered by a dark-colored jacket. His hair appeared to be black, but it could have been dark brown. And if she couldn't make out his eye color, she could see the compassion in them.

She dropped the bag of coins next to the scoundrel Cullen had knocked out. "Thank you, sir."

He stared at her for a few moments, then shook his head as if to clear his vision. "I am afraid I can't stay and deal with the constable." He glanced behind him. "In fact, I must go. There are others waiting for me. I am helping a neighbor recover his daughter."

Henrietta could not imagine what Merton would say if she became involved with the law. Whatever it was, it would not be good. "I will only remain if one comes before I depart. Otherwise, my brother-in-law will take care of it."

The gentleman seemed to think about that before saying, "I see your point." He held out his arm. "Would you allow me to escort you to your coach? It's on my way."

"Yes. Thank you." The tension that had coiled within her during the fight fled, and she smiled. "I would appreciate that." Henrietta placed her hand on his arm, and immediately her fingers started to tingle, as if they had been cold before and were now being warmed. She glanced up at him as he was looking down at her. He smiled a bit shyly, and she returned his smile. He carried the baby tucked in his other arm as if he had a lot of experience carrying children.

Cullen followed behind them until they reached the larger street, then dashed ahead to open the carriage door. Henrietta was glad to see there was not a constable in sight. She'd put her pistol back in her pocket, but her hand still clutched the butt. She had never shot another person before, and she had no idea whether or not she'd killed the scoundrel. He deserved to be shot, but, eventually, all of it was bound to affect her somehow.

The gentleman stopped in front of the coach door. "I wish you a better evening than the one you have had thus far."

"I hope you prosper in what you are doing." In the coach lights, she could see that although he was dressed neatly, his clothes had not been made by any of the London tailors, nor were they in the latest fashion.

He glanced at the other coach and his lips tilted up. "I think that is going very well indeed."

She dropped her hand from his arm. "Thank you again, and farewell."

He started to turn and stopped. "I am glad I was able to help you."

Henrietta's heart started to beat harder. "As am I."

He was staring at her again and opened his mouth, but closed it again, then said, "Perhaps we will meet again."

What had he been going to say? She slid a glance at the large traveling carriage. He was probably returning to the country. The chances of them meeting again were slim. "I would like that."

"I suppose you want the babe."

"Yes, of course. That is the reason I am here." Henrietta could not believe she had almost forgotten the child. The poor thing was so quiet.

"Please, allow me to assist you." He handed her into the carriage and, once she was settled, gave her the baby.

"Thank you."

"It was my pleasure." He lingered while Henrietta wrapped the child in a flannel blanket. "I must go."

"I as well." He walked away, and she turned her attention to the child, wondering how badly off the infant was. If only there was something she could do before she arrived at Merton House, but there was nothing. The babe needed to be fed. Only then would she know if a doctor needed to be fetched. Fortunately, they had a good one they could call upon at any time. Another former military man.

The coach lights were lit on the traveling coach, and she could see an older man and a girl who looked to be about the same age as she was in the other coach, gazing out the window, waiting for the gentleman. He had said he

was helping a neighbor. She hoped they did not have far
to travel this evening.

The coach started forward and turned around to face
the way they had come in. Henrietta looked back, but she
was on the wrong side of the carriage to see him well. It
was a shame he would not be one of the gentlemen she
met this Season.

The baby began to whimper, and she hugged it close to
her. He or she was too light and too cold, yet still it lived.
"Not long now, sweetie, and you will be fed. From now on
your life will be much better. I promise you that."

Fortunately, it was the time of day where traffic had
lightened and the drive home didn't take as long. Once
they arrived, Cullen opened the door, and she handed him
the baby, then descended the steps by herself before taking
the child again. "It needs to be fed immediately."

The footman nodded, rushed up the steps, and had
raised his hand to the door knocker when it opened. Parkin
stood in the doorway. "The wet nurse is waiting."

"Good. I will take the babe up straightaway." Henrietta
decided not to wait for Nurse's assessment of the child.
"Fetch the doctor."

"Yes, miss." Cullen strode down the steps.

Henrietta grabbed a fistful of her skirts and raced up
the stairs to the nursery as quickly as possible with the
child in her arms. Her heart pounded as she handed over
the child. "I fear this one's health is in danger."

Mrs. Roberts, the wet nurse, took the babe. "If it'll nurse,
that's half the battle."

She slipped down the blanket, exposing a pale head with
fine white hair, and set the babe to her breast. Henrietta
closed her eyes and prayed the poor little thing would eat.

"There you go, precious," Mrs. Roberts said. Thank God. Henrietta swiped at a tear that had somehow got into her eyes. "You can leave it with me now. We'll find out what we have when I'm done."

"Thank you." She blinked the other tears back. "I was afraid I was too late."

The other woman smiled. "Not this time."

CHAPTER THREE

Henrietta made her way to her rooms and stared out the window into the dark garden below, letting the tears flow down her cheeks. Not, she decided, for the man she might have killed. But for the innocent child they had used to try to get to her. She almost dismissed their actions as chance, but there had been three of them, and one of the black-guards had been hiding. Had they done something like this before, abducted a woman coming for a baby? Her sister's charity was not the only one attempting to save children by offering payment for them. The conditions so many of the poor suffered were heartbreaking. Henrietta couldn't imagine having to give up a child. But many of them would not live to see out their first year, and for those who did, their lives held little hope. If only the government would pass laws to help. She knew Merton and his friends tried. New workhouses were being planned. Yet she could not think that was enough. Something, some sort of major reform, had to occur. But what?

Henrietta gave herself a shake. Until she or someone else came up with a scheme, she could only support the work they were doing. At least the children they saved would have better lives.

A household maid entered the room, and lights flared and the fire was built up. "I'll have everything ready in no time, miss." Her lady's maid handed her a cup of tea. "Mr. Parkin just informed me you were back. I thought you could use a nice cup of tea. The doctor arrived before his lordship and her ladyship."

"Thank you." Henrietta wiped the tears away and gratefully drank the tea. As soon as Merton found out about the trouble, he would want to have a "talk" with her. She supposed she should tell him first. "Thank you for telling me, Spyer. Where is his lordship?"

"They're both in the nursery." Spyer handed Henrietta a damp cloth. "Best to catch them when they're with Lady Vivienne."

That was a true statement. Merton doted on his three-year-old daughter. By this time next year, there would be a second child. "I'll go now."

Henrietta retraced her way back to the nursery, heading to the other end, where her niece, Vivienne, had her rooms. A fire burned, warming the cozy bedroom that had been painted the color of butter to brighten it. Only a few candles remained lit and a nursery maid was cleaning up the remnants of her niece's dinner. Dotty was sitting in a bedroom chair gently rocking her daughter, but gazing at her husband as she did so. Cyrille, Merton's Chartreux cat, sat on the floor leaning against one of Merton's boots as he lounged in the chair next to Dotty's, reading a book to the little girl.

After the maid left, knowing better than to interrupt reading time, Henrietta leaned against the doorpost and listened. The nursery maid came in again and warmed the sheets of Vivienne's bed. Soon the little girl's eyes drooped, then shut, and when her breathing was even, Dotty placed her in her bed and pulled the covers over the child.

As she stood, her eyes caught Henrietta's, and traveled down to the gown she had not taken the trouble to change. "I take it there is something you wish to tell us?"

Straightening, Henrietta nodded. "There is a baby down the corridor. However, there was some trouble when we fetched her."

Dotty's lips flattened. "Where was Mrs. Perriman?"

"Out seeing to another child." Henrietta related what Toby had told her.

Her sister motioned at the sleeping girl and went into the corridor. "Was it necessary for you to go immediately?"

"According to the message I received, yes. Even Parkin agreed I should go. I took Cullen with me."

Merton, who had taken time to put the book back on a shelf, joined them. "Let's look in on our new guest first. Then we can discuss it."

They met the doctor leaving the room the baby was in. "One of the nursemaids is bathing her. She has sores all over her body." He grimaced. "Bites of some sort, I imagine. And she is severely malnourished. You are lucky you got her when you did. She would not have lived much longer."

For Henrietta, hearing that made it all worthwhile. "Thank you, Doctor."

He bowed to them. "I'll be back in two days to look in on her." His face lost some of its seriousness. "Perhaps by then you'll have a name for her."

"Deciding on a name will be much more fun than worrying about her health," her sister said.

They entered the room and watched as Nurse rubbed

salve on the bites. Henrietta shuddered. How anyone could allow that to happen to any child, especially one so young, she could not comprehend.

"It appears you were right to go and get her," Dotty said.

Merton nodded in agreement.

Henrietta dearly wanted to hold the baby, but she knew better than to allow herself to become attached. She'd done that once before, and it had broken her heart to have to give the child up. No more holding infants except when they were being rescued. No more feeding and playing with them. Now she forced herself to keep her hands and arms and heart to herself.

They repaired to Merton's study, where she made herself comfortable on the plush leather chair. Her sister sat on the sofa.

Merton handed them glasses of wine before joining his wife. "Tell us exactly what happened."

She told him the complete story. "We were lucky the gentleman came along."

The whole time she had given her account, she could feel her sister's eyes on her. Dotty took a sip of wine. "It is a shame we do not know who he is."

"I doubt we ever will." Henrietta had the same wish, but knew it would never be realized. He could live anywhere in the country. "I expect he will depart for his home by tomorrow."

She was glad she'd gone, but she was pretty sure today was the last time she would be allowed to go alone.

Merton cleared his throat. "We can't depend upon the intervention of helpful strangers. I shall have to ensure that more than one footman is available to assist you if this occurs again." He gave her a pointed look over his glass. "However, I do not want you to make a habit of it. This is just the sort of thing gossips will latch on to. I will also see about hiring someone to assist Mrs. Perriman."

Henrietta had not considered the possibility of gossip. Part of her wanted to protest, say she did not care, but being involved in a scandal was never pleasant. "You are right, of course."

He gave Dotty a smug smile, and she stared at the ceiling. "Please do not tell him that too often. It took his mother and me a long time to convince him even he was fallible."

Henrietta grinned. She had heard how stuffy Merton had been before falling in love with her sister. "I shall endeavor not to." Setting down her glass, she rose. "I suppose I should change for dinner."

"We shall see you in the drawing room," Merton said.

"Until then." Henrietta wondered what would happen if it got around that she had rescued a child without her sister or brother-in-law being present.

Her parents would be proud of her, especially her father. But he was probably the exception rather than the rule. Papa had been a vicar before his elder brother died, leaving him the baronetcy. And he had what some considered to be radical views on what reforms should be made to help others. He did not even believe the peerage should exist. Yet that brought up an interesting point when it came to any gentleman she might wed. Whoever the gentleman was, he would have to agree that she could remain involved in her sister's charitable work, even if it meant rescuing children herself. That alone was bound to limit the number of men she could consider. Her thoughts drifted back to the gentleman who had assisted her. Unfortunately, there was no point thinking about him. If he was not already on the road out of London, he soon would be.

* * *

Nate glanced back over his shoulder, but the lady's coach was already turning around. When she'd first faced him with her brows imperiously raised, he'd thought she was Dotty Stern, but that was impossible. Miss Stern had married the Marquis of Merton shortly after Nate had left Town four years before. Surely Merton would not allow his wife to engage in that type of activity. Also, the lady looked like Miss Stern had four years ago.

Whoever she was, she was beautiful. Her hair was as black as night, and her eyes appeared as if they might be light. But what struck him most was her courage. He'd never met a female who had so little fear of using a weapon to shoot a man. Yet even though she was a lady—a fact that had been clear once she'd abandoned her country accent—she was not dressed like a female who would be attending the Season. The cloth was good enough, but the styling was not that of a London modiste. At one time, when he'd been a well-known Dandy, those things had actually mattered to him. He was still able to recognize the differences, but he didn't care about them anymore. Now, he was much more interested in the person instead of the way they dressed.

Yet, because he was a gentleman and she was a lady, he could not insult her by introducing himself. That was unfortunate.

He hoped the infant lived. Most babes would have given a loud screech when tossed. This one had only a small, pathetic cry.

Her carriage traveled up the street at a smart pace, and he went around to the door of his coach and found

Mr. Odell, Miss Bywater, and her child already inside. "I see you are ready to leave."

"We are." Odell's smile was wider than Nate had ever seen it as he gazed at the infant in his arms. "Emily has agreed to be our daughter, just as if she and John had wed."

Emily's tears were gone and she too was smiling broadly. "From now on I am Emily Odell."

"What is the child's name?" Nate climbed into the coach.

"John for his father. Papa"—she looked shyly at Mr. Odell—"said that he was to have the same rights as if John and I had married."

That did not surprise Nate at all. Odell and his wife had several daughters, all of whom had married well, and one remaining son. The younger son was studying to be a lawyer and had taken little interest in the farm. And there were no entailments to stop Odell and his wife from leaving the property as they wished.

Today had definitely been a good day. Nate returned her smile. "I'm glad to hear it."

"Papa"—Nate was pleased to see how comfortable she was calling Odell "Papa." But she would have known them fairly well. Nate briefly wondered why she hadn't gone to the Odells in the first place, but not only was it water under the bridge, it wasn't his business —"told me how hard you looked for me," Emily said as the coach started. "If I live to be a hundred, I don't think I'll find a lord as good as you are."

A flush heated Nate's neck. "Thank you. I'm glad I was able to help." The coach had turned and was headed back up the street. "Mrs. Odell should be at Fotherby House by now." He decided to ask a question that had been bothering him. "How did you survive?"

"My, my." She straightened her shoulders. "*Mr. Bywater*

made me leave. But my mother gave me all the money she had been able to save, and I got work sewing. But after the baby came . . ."

"Well"—Odell's voice was rough with emotion—"at least you had the sense to go to the workhouse. That's the only way we found you."

"Yes." Her tone was barely above a whisper. "It was really my only choice."

Nate and the older man exchanged a glance. They were both glad she thought that way. Too many young women and girls on their own were forced into prostitution.

Upon arriving at his house, he learned that Mrs. Odell had got there not long before they did. His housekeeper, Mrs. Garford, had assigned his guests rooms and ordered baths and a cold collation to hold them until dinner. "As you know, my lord, I'll do my best until the rest of the staff gets here."

"I do know, and I value all you do for me." A footman he didn't know climbed the stairs carrying two bags. Mrs. Odell had prepared well.

"Fortunately, we've got enough staff to serve you and your guests."

Only because the housekeeper insisted on having more than a skeleton staff when the family wasn't in residence. Another footman came in carrying one of his bags, and Nate gave thanks for his valet. He hadn't even thought about clothing. "The rest of the staff will arrive within the next day or so."

Mrs. Garford nodded. "How long do you think your guests will be here?"

With Miss By—no, Miss Odell—thin, but healthy, it wouldn't be long. "I would not be surprised if they left tomorrow or the next day. I'll ask Mr. Odell after they've settled in."

"Very well, my lord. I'll be off to see about dinner. It will be ready in a little more than two hours. Nothing fancy. I haven't had time." She looked as if she was thinking something over and said, "Would you prefer to eat in the breakfast room?"

"Yes, thank you." Not fancy was fine with him, and the room had always seemed warm and cozy. He had forgotten to ask if the Odells wished to dine with him. If not, he'd be eating by himself in solitary splendor. Well, perhaps not splendor, but very much alone. Another footman passed by. "You there." The servant stopped. "Please tell Mr. and Mrs. Odell and Miss Odell that I would be pleased if they would join me for dinner in about two hours. A maid will tend to the child."

"Yes, my lord."

"I'll be in my apartments." His voice followed the man up the stairs, and Nate hoped he'd been heard. Then he shrugged. Someone would find him with the answer.

He was in his bathing room watching a bathtub being filled when the footman found him. "Mrs. Odell said they'd be happy to join you, my lord."

"Thank you. What is your name?"

The young man flushed. "Garford, my lord. Mrs. Garford is my aunt."

It wasn't the first time, nor would it be the last, family members were hired. And that wasn't a bad thing. Unlike many members of the *ton* who thought their relatives could do no wrong, servants wouldn't tolerate sloppy work from a relative. In fact, they were likely to be harder on them. "I'm sure she knew what she was doing."

"Thank you. If you need someone to act as your valet until yours arrives, I'd be happy to perform the duty."

"Thank you. I'd appreciate that." Nate would have to remember the man might like to train as a valet.

A swift smile appeared on the young man's face. "I'll just go tell Mrs. Garford."

He turned to walk out the door, and Nate stopped him. "If you wish to act as a valet, you must learn to tell others to send your messages."

Garford's eyes widened; then he glanced at the boy filling the tub. "George, when you go back downstairs, please inform Mrs. Garford I am assisting his lordship."

The boy gave him a pert wink. "I'll do it right away."

Nate untied his cravat and hung it over a chair while his temporary valet tested the water and laid a towel on a rack in front of the fire to warm it. While Garford unpacked Nate's kit, he sank into the hot tub and almost wished he could go straight to bed. But there were the Odells to consider. Fortunately, it wouldn't be a late night. They would want to be up early for their journey home.

Shortly after he'd bathed and changed, Nate entered the drawing room, and his guests joined him. "Would you like claret or sherry?"

"Thank you, we would," Mr. Odell's hearty voice boomed in the room. "The claret for all of us."

Nate was glad he had changed, as his guests had done so. Even Emily wore a different gown. Once he had served them, he held up his glass. "To a successful day." He glanced at Mrs. Odell. "I am glad you were able to arrive so quickly."

"That was due to your orders to see to my horses." She grinned. "I've never been seen to so quickly or with so much consideration." She held up her glass. "Thank you for finding our Emily and the babe. I don't think we could have done it without your help."

One of the footmen came in and announced dinner. "We are dining in the breakfast room. It's much more comfortable than the main dining room."

He held out his arm to Mrs. Odell, and she blushed like a young girl. "You're going to turn my head." She laughed as she took his arm. "I feel like a grand lady."

"That's it." Mr. Odell chuckled. "I'll never keep her on the farm now."

She stuck her nose in the air, and they all laughed.

Nate was happy that the meal was indeed simple, consisting of roasted chickens, salad, potatoes, glazed carrots, and a preserved pear fool for dessert.

"Who was the woman you were with?" Miss Odell asked after she had taken some of the chicken.

"She works for a charity that saves children." There was no need to tell her that payment was always offered. "I was able to be of assistance in fetching the baby."

Mrs. Odell nodded. "I'm sure she was glad you were there."

Nate was as well. If only he'd been able to ask the lady's name. But what he might be able to do was discover by which charity she was employed. He wondered who her brother-in-law was that could help her handle the constables. Perhaps a barrister.

Instead of removing to the drawing room, he ordered tea and port served at the table.

After he and Mr. Odell had one glass of port, Mrs. Odell rose. "We have enjoyed our evening, my lord, but it's time we find our beds. I'd like to be off first thing in the morning."

"Of course." Nate walked them to the door. "I hope you sleep well."

He had one more glass of the fortified wine and made his way to his bedchamber, where Garford was waiting.

"Sir," the younger man said. "Will you be going to a tailor while you're here?"

Given how precipitous this bolt to Town had been, he hadn't given it any thought. But if he was going to attend the Season, he must have more appropriate clothing. "Yes." But not the tailor he had used before. He had no interest in flamboyant clothing. This time he would take his custom to Weston. Nate was glad he had some time before the Season began. "Yes. I believe I must. I shall write a note to Weston asking him to attend me."

"Very good, my lord." Garford helped Nate out of his jacket. "I'll be happy to take it over in the morning."

"Thank you." It occurred to him that he would need a whole new wardrobe, and he wasn't looking forward to it. Yet needs must. Even if he decided what he had was good enough, his mother would disagree. Suddenly, he wished he was traveling back to the country as well. Then again, if he found the lady, and they had as much in common as he thought they would, he might be lucky enough not to have to remain for the whole Season.

CHAPTER FOUR

Henrietta woke the next morning, donned a robe, shoved her feet into a pair of slippers her younger sister had embroidered her for Christmas, and went to the nursery room where the baby girl she had saved yesterday was located.

She quietly slipped into the chamber to find the child nursing. "Good morning. How is she?"

"Much better." Mrs. Roberts lifted the child to her shoulder and patted the babe's back. "I've never had a child this young sleep thought the night, but she was ravenous this morning."

Henrietta sat in a wooden chair. "Do we know how old she is?"

"It's hard to say exactly." The baby let out a soft belch. "She was so mistreated, she might be older than we think she is, but the doctor and I agreed she's most likely around three months old."

She did not and would never understand how anyone could mistreat a child. "What do you think of Margaret for a name? We could call her Meg or Meggie."

"That sounds like a good, solid name," Mrs. Roberts agreed. "Well, Meggie. What do you think about having a name?" Meggie gurgled and grabbed one of Mrs. Roberts's fingers. "Do you want me to stay with her when she can travel?"

Mrs. Roberts came to them after the death of her husband and baby. She resided in London, but Henrietta wondered if she would like to move to the country. They had a house in Richmond they used for younger children. "Would you care to remain with her? We can send the two of you to Richmond."

A small smile settled on Mrs. Roberts's face. "Yes, I would be interested that. Although you'll have to find another wet nurse for emergencies."

"I'll speak to my sister about it." Henrietta rose. Seeing little Meggie reach up and touch Mrs. Roberts's face made Henrietta smile. "I'll look in on you later."

After dressing for the day, she entered the breakfast room as Dotty was pouring a cup of tea. "Good morning. I've been to see the baby." Henrietta sat next to her sister and reached for the tea-pot. "I would like to name her Margaret and call her Meggie."

Dotty savored her first sip of tea before answering, "I think that is a lovely name."

"Do you think Mrs. Roberts could remain with her, and that we could send them to Richmond?"

Dotty raised a brow. "Could I finish my tea before we have this conversation? Get your breakfast. I'll be done by the time you sit back down."

Henrietta went to the sideboard and selected two baked eggs. Once she had regained her seat, she took a piece of toast from the rack, then waited for her sister to finish the cup of tea.

"Now I am ready for this conversation." Dotty rubbed her stomach. "The baby was quite active last night."

"Ah." It wasn't until then that Henrietta noticed dark smudges under her sister's eyes. No wonder Dotty was a bit surly. "Forgive me. I seem to have had nothing on my mind but Meggie."

"That is understandable." Dotty poured another cup of tea and placed a piece of toast on her plate. "I'm not happy with what occurred, but you behaved just as you ought. Merton went out early this morning to discover what he could about the man you shot."

After hearing about Meggie's condition, Henrietta had no regrets over shooting the man. "I hope I did not kill him."

"We shall find out sooner or later." For a few minutes they were silent as they ate. Then her sister said, "You have an appointment at the modiste today."

"I remember." What she had forgotten to do was send a message around to her friend, Dorie, who she had met a year ago and was now married to the Marquis of Exeter, asking if she would like to join her. "At eleven."

Dotty nodded. "I might go back to bed for a while. I do not remember Vivi being this active. I feel as if I am being beaten up from inside."

Unable to offer an opinion, Henrietta applied herself to her breakfast.

Her sister rose first. "Take the town coach and a footman. I will see you when you return."

She nodded and finished her second cup of tea before writing to Dorie.

By eleven they were at Madame Lisette's shop, looking at the latest styles in *La Belle Assembleé*.

"The skirts are much wider at the bottom," Henrietta mused, wondering if she was too short to wear them.

"They are," Dorie, who was a few inches taller, agreed.

"*Bonjour.*" Madame was a slim, fashionable Frenchwoman with dark hair and eyes. She glanced at the gown Dorie and Henrietta were studying. "It will be very nice on Lady Exeter, but Miss Stern, we must do something else for you."

It was nice to be proven right even if she would not be dressed in the newest of fashion. "That is exactly what I had thought."

"Never fear. *Moi,* I know what I am doing." Madame ushered Henrietta behind a curtain into a room where one of her workers waited. "I do not believe your measurements have changed much, but we will see."

After her measurements were confirmed, Madame took Henrietta to a room where she had drawings stacked on a long table. The sketches depicted everything from day dresses to evening gowns. There was another stack of fabric samples. Not that Henrietta had much choice in colors. They all had to be pale. As far as she was concerned, she had enough day dresses, but it was important to have new clothing for entertainments, walking, and carriage rides. In the end, the order was larger than she expected it would be. But the time it took to order all the gowns was not nearly as long as it had been at the beginning of last Season.

She joined Dorie in the waiting area. "Are you ready to visit Hatchards?"

"Yes. I forgot to tell you that I heard from Georgie. She and Turley will arrive within a few days or a week if not sooner." Dorie grinned. "She complained that Turley is treating her as if she is an invalid."

"There is no surprise there." Exeter had done the same with Dorie, and Littleton had been almost as bad with Adeline. "It will be good to see her again." At least they would have three of the original five of them together. "I suppose there is no point in even attempting to talk Adeline into coming to Town."

"That would be a waste of time and effort." Dorie rose and shook out her deep pink skirts.

Lady Adeline Wively had married Lord Littleton late last spring. Since then the only time they had come to Town was when Georgie Featherton had wed Viscount Turley in the autumn. Now Adeline was the mother of twins, a boy and a girl, and Georgie was in a delicate condition. Until they had gradually married, the five of them had been inseparable. This Season would be much different. Henrietta was the only unmarried one. And seeing how happy her friends were, she hoped she would find a gentleman she could envision herself living with for the rest of her life. But that would mean someone new would have to come to Town. None of the gentlemen she had met last Season had interested her. Once again, her mind reflected back on the country gentleman. It was too bad that he was not likely to be here for the Season. She would have enjoyed getting to know him better. Henrietta considered telling her friend about the gentleman she had met, but what was the point when he was not in Town?

Sometime after luncheon, a dog's bark roused Nate, and he strode to the hall. His butler, secretary, valet, and Padraig were gathered there.

"Cook is here with us. Her ladyship will be here tomorrow," Hulatt said. "Her ladyship decided to use the smaller carriage, but stopped in Stevenage when we saw your coach."

"Very well." Nate wondered why she hadn't waited. As much as he loved his mother and enjoyed her company, he had wanted a day or two to settle in before she arrived. Padraig leaned against Nate's leg, and he stroked the dog's head. His valet, carrying two satchels, had one foot on the stairs. "Styles."

"Yes, my lord."

"There is a footman here, Mrs. Gorman, the house-keeper's nephew, who wishes to train as a valet. Would you mind if he studied under you?"

"Not at all, my lord." Styles nodded slowly. "There will be plenty to do now that we're in Town."

"Thank you." Nate scratched his dog's head. "Let's take you for a walk." It would feel good to stretch his legs.

"My lord," Chetwin said. "Did all go well with Mr. and Mrs. Odell?"

"Yes, it did. Very well indeed. They left this morning. You probably passed them on the road." Nate took his dog's lead. As he attached it, he had an idea. "Could you discover the names of charities that save children in places like Whitechapel and other poor areas?"

"If you wish." Unlike his valet and butler, his secretary didn't hide his expressions. And the man was more than a little bemused.

Nate grinned. "I do." He led Padraig out the door and down the three shallow steps, then mumbled to himself, "The real question is what my mother is going to say when I find her."

It was still much too early for the Grand Strut, which was fine with him. He walked his Wolfhound past the entrance to Grosvenor Square, where Merton House was clearly visible. Seeing Merton again was a bridge Nate would cross when he got there. The man used to be his closest friend, but he hadn't seen him since he had abducted Merton's betrothed. Granted, Nate had had his friend's best interests at heart. At least that was what he'd told himself. Albeit, if he'd been less busy worrying about losing his friend and more interested in seeing how happy Miss Stern made Merton, Nate never would have made such a horrible mistake. His folly had led to a rift between them that he regretted and didn't know could be healed. The punishment had been leasing his house in Richmond to Merton for a period of ten years and exile to the country. Yet for all he had resented the banishment at first, it finally made him grow up and take his responsibilities seriously. Surprisingly, he'd found that he liked them. Padraig paced beside Nate. He liked having a dog as well. Another thing he'd never looked for. To his eternal shame, he'd had a fear of dogs since he was young. Then, on a trip to Ireland to buy his horse, he'd seen the Wolfhound puppies, and Padraig had come right up to him demanding to be picked up. Once Nate did, it seemed like the most natural thing in the world to have a dog. That had been just over three years ago.

They reached the Park, and he found a stick to throw for the dog. Being raised to hunt wolves, Wolfhounds were known as sighthounds. A stick wasn't a wolf, and Padraig knew it. Nate was certain that the only reason the dog would bring the stick back to him at all was due to the resulting rewards. Still, four throws was all it took for the Wolfhound to tire of the game. Afterward, they strolled along The Serpentine until Nate turned them back toward Grosvenor gate. They had just crossed Park Street when he saw Merton drive by. Nate's former friend glanced briefly his way and looked again with a confused expression on his mien, then faced forward. He didn't think he'd been cut—although he wouldn't blame Merton if he had—

but Nate also did not think he'd been recognized. That was interesting.

He traced his way back to his house and was surprised to find his mother had arrived. He offered her his cheek to be kissed. "I didn't think you were going to be here until tomorrow."

"And that is exactly what I said, but after having a rather mediocre luncheon, I discovered I would much rather continue on." She wrapped her hands around his arm. "Please tell me you have had the time to think about a new wardrobe."

"I sent a note to Weston this morning, asking if he could wait on me."

One dark brow rose. "Weston?" He nodded. "A very good choice. Much better than that other man. What was his name, Nagey or something like that?"

"Something like that." Nate escorted her up the stairs. "I decided I no longer cared for his styles."

His mother inclined her head. "I think Weston will do an excellent job."

"I believe he will as well." Nate just had to live through the fittings. To think that once he had reveled in that sort of activity.

The door opened and Hulatt bowed. "My lady, I am glad to see you safely arrived."

"Thank you, Hulatt. I am glad to be here. Please inform Cook that there will be one more for dinner." She turned a stricken look at Nate. "Dear me. I should have asked if you are dining in this evening."

"I am." He would make the round of his clubs, but not until after he'd refurbished his wardrobe. Despite how he normally dressed, he could not look like a provincial in Town.

"Good. I shall see you at seven. Or had you planned to dine earlier?"

"Seven is fine." He'd have to get used to Town hours again and might as well begin now. "If you will excuse me, I have to see what Chetwin has brought me."

"Of course, my dear."

He walked down the corridor to his secretary's study and entered. "I trust nothing of import occurred in the past day."

"No, my lord, just the normal correspondence. I have sent out one of the London footmen to research charities and hope to have something soon." He held up a card. "This arrived for you before I left. It is an invitation from a Lord Fallows inviting you to a small gathering."

Fallows was one of the gentlemen Nate had been friendly with before. Even after he had been banished to the country, every year an invitation was sent to his London house. Had Fallows even known Nate wasn't in Town? One would think that after he had stopped responding to the invitations, the invitations would have stopped as well. He wondered if the man still spent his time drinking and gambling. "Send my regrets. In fact, the only events I plan to attend are the ones chosen by my mother."

Chetwin's eyes widened. "You are really going to look for a wife?"

He took a breath. "I am. Drat"—he knew he'd forgotten something—"I must speak with my mother."

She was probably going to think he was mad, but whether or not he found the lady he was looking for, she needed to know what he wanted in a wife. Otherwise, this would all be for naught. Nate strode to the hall and took the stairs two at a time, then turned down a corridor to the rooms his mother had taken after his father and older brother had died.

He knocked on the door, and her maid opened it.

"My lady, it is his lordship."

"Tell him to come in."

The rooms had been redone in his mother's favorite colors, pink and white. The windows looked out on the side garden, which faced south. His mother was sitting on a small sofa and a tea tray had been placed on the low table in front of it. "Fotherby, I thought you had work to do."

"There was nothing pressing, but I realized that as soon as people know we are here, we will begin receiving invitations. And we have never discussed what I want in a wife." He didn't quite know how to bring up the lady he'd assisted. There was always the chance his mother knew her family. He might as well just say it. "While I was at the workhouse, fetching Miss Odell and her baby, I discovered that there are charities that save children. That is something I would be interested in. Do you know any of them?"

"Please stop looming over me and have a cup of tea. We shall address the requirement of a wife first. Then I shall give some thought to the charities." He selected a chintz-covered chair, and she handed him a cup. "What do you want in a wife?"

"I want her to be practical and not pretentious, and"— he wanted to say "courageous," but how to explain that?— "and be equal to me." He'd seen that in the Odells and some other couples. "But not stuffy or too serious." He wanted her to love him, not who he was. He'd heard Merton had found that and was happier for it.

"Well, that is an interesting combination." She sipped her tea. "Do you want beauty and grace?"

A pair of light eyes—he wished he knew the color—under long, thick, black lashes passed through his mind. "Some beauty. I do like the combination of black hair and light eyes. I suppose most ladies are graceful."

"Yes, most are." His mother turned to her maid. "Bring me my pocketbook." Once it was handed to her, she began making notes. "Is there anything else?"

He thought about the lady again. "Someone not in her first Season. I want someone who has maturity, if not in age, then in behavior."

Mama drew her lips under as she wrote again. "Very well. I shall see who is here for the Season." She put the pocketbook on a side table. "Do you know anyone who meets these criterion?"

Nate felt heat rise in his neck. "I did, in a loose meaning of the term, meet a lady." He supposed he'd now have to tell his mother where. "When Mr. Odell was in speaking with Miss Bywater—although she is now Miss Odell—I saw a lady in need of assistance."

His mother pursed her lips. "And you were able to render it?"

"Yes." Damn, he never should have said anything.

"You are certain she is a lady?"

"Absolutely certain."

Her brows rose. "And would this have anything to do with searching for a charity?"

"Er. Yes." He downed his tea. "I believe she is working for a charity."

"You do know that if she is working, she will not have a dowry." Mama's face was a mask, and he wished he knew what she was thinking. Still, he did not think she disapproved.

"That does not matter to me. What I want is a lady of

character and compassion." After all, he was the one who would have to live with her.

She met his gaze and seemed to study him for a long few moments. Finally she nodded. "Very well. I shall make inquiries. I hope for your sake that she *is* a lady."

"She *is* a lady." He almost growled the words. He did not have to hope at all. He, like everyone else, knew when a female was a lady. Nate rose. "I am well acquainted with the breed. I'll see you in the drawing room."

CHAPTER FIVE

Merton arrived home from seeing about the man she had shot as Henrietta was taking off her gloves. Even if the blackguard deserved to have a hole put through him, she did not like the idea she might have killed a man. Taking a life was rarely a good thing. Although there were times it was necessary. Strangely, she had not had the delayed reaction she thought she would. It bothered her a little that she had few if any sensibilities about the ruffian or the incident in general. "What did you discover?"

"There was no body, but the blood was being washed away as I arrived. I asked the shopkeeper who was cleaning the pavement what he knew. He lives above his business and told me that he heard the commotion and the shot. When he finally looked out the window, no one was on the street."

That was most likely all she would be able to learn. "Thank you for looking into it."

"You Sterns are a great deal of work." He gave a rueful grin. "Before last Season I thought it was just my darling wife, but it appears you have the same traits."

Henrietta grinned. "You can blame our parents. Well, mostly Papa."

Merton raised a haughty brow. "I know exactly from where your compulsion to save the world comes. Speaking of Sterns, have you seen my wife?"

"Earlier in the breakfast room, but she was tired and went back to bed. I had a modiste appointment and have just returned. She might be awake by now."

"Tired?" He had that ominous tone that crept into his voice when he was worried about Dotty.

"The baby was active last night." Henrietta wondered what it would be like to have a gentleman love her as much as Merton loved her sister.

"I'll go look in on her." He started toward the stairs.

She followed. "I'll come with you. I want to tell her about the gowns I ordered.

When they reached her sister's parlor, she was sitting at her desk with the cook standing in front of her. "This will do nicely, thank you, Henri."

"*Merci*, Madame." The cook bowed. "My lord, *et* mademoiselle." The man bowed again.

Once Cook left, Merton kissed Dotty's cheek. "I hear our child kept you from sleeping well. Why didn't you wake me?"

"And have us both exhausted in the morning?" She placed a palm on his face and returned his kiss. "No. I can nap." His brows lowered as he glanced at Henrietta. "I have asked your mother to come help chaperone Henrietta. She will arrive either later today or tomorrow. I will not have you"—her sister gave her a pointed look—"stuck at home if I am unable to accompany you."

"Thank you. I'll be happy to have her chaperone me." The dowager Lady Merton was one of Henrietta's favorite people. The other one was her grandmother, the duchess. "I assure you that I still intend to come home after supper."

"That is an excellent tactic." Merton sprawled on the chair in front of Dotty's desk. "I had an odd experience today. I could have sworn I saw Fotherby."

Dotty's eyes narrowed and her expression darkened forbiddingly. "Indeed."

Henrietta had never heard her sister speak in such an icy tone.

"But it couldn't have been." Merton shook his head, as if he was bemused. "The man was dressed like a provincial, and he had a fully grown Wolfhound with him."

"You're right." Her sister's expression relaxed.

What was going on?

"That does not sound like him at all." The warmth had returned to Dotty's voice. "Do you have any idea when he does plan to appear in Town again?"

"No. I have not been in contact with him since"—he glanced at Henrietta—"since that day."

She closed her eyes, then raised them to the ceiling. "You might as well tell me in the event he does come to Town." Her sister's lips flattened into a thin line. Good Lord. She was not a child any longer. "Especially if I am to have nothing to do with him."

"Very well." Dotty sighed. "Lord Fotherby abducted me to stop me from marrying Dom. He and Matt Worthington"—Worthington Merton's cousin, thus her and Henrietta's cousin by marriage—"came to rescue me."

"Only to find that she had escaped on her own." Merton grinned. "It was Thea's idea to allow his mother to deal with him, and she decreed he was to be banished to the country until he learned his lesson and gained sufficient maturity to be let loose again."

How horrible that he would do something like that! Henrietta did not blame her sister at all for still being angry. "But why did he want to stop the marriage?"

"He got it into his head that I was not worthy of being the Marchioness of Merton, and Dom would never be happy with me."

Henrietta stared at her brother-in-law. "Other than the dog, how do you know the man was not him?"

"Fotherby is a Dandy. He delighted in . . . hmm . . . shall we say interesting colors in clothing and the newest styles. He wouldn't be caught dead in a plain suit from a country tailor."

"I had never seen a man with so many fobs hanging from him," Dotty added. "He even had gold tassels on his boots."

Merton barked a laugh. "A puppy got loose and went straight for the tassels." He glanced lovingly at Dotty. "That's when I first met your sister. She ran up as he was trying to kick the puppy, and she gave him one of the best dressings down I'd ever heard. You see, he's been afraid of dogs since he was a boy."

"Afraid of dogs?" Henrietta had never heard of such a thing. "Isn't that, umm, rather un-English?"

Dotty emitted a thrill of laughter. "That's what Dom said. It was the first time I had noticed him standing there. And he made Louisa introduce us."

That was confusing. "I thought Cousin Louisa likes Merton."

"She does now." Dotty grinned. "But she did not like him at all back then and was against our marriage."

"Worthington felt the same," Merton added. "Fortunately, we have all resolved our differences."

"I'm glad about that." The Worthingtons and the

Mertons were all very close now. Henrietta recalled what her brother-in-law had said about the gentleman he saw and wondered if he could be the gentleman who had helped her. "Can you describe the man you saw walking the Wolfhound?"

"About my height. Chestnut-colored hair." He shrugged.

That was not very helpful. "Are his shoulders broad like yours?"

He exchanged a look with her sister, who tried to stifle a chuckle. "I suppose so. I must say that I don't make a point of spending time thinking about a man's physical attributes. I am more likely to notice how he is dressed so that I know his status."

That was what everyone did. Dress and the way one spoke could tell one everything one needed to know about their place in life. "I asked because he sounds like the gentleman I saw in Whitechapel."

"If he is someone you should meet, he will be at the same entertainments this Season," Merton said in a way that she knew meant he wouldn't budge.

"But what if he is not part of the *haut ton*?" It was a good question. Quite eligible gentlemen did not always attend the balls and other events she attended.

"The next time I see him, I shall make a point of discovering his identity."

And that was all she could hope for. "Thank you." She glanced at her sister. "Do you want to hear about the gowns I ordered?"

"If you wish to tell me, but I already received the list from Madame. I must say, you were rather frugal."

Henrietta shrugged. "I did not see the point in new day dresses when we can add new trim. The most important thing that has changed is that the skirts are much wider, which does not help me at all, being as short as I am."

"That is unfortunate." Her sister, who was the same height, pulled a face. "Did you get any other shopping accomplished?"

"Yes, Dorie came with me, and we went to Hatchards, then to the bazaar for stockings and other things. Madame will send over swatches of cloth to the shoemaker. I asked her to pick the colors for my gowns. It will be nice to be surprised. I'll purchase new bonnets later." Henrietta rose. Merton had moved behind her sister, placing his palms on her shoulders. Clearly, her sister and brother-in-law wished to spend time together.

The longing she had begun to feel rose within her. Someday, she would have a husband. Perhaps before this Season was finished.

After Fotherby closed the door on his retreat, Catherine, Viscountess Fotherby, glanced at her dresser of many years. "I believe we have a problem."

The dresser nodded sagely. "What are you going to do about it?"

"Write a letter to the duchess." Catherine went to her desk and pulled out a piece of pressed paper. "This must go by messenger. If she is not at her estate, he will have to find her."

"Yes, my lady."

Two days later, she received a missive asking her to visit the Dowager Duchess of Bristol, grandmother of the Marchioness of Merton and Miss Stern, at the duchess's suite in the Pulteney Hotel. Catherine and her old friend had exchanged correspondence for years. After the "incident," their exchange of letters had increased, with the duchess making a point of asking about Fotherby's progress. And Catherine was extremely glad she had. Not that she in any way thought the duchess was prescient enough to foresee this complication. Yet the lady her son had described sounded too much like Henrietta Stern for Catherine to be sanguine. Fotherby had acted horrendously toward Lady Merton before her marriage, and Catherine had to discover whether the Mertons were ready to forgive him. If not, and the lady *was* Miss Stern—which was not as yet certain—Fotherby had a long, hard road to travel if he wished to gain the lady's affections. And that was if Miss Stern would have anything to do with him. Would he then return to the country? He was nearing thirty and must think about an heir. Which meant he had to marry.

Catherine, as always, dressed with care. There was never any point in putting others off because of one's appearance, and took the town coach to the Pulteney, where the duchess's butler announced her.

She entered, holding out her hands. "Duchess, I am so glad you are in Town."

"Catherine." The older woman took her hands and bussed her cheek. "I did not come last Season because I was certain Henrietta would take." The duchess frowned. "Well, she did, but she liked none of them enough to wed. Not that any of us are in a rush, but one must admit that the longer one waits, the harder it is."

Catherine removed her gloves and handed them to the butler. "Yes, well, we might have a small problem in that regard."

The duchess drew her into a well-appointed parlor that, as always, was decorated with the duchess's own possessions, including paintings on the walls. Her friend led her to a sofa covered in a silvery-blue velvet. "Please, let us be comfortable and have a cup of tea. I always find tea helps smooth over difficulties of all sorts."

Once the tea tray arrived and the duchess poured them both cups, she asked, "You mentioned a possible problem in your letter. What is it?"

Catherine took a breath and hoped that her dear friend would think as she did. "You remember, probably all too well, what Fotherby did to your granddaughter, and my promise to keep him in the country until he matured."

"Yes." Her friend nodded. "I understand from your letters over the years that he has changed a great deal."

"Indeed he has." In fact, he was now a son of whom she was proud. She felt her lips forming a small smile. "I have never seen a more dramatic transformation. The only reason he came to Town, and decided to stay for the Season since he was here, is that neighbors, a gentleman farmer and his wife, lost their son before his marriage. The girl was made to leave her home. We could only imagine she was with child. He hired a runner and refused to allow the Odells to pay the whole of the fee. Then, when she was found, he brought them to Town to fetch her." Catherine took a sip of tea. "And that is when I believe he met your granddaughter Henrietta. Naturally, he did not introduce himself, nor did she introduce herself. But his description was striking, and they met in Whitechapel, where she was rescuing a child. He thinks she works for a charity."

"And that does not bother him?" the duchess asked in a curious tone.

"Not in any way." Catherine wondered why she had not been more surprised. Before, he had always been concerned about bloodlines, dowries, and the advantages a wife might bring to the marriage. "All he knows is that she is a lady. He simply believes she must work for a living."

Her friend's black brows rose. "Well, this ought to be interesting." The duchess set down her cup, rose, and brought over a decanter of claret from the sideboard. "I believe wine might be more helpful." She poured two glasses and handed one to Catherine. "If he has changed that dramatically, I would not be surprised if Henrietta might be interested in him as well. Especially because she met him under such circumstances."

Catherine's thoughts exactly. "He is currently in the process of acquiring a new wardrobe from Weston. Thankfully, he has enough sense not to appear at his clubs or about Town looking like a country gentleman. He thinks Merton saw him, but did not recognize him."

"This becomes more and more curious." The duchess sipped her wine. "For some reason I cannot imagine your son taking his custom to a country tailor, nor going to Weston."

She did not know if the duchess knew of her son's fear of dogs but said, "He also has a dog. An Irish Wolfhound."

As she hoped, her old friend laughed. "I must meet this new Fotherby. Although you understand that if my granddaughter Merton still holds his actions against him, I do not know how we will get them together. If indeed they did meet, and we are not worrying over nothing." She took another drink of wine. "Although that I can discover. I shall invite Henrietta to visit me."

Catherine had the urge to drink down the whole glass of wine at once. How had what was to have been an uncomplicated Season to find her son a wife become so fraught? "I cannot think it would be only Lady Merton who might have trouble forgiving him. Lord Merton was furious."

"Yes, as well as Lord Worthington and Dorothea's father and mother. If this situation is as we think it, I will have to involve them as well. We do not want them enacting some sort of ridiculous Cheltenham tragedy. Although I do believe that Henrietta is much too practical for that."

"It could very well be that once she discovers what Fotherby did, Miss Stern will not want to have anything to do with him."

"I would expect nothing else from her, but if he is the man you think he is, he will bring her around. Then the problem becomes her family."

"This is not going to be easy." Catherine took a large drink of wine.

"No, it will not. But none of the best results are." The duchess saluted her with the wineglass. "This is what grandmothers and mothers are for. Is it not?"

Catherine held up her glass. "I sincerely hope that is the case."

"Come now, we trusted you to bring about change, and you have succeeded beyond anyone's expectations. There must be a reward."

"But your granddaughter and my son?" Catherine blew out a frustrated breath. "Could he have not chosen someone else?"

"He might have." The duchess raised an imperious brow. "But if it is indeed Henrietta, he could not have chosen better. She could have any gentleman she wants. I would venture to say with her maturity, her connections, and her dowry, she is the most eligible lady in London."

"And she would be the most eligible bride." Catherine

nodded. In for a penny, in for a pound. "What is our first plan?"

"You shall invite me to dine with you, but not, I think, as the Duchess of Bristol. I shall be"—a sly twinkle entered the duchess's eyes—"I shall be Lady Fitzwilliam. It was a lesser title of my husband's. We do not want him associating me with Merton."

Catherine was certain Fotherby had discovered Lady Merton's grandmother was a duchess, after the fact, naturally. "Excellent. It must be soon. Before he has suitable clothing in which to go about Town. Shall we say tomorrow evening?"

The duchess inclined her head. "I shall arrive at eight."

CHAPTER SIX

The next morning Nate found a note on his desk from his secretary and entered Chetwin's office. "What have you discovered?"

"Well, there seem to be an abundance of charities for different purposes, but only three of them let it be known that they will rescue children for payment." He pushed a cut sheet of foolscap cross the desk. "Here are the names and addresses."

The Ladies Society for the Benefit of Orphans and Other Unfortunates, 2 Old Compton Street
The London Society to Promote the Well Being of Children and Mothers, 17 Stacy Street
The Phoenix Society for the Aid of Children, Families, and Widows, 12 Phoenix Street

"All of them are located near Covent Garden," Chetwin added.

"Close enough to St Giles and Seven Dials that word could get to them, but not so close the people working at the charities could be in danger." That made sense. "I suppose I must visit each of them."

"I could send a footman if you wish," his secretary offered.

"Thank you, but no. This is something I must do myself." He pulled out his pocket watch. "Padraig needs a good walk." What Nate didn't know was what he would say when he found the right place. Would there even be someone there who could introduce him to the lady? There was only one way to find out. "If my mother asks, tell her I'm running an errand, and I will return in time to change for dinner." Visiting the charities probably wouldn't take long at all, but if he did find her, he wanted to make sure he did not have to rush home for some reason.

"I hope your search is productive." His secretary's tone was doubtful.

"I do as well." Nate strolled into his study, where Padraig had taken up residence near the fireplace. "Come, boy. We're going for a nice, long walk." The Wolfhound rose, slowly stretching as he did. It wasn't until he was fully standing that he turned his golden-brown eyes on Nate and his tail started to wag. Nate grabbed the lead. "You are going to discover all sorts of things you've never seen before, including pigeons. You are not to chase them. Do you understand?" Padraig leaned against Nate's leg as he attached the lead to the dog's thick leather collar. "Let's see if we can hunt down the lady I'm looking for."

He arrived at the Old Compton Street address first and knocked on the door. A young man dressed neatly, but not as a footman or a butler, opened it. "May I help you?"

"Yes. I was able to assist a young lady who fetched an infant from the area near the Whitechapel workhouse a few

days ago. I wished to discover how the child was doing."
Not a lie, but not the whole truth.

The lad scratched his head. "Don't think it was us, but if you want to come in, I'll ask Mrs. Denison."

"Thank you." He shortened Padraig's lead to keep him by his side.

As Nate started forward, the young man's eyes fixed on the Wolfhound, and his eyes widened. "Is he safe?"

"Perfectly. He loves people if you would like to stroke him."

The lad swallowed hard. "Maybe later." He backed away. "I'll go ask Mrs. Denison."

A few minutes later, the aforementioned Mrs. Denison entered the hall. "Ah, I see what Johnny was talking about." She held her hand out to Padraig's nose. "He's a fine-looking fellow."

"That he is." Nate waited until the lady gave his dog a few pats on the head. "Did, er, Johnny tell you what I came about?"

"Just barely." She smiled. "He was much more impressed by your dog. He has probably never seen one so large." She glanced at Padraig again. "I can tell you that we have not had a rescue in Whitechapel recently. I suggest you call at The London Society to Promote the Well Being of Children and Mothers"—she wrinkled her nose—"or the Phoenix Society for the Aid of Children, Families, and Widows. I would try the Phoenix Society first. It is closer, and you are more likely to find what you are looking for."

Nate bowed. "Thank you for your help."

She curtseyed neatly. "It is my pleasure to assist anyone who is interested in saving children's lives."

Once back on the pavement, he set course for Phoenix Street, where he found the Phoenix Society. It was a well-kept building painted white with black shutters. Nate knocked on the door and found himself facing a large man in his mid- to late-twenties who had the look of a soldier about him.

The man ran an expert eye over him before saying, "May I help you?"

"I hope so. . . ." he repeated his request.

"Yes, we had a child rescued there not long ago." The man stepped back. "If you will take a seat in the parlor, I'll fetch Mrs. Perriman."

"Thank you." Padraig entered with Nate, but the man didn't say a word about him. "Are you used to large dogs?"

"As a matter of fact"—he grinned—"I've met a few of them. Mostly Great Danes. I'll be back in a minute."

He led Nate into a parlor facing the street and took himself off toward the back of the building.

Shortly thereafter, a woman dressed plainly but with propriety entered the room. "Good day, Mr. . . ." She raised a brow.

"Meadows." That hadn't been his name for a few years now, but he'd used it longer than he had Fotherby. The question he had to ask himself was why he hadn't used his current name and rank? He'd think about that later.

"Well, Mr. Meadows, I must thank you for your assistance. It came as an urgent request and we were short of people. I am grateful for your help."

He crossed his fingers and sent up a prayer. "Can you tell me if the lady who was there that afternoon is here?"

"I am sorry, she is not. She—"Mrs. Perriman's forehead creased—"she does not actually work here. Both she and her sister help when necessary. They are patrons, and I cannot reveal to you her name."

"I see," he said, but he wasn't at all sure that he did.

Then he thought about what some members of Polite Society would say about a young lady rescuing children in Whitechapel, and everything was clear. "Can you tell me how the child is doing?"

She gave a relieved smile. "Yes, of course. The baby is doing well. She will be sent to the country in a week or so."

Thank God the child had lived. He let out the breath he'd been holding. "Excellent. I'm glad to hear that you have a place in the country for the children."

"We have several houses we use. This one is in Richmond, so the journey will not overtax her."

Richmond? The hairs on the back of his neck prickled, and Padraig stood straighter, as if he sensed something was wrong. "She is a girl?"

"Yes. Of course, you could not have known that when you helped rescue her," Mrs. Perriman said.

"If you require any assistance in the future, I would be happy to be of service again." Maybe that way he could discover who his lady was.

"Thank you for your very kind offer." She smiled. "Our staff has been augmented, but if you will leave your direction, I will call upon you if there is a need. There might very well be. We see an increase in children needing homes this time of year."

The question was, should he give his house address? He'd already misled her about his name, but he could always say that he felt it was safer. That excuse sounded lame even to him. He'd better not mislead her about his address. "A message sent to Forty-five Grosvenor Street will find me."

"Grosvenor Street." Somewhere in the house a door slammed, and she suddenly rose and ushered him out of the parlor and into the hall. "Thank you, Mr. Meadows."

Nate bowed. "Good-bye, Mrs. Perriman."

"Farewell. I hope that we do not have to call on you, but it is nice to know that we may."

As he turned to leave, a boy of about ten or eleven almost ran into him. "Sorry, sir."

"It's no matter." Nate and Padraig regained the pavement. "Did you notice that she did not acknowledge you at all?" he asked the dog. "I find that interesting. And after I gave her the address, she couldn't get me out fast enough. Of course, it could have something to do with the boy coming in. What do you think, Padraig? Is she merely protecting the lady?"

Then the mention of a house in Richmond came back to him, and he stopped walking. Oh, good God! She . . . his lady . . . could not possibly be related to Merton. Or could she? Nate resumed his stroll back toward Mayfair. No, not Merton. His wife. That was the reason she resembled Miss Stern so strongly. She was another Miss Stern.

But what was he going to do about it? He didn't want to give up on her without at least trying to attach her attentions. She really was the most remarkable female he'd ever met. "Padraig, old boy, I think I'm in trouble."

The following morning, Henrietta ate a piece of toast and drank her tea as her maid fixed her hair. Dorie was finally able to ride again after having the baby and they had agreed to meet in the mornings for a short while.

"That should stay up," Spyer said as she put away the rest of the pins. "I'll arrange it more becomingly after you return."

"Thank you." Henrietta grabbed her bonnet and fixed

it with a hat pin. It was almost eight o'clock, but the sun had just made a showing. "I won't be long."

"I'll have a tub ready when you return," her maid called after her.

"Thank you." No matter how little time one spent on a horse, one always smelled like the stables afterward. She hurried down to the hall and out the door where one of Merton's grooms stood with Lilly, her black mare. The groom assisted her into the saddle, and she started toward Exeter House on the other side of the square.

She arrived just as Exeter was lifting Dorie onto her horse. "Remember what the doctor said, and take it easy the first few times out." He turned. "Good morning, Miss Stern."

"Good morning." She was extremely happy that Exeter and Dorie had worked out their problems and had wed.

"I shall." Dorie leaned down and kissed him. "We will not be long." She glanced at Henrietta. "Shall we go?"

"Yes."

They made their way through the heavy morning traffic to the Grosvenor gate into the Park. "I liked riding in April and May better," Dorie said. "There were not so many drays and other vehicles."

"Because we ride earlier." Henrietta grinned. When he was attempting to court Dorie, poor Exeter had not realized that she rode at sunrise, not according to a clock, and had frequently missed Dorie. "As long as you are able, we can depart just before sunrise for the rest of the Season, and there will be less and less traffic."

She closed her eyes for a moment. "And as long as little David decides to sleep. He wakes up hungry."

"Keep the room dark until you return." Due to Henrietta's parents' more advanced ideas on raising children, she had been required to assist her mother looking in on tenants and had not been made to leave the room when womanly subjects had been discussed. "It is easier to keep the baby on a schedule of sorts that way."

"I am surprised Nurse did not say anything." Dorie pulled a face. "Then again, she does not approve of me nursing the baby."

That was something Henrietta would not tolerate. "It is not for her to approve or disapprove."

"I know." Her friend sighed. "I had hoped she would wish to retire, but she fell in love with little David and cannot bring herself to leave." Dorie shrugged. "It is always hard with old retainers, particularly when they are not one's own. Exeter had a word with her, and she no longer says anything."

"But the disapproval is still plain?" Despite her previous thoughts, Henrietta wondered if she would eventually have the same problem.

"Yes, but not as much as before." Her friend smiled. "She might be coming around. Enough about me. What have you been up to since yesterday?"

"Well"—Henrietta felt a thrill of happiness rush through her body—"I met a gentleman a few days ago, but I thought he had gone back to the country. Then yesterday Merton told me he had seen a man who matches the description of the gentleman I met walking his dog."

Dorie brought her horse to a halt. "Wait. When and where did you meet this man, and why did I not hear about it yesterday?"

"You know that occasionally my sister and I would help fetch children we rescue?" Dorie and their other two friends were the only ones Henrietta had told about some of the dangers. Dorie nodded. "I ran into a bit of trouble, and he was suddenly there to help."

Dorie's brows rose. "Do I want to know where you were and why your sister and her husband were not there as well?"

"I thought it was safe." Henrietta closed her eyes for a moment and shook her head. "However, Whitechapel seems to be suffering some difficulties. In any event, the gentleman was assisting one of his neighbors from the country. There was no one present who could introduce us. Therefore, I do not know his name. And I assumed he had returned to the country. But if the gentleman Merton saw is the same one, then perhaps I will meet him properly."

"Ohhh, Henrietta, he sounds just like the type of gentleman who would appeal to you." Dorie smiled broadly. She and Henrietta's other friends wanted the same happiness for her that they had found. "What does he look like?"

She described his physical description down to his country-made clothing . . . "and he has a lovely rich voice, and looks as if he spends a great deal of time out of doors."

"And a dog." Dorie had been lucky enough to acquire one of the Worthington Great Dane puppies. "What kind of dog?"

"An Irish Wolfhound. I found information about the breed in one of the books in Merton's library. They are a very old race. The book mentioned a saga from Iceland called the 'Saga of the Burnt Njal'—I hope I pronounced the name correctly."

"If Augusta were here, she could have told you," Dorie said.

"I miss her." Lady Augusta Vivers, now Lady Phineas Carter-Woods, had wanted to attend the university in Padua and thought she'd been accepted, only to discover after she arrived that she had not. However, her husband argued that she should be allowed to take the final examinations, and she was granted her degree. The last Henrietta had heard from her friend, they had traveled to Turkey after leaving Egypt. Augusta knew more about languages than almost anyone in or out of a university. "Let me tell you about the breed. I memorized the part because it was so interesting. In the tenth century, Olaf, a Norwegian, son of an Irish princess, told his friend, Gunnar, 'I will give thee a hound that was given to me in Ireland; he is big and no worse than a stout man. Besides, it is part of his nature that he has a man's wit, and he will bay at every man that he knows to be thy foe, but never at thy friends. He can see too in any man's face whether he means thee well or ill, and he will lay down his life to be true to thee. This hound's name is SAMR.' Isn't that interesting?"

Dorie frowned, as if trying to envision the dog. "What do they look like?"

"They have a sort of rectangular head, and from the drawing, the fur looks rough. I would love to see one."

"I find it interesting," Dorie said, "that ever since meeting Augusta's family's Great Danes, we have all fallen in love with giant dogs. And that some of us have been fortunate enough to have one of our own."

"We have, haven't we?" Henrietta shrugged. Neither she nor Georgie had been able to take one of the Worthington Danes. "They are much nicer than smaller dogs. I do hope that the man Merton saw is the same gentleman I met."

"It is a shame that he did not have the dog with him when you met him."

"Then I would be certain." She wondered what the dog would have done to the blackguards when they had threatened her. "Unfortunately, I have no recourse other than to wait and hope that I see him again."

"And that you are in a place where someone can introduce you," Dorie added.

"That too." Henrietta sighed. "There are times when the rules governing young ladies are not very practical." If she'd had her way, she would have introduced herself. But even her father would not have approved of that.

"It will work out the way it is supposed to." Her friend grinned at her. "Is that not what you used to tell me?"

"Yes." Henrietta knew she sounded disgruntled. "But being on the receiving end of that statement is not helpful."

Dorie let out a thrill of laughter. "Come, let us see if I still know how to gallop."

Henrietta urged her horse into a trot, then a canter, and a faster gallop. One way or another, she would find her gentleman.

CHAPTER SEVEN

Nate was beginning to chafe at not being able to go anywhere. Fortunately, Weston had sent over one suit of clothing consisting of a jacket and pantaloons in Prussian blue, and a waistcoat embroidered in blue, green, and gold thread. Nate had soundly rejected the new frock coat that was so long it reminded him of a banyan, and had insisted that his jacket fit loosely enough that he wasn't in danger of splitting the seams. His new shoes had also been delivered, not that they looked much different from his old ones, but he had needed new shoes. The boots would take a bit more time. His valet kept his older ones highly shined, but he had just the one pair in Town. The only problem with his new clothing was that it could not be worn for dinner this evening. From what he understood, breeches were still worn in the evening. His mother had invited a friend to dine with them and wished him to attend. Ergo, he would have to wear his older clothing.

His valet stood back as Nate tied his cravat, then helped him into his jacket. He affixed his pocket watch, the only fob he wore these days other than, occasionally, his quizzer. Thanks to Garford, Nate's shirt and stockings were new.

He gave his image in the mirror a hard look. The dark-green jacket and breeches still looked well. He had been able to wear his new waistcoat. He no longer had the tan he'd had last summer, but neither was he pale. He wondered what the lady had seen when she'd looked at him. Padraig rose. "You cannot come down this evening. Her ladyship specifically asked that you wait until after dinner."

"I'll bring him down when you send the word," Styles said, holding onto the dog's collar.

"Thank you." Normally, the hound went everywhere with Nate, and lately he hadn't been able to. This week must have been particularly hard on Padraig. First, Nate had left home without the dog, and now he was not allowed in the dining room. "The transition to Town life will not be easy for him."

"It is a shame you can't find some other dogs for him to play with," his valet said.

"That's an excellent idea. I'll ask around." He attached an emerald tie-pin to his cravat. At least he wouldn't put his mother to shame. "I won't be late. Darragh arrived not long ago, and I want to take him for a gentle ride in the morning." When no one would care how he dressed or if he was accompanied by a large dog.

Nate joined his mother in the drawing room, and several minutes later his butler announced Lady Fitzwilliam. He had propped himself up against the fireplace and had a perfect view of their guest as his mother rose to meet her. Lady Fitzwilliam was a short, neatly built lady. One might say almost dainty, but she gave the impression of being much taller than she was. Her silver hair was piled on top of her head in an elaborate design, making him think that she was older than his mother, even though she had very few lines on her face. But what struck him were her black brows, which rose in a graceful arch over arresting, bright moss-green eyes. Her demeanor was such that he straightened immediately and strode over to be introduced. She reminded him of someone, but at the moment he could not think of whom.

"Ah, Fotherby, my dear." His mother took his arm.

"Er"—she paused, and he wondered why—"Lady Fitzwilliam, may I present my son to you?"

"A pleasure to finally make your acquaintance." The lady held out her hand. "You mother has told me much about you." Nate bowed.

He straightened. "I am pleased to meet you."

She looked at him as if she was memorizing his features. "I am happy to meet a young man who does not dress to extremes. I have a nephew whose shirt points are so tall they will poke his eyes out one day."

Nate chuckled, as he was meant to. "I believe many young men fall to the excesses of fashion when they are young." Or not so young.

"I cannot believe you did such a thing." One of her brows rose as she ended the sentence.

"Much to my chagrin, I spent several years as a Dandy."

Her gaze was steady as she said, "But you have learned your lesson."

He had the feeling she meant more than his clothing. Who was this woman? "Indeed I have." He stepped back. "Would you care for a glass of sherry or wine?"

"A sherry if you will be so kind." His mother led the lady to the sofa upon which she had been sitting when Lady Fitzwilliam arrived.

He poured a glass and handed it to her before lowering

himself into one of the cane-backed chairs across from them. He was being kept in the dark about something, but he wouldn't embarrass his mother by asking now. That would wait until after their guest had departed. "Do you spend much time in Town, my lady?"

"Oh, not so very much." She took a sip of wine. "I was here several years ago, but this is the first time I have been back since then. After Napoleon was once more tucked safely away, I decided I would visit the Continent. It had been too many years since my last trip. The damage from the war was, as one would expect, appalling. And in France there were not many of my old friends left. Austria and Germany were more pleasant experiences." She turned to his mother. "You really must travel more, my dear. I recommend you do it by boat. The roads from Calais to Paris were so horrible I forsook them after that."

"I remember you mentioning that to me," his mother said. "Your letters were most vivid."

The two ladies talked of travel until they were called to dinner. Yet despite the fact that neither of them had paid the least amount of attention to him after Lady Fitzwilliam's initial greetings, he had the feeling there was something more to this visit, and that was making his shoulders tense.

They dined in the family dining room, where the table had been reduced to seat four. He and his mother sat at either end of the table and Lady Fitzwilliam was between them.

After the first course had been served, she turned her attention to him. "I understand you have not been in Town recently either. What have you been doing to entertain yourself?"

"There was a great deal to keep me busy at my estates."

Nate felt his fingers curl tightly around the stem of his wineglass and loosened them. "I was, unfortunately, not up to the task when my brother died, and he allowed stewards to advise him instead of going around himself. I have come to realize that is not a satisfactory way to run estates and care for one's dependents."

"I understand you have decided to look for a wife." She pierced a piece of fish, but her sharp gaze stayed on him.

"I have. Now that I have things in order, it is time for me to find a helpmate." He took a drink, willing himself to sip his wine slowly.

"A helpmate." The lady's brows shot up, again, reminding him of someone else. "Am I correct in assuming from that remark that you wish to have a partnership with a lady?"

"Yes." He was absolutely certain about that. "I have discovered the value of a woman's opinion. Much of the time you ladies, and others of your gender, have different ways of looking at things than we gentlemen have. At first I was surprised, but I should not have been." He inclined his head toward his mother. "After all, I had an excellent example of the common sense a lady can bring to a matter." And in the Odells a good example of how a couple working together can accomplish what they want.

Her ladyship swallowed a piece of fish. "Are you seeking a love match?"

Nate felt as if he was taking an examination for which he had not studied and did not know the correct answers. His normally healthy appetite was rapidly deserting him. "I would prefer one." From the corner of his eye, he caught his mother's surprised expression. It was not something he'd have wanted before. Yet he'd heard that Merton had benefited greatly from his love match. "I believe there are good arguments to be made for them."

"I am not arguing against them at all," Lady Fitzwilliam said. "When they are based upon mutual respect as well as passion, they work quite well. It is when there is only lust and nothing else that problems arise."

Nate quickly swallowed a large portion of wine as she went back to the fish as if she hadn't said anything out of the ordinary.

"Are you all right, my dear?" Mama asked. "You are not eating much."

He had to clear his throat before he could answer her question. "I am fine." But who the devil was that woman? Lady Fitzwilliam's lips twitched, and for a moment he wondered if he asked the question out loud. "I just don't seem to have much of an appetite this evening."

His mother stared at him. "You do look a little peaked. We will understand if you would like to be excused."

"Yes." He rose. "I think I will go to my room." He could order a tray from the kitchen. Nate bowed to his mother and her friend. "Please enjoy the rest of your meal."

He strode straight to the door and into the corridor, closing the dining room door behind him, and leaning against it.

"Catherine, do you think he suspects?" Lady Fitzwilliam asked.

Suspects what? What the devil is going on?

"My dear Duchess, he's not stupid, but it would be a great leap for him to connect you with your granddaughter."

Duchess? Damn! That was who she reminded him of. *Both of her granddaughters.* He almost went back into the dining room, but that would be foolish. Somehow, he'd work out why she was here and what was going on, but it would take some thought. He stepped quietly onto the thick corridor carpet knowing it would muffle his footsteps, and made his way to his chamber. The only reason that immediately came to mind for his mother to invite the Duchess of Bristol to dine with them and for the duchess to assume another name was if his mother had recognized the lady he'd told her about. And she was here to look him over, as it were.

He opened the door to his parlor and was greeted by Padraig. "Well, old boy, I think our lives might soon become interesting." Tail wagging, the Wolfhound leaned against Nate as he tugged the bell-pull. When Styles answered Nate ordered a tray. "We're going for a ride in the morning even if it's raining. I need some space. Clearly, I've been away from Town too long to enjoy the machinations of the ladies."

For the first time in four years, he felt as if his life was not completely in his control, and he didn't like it at all.

Henrietta jumped out of bed and ran to the window. Light-gray clouds were gathering in the sky, but there should be enough time to have a ride.

Spyer entered the bedchamber from the dressing room carrying Henrietta's dark-green habit. "You must hurry if you wish to do more than get to the Park and return."

"So I surmised." She barely had enough time to gulp her tea and eat the toast before she was dressed and her hair done.

When she reached the hall, one of the footmen held open the door. "Have a good ride, miss."

"I shall." She wondered how wet she would be when she arrived home.

Fortunately, Dorie was already mounted. "It looks like rain."

Henrietta glanced at the sky. "All the more reason to hurry."

They urged their horses into trots and in a few minutes entered the Park.

"Gallop?" Dorie asked.

"Yes." Henrietta had fidgets she was unable to get rid of, and she did not even know the cause of them.

They flew down the carriage way, then off though the trees, coming to a halt near the Serpentine. She leaned down and patted Lilly's neck. "That was fun."

"It was," Dorie agreed, turning her horse. "We should probably head back. Our stable master sent word with my groom that he thought it would be raining within the hour."

"That is what I thought as well. I hope this is not going to be a wet year." Only three years before, they did not even have a summer, and that was the least of it. Crops had failed all over England. "How is your son?"

Dorie glanced at Henrietta with her marchioness look on her countenance. "I had a discussion with Nurse, and we have come to a resolution. She will do as I wish unless she believes it threatens David's health. Then we will discuss the matter."

"A fair compromise." Although Henrietta could not for the life of her think of anything her friend would do to harm her own child.

"I agree." Dorie nodded. "Other than feeding him when he is hungry, we have agreed on a schedule of sorts. Nurse firmly believes that children need to know what to expect in order to be happy."

"That makes sense too." Were children raised in other ways? If so, Henrietta did not know of it.

"It does." Dorie glanced at Henrietta. "I did manage to convince her that my milk was the best for him. My sister-in-law was a great help. Apparently, she had to have the same discussion with my old nurse."

Henrietta chuckled at an image of nurses rising up to protect the status quo. "It sounds like a revolution of modern mothers. Or perhaps I mean mothers from a certain set. My mother nursed us, and my father supported her fully."

"Yes, but your father is a Radical," Dorie pointed out. "I doubt Exeter had given it a second's thought."

"True." If it was up to Henrietta's father, the peerage would no longer exist. Every citizen would have the right to vote, male and female, and the right to run for office. He would also abolish the laws pertaining to a married woman's property and identity.

"Who is that?" Dorie was staring across the way. "And what kind of beast is with him?"

Henrietta swung her head around. "An Irish Wolfhound." Her heart started to beat a rapid tattoo as she took in the dark-haired gentleman on a chestnut horse. It must be the man Merton had seen. But was it her gentleman? "Can we ride a little closer to him without attracting his attention?"

"You think it is *him*?" Dorie's eyes seemed riveted on the rider.

"I think it might be." Henrietta turned her horse toward the man. "Come, we do not need to get very close. I should be able to recognize him."

Her friend followed suit. "How wonderful if it does turn out to be him. It is a pity that there is still no one to introduce you."

They closed the distance until she had a better look at the gentleman. "I believe it is the same gentleman."

"That suit was definitely not made in Town."

She had to agree with her friend's opinion. "It was not."

"He has an excellent seat," Dorie opined. "I wish I could see his face."

"If we ride a little to the right, and he is going toward the Grosvenor gate, then we should be able to catch a glimpse of his face." Or Henrietta hoped they would.

Dorie laughed and clasped a hand over her mouth. "Forgive me. It simply struck me as ridiculous that we are trailing a gentleman. There must be a better way to do this."

"I am all ears, if you are able to think of one." Henrietta could not quite keep the sarcasm from her tone.

Just then he turned, and her heart stopped. It was him! She held out her hand to halt her friend, but Dorie had already stopped. "Yes."

"You are sure?"

"I would know him anywhere." Now what? Dorie was correct. Henrietta had no one to introduce him to her.

"If we knew who he was or where he lived, I could ask Exeter to discover more about him," her friend suggested.

"Do you think we could follow him without being seen?" It would be embarrassing in the extreme to be caught following the gentleman.

"It is not as if we are the only ones out." As if to prove her point, a milk wagon passed by on the road.

"My lady?" Dorie's groom, who was so discreet Henrietta always forgot he was there, motioned toward the sky. "We need to be going if you don't want to get wet."

"There, you see?" She smiled slyly. "We have a perfect excuse."

"I suppose so." *Why am I so shy about him seeing me?* "Of course we do."

They had almost got right behind him when the heavens opened, and they made a dash into Grosvenor Square and to their respective houses. But when Dorie passed by, the groom was not in sight. Henrietta glanced to her right and saw the servant behind the gentleman. It looked as if she was going to know the identity of her mystery gentleman sooner rather than later.

CHAPTER EIGHT

Nate rose just before dawn and looked out the window. In the east the sky was growing lighter, but clouds impeded the sun's progress. If he was going riding it was now or never. Padraig shifted in his sleep while Nate donned the clothing his valet had left out.

He slipped his watch into his pocket. "Come on, boy. Let's go get Darragh."

The Wolfhound lifted his head and stretched before getting to his feet and stretching again and going to the door. Whoever he married would have to like having dogs in the house. He hoped Miss Stern liked dogs. When they reached the stable, he waved away the stable boy, who was already mucking out the stalls, and saddled his horse.

"Have a good ride, my lord."

"I only hope I don't get too wet." Darragh's hooves clattered on the cobblestone street.

Soon his little group entered the Park. Nate paused for a moment and gazed around. Most of the trees had buds but wouldn't be in full leaf for another few weeks. Early spring flowers dotted the lawn, and birds flitted from place to place searching for food. It was the first time he'd been here this early, when no one else was around. He moved the horse forward and let Darragh set the pace. For several minutes the horse went no faster than a walk. Traveling in a wagon must be as tiring on a horse as it was on a human. Perhaps Nate should have waited another day or so. Padraig amused himself by chasing the birds and came back looking pleased with himself.

Now that Nate had a suit of clothes he could go to one of his clubs, but he was undecided as to which one he wanted to visit. White's would be the most obvious choice. Or would have been. He had a membership at Brooks's as well, but he'd never been there. He supposed he'd have to decide whether he wanted to brave the chance of running into Worthington or Merton. Early in his time at home, Nate had received letters complaining that his old friend had changed parties and was now a Whig. That was a decision he'd have to make as well. He doubted his current views agreed with the Tories. Most of the laws they passed seemed to benefit themselves and not the populace in general.

He glanced at the sky and patted his horse's neck. "It's time to start back. Padraig might not care about the rain, but you don't like it at all."

Just as he reached the turn for Grosvenor Square and South Audley Street, rain started pelting down, convincing the horse to trot instead of walking. Nate glanced to the left, making sure Padraig was still near him, and saw two ladies riding into Grosvenor Square. Both had dark hair. But only one of them looked familiar. Two thoughts came to him at the same time. It was her, and Merton lived in Grosvenor Square. Nate heard himself groan. He might just as well return to Ouse Tower. If he'd had any doubts at all about her relationship to Lady Merton, they had ended.

Merton and his wife wouldn't allow Nate within a mile of her sister. Not after what he'd done. "My life has become much too complicated lately."

He guided the horse to his stables, and his groom came running up.

"The boy said you'd gone out." Jones stroked Darragh's nose, and Nate swung down from the horse. "We'll get you dry." The groom glanced at him. "You best get dry too. Padraig looks like a drowned rat. Do you want me to keep him here until he won't make so much of a mess?"

"It won't do any good. This rain looks like it's here to stay for a while. Give me something, and I'll dry him when I get to the house."

Jones handed Nate a large, folded cotton cloth. "That should do it."

He tucked the towel in his jacket. "Thank you. Padraig, come." He raced to the house and entered through a door the servants used. Before he could unfold the towel, the dog started shaking the water off him. "If I wasn't already soaked, I would be now." Nate covered the hound with the cloth and started to rub, but the dog kept moving around, trying to direct his drying efforts. "Hold still." By the time he was done, a puddle of water had formed on the floor, and he dropped the soaked towel over it. "That's not going to do much good. We need to find someone to clean it up. I'm pretty sure they won't let me do it."

He took the servants' stairs to his rooms, then tugged the bell-pull. Styles poked his head out of the dressing room. "Are you ready for a bath?"

"I am. We left a puddle of water near the back door. I tried to take care of the mess myself, but—"

"I'll send someone to clean it up." The valet grinned. "I've never seen a dog hold so much water."

"Only because the other dogs around have short hair."
Nate stripped down as pails of hot water were brought in.
"You timed that nicely."

"Even Padraig doesn't like cold rain. I expected the
horse to rush to the stables but remembered that he might
not know the way back yet."

"He quickened his step. Fortunately, we weren't far."
The footman left, and he padded over to the tub, sinking
into the hot water. "I suppose it's a good thing I wasn't
wearing new kit."

Styles glanced down at Nate's boots. "The wool is fine.
It's the boots that are going to be a problem. You'll be
wearing shoes or slippers until these dry and I can get
them polished."

"My new ones should be here soon." Nate took the
scrap of linen hanging on the side of the tub and ran soap
over it. "I'll order a second pair as well. I should have
brought my others, but they're well-worn and look it."

His valet picked up the boots and stuffed them with
rags. "Did you plan to go anywhere today?"

Not now. He wasn't going to take the chance of ruining
his shoes as well. His wet boots shouldn't feel like a gift
from fate, but they did. Still, he couldn't put off making
the rounds too long. "No. I must look over some correspondence."

"I'll have them ready by morning at the latest." Styles
set the Hessians back a bit from the fire.

It was good to have a valet who didn't become miffed
at wet boots or other things. Nate's old valet had left not
even five months after he'd been sent down from London.
He'd gone without—which had *not* been fun—for almost
a month before he'd found Styles. Nate had never had a
more pragmatic valet before. Then again, he'd only had

one other valet. He grinned to himself. The day he'd come home with mangled gold tassels on his boots, his old valet had broken into tears. Nate didn't even want to think what the state of the tassels would have been if Padraig had got hold of them when he was a puppy. Nate shook his head. How could he have been so unkind to that other puppy? Lady Merton had been right to have rung a peal over his head.

"Are you ready to rinse, my lord?"

He looked down at the soapy water. He hadn't even remembered washing himself. Not that it took much thought. "Er, yes." He stood and dumped a bucket of clean water over himself. "I'm becoming distracted."

"It happens to everyone at some point or another." He was glad for the valet's calm good sense.

"I suppose it does." But it hadn't happened to him in several years.

It occurred to him that he had a lot to think about before appearing in public. If only he hadn't listened to Lady Manners when she'd told him Merton truly did not wish to marry Dotty Stern. Yet Nate had been all too willing to believe the worst of the young lady. Even her argument that he could very well ruin her reputation hadn't made him change his mind. Recalling the conversation made him cringe. It was almost worse that very few people knew about what had occurred. Merton, his wife, his mother, and in-laws, and Worthington, his wife, and who knew how many of the others. Merton's cousin Louisa would know, as would Lady Charlotte Carpenter, Lady Worthington's sister. But he'd heard she had married as well. Who was it? Ah, yes, Kenilworth. And Louisa had wed a duke. Nate pulled on a pair of old buckskin breeches. If they chose, they could make life extremely uncomfortable for him. Not that he didn't deserve it.

The door to the room opened and closed. Perhaps he should have stayed away for another four years. But it was time he faced up to his misdeeds. At least now he knew he could live, and live well, in the country. In fact, he preferred it to Town. If only he hadn't met Miss Stern, he'd probably flee back to Ouse Tower.

Padraig, who had been lying between the tub and the fireplace, shoved his head into Nate's hand and, recognizing the command, he started stroking the dog. There was one being who didn't care what had happened before. But he had to find a way to move past what he'd done and make amends to those he had harmed. And, possibly, gain permission to meet Miss Stern. The question was how.

Henrietta slid off her horse before the groom could help her down and dashed to the front door. Her small, round hat adorned with a long feather was most likely ruined. Her boots were fairly dry, but her habit was drenched.

The door opened as she approached, and Parkin grimaced as he bowed. "Is it worse than I think it is?"

"No, Miss Henrietta. There is just the matter of the red feather leaving some of its dye on your face."

Lovely. She hoped it came off her as easily as it had come off the feather. She pulled out the hat-pin and removed the bonnet only to have red dye on her fingers as well. The hat, made of cork, looked as if it was still in good shape, but only time would tell. "I'm going to change."

"Yes, miss." He gazed pointedly down at the floor. For the first time she understood why Merton wished his butler was more stoic. She had not needed to know a puddle was forming at her feet.

Taking the stairs as quickly as she could, she rushed to her chamber. "Spyer, I am a mess."

"That's not surprising in the least. As soon as it started to rain I pulled out the tub and sent for hot water. Let's get you out of those clothes."

Henrietta held up the hat. "Do you think it can be saved?"

"Not the feather." Her maid took the bonnet. "Go wash your hands and face. I hope it comes off."

She went behind the screen and grabbed the soap. It took a little scrubbing, but soon the red dye was gone. By the time she was done, hot water was in the bathtub and she was starting to shiver. Spyer had Henrietta undressed in almost no time and into the hot water.

"I hope you don't take a chill."

"We almost made it. It only started to pour when we reached the entrance to the square."

Spyer's tightly closed lips indicated that she was not impressed. "Next time—and I assume there will be a next time—try to pay a little more attention to the weather."

"I will. I hope I did not ruin my habit." It was her favorite one.

"I'll do what I can." Her maid's tone was not promising.

"Thank you." It was not fashionable to thank servants, even senior staff, but her mother, the daughter of a duchess, maintained that being kind and respectful to servants prompted them to give better service, and she liked thanking people for their work. Everyone should be appreciated for doing a good job. Henrietta sank into the warm water.

"You're welcome, Miss Henrietta. You know I will always do my best for you."

"I do know it"—she smiled to herself—"and I do not know what I would do without you."

"Well, pray God we never find out." Her maid gave a rare sniff.

She really could not complain. The only time Spyer was put out was when she thought Henrietta had endangered her health. Coming back cold and wet was high on the list of things being dangerous to one's health. "I will not tell you there is no need to be concerned. Although I do think that I was able to get warm before any damage was done."

Two buckets of hot water later, Henrietta's skin was a rosy shade of pink. Standing, she stepped into a warm towel. She would be fine. But she did worry about Dorie. Although she was surely receiving the same treatment as Henrietta. Shortly after her hair was dried and pinned up, she dressed in a light, woolen day dress and went down to the breakfast room.

CHAPTER NINE

When Henrietta arrived for breakfast, only Merton was there. "Is Dotty not feeling well?"

He finished chewing and swallowed. "It's the baby again. I suggested she take her breakfast in her chamber, and she agreed." He pulled a face. "Unfortunately, I was unsuccessful at convincing her she should remain in bed for the rest of the day."

Poor Merton. He so much wanted to protect Dotty, and she would only allow a certain amount of coddling. "I'm sure she will be fine. This baby seems very different from the first one. Do you think it's a sign of a boy?"

"It could be, but that means nothing to me if she is not well." He picked up a piece of toast and frowned.

"Is there anyone you could ask?" Maybe being around one of his friends who had gone through this would help him.

He stared at Henrietta as if she were an aberration. "That's an excellent idea. Kenilworth and Rothwell will be in Town soon. I'll visit them when they arrive." He frowned again. "I am right that Louisa had a boy, am I not?"

"Yes." Henrietta hid her smile. "In December."

"I thought Thea had mentioned it. It's the off year when I have trouble keeping track of everyone."

That confused Henrietta until she remembered that every other year Louisa and the Worthington family spent Christmas together, and last year everyone remained at their own homes. Dotty and Merton joined in the rota because the gathering was always at Stanwood House, Grace Worthington's family home, which was close to Dotty and Henrietta's family. But Henrietta wondered if they would go there this year; Charlie, Earl of Stanwood, would still be on his Grand Tour. She gave herself a shake. Her close and extended family was growing by the year. Not a month ago, her friend, Adeline Littleton, had given birth to twins, a boy and a girl. Dorie had a baby, and Georgie would have one this year. Of the five of them, only Henrietta and Augusta were not filling their nurseries. But at least Augusta was married.

Henrietta nibbled on a piece of toast. Stupidly, she had not thought it would affect her that her friends were all married, but she was definitely starting to feel left out. Of course, none of them purposely spent less time with her, but they had their own families. Had she been too hasty in rejecting the offers she received last Season? She speared a piece of her baked egg. No, none of them had been the right gentleman. And marrying simply to wed and have a family was not the answer. Not for her. Her mind drifted to the gentleman with the dog. Would he be the right one? He had not seemed to think it strange that she was rescuing children. And as it was something she was determined to continue to do after she married, any husband she had would have to agree.

Merton stood. "I must be off."

"Have a good day." She finished eating and went to the library. The room was almost two stories high with a balcony that went around the upper floor, and a spiral staircase connecting the balcony to the ground floor. Books dating back centuries could be found, and they were all shelved by subject and author. Two large fireplaces were kept lit, warming the room, until late in the evening because Merton, Dotty, Henrietta, and the Dowager Lady Merton when she was in residence frequented the room on a regular basis. Henrietta found a book she had loathed when she was still in the schoolroom a few years before written by Ovid, in Greek. Her father did not believe that ladies should be taught less than gentlemen. Which meant that in addition to all the things she and her sisters had to learn to be proper ladies, they also had to study Latin, Greek, and the higher maths. She remembered an argument she'd had with her sister, attempting to maintain that men did not want intelligent and educated females. It had not taken long for Henrietta to be proven wrong. At least about any gentleman she would want to wed.

She curled up in a large, brown velvet chair and opened the book, which had become an old friend. About a half hour later a tea tray arrived with slices of lemon cake and two ginger biscuits. The footman had entered the room and left before the scents reached her nose. She poured a cup of tea, selected a biscuit, and got lost in the story again.

"Miss," Parkin said rather loudly. "A letter from Exeter House has arrived for you."

"Thank you." She held out her hand for the missive, written on finely pressed paper.

Placing the book on a small, round cherry table next to the chair, she popped open the seal.

> *My dearest Henrietta,*
>
> *I had my groom follow "the gentleman." He turned onto Charles Street and into the mews, and stopped at the first stables. According to my map, that puts him at Forty Grosvenor Street. That house has been occupied by the Fotherby family since it was built. I trust this information is helpful.*
>
> > *Yr. devoted friend,*
> > *D.*

"Oh, God." Henrietta covered her eyes and groaned. "It needed only this. Why is it that the only gentleman who has interested me at all abducted my sister?"

She closed the book. Even Ovid would not be able to distract her now. She supposed she should forget about Lord Fotherby. After all, they had not even been properly introduced. She munched on a ginger cookie, swallowed, and took a sip of tea. He must have been a truly horrid person. But the gentleman she had met was in no way objectionable. On the contrary, he had been extremely helpful and polite. And he had not judged her actions. What was it Merton had said?

It was Thea's idea to allow his mother to deal with him, and Lady Fotherby decreed he was to be banished to the country until he learned his lesson and gained sufficient maturity to be let loose again.

Therefore, if Lord Fotherby—even if it was the wrong name, it was nice to have a name for him—was in Town, presumably his mother had decided he had changed sufficiently. That would explain his clothing and the dog, and the way he'd behaved toward her. Merton had also mentioned that his cousin had not liked him at the time he'd met her sister. Had Merton changed? If so, perhaps he would acknowledge that Lord Fotherby had changed as well. Still, if she was not to have anything to do with him, how would she find out? She reviewed the conversation again. No one had actually said she could not dance with him. Of course, no one knew he was in Town. Perhaps this might be one of those cases where it was easier to get forgiveness than permission. If, that was, she could find someone to introduce them. She glanced at Dorie's letter again. A meeting might already be planned.

Nate finished dressing and went to the breakfast room, Padraig at his heel. He was surprised to find his mother already there. "Good morning. You are up early."

"Good morning, dear. I have a great deal to do today." She folded the newssheet she'd been reading and placed it on the table by her elbow. "Are you feeling better today?"

"Yes." He should ask her about the duchess, but first he needed food and tea.

"The bacon is particularly good this morning." Mama cut a piece of the bacon. "I think Cook must have found a new supplier."

Stepping over to the sideboard, he lifted the lid on the first tray and found poached eggs. He took two, then found the bacon, added some ham, and went back to the table. A fresh rack of toast had just been brought in, and his mother handed him a cup of tea.

"What are your plans for today?" she asked.

"I was going to visit one or two of my clubs, but I went

riding this morning and my boots are soaked. The pair I ordered from Hoby have not yet arrived, and I don't want to ruin my shoes, so I'm staying home." He cut an egg and dipped a piece of toast in it. "Do you have plans for the day?"

"I have an appointment with my modiste." She sipped her tea. "When do you expect to receive more footwear?"

"Soon. If nothing has arrived by this afternoon, I'll have Styles look into it." He finished the toast and took another. "Mama, what was the Duchess of Bristol doing here last evening, and why did the two of you attempt to mislead me as to her identity?"

His mother had just taken another sip of tea and quickly held a serviette to her lips. "I would not say that we misled you."

If not misleading, Nate would like to know what she called it. He raised a brow. "Indeed?"

"Quite." His mother matched his look with a completely unrepentant one of her own. "We lied to you quite purposefully."

This time Nate almost spewed the tea from this mouth. "Good Lord, why?"

"Well, you see, she was the one who approached me after you had the poor sense to abduct her granddaughter. I surmised from your description of the lady you met that it was Henrietta Stern." Now he had a name. Henrietta was a strong name, and it suited her. "I decided if you were to have any sort of opportunity to be introduced to the young lady, it might be helpful to approach her grandmother. Fortunately, we have been friends for many years, and in my letters to her I mentioned your progress."

He'd had no idea his mother could be so devious. "In effect, you came up with the lie together?"

"Not precisely." She picked up her cup again. "The duchess wished to meet you. And she decided to use one of her late husband's minor titles."

"So that I would not know who she was." No wonder he'd felt as if his life was out of his control. A duchess, of all people, was meddling in it.

"Yes." His mother took a sip of tea and set it down, then proceeded to twist the cup around on the saucer. "If it makes any difference, she formed an excellent opinion of you."

Nate pinched the bridge of his nose. He had spent the last four years learning to stand on his own two feet. To direct the course his life would take. And even though his mother and the duchess obviously had his best interests at heart, he did not want to be handled, and he had the feeling they were more than capable of doing just that. Then again, he did not wish to be perverse. He might—hell, he *would*—require their help even to gain an introduction to Henrietta Stern. And that was assuming she would have anything to do with him. Although, from the way she had acted after he had assisted her, he was certain there was something—an attraction—between them. Yet, he didn't for a moment doubt that when Merton or her sister discovered he was in Town, they would warn her against him. It amazed him that the Duchess of Bristol had considered meeting him at all. And that must have been the reason for the subterfuge. If she had found him lacking, he would have been none the wiser.

"Fotherby, do you have nothing to say?" His mother sounded concerned.

"I am not quite sure what *to* say." He wished he'd not so

thoroughly complicated his life. The desire to return home was stronger than ever. Then again, so was his desire to properly meet Miss Stern. "We only met once and the meeting did not last long." Although, he would *like* to get to know her better. Nay, he was *determined* to know her better.

"You could forget about Miss Stern and look for another lady." His mother's nose wrinkled. "I am sure I could find you a lady with *some* of the characteristics you want."

He could not imagine any other lady with her bravery. "I could return to Ouse Tower." But did he truly wish to run home? Because that would be exactly what he would be doing. Running away from anyone who knew of his wrongdoing, and from a lady he might want to wed. "I simply wish the situation was not so problematical."

"You have at least one thing in common." He raised a brow. How could she possibly know he and Miss Stern had anything in common? "You both put yourselves forward to help others."

Mama was right about that. "I suppose we do."

She placed her serviette next to her plate and rose, prompting him to stand. "Give it some thought. You do not have to do anything today."

"I shall. Thank you for your assistance."

"I am always glad to help you." A wrinkle creased her still-smooth forehead. "If you are able, I would like you to escort me to Lady Thornhill's drawing room in two days' time."

He'd never been to one of her ladyship's drawing rooms. Before, he had considered the entertainment a hotbed of radicalism. He even remembered how appalled he'd been when Merton mentioned attending. Of its own volition, one corner of his mouth rose. He'd finally get to see why it was so disdained in Tory circles. "I would be delighted."

"Oh, I am glad." His mother smiled. "I think you will enjoy yourself. There are, naturally, any number of artists who attend, but also inventors."

New inventions always interested him. Attending would also give him another way to ease himself back into the *ton* than attending one of his clubs. Nate inclined his head. "I look forward to it."

The wolfhound had opened one eye, but when he went back to his seat, Padraig shut it again. After this morning's exercise, he'd probably sleep most of the day. Nate finished his breakfast, then headed to his study. A packet from Ouse Tower had arrived yesterday. By now his secretary would have sorted through it. When he entered the room he was pleased to see three neat stacks of letters. The first for bills, the second, and smallest, from tenants, and the third regular correspondence. One letter was placed in the middle of his desk. He picked it up and shook it out.

To Viscount Fotherby,

We thought you might like to know that we arrived home safely, and Emily and little John are doing well and already putting on some much-needed flesh.

Yr. Servant,
Odell

Nate grinned to himself. Little had given him more pleasure than helping to find Emily and her son. He opened the center drawer, tucked the letter away, and started on the bills. When he was finished, his mind strayed back to the day he'd arrived in Town. The other thing in which he'd been more than happy to assist was rescuing the baby. He would like to help fund the effort as well. He dipped his pen in the standish and started to write a cheque, then realized that all of his cheques now had his name printed on them. That wouldn't do at all. He wasn't ready for his former friend to know he was in Town. He'd have to have his secretary take the funds to them. He wrote a cheque for Chetwin to draw the funds from the bank. Nate also needed money for the household account. He wrote another cheque.

Gathering up the payments for the invoices, he strolled into his secretary's office. "These are ready to be sent." He set the cheques on Chetwin's desk. "There is another matter I'd like you to see to. I wish to make a donation to the Phoenix Street charity, but I want you to take the funds to them and use the name Meadows if asked who made the donation"—but did he really want the money traced back to him?—"No, better the gift is given anonymously."

Chetwin opened his mouth, shook his head, and closed his lips. "Yes, my lord. What amount would you like to give?"

"One thousand pounds." Nate had no idea of their expenses, but had gathered there were several properties and many children and women involved.

"I take it the rest is to have on hand."

"It is. I do not yet know how much we'll require on a weekly basis, but we can start with five hundred." Nate glanced out the window. He'd almost forgotten it was raining. "Tomorrow will be soon enough."

"If it stops pouring?" his secretary gave a wry smile. "It is England."

"I suppose you're right. If I had more than one pair of boots, I'd go out. But Styles was right when he said that only one of my pairs was suitable for Town and advised leaving the other pair at home."

"I'll send a footman to the post office and I'll go to the bank." Styles pulled out a large piece of foolscap and began to cut it. "They will be ready soon."

"I'll have the town coach brought around for you. That will keep you a little dryer." Nate would have to send for the unmarked carriage. Fortunately, the vehicle had a convertible cover to protect the coachman from the weather.

"Thank you."

"You're welcome." It was the least he could do.

Now if only he could work out a way to see Miss Stern again and be properly introduced to her. On the other hand, he might be better served waiting for his mother to arrange it. The question was, how long would it take?

CHAPTER TEN

After consuming the tea and biscuits, Henrietta decided to move to her parlor. The rain was still coming down in buckets, and there was no sign at all that it would end soon. Fortunately, one of the things she had purchased was a stout umbrella. As soon as it arrived, she could take advantage of it. But for now, she could curl up on the comfortable sofa in her parlor, which was warmed by the fire. She had removed her slippers and tucked her feet under the light, cashmere day dress she had donned.

A few minutes later, Parkin knocked on the door of her parlor and entered. "Miss Henrietta, a letter has arrived for you from the Duchess of Bristol."

"Thank you, Parkin." She took the letter, popped the seal, and opened it.

My dearest Henrietta,

I arrived in Town and am residing at the Pultney Hotel. I would like you to join me for luncheon the day after tomorrow. After which we shall find something to occupy our time.

> *Your Grandmother,*
> *B.*

"I did not even know she was back in the country. I wonder what brought her to Town?" she mused to herself.

"I couldn't say, miss," Parkin said. "Will you respond to her missive?"

She had forgotten he was still there and smiled ruefully. "Even though this is more in the line of a royal command than a request, I suppose I should."

"I should say so." He sounded so offended at the notion that she might not send her grandmother an answer, she almost laughed.

"Give me a few moments." She went to her desk and scribbled a hasty note, telling her grandmother how happy she was to be able to see her again. Once Henrietta had sealed it, she handed the letter to him. "There you are."

"Thank you, miss." The butler bowed and left.

She wondered if her sister knew their grandmother was here. No. Dotty would have mentioned it. And when had Grandmamma returned from the Continent? Henrietta supposed all her questions would have to wait to be answered. What she really wanted was to know what to do about Fotherby. She could not see her grandmother helping with that problem. In fact, none of her family would be helpful. Dorie might be able to assist, but the problem was that she had not met him either.

Henrietta pulled out a piece of paper and was sharpening her pen when a knock sounded on her door and it opened.

Parkin entered and bowed. "The Marchioness of Exeter to see you, miss."

"Dorie, I was just thinking of you." Henrietta led her friend to a small sofa. "But what are you doing out in this weather?"

"Oh, pooh. I am not going to let a bit of rain keep me

inside." The corners of her lips twitched. "I have been terribly extravagant. I had them bring the coach around, and a footman armed with a large umbrella escorted me to and from the carriage. I will have to send a note when I wish to return."

"I can send you safely home with a footman and the large umbrella." Henrietta frowned. "If Merton has not taken it." The thing was so big and heavy, she had never been tempted to use it herself. "I do not suppose the umbrella you bought has arrived yet?"

"No. I do not expect to see it until later today or tomorrow." Dorie sank on to the sofa. "It is nice and warm in here."

"It is. I was in the library and it started to become a bit chilly. This room is much easier to keep warm."

Henrietta moved to the bell-pull to order tea, but the door opened again, and Parkin entered carrying a large tray with tea, biscuits, and sandwiches. "I thought you might wish some sustenance."

Her friend slid her a look and almost made her laugh. "Thank you, Parkin. I was just going to ask for a tray."

"Yes, miss. I know." He set down the tray on a round table with two chairs and unloaded the tray, placing everything precisely before leaving the room.

Once the door closed, Dorie went off into a peel of giggles. "I have never in my life seen such an unusual butler."

"I adore him." Henrietta waved her friend to the table. "Although Merton bemoans that he is not stiff and formal like most of the breed." She poured two cups of tea and handed Dorie one. "His cousin Matt Worthington maintains that Merton was so stuffy it was good for him to have a butler who was not."

"I always forget they are related. Were their mothers sisters?" Dorie picked up a lemon biscuit and bit into it.

"No. It's actually a distant connection, although the two branches remained close. In fact, Merton was Matt's heir until Grace had their little boy." Henrietta ate a lemon biscuit, but her friend's brows rose, wanting the rest of the story. "Matt's several times grandfather was a younger son who married the daughter of an earl. The earl had no male heirs. Matt's ancestor had to agree to take the Vivers name, and there was something in the letter of patent that allowed his son to take the title."

"How exciting!" Dorie's face lit up. "The lady must have been a countess in her own right after her father died. It is much more common among barons for that to happen."

"I suppose so." Henrietta shrugged. "That part was never made clear to me. I wonder what it would be like to have one's own title?"

"We could ask the Duchess of Wharton when she comes to Town," Dorie said. "I think it is dreadfully unfair that she cannot sit in the Lords. Or at least allow her husband to sit in the Lords, but that ended sometime in the late sixteenth century."

Henrietta had consumed one of the chicken sandwiches while her friend was talking. "You know a great deal about this sort of thing."

"My father's titles include a barony, and if there are no male heirs, it would go to the eldest female. That in itself is different because many times in cases like that someone would choose which daughter would take the title."

"Almost as if they do not trust that the older daughter might not be able to perform the tasks."

"It would not be a bad thing if they did that with the

gentlemen," Dorie said, her voice as dry as sand. "Some of the ones who are the heirs have very little sense."

Well, this had been a pleasant and welcome diversion, but it still did not help with Henrietta's problem with Fotherby.

"Speaking of peers." Dorie put down her cup. "I asked Exeter if he knew Lord Fotherby. He did not. However, he will make a point of introducing himself. After which, I shall arrange for him to be presented to you." She smiled smugly.

"That is a wonderful idea! Thank you." Now the only thing Henrietta had to do was to make sure that she could find a way for her family not to forbid her to dance with him.

Her friend rose and moved over to a window. "It has stopped raining. Shall we ride in the morning?"

"Yes. Let's do." She walked Dorie to the front door. "I wonder how long it will take Exeter to meet"—Henrietta did not dare mention Fotherby's name out loud—"the gentleman."

"Not long at all." Dorie bussed Henrietta's cheek. "Until later."

Once Dorie left, Henrietta tried to think of a way to approach her sister and brother-in-law about Fotherby. She could wait until she knew if she truly did like him, but that might be too late. Yet what if her sister forbade the connection? If only she knew what to do. Dotty had been furious when Merton had mentioned Fotherby. Henrietta had never seen her sister react that way before. She stood at one of the windows in her parlor, attempting to think of someone, anyone, who might be able to help.

Lady Worthington, a voice whispered in Henrietta's mind.

Lady Worthington was the perfect person to assist her.

She was the most understanding person Henrietta knew. Grace Worthington had even arranged for Augusta to travel to Europe. And it was not as if Henrietta and Grace were not related. She was a cousin by marriage.

"If she could manage a European trip for her sister, she should be able to help me." She was also someone Dottie had known all her life and would listen to. Henrietta hoped.

Hulatt entered Nate's study and bowed. "The Marquis of Exeter would like to see you, my lord."

Exeter? Nate had never met the man. When his father and brother had been alive, he remembered his father had mentioned him when speaking with his older brother. Nate, of course, had never been involved in those conversations. He wondered what his lordship wanted. "Show him in."

"Yes, my lord." Less than two minutes later, his butler returned. "The Marquis of Exeter."

Standing, Nate began to wave his guest to a chair in front of his desk, then noticed the man was probably about the same age he was. This couldn't be the gentleman his father knew. "Please have a seat."

"Thank you." The man inclined his head.

Once Exeter had lowered himself into the chair, Nate came around his desk and took the second chair. Was the door knocker even up? "To what do I owe your visit?"

"My wife." Exeter had a fond look on his face that was obviously not because of Nate. "She is a force of nature."

"I do not believe I have met her." He spoke slowly, trying to place the lady.

"I have no doubt about that." Exeter's lips twitched and

laughter filled his eyes. "You did, however, meet one of her friends."

Hulatt brought in a tea tray and set it on Nate's desk. As he poured, he tried to think of any ladies he'd met—Miss Stern? It had to be. Was Lady Exeter merely meddling—he already had two females doing that—or did Miss Stern really wish to meet him? Or was it some other lady who had seen him? Although when another lady could have seen him, he didn't know. The only places he'd been was at the Park and to and from there. But no. It was a lady he had met, though obviously not properly. Ergo, it had to be Miss Stern.

Exeter took the cup. "I am here to invite you to tea. Tomorrow, if you are available."

"Tomorrow?" He nodded. "Yes. I am free." Nate wanted to ask more questions.

He must have opened his mouth, for Exeter shook his head. "I know little more. My wife and her friend saw you riding this morning. She sent her groom to find your house. Once he reported back, she discovered you are the gentleman her friend met." He finished his cup of tea, rose, and with a graceful gesture, indicated himself. "Hence my visit."

Nate stood as well. "I suppose I should instruct my staff to put up the knocker if it has not already been done."

"It has not." His lordship grinned. "May I ask to which party you belong?"

That was the exact question with which he'd been wrestling. "I used to claim the Tories. But now I believe I might do better with the Whig party."

Exeter nodded. "I was in the exact same position. My father was a Tory, but I am more comfortable being a Whig. Are you a member of Brooks's?"

"Yes. Since birth. I was signed up for White's, Boodle's, and Brooks's. Although I have only visited White's, and that not for several years."

"Again, exactly my position." He nodded again. "If you'd like, I'd be happy to take you around."

"Thank you. We might wish to have tea first." When Exeter discovered what Nate had done, would he still wish to spend time with him? Today was not the day to find out. After he went to Exeter House for tea would be a better time. And would Miss Stern still wish to know him? He could not believe she knew of his wrong doing.

"Of course. I shall see you tomorrow at three." Exeter inclined his head again. "Until then."

"Yes, and thank you." Feeling more than a little non-plussed by this turn of events, Nate walked with his lordship to the door. "Until tomorrow."

He watched as the man reached the pavement and strode down the street. "Hulatt, you may put up the knocker."

"Yes, my lord."

Nate wondered who, if anyone, would arrive next. He glanced at the clock and whistled. Not a second later, the sound of Padraig running from Nate's study echoed. "Good boy. Let's take a short walk. Not that you need one, but I do." He attached the lead and stepped outside. Had Miss Stern really told Lady Exeter about him? It seemed incredible. He'd been right. It had been Miss Stern he'd seen this morning, and the other lady must have been Lady Exeter. Why did he suddenly feel as if he was think-ing underwater? Lady Exeter knew who he was, but had she told Miss Stern? Or was her ladyship one of those women who insisted on arranging things to her own sat-isfaction? He shrugged. No matter what it was, he'd find out tomorrow.

Several fashionable carriages drove by headed toward the Park. Nate was not ready to see many people yet. "We're not going to the Park today. I'd take you to Green Park, but you might be too interested in the cows." Padraig glanced up, his tongue lolling out of his mouth. Perhaps the cows wouldn't be there in the afternoon. "Very well, Green Park it is."

When he arrived, the cows were grazing, but he was able to take a path that avoided the animals. Strange; he'd spent years coming to Town and had never before known there were various paths. In many ways, he was seeing London through different eyes. They reached the south side of the park and crossed Piccadilly. As he approached Grosvenor Square, he found his steps slowing. What if he were to leave his card at Merton House? Shaking his head, he walked on. He had to find some way of reintroducing himself to Merton.

Perhaps he'd be better off waiting to see if the attraction he thought was between Miss Stern and himself was actually there. It might have been a temporary result of the way they met. He nodded to himself. That was what he'd do. Discover if what he thought he felt about Henrietta Stern was true. If it was, then something would have to be done about his relations with the Mertons. Nate didn't like all this uncertainty. Nor did he like feeling as if a building was about to fall on his head, or his lack of self-confidence about the matter. Then again, there was no point worrying about it at the moment. There were too many variables. He and Miss Stern could see each other again and not be at all interested. He really couldn't believe that would happen, but it might. Almost anything was possible.

Nate strolled into his town house and back to his study

and found Chetwin had returned. "Were you able to deliver the donation?"

"I was." He grinned. "It was most appreciated. The manager—Mrs. Perriman, I believe her name is—tried to get me to tell her who the donor was, but I told her I had other errands and must leave."

"Good man." That had gone well. Nate trusted that the funds would be promptly deposited in the bank.

"My lord," Garford said from the door. "Your new boots have arrived. Mr. Styles would like you to try them on."

"Tell him I will be there in a few moments."

The servant bowed. "Yes, my lord."

Despite some of Nate's worries, this was turning into a very good day indeed. Hopefully, tomorrow would be even better.

CHAPTER ELEVEN

Taking advantage of the cessation of rain, Henrietta rang for her maid, changed into a walking gown, donned a spencer, and went downstairs. One of the footmen was speaking with Parkin. "May I borrow Jack for a while? I have decided to go to Worthington House."

"Yes, of course, miss," Parkin said.

"Thank you."

Followed by the footman, Henrietta walked to Berkeley Square and up the steps to Worthington House.

Thorton, the Worthington butler, opened the door. "Good day, miss. We have not seen you for some time."

"Good day, Thorton. Is her ladyship at home?"

He waved her into a small parlor. "Allow me to ascertain if she is receiving."

"Thank you." Henrietta was too nervous to sit and walked around the room, looking at the paintings on the wall. Some of them appeared to have been painted overseas.

Before she even finished looking at all of them, Thorton returned. "Miss Stern, please follow me."

She was led down the familiar corridor to Grace Worthington's study. The room was arranged for comfort rather than elegance. A cherry-wood desk with drawers anchored the center of the room against the wall. In front of the fireplace, two sofas faced each other over a low table, and a scattering of chairs were against the walls. The view out the window led onto the garden, and a glass door was situated next to the window. Everything about the room was light, airy, and comfortable, even on a gloomy day.

Grace smiled as Henrietta entered. Although approaching her thirtieth year, no lines marred her complexion, and her golden-blond hair showed no white. What was noticeable was that she was once again expecting a child.

Rising, she held out her hand. "This is a pleasant surprise."

Henrietta squeezed Grace's hands. "I have a problem."

"Oh dear." Consciously or unconsciously, Grace touched her stomach.

"No, not that." As liberal as Henrietta's parents were, their expectations of her did not include becoming pregnant without benefit of marriage. "Although congratulations on the next baby seem to be in order."

"Thank you." Grace smiled softly. "It is not due until late this summer." To Henrietta's mind, Grace looked farther along than that. "Let us be comfortable. Thorton will be here shortly with tea. Until then, tell me how Dotty, Merton, and your niece are doing."

"Dotty has decided to have another baby as well. She is due in September." Henrietta frowned to herself. "She is having a difficult time with this one. It is keeping her awake at night."

"That is never good. I do hope she is resting when she can. I shall make a point of visiting her." Grace grinned. "The children will not be far apart."

As she predicted, tea was brought, along with a generous selection of biscuits, tarts, and slices of lemon cake.

Henrietta took a cup from her ladyship, as well as a lemon curd tart.

Grace leaned slightly back against a large pillow. "Now tell me what is troubling you."

Henrietta thought about easing into the issue, but there really was no way to do it. "Do you remember when Dotty was abducted by Lord Fotherby?"

"I do." Although Grace's eyes had widened, there was no other indication that she was upset.

"Well"—Henrietta fiddled with the fringe on her spencer—"I met him by pure chance when I went to rescue a baby from Whitechapel."

Grace's brows drew together. "Were Dotty and Merton not with you?"

"No. They were out. Mrs. Perriman was on another call and the message was urgent."

"I see." And Grace did. She was the one who had encouraged Dotty to set up the charity and was still a patron.

"I took a footman who had fighting experience, a groom, and the coachman. But there was a problem. I had to shoot one of the men, causing one of his fellows to toss the infant toward me and run away. Then a strange gentleman caught the babe while the footman knocked out the third man." She took a sip of tea and a bite of the tart. The events seemed so far away now that it was almost as if it had happened to someone else. "He was dressed as a country gentleman and said he was in Town helping a neighbor fetch his daughter. And, indeed, there was a large traveling coach outside of the workhouse. I thought he was returning to the country, and that I would never see him again." She looked up and met Grace's eyes. "I was not happy about that certainty. He went to the coach, and we left."

A crease marred Grace's forehead. "Are you certain it

was Fotherby? I never met him, but Louisa has, and she said he was a Dandy."

"Merton said the same thing." Henrietta finished her tea and held her cup out for more. "Other than me, he was the first to see Lord Fotherby, but he did not recognize him as his former friend. You see, his lordship has changed. At least in the way he looks, and possibly in the way he thinks as well. He has an Irish Wolfhound. Merton said he was afraid of dogs."

Grace frowned slightly. "How do you know the gentleman you met is Lord Fotherby? I take it that you have not actually been introduced."

"No, we have not. I did not know who he was. I was riding with Dorie Exeter in the Park early this morning. And I saw him"—she grinned at their behavior—"we got a little closer so I could be sure it *was* him. Then it started to rain." There was no point in relating their decision to follow the man. "We dashed home, but Dorie sent her groom to find out where he lived."

"And now you know it is Lord Fotherby," Grace stated.

"Yes. I can only assume he is here for the Season. Why else would he remain in Town? Merton does not know the man he saw was Lord Fotherby. He told Dotty he thought at first it was him, but . . . ."

Grace's brows knitted as if she was thinking. "But there was nothing about him that was familiar?"

"Yes." Henrietta was glad Grace had seen the problem. "That is when they told me about him abducting Dotty." Henrietta sipped her tea and waited.

"This is quite a pickle." Grace poured herself another cup of tea. "Am I correct in assuming that if they do discover he is in Town, you will be forbidden from dancing with him?"

"Yes." Henrietta heaved a sigh. "At least, I believe that will be the case. Dorie is arranging for her husband to meet him so that he can be introduced to me."

Suddenly a door at the back of the room opened, and out spilled Eleanor and Alice, the Carpenter twins, Grace's sisters, and Madeline Vivers, Matt Worthington's sister.

"I told you you were leaning too much on the door. The latch is not secure," Alice said to Eleanor.

"Well, if you and Madeline had not been pushing against me, I would not have been 'leaning heavily.'"

"But we could not hear," Madeline protested.

The commotion must have awoken Daisy, Grace's Great Dane, and, recognizing Henrietta as someone she had not seen in a while, came to her. Without even thinking about it, she started stroking the dog.

Grace cast her gaze to the ceiling. "We were having a private discussion that did not include the three of you." Then she narrowed her eyes at the girls. "And what are you doing out of the schoolroom?"

"We were sent to get our cloaks," Alice mumbled.

"And we heard Henrietta being brought to you," Eleanor said.

"So we thought we would discover what was going on. After all, since Augusta left, she has never come without Dotty," Alice added proudly. "We might be able to help. Mrs. Winters"—last year the governess, Miss Tallerton, had married the tutor, Mr. Winters—"said we are extremely creative."

Henrietta bit her lip, trying not to laugh. She remembered Worthington telling Merton that when the three of them made their come out it would be all hands on deck for the Season. Which she assumed meant that all their relations were required to assist in chaperoning the girls. Even at sixteen, they made a striking trio. The twins had golden hair and summer-blue eyes, while Madeline had the Vivers dark brown hair and lapis eyes. Henrietta recalled that her sister, Charlotte, and Louisa had been called "the Three Graces." Henrietta wondered what appellation these three would have.

She thought they would be banished from the room, but Grace surprised her. "How much did you hear?"

The girls glanced at each other, then Alice said, "We know that Henrietta has an interest in Lord Fotherby."

"He was the one with Merton when he met Dotty who Louisa did not like," Madeline said. "I remember because none of us liked Merton, and Matt was furious when they became betrothed, and none of us wanted Dotty to marry him, not even Mama."

Henrietta had known that none of Matt's family had liked Merton, but she had not understood how vehemently they had been against him and the match. "But he changed, did he not?"

"Yes." Madeline nodded. "Dotty brought out a side of him no one knew existed."

"As I recall," Grace said, "his mother told him some things about which he had been unaware. That helped change his attitude as well."

Alice tilted her head. "Could that be true of your Lord Fotherby as well?"

"I really cannot call him *my* Lord Fotherby. We have not even been introduced, but yes. I think you might be right. He appears to be much different from the gentleman Merton knew before." Henrietta finished the tart. "The question is, if I am not allowed to even meet him, how am I to know if we would suit?"

The girls each took a biscuit and sat on a small sofa facing Grace with intent expressions gracing their countenances. After a few moments Madeline finished the last of her biscuit. "Dotty is expecting a baby. Will she be your only chaperone?"

"No, Merton's mother is coming to Town. She will accompany me when Dotty cannot."

"Hmm." Alice lifted the tea-pot and rang the bell-pull. "Is there anyone else who could chaperone you?"

"My grandmother wrote to me and asked me to have luncheon with her. But I have never heard of her chaperoning anyone."

"Still, she could," Eleanor said.

"I suppose I might be able to talk her into it." Henrietta tried to think of that possibility. Grandmamma had not even come to Town for her Season last year. She had been traveling, and who knew how long she would be here?

For the first time since the girls had become involved in the conversation, Grace said, "She helped Dotty and Merton. I am not quite sure *how* she did it, but I know that she promoted their marriage." A fresh pot of tea had arrived, and Grace poured them all cups. "And she knows Fotherby's mother."

Henrietta couldn't believe what she had just heard. Her grandmother had been involved in her sister's marriage? "I beg your pardon?"

"Yes." Grace stared at a far wall, then her eyes focused on Henrietta. "Yes. There was a discussion as to what to do with Fotherby, and Dotty suggested that he be left to his mother. Your grandmother informed her what her son had done, and he was banished from Town until he matured."

"There you have it," the three girls said at the same time.

"Just like Lady Merton helped Merton," Madeline said.

"Your grandmother can help Fotherby," Alice finished.

"You will have to make sure your grandmother speaks with Lady Fotherby," Eleanor finished.

Henrietta stared at the three girls, and the only thing that she could think was that they would be forces to be reckoned with when they were older. "You might have the solution."

The three of them seemed to revert to the schoolroom girls they were as they grinned with satisfaction.

"Girls." Grace clapped her hands. "Mrs. Winters will be looking for you. It's time to go."

They rose as one from the sofa.

"You will tell us what happens, will you not?" Madeline asked.

"Silly, we'll be at the wedding or at the wedding breakfast," Alice said.

They all waved and strode out the door.

Henrietta thought they might wait yet another year for the three of them to make their introduction to Polite Society, and glanced at Grace. "When do they come out?"

"Two more years. We are recruiting friends to help us." She broke out into laughter. "At this point, I don't know if we will have silly young ladies or younger replicas of Lady Bellamny."

Lady Bellamny was one of the influential ladies of the *ton* and a force of her own. "It will be interesting to be sure." Henrietta drank the rest of her tea. "Thank you. You and the girls have given me a place to start."

"I hope he is worth the trouble." Grace rose.

"We shall see. If not, I will continue searching for the right gentleman. A gentleman who *is* worth the trouble."

Standing, Henrietta took her cousin's hand. "I will keep you informed."

Grace smiled. "I shall hold you to that. Good luck."

"Thank you. I have a feeling I will need it." Fortunately, if Exeter was successful, she would meet Lord Fotherby tomorrow. With any luck at all, she would learn if she wished to know him better.

She returned home to find another note from Dorie.

Dearest Henrietta,

   Please join us for tea tomorrow at three o'clock. I think you will be interested in the other person who will be there. We can discuss it further in the morning.

                    Your friend,
                    D.

Henrietta's hands shook slightly with excitement as she refolded the missive. This must mean that Exeter had succeeded in inviting Lord Fotherby to tea. Did he know she would be there as well?

Whitechapel, London

"Augie's dead," their gran said, pulling aside the blanket separating the room Bart and his brothers shared. "Couldn't get the fever down."

The only thing that'd surprised him was that his brother had hung on fer so long.

"It's all that bitch's fault." Cager, his youngest brother, growled.

"It's ye're own fault for not just hand'n over the babe." Gran scowled. "What the 'ell was ye think'n?"

"More money for the mort," Bart muttered. They'd all thought it were a good idea. "Didn't know she had a pop."

"Didn't think she'd use it," Cager muttered. "She weren't no rum mort."

"But she might work for one. Never thought ye was a knowing one, but I didn't think ye was pudding-headed." Gran shook her head. "I told ye 'afore. Leave the morts to a flash man. We got a good thing go'in here." Find'en and selling brats had made them enough to leave St Giles. "Ain't no one gonna complain about giv'n a brat to one of them charities. Everyone gets what they want. But ye start grabbing morts, and the pigs'll be look'in fer us. Leave it be." She grabbed a bag she held the coins in and counted out several. "Yer lucky she paid ye at all. I'd say she's cannier than ye are."

Bart took the balsam. He knew his gran was right. Him and Cager couldn't go look'in for the mort. But if they found 'er agin, 'e'd make sure she paid for killing his brother. This time 'e'd just put a hole in 'er like she did to Augie. He'd have ta find a pop first. Bart wished 'e knew which charity the mort was from. Meebe if they saw the same shaver he'd tell 'im.

"Go find me some'un to take Augie," Gran ordered. "Then ye can go get another brat or two to save."

Bart jerked his head for Cager to follow him. They went to the house of a night-soil man and left a message with his woman to come and take their brother. Then they went over to St Giles and started look'in and ask'in around fer more brats. They was never too hard to find.

CHAPTER TWELVE

The next morning Nate rose just before the sun and set out on a ride with Padraig prancing alongside the horse. As he did before, he roamed the Park, allowing Darragh to set the pace. The horse was recovering nicely from his journey to Town. As Nate was leaving, he saw the same two ladies he'd seen before. If it were not for the rules of Polite Society, it would have been easy to join them and introduce himself. But there were rules, and he was not in a position to break them. Still, he'd meet Miss Stern today. Tea might be hours away, but it would be to his benefit to wait. Then, with any luck, he might be able to speak with her the next time he saw her. If she didn't reject him.

He turned toward the gate and home. He was glad his new boots had arrived yesterday. He wanted to make as good an impression as he could, especially if she knew what he'd done. But did she? It was hard to believe that if she knew she would still want to meet him. One way or the other, he'd find out soon.

After bathing and dressing, he headed to the breakfast room, where the scent of bacon seemed to drift on the air. Once again, his mother was before him.

"Good morning, dear." She folded the newssheet she'd been reading and set it next to her plate on the table. "How was your ride?"

"Better than yesterday." He went to the sideboard and found baked eggs topped with bacon and cheese. "At least I didn't come home soaked."

"Very true. I noticed the knocker had been put up." A question lingered in her tone.

"Yes." Nate added ham to his plate, took his seat, and pulled over a fresh rack of toast. "I had a visit from Lord Exeter. After that, I decided there was no point in not having it put up. Were you aware that his father, Papa's acquaintance, had died?"

"Yes, I was. It took some time for the lawyers to find the new Lord Exeter. He had been on his Grand Tour. He arrived shortly after the last year's Season began. I had the pleasure of meeting the new Exeter. He married Lady Dorcus Calthorp. The daughter of the Marquis of Huntingdon. It was her second Season, but I think it was worth the wait."

Naturally, as the mother of three daughters who married well, Mama would think of the status of the gentlemen involved. A mother could easily forgive a daughter for not marrying in her first Season when her second or subsequent Season was so successful. He had been too young to remember much about his sisters' Seasons. Yet, he thought he remembered that one of them had taken more than one Season to wed.

Nate thought about the look Exeter had on his face when he mentioned his wife. "He seems much taken with her."

"It was one of the well-known love matches last spring." Mama spread marmalade on a piece of toast and ate it.

Nate's jaw almost dropped. Was this his mother? He remembered a time when she disapproved of love matches. "They don't bother you?"

She waved another piece of toast in the air. This one, fortunately, did not have marmalade on it. "Not at all. I have come to understand the value in them. Provided, of course, the couple has fallen in love for the right reasons and to the right sort of person. It would not do, for example, for a lady to marry a man from the middling class or for a gentleman to marry a woman from St. Giles, for example. Unless there is an issue of money." She gave him a pointed look. "That is a difficulty we do not have."

"No, we do not." Once Nate had found his way, he'd made sure that the viscounty was on firm footing. Something that neither his father nor his brother had done. "And we will not."

"From what I have seen, many of the love matches are doing quite well." She ate another piece of toast and some of her baked egg. "I do like the eggs prepared this way."

While she'd been talking, he'd had a chance to finish one of his eggs and start on the other. "As do I. The bacon is particularly good."

"I am glad you like it. It was a gift from a friend." She tapped her fingers gently on the newssheet. "You do know that since the knocker is up, it will be reported that we are in Town."

No. He'd not thought of that at all. "Perhaps people will think you are here by yourself, as you have been lately."

She gave him a sardonic look. "Are you planning to become a hermit?"

Even if he tried, he couldn't hide forever. Exeter had already found him. "No. I just wish I knew how to approach certain people."

"Ahh." She took a sip of tea. "I am sure you will work it out somehow. When you finally meet Miss Stern, and if the two of you get on well, Merton will have to come around . . . eventually. Especially if the duchess approves of you." Mama studied Nate for several seconds. "You have changed immensely. I do not say it enough, but I am very proud of you."

"Thank you." A lump formed in his throat, and he coughed to clear it. "That means a great deal to me."

"Yes, well, now it is up to you to show others how much you have matured." His mother finished her tea. "I shall see you later. It is time for me to discover who is holding morning visits this early in the Season."

"I'm going to Exeter House for tea this afternoon." Nate took a breath. He had originally decided to wait until after the visit before telling his mother. "Miss Stern will be present."

He'd never seen his mother's face show such pure joy. "I am delighted. You will tell me how it goes?"

"Of course." Even he felt a smile tug the corners of his lips. "I am a little nervous. Well, perhaps a bit more than a little. For all I know, she is coming to berate me. Or because Lady Exeter has not told her who I am." He shook his head. "All I can do is see what happens."

His mother was still beaming. "I have some acquaintance with both Lady Exeter and Miss Stern. They are very close friends. I have a strong feeling that Miss Stern knows exactly who you are, and that you will be there."

"But to what end?" Despite having tried to bury his worries, all his fears about the meeting came rushing back.

"Unlike many young ladies I have known, neither Lady Exeter nor Miss Stern is cruel." His mother rose. "I wish you luck."

"Thank you." He watched his mother leave the breakfast room. When she could no longer be seen, he muttered to himself, "I wish I was as confident."

He half expected to be sent away with a flea in his ear. What would he do then? The easy answer was to return to the country. Yet, he did have to find a wife. His cousin was currently Nate's heir, and the boy was still in the school-room.

Padraig wandered into the breakfast room and nudged Nate's arm with his head. "Finished with your breakfast already?"

The Wolfhound eyed his plate. "No. You're not going to join me at meals here. That would be a bad habit to start." He stroked the dog's head as he finished his egg and the last two pieces of toast. "Come. You can take a nap while I work."

Nate wondered if Miss Stern liked dogs, and hoped she did. It could be a problem if she did not.

"There he is." Henrietta and Dorie were cooling down their horses from a gallop when she pointed to the gentle-man riding with a Wolfhound. "It is such a pity we cannot simply introduce ourselves."

Henrietta stared at Fotherby's back, then at his profile as he glanced down at his dog. "That would be so much easier." But rules must be obeyed. Even her sister would send her back home for such a breach in conduct. "Then again, I will meet him this afternoon. I must remember to thank Exeter for arranging it."

"Yes." A dreamy smile dawned on Dorie's face. "He is wonderful and exceedingly helpful. I could not have married a more perfect gentleman for me."

"I agree." Henrietta stifled a laugh. Her friend had fought so hard to not even like Exeter, but just when she realized that she was in love and thought she'd lost him, he'd declared his love for her and proposed. More or less. "I think everyone has done stupendously well. I could not think of a better gentleman for Adeline than Littleton."

Dorie pulled a face. "And I almost caused the match to never happen."

"You had your reasons." Henrietta let her smile show. Dorie had thought Littleton was going to make her an offer when he left Town two years previously. She had been so angry and hurt that she spoke against him to Adeline. "I suppose we can thank the rules for making it impossible for her to refuse to dance and ride with him."

"Yes, they were helpful for that." Dorie smiled as well. "And now they have twins! I am so happy for them. Not that *I* want twins, but they are in Heaven."

"And Turley is the perfect gentleman for Georgie." Henrietta grinned as she thought of the trouble they had given him because he would not admit he loved Georgie. "Although it was ridiculous that he almost had to lose her before he realized he'd been in love the whole time."

Dorie heaved a sigh. "Apparently it takes some gentlemen longer than others." She turned to Henrietta and grinned. "I do hope Fotherby turns out to be the right gentleman for you."

"If he does, the problem will be bringing my family around." Henrietta pulled a face. "That will not be easy, and I am not looking forward to the fight."

Dorie raised a brow, making her look as imperious as her mother. "But really, what could your sister and brother-in-law do?"

"Send me home." Fotherby had left the Park. Perhaps the next time they rode, he could accompany them.

"In that case, you will stay with me. I am perfectly capable of chaperoning you, and my consequence will not suffer Merton's disappointment."

It must be wonderful to have such well-deserved confidence. "But you cannot keep me from my parents," Henrietta pointed out.

Dorie's face fell. "That is true."

Henrietta stared at the direction Fotherby had gone. "If we do suit, and even though it would only be a year and a half, I do not wish to wait until I am one and twenty to wed."

"I can see where that would be a problem." Dorie turned her horse toward the gate. "Once Exeter and I decided to wed, I wanted the ceremony to take place immediately." Her lips tightened as she frowned. Then her face cleared. "I have an idea. After the Season, Exeter and I could escort you to Scotland. We have a very nice castle there."

"I will keep your offer in mind." Technically, that would not be eloping. "But we are getting quite a bit ahead of ourselves. I do not even know if I will like him." Henrietta thought she would. She had when she and he had first seen each other. Still, there was no getting around the fact that he *had* abducted her sister. And although from his behavior in Whitechapel it appeared he had changed for the better, she would be wise to take this—whatever it was—slowly.

"You are right." Dorie sighed again. "I simply want you to find the happiness the rest of us have found."

"I know. And I will." Henrietta attempted to stamp down her expectations for this afternoon. "Whether or not it is with Fotherby still remains to be seen."

"It is clear he must explain himself."

"Yes. That is the one thing that must occur." She wondered what he would say. "I have to find something to do between breakfast and tea." If she did not, she was certain to drive herself mad wondering what would happen.

"Shopping," Dorie said firmly. "You still need bonnets for your new walking and carriage gowns."

"What a brilliant idea." They could take hours shopping and the time would go quickly. "I do hope Georgie arrives sooner rather than later." Henrietta had received a letter from her friend announcing that Georgie was expecting a blessed event in July, but no word at all about how long they would stay in the metropolis.

"We should hear about her plans soon. Although I suppose she will want to be back in the country by the end of May at the latest."

Dorie was right. The four of them exchanged letters at least once a week. Even Augusta, who was last in Egypt, wrote frequently. They turned into Grosvenor Square. "When do you want to leave?"

"Two hours?" Dorie asked. "I want to spend time with my son."

"Very well. Will you come for me?" They generally took the town coach her husband had made specifically for her.

"Of course."

They had reached Merton House and Henrietta slid down from her mare, then handed the reins to a footman. "I shall see you then."

She strolled up the shallow steps and into the house.

"Miss, you have received a hand-delivered letter," Parkin said. "I believe it is from Lady Turley."

"That is wonderful." Or it would be if Georgie was arriving soon. Henrietta took the letter from the silver salver he held and ascended the stairs. As soon as she reached her apartments, she opened the missive.

My dearest Henrietta,

Turley and I arrived late yesterday afternoon. I have been ordered to rest this morning, but if you are doing nothing more strenuous than shopping, I would love to join you. My modiste appointment is not until tomorrow, but I am certain I require many other new items.

> *Your loyal friend,*
> *G.T.*

Henrietta started to chuckle as she imagined Georgie explaining to Turley that shopping took almost no energy at all. There was no need to write to Dorie; Georgie would have written her as well. If only Adeline would agree to come to Town, they could all be together again.

Spyer entered the parlor. "Your bath is being filled."

"Thank you." Henrietta removed her riding habit, handing the pieces to her maid as she did.

After washing her face, she sank into the hot water, and then a thought made her sit up. It was a certainty that Dorie would invite Georgie and Turley to tea. In fact, it was impossible that the couple would not be invited. Which meant she would have to explain everything to Georgie before then. Oh, well. Henrietta leaned back against the towel her maid had placed on the tub. There was nothing she could do about it. And, after all, there was safety in numbers. And if she and Fotherby did decide to see if they would suit, he had to get on with her friends and their husbands. He might be a little older than the other gentlemen, but at their ages it did not matter very much. He would need friends, as it was probable that neither Merton nor Matt Worthington would be welcoming toward him.

Less than two hours later Henrietta was dressed in a walking gown she had purchased last autumn and was just setting the bonnet on her head when a footman announced Lady Exeter had arrived.

On his heels, Dorie strode into the room. "I decided not to wait downstairs. We are picking up Georgie."

"I thought we must be." Henrietta tilted the bonnet at a jaunty angle. "I gather you had a letter waiting for you as well?"

"Yes." Her friend gave her a critical look. "I like that hat."

"Thank you." Trimmed with red ribbons to match her spencer, it was made of straw with a fairly wide brim and a shallow crown. "It is one of my favorites."

"Come along. We do not wish to keep Georgie waiting." Dorie headed toward the stairs.

Henrietta grabbed her gloves and reticule and hurried after her friend.

Soon they were at Turley House on Green Street. When Georgie came down the steps, Henrietta noticed her girth. It looked to be the same as her sister's. How was that possible when Dotty was not due until early autumn? Come to think of it, Grace was the same size as Dotty.

Once Georgie settled onto the plush carriage bench, Henrietta asked, "When are you due?"

"In July." Georgie grinned. "I have sufficient time to visit Town before returning to the country to have the baby."

Several minutes later they arrived at the milliner they

liked on Bruton Street. By then Henrietta had told the story of Lord Fotherby to Georgie.

"This should be interesting." She frowned as they strolled into the shop. "Why is it nothing can be easy for any of us?"

"If I knew the answer to that question." Henrietta blew out a frustrated breath. "I would have saved us all a great deal of trouble." She glanced at Dorie. "Although I did suggest you marry Exeter, and you insisted you were not interested."

Dorie grinned. "Very true, but I am not sure that we would have realized I loved him if I had agreed at the beginning."

"Turley and me," Georgie quipped. "Perhaps it is true that one appreciates things that one must work for."

The hours passed and, surprisingly, all their purchases fit in the areas Exeter had designed for package storage in the carriage.

By the time they turned into the Square, Henrietta was more nervous about meeting Fotherby than she thought she would be. Perhaps a brisk walk to Exeter House would be helpful.

The coach drove past her house, and she felt her eyes widen. "Am I not going home first?"

Both her friends shook their heads.

"We thought it would be easier this way," Georgie said. "I remember when Turley finally came to Littlewood. We had been out looking at the follies, and I felt very much at a disadvantage by not being there when he first arrived."

"If you think it is best." Henrietta tried not to cringe and hoped they were right.

CHAPTER THIRTEEN

Nate wiped his hands down the sides of his pantaloons for the second time as he walked from his house to Exeter House. He entered the Square at the other end of where Merton House was located to avoid anyone seeing him, and donned his gloves. He'd been afraid that they'd be damp before he arrived.

Coward.

"Well, I have some reason to be concerned," he muttered to himself. Even now he was entering an uncertain situation.

Before he was ready he was climbing the steps to Exeter House. When he reached the top tread, the door opened and a butler bowed. "Lord Fotherby, please follow me."

He followed the servant down a corridor to a room at the end. The sounds of people laughing could be heard as he neared.

The butler entered, then stood to the side. "Viscount Fotherby."

Exeter strode forward, holding out his hand. "I am pleased to see you again." He turned and spread his arm to indicate the others in the bright, cozy room. "Allow me to introduce you. My dear, may I present Lord Fotherby?"

A dark-haired lady curtseyed and held out her hand. He bowed over it. "A pleasure to finally meet you, my lord. I believe I have seen you riding in the Park."

"Yes. I have seen you as well." From the corner of his eye, Nate could see Miss Stern standing witha blond-haired lady.

"Lady Turley," Exeter said, "May I introduce Lord Fotherby?"

She smiled and held out her hand as well. "Good afternoon, my lord."

After Nate straightened, Exeter continued, "And this is Lord Turley."

They shook hands.

Nate willed his hands not to start sweating again.

Exeter stepped over to his wife, who was standing next to Miss Stern. "Miss Stern, may I present Lord Fotherby?"

If she was as nervous as Nate was, he could not see it. She looked as cool as a glass of iced lemonade on a hot day.

"It is very nice to finally make your acquaintance, my lord." He thought her lips tilted up at the corners, but it was hard to tell, for the corners of her mouth rose naturally.

She held out her hand, and he remembered to bow, and take the slender digits in his. She was not wearing gloves, and he wished he was not either. Nate remembered he'd have to remove them to drink his tea. Still, he fought to keep his fingers from closing tightly around hers. "Yes. It is"—splendid. No, he couldn't say that—"delightful to meet you. It *was* you riding in the Park with Lady Exeter."

"It was." Her bright, moss-green eyes met his and searched them. Still, she left her hand in his, but pulled her plump lower lip between small white teeth. "I think we must have a conversation. Do you not agree?" He glanced at the others. "They know all of it."

"I see." Knowing that, he was shocked her friend had arranged this meeting. "We must indeed speak."

Lady Exeter came over, and Miss Stern removed her fingers from his. Her ladyship handed Miss Stern a cup and waited for him to remove his gloves before giving him his cup. "I hope you like the way I prepared it, one lump of sugar and a splash of milk."

At this point he'd agree to anything. "Yes, thank you."

Her ladyship pointed to a spot on the other side of the room. "There is a very interesting painting that my husband picked up while he was in Italy. It is on the far wall."

That was well done of Lady Exeter.

"Thank you." Miss Stern gave her friend a relieved smile. "I thought I had looked at them all, but I see this has just been hung."

"It took me some time to decide on the right frame." Her ladyship smiled as well. "I shall save you each a slice of spice cake."

"How very kind of you." Miss Stern's smile broadened. "It is definitely my favorite receipt for spice cake."

"Naturally it is." Her ladyship returned Miss Stern's smile.

Nate glanced at both ladies. There was some sort of private joke about the cake. He wished he knew what it was.

Lady Exeter raised her brows and glanced toward the painting. "I cannot save the cake for long. Both Exeter and Turley have developed a fondness for it."

Nate was sure he saw Miss Stern almost roll her eyes, but she placed her hand on his arm. "We had better get to it. The spice cake is truly wonderful. Lady Turley and another of our friends stole the receipt and shared it." Miss Stern's lips twisted as she wrinkled her nose. "Well, perhaps 'stolen' is not the right word. They took a piece of the cake and asked Lady Littleton's cook to replicate it."

A smile tugged on his lips. He had only just met her and her friends, but he liked them already. They were more fun than any of his previous chums had been. "Definitely not stolen, then. More like 'copied' in the way that many artists copy the works of famous painters in order to learn."

"Well said, my lord," Lady Exeter announced. "That is a much better way to look at it. They did the same with the lemon biscuits."

Nate couldn't stop himself from chuckling. "You have enterprising friends."

"Oh, you have no idea," Miss Stern muttered under her breath. "We had better look at the painting."

They ambled to the far end of the room and stood before a newly framed painting, with their backs to the others.

At first he wondered if he should start speaking or if she would ask, then she said, "Please tell me what exactly happened. Why did you abduct my sister?"

"I was stupid." That was the short answer. However, the one raised brow and the imperious look on her face that reminded him of her grandmother informed him that she wanted a longer explanation. "I would like to blame it on a lady who had told me your sister had compromised Merton with the intention of marrying him, and he really wanted to marry her cousin. A lady who was on his list." Miss Stern's eyes flew wide. Nate gave her a rueful look. "Yes, he had a list he'd decided to choose from. That, though, is but part of the story. You see, I was not present that evening. The evening Merton and your sister were caught together."

Miss Stern's jaw dropped for a second before she recovered herself. "They were caught together? No one told me that part."

"They were. But as I said, I was not there, and I really didn't know her. I wanted to believe it was true. That she was so desperate to marry, she would do something like that to catch a husband. Knowing Merton as I did—he and I had been friends since we were children—I knew he was too honorable not to wed her. Not only that, but I knew she was not on his list. Suffice it to say that Merton and I were very high sticklers. We were members of the Tory party and believed many things I now think are not only questionable but wrong. I digress."

A line formed between Miss Stern's brows. "How did you meet him?"

"I was a second son with not much to do. My family did not have any traditional professions for second sons. I was introduced to him as a suitable friend." He sipped his tea, glad that it wasn't brandy or he'd never get through this. "I suppose that is a much longer story." Nate really did not want to have to bear his soul, but pressed on. "I was also jealous of your sister. Merton had come to Town to find a bride with his list of suitable ladies. As far as I knew, your sister was anything but suitable, yet he was determined to marry her." Nate took a large drink of tea and drained the cup.

"You thought you were losing your best friend?" Miss Stern asked.

"Yes, and to a scheming woman." Part of the pain Nate had felt rose up. Instead of helping he'd lost his only real friend. "I later discovered that they were in love. We had both been raised to think love matches were vulgar, and it never occurred to me he was in love. Then, suddenly, there was a wedding date. Ergo, when the lady approached me with her story I wanted to believe that I was saving him from marrying someone who would make his life miserable by taking your sister out of Town until after the date of the wedding. When I planned the—the abduction it honestly never occurred to me that I might hurt her reputation. When she mentioned it I had a twinge of conscience, but continued on. None of it was well done of me. I truly never dreamed Merton would come after her."

"And she escaped herself." Miss Stern smiled again.

"Did she?" Nate couldn't help but smile at the news. "Your sister is an extremely resourceful lady. After my mother was told what I'd done she sent me back to Ouse Tower and refused to allow me to return to Town until I mended my ways." He gave her a rueful grin. "You see, she was, and still is, my trustee. It took me almost a year before I stopped resisting my punishment. After that I dived into what I needed to learn and had not. I understood how much better I could make the lives of not only my dependents, but others in the neighborhood by helping anyone who would let me. I learned the difference between giving a person something and allowing them to keep their pride by not helping too much, or in a more creative way. I also learned to recognize when a family was in danger of starving and would go hungry if I did not find a way to feed them."

She nodded slowly. "I was raised knowing the difference, but I have seen Merton struggle with the concept. Thank God he finally learned."

"I have not had any contact with him since . . . since

then." Nate pressed his lips together for a moment. It had taken him too long to realize that if he was not a peer, his punishment would have been much harsher. "I deeply regret what I did. But I do not know how to make up for it."

Henrietta had to think, and she needed to do it quickly. He had done something horrible. Yes, it had been based on a lie he was told, but he was still responsible for his actions. She wanted to believe that given the same choice now, he would do the right thing. That he had truly changed. The problem was, how was she to be certain? "Can you tell me more about the day in Whitechapel?"

Fotherby seemed grateful to change the topic. "Of course. A year prior, shortly after the young woman had been made to leave her home, a neighbor of mine, a gentleman farmer, asked for my help in contacting a runner. I found someone who could give me a name, and I hired the man. I did not tell the farmer the full cost. I was fairly sure he could not afford it. When we found the woman and her child, I offered to bring him to Town. I, or rather my mother, had horses stationed at posting inns along the way. His wife insisted on taking their own coach, but I tried to ensure that her travel was easier." Lord Fotherby smiled. "I'm glad she accepted the assistance. In any event, the woman we were searching for was to have married his eldest son, but the son died before they could wed. The man's plan was to have her accept the family's name as if she had been married and raise the child as his heir. He wrote me saying all was well." Nate shook his head. "He did not like accepting my assistance. He would rather there was no peerage. Fortunately, he does not know the whole."

"That you paid most of the fee." Henrietta couldn't stop

her grin. "My father is also a Radical. He was not at all happy Merton is a marquis."

Fotherby took her hands, warming them as no other gentleman had done before, and sending tingles through her body. His face, his eyes, were so intent, she almost backed away. "The night I was able to assist you. That is the man I have become. I hope you can bring yourself to believe me."

Henrietta thought she did believe him. And she liked what she saw. Yet that was only part of the battle. If she decided to see where, if anywhere, this led, she would be going against her family's desires. She had been raised to put her family and her community first. Fotherby, even a friendship with him, would violate that tenant of her upbringing. Unless she could bring her sister and Merton around. She wanted to slide a glance at her friends, but Lord Fotherby's focus on her was so strong she could feel him.

She raised her gaze to his and became distracted by how beautiful his turquoise eyes were. They looked like the water in a painting of the West Indies she had once seen. "I do think you have told me the truth. From what I have heard about you, I am certain you have changed as well. But despite my going out to rescue children, I am rather careful." She frowned to herself. How best to put this? "You, my lord, are a complication. No, that's not the right word."

"I am a problem you might not want to take on?" His tone was soft . . . and dolorous. The sadness twisted her heart.

"I do not think it is that either. I cannot simply ask you to tea." Henrietta did not even want to know what her sister would say if he simply showed up at Merton House.

"No. I do understand that would not be possible." He

looked and sounded a little more hopeful. "Perhaps we can get to know each other. Slowly. After all, the Season has not yet begun in earnest."

He was so handsome. She had not got that impression from the people she had spoken with. He seemed to have been a bit ridiculous before. "I think we can do that."

The tension visibly left him. His shoulders dropped, and the tightness around his eyes and mouth—she really did not need to think about his perfectly formed mouth—dissolved. "Thank you."

Henrietta had never been drawn to a man before. Part of her wanted to argue with the fates, why him? She gave herself an inner shrug. Now she did glance at her friends, who she caught sliding looks at her and Fotherby. "We must go about this, whatever this is, carefully. I will not lie to my sister, but nor do I wish to get into a confrontation with her." Dorie and Georgie would have ideas about how to avoid that. "Let us go back to the others."

He inclined his head, and a chestnut curl dropped onto his forehead. Henrietta fought the urge to put his hair back in order. "As you wish."

He held out his arm, and she carefully placed her hand on it. It felt much more comfortable than it had before. Instead of the disturbing, tingling feeling, it felt as if her hand belonged on his arm. This time she noticed how hard it was, as if he had been engaged in physical work. "Will you seek out Merton?"

"I haven't decided. Part of me wants to do just that, as soon as possible, but another part of me cautions me to wait." Fotherby grinned at her. "I would like him to see the changes I've made before meeting him again."

"I can understand." And the best place for the meeting

would be in the Lords. "Perhaps you can discuss a bill that is already being drafted with Exeter and Turley."

"You mean move formally, from the Tories to the Whigs?" Fotherby said lightheartedly.

"Yes. There is no better way to make the point than showing how you have changed." They had almost reached her friends. "After all, Merton made the same transition."

"You have a good idea." Fotherby gave a slight smile, and she wondered what he thought about being drawn to her. Or rather if she was worth the trouble to him.

CHAPTER FOURTEEN

Henrietta and Fotherby reached the rest of the group, and she took a cup and plate from Dorie. He accepted another cup of tea and a plate with a slice of spice cake as well. As if planned—and Henrietta had no doubt it was—the gentlemen walked off with Fotherby, and Dorie and Georgie drew Henrietta between them.

"Well?" Dorie asked.

Henrietta had taken a bite of the cake so that she had time to think of her answer. She swallowed. "I like him. He has promise."

"I thought so as well," Georgie added. "He seems very taken with you."

As Henrietta was with him. Still, it was much too early for that sort of talk. "You do realize this is something I cannot rush in to." Henrietta grinned into her cup and drawled, "Not that either of you jumped into marriage."

"I knew fairly quickly after meeting Gavin that he was the right gentleman for me. I probably would have been married much"—Georgie slid a look at her husband—"much sooner if he had not been so, er, confused."

"That is one way to put it." If Turley had not been so

slow about declaring his love, they would have been married for almost a year.

"And I did not know what I wanted." Dorie's brows lowered. "Or I thought I did, but I was mistaken."

Henrietta had put her cup on the low table in front of the sofa, and Georgie took her hands. "What do you want us to do?"

"I do not know." That was the question that had begun to plague Henrietta. Despite the reassurances she had received from Grace, and the support of her friends, Henrietta was at a loss. Perhaps nervous was a better word. "This is such a quandary. One I had not ever thought to have." On the other hand, this *was* her life, and she had to be happy with her choice of husband.

Georgie sighed. "This courting and marriage thing is much more difficult than one would assume."

Dorie nodded. "I must say I agree." She glanced at her husband and the other men. "Although displaying his rehabilitation might be the first step."

"That was my idea as well." If Henrietta was going to be able to dance with Fotherby, gaining permission had to be accomplished before the Season proper started. The Dowager Lady Merton had no love for him either, which might cause even more problems.

"Hmm." Georgie pressed a finger in the last crumbs of spice cake on her plate. "There are a few new bills Turley has been working on and, of course, the old ones for which we never seemed to gather enough support." She placed the tip of her finger in front of her mouth. "I think I will hold a soirée to discuss the bills."

"What a brilliant idea." Dorie looked down at her plate and frowned. "Most of the political sorts are already in Town. I could hold one as well."

Henrietta had moved her plate to her lap and was slowly finishing the last of the cake. It was unusual for unmarried young ladies to be at political events, but these were her friends. "I would love to be included."

Actually, she would give a lot to be present when Merton first saw Fotherby and recognized him. But she did not at all want to be there when her sister did. If she and Lord Fotherby formed even more of an attraction than they already seemed to have, something had to be done about Dotty. Before coming to Town last year, she had just been an older sister with whom Henrietta was not particularly close. She never thought she would have much in common with Dotty. But as they spent more time together, she and Henrietta had become extremely close. She would hate to lose that friendship. But if she and Fotherby fell in love, she did not want to lose that either. She blew out a huff of air. This whole situation was unfair. Why could she not have been attracted to a gentleman who did not have problematical relations with her family?

Dorie slid Henrietta a look, and she gave an imperceptible shake of her head.

Next to her, Fotherby moved. She could feel his gaze settle on her cheek. "Miss Stern. Is there anything wrong?"

"Oh, no." She smiled at his troubled face. "I am simply thinking."

"Henrietta likes to have things planned out," Dorie explained. "Even when we go shopping, she will have a list of what she needs, and a logical way to visit all the stores."

"I like order." Henrietta took another bite of the cake and chewed.

"As do I." He grinned at her. "Although you would never know it by the state of my desk. My secretary calls it 'organized chaos.'"

Georgie waved an airy hand. "I always find that if I make plans, something will come along and toss them into the wind like flower petals. Therefore I rarely bother." She smiled teasingly. "That is the reason I have friends who enjoy organizing."

Nate chuckled when Henrietta and Lady Exeter cast their gazes to the ceiling. He was more than pleased about how his conversation with Miss Stern had gone. He'd tried to be as honest about the events as he could be and did not allow himself to blame anyone else. Still, she was cautious, and he couldn't blame her. He would have to prove himself not only to her, but to her family as well.

"I always plan my day, but I am often interrupted by events that occur with my tenants or in the town. Although that is the way I wish it. I want them to know they can come to me with their problems."

Miss Stern tilted her head slightly. "When my uncle was the baronet he kept a distance from his tenants. But when my father took over, he made sure everyone knew he was there to assist them. Was it like that before you came into the title?"

"It was. Though, to be honest, it took me some time to see the merits in becoming more involved with my dependents."

She shifted on the sofa, enabling her to see him better. "What made you change?"

"A small child was injured by a roof falling in. The damage to the roof had been reported to my steward, but he failed to have it repaired." Nate placed his empty cup on the round wood and marble table to the side of the sofa. "I was notified and went immediately, and sent for the physician who serves our area to meet me at the cottage. When I arrived and saw the damage it was clear there was no way the family could remain in the house with half the roof gone. The nearby market town has a thatcher, so I sent for him as well. While we were waiting for the doctor and the thatcher, I started talking with the child's parents, and a few more of my tenants, who'd come to help, and discovered that for too long a time the viscountcy had not lived up to its duties. I was lucky. I knew a chum of mine from Oxford was looking for a new position as a land steward. My old steward was of an age to be pensioned. I did that as soon as possible."

"That was good luck," Miss Stern commented. "Was he ready to be pensioned?"

"Yes. He had expected to leave when my brother died, but no provision had been made for him."

She bit down on her plump lower lip. "How did the child fare?"

"I was fortunate that a midwife was also called. She came. The doctor did not. The child had a broken arm, and she set it. The little girl is completely well. As you can imagine, I was not pleased with the doctor. Injuries occur on farms. They must be taken care of immediately. When I arrived home, I found my mother with the rector's wife, and I decided to tell her my problem. She had a friend whose son had graduated from the medical school at St. Andrews in Scotland. He was currently working for a London doctor but missed the country. He also had a strong belief that a trained physician should do more than give his opinion and prescribe medicines. In his spare time, he started working with a surgeon at one of the hospitals. I obtained his direction and offered him a position. I would pay him a certain amount to see to my tenants and the town's people that was over and above the fees he earned. It has worked out well for both of us and my tenants. They never have to worry if a doctor will be available."

"A brilliant idea." His chest tightened when Miss Stern looked at him as if he had worked a miracle. "Absolutely brilliant."

"I'm glad you approve. I had no idea before then that most doctors are in cities and not in the country."

"It does not seem right. It is not as if those in the country do not need a doctor."

"Miss Stern." Turley bowed. "Do you mind if I take Fotherby away? Exeter and I would like to discuss something with him."

"Not at all." She smiled at Nate when he rose and let himself be led away by Lords Exeter and Turley for the inevitable political talk. Even though he'd not attended the Lords for several years, he did try to stay abreast of events.

"As you probably know," Turley said, "we have not been successful at rescinding the Corn Laws." A law Nate had originally supported, but had come to believe was responsible for the lack of affordable food for the majority of English families.

"Yes. I am aware." Now that he was back in Town, he'd be happy to work on yet another bill. Eventually, it had to pass. The situation was becoming much too dire.

"Nor have any of the bills we've presented to abolish slavery in the colonies been passed," Exeter added.

"My understanding is that the slave owners are demanding an extraordinary amount of compensation." Nate had been shocked at the amount requested. It was almost twenty million pounds sterling.

"Yes, that's true." A fresh pot of tea had been brought, and Exeter poured a cup for himself, then held it up to the others.

Nate held out his cup. "I think that one must take into consideration the suffering of those held in slavery. If I had my way, the slave owners would not be compensated at all."

"I agree." Exeter took a sip of tea. "They have already benefited. However, that would create more problems than it would solve."

"I suppose you are correct." Nate still thought that the slave owners had been given enough "free" labor. "They've come to believe they need slaves in order to make a living. Yet we in England do not have the benefit of free workers, and if one takes care of one's holdings, it is not difficult to live well." Still, it was clear that other investments were necessary to protect against bad years for agriculture. It wouldn't be long before farming would not produce the needed income.

"We had serfs," Turley said dryly. "Slaves by another name."

"Not since the sixteenth century," Nate countered, trying to remain calm. There had also been more of a social contract with serfs than with slaves. Once he'd had time to consider it, he was of the firm opinion that England had been wrong to allow the slave trade to exist at all. "A system of tenant farms could be established."

"You will never get the owners to agree," Exeter countered, his tone a little louder than it had been. "We must be flexible enough to accomplish the greater good."

"What are you gentlemen arguing about?" Lady Exeter and the other ladies were staring at them.

"Abolishing the slave trade," Exeter said.

"Does one of you think it should not be ended?" Lady Turley asked.

"No," her husband responded. "Fotherby thinks the slave owners should not be compensated for the loss of what they consider to be property."

The ladies' gazes switched to Nate.

Miss Stern raised her chin and one dark brow rose with it. "I, for one, happen to agree with Lord Fotherby. Owning another human being is wicked."

"We all agree with you," Lady Exeter said. "But to end the trade, we must be practical. If they are not paid something, it is not inconceivable that the colonies could declare independence. Then where would we be?"

"In a war." Nate's words sounded flat even to himself. He did not actually think it was probable that would happen. Then again, Britain had already fought two wars trying to keep their former colonies and lost both of them. "Very well. I concede the point. That does not mean I have to like it."

"I agree with you." Miss Stern inclined her head in his direction. "Even though I believe it is a devil's bargain, another war would be worse than paying the slave owners."

"Well"—Lady Exeter rose—"I am glad we settled that."

Nate glanced at a large, elegant ormolu clock decorated with figures playing various musical instruments. He had been there over two hours. He bowed to her. "Thank you for inviting me. I have had an enjoyable time."

She smiled. "We will have to do it again."

"Lady Turley, Miss Stern." He bowed to the other ladies, but wished he could speak with Miss Stern alone before he left. "It has been a pleasure to meet you."

"Do you ride every morning?" Lady Exeter asked.

"Yes." Thinking about Padraig going without his morning run made him smile, even though there would be nothing humorous about what he'd get in to. "My horse, the dog, and I all require the exercise."

"In that event, we shall probably see you." She cut a look at Miss Stern. "We ride shortly after dawn in order to avoid crowds."

Not that there were "crowds" that early in the morning, but there could be wagging tongues. "I understand. I am certain we will see one another."

"Come." Exeter and Turley stepped over to Nate. "We will walk you out. We'd very much like it if you would join our circle for luncheon on Wednesdays," Exeter said. "We spend most of the time discussing legislation. We meet at Brooks's."

"Thank you." Perhaps that was when Nate would meet Merton again. The confrontation would have to come soon. And Nate welcomed it. It was time to take back his life.

When they reached the front door, Turley surprised Nate by leaving with him. "Will you not wait for your wife?"

Turley grinned. "They are taking Lady Exeter's new barouche to the Park for a short visit. Even though the ladies exchange letters at least once a week when they are all in the country, they have not had time for a comfortable coze. Exeter and I will ride our horses alongside the carriage. You are welcome to join us if you wish. We will depart from Exeter House in a half hour."

The question was, should he? Miss Stern seemed as if she would like to be interested in him, but he didn't want to make her uncomfortable by pushing things along too quickly. At least not yet. "Perhaps it would be better if I see you there."

Turley tilted his head to one side. "That might be a better strategy, at that."

"Strategy?" Nate didn't understand.

"Of course." Turley seemed surprised. "One must have a plan of action if one wishes the lady he desires to return his affections. There is no use leaving it to fate." Then he grimaced. "On the other hand, I was extremely happy when fate intervened with my plan."

Nate hid his smile. "I take it your scheme was not working?"

"That would be one way of putting it." Turley had a rueful smile on his face. "Fortunately, it all turned out well in the end."

"The two of you look very happy." As did Exeter and his lady. There were two more couples that had successful love matches to add to his count.

"We are. Of course, we would have been happier longer if I'd taken any advice, but I was determined to do it my way." Turley pulled a face. "Do not make my mistake."

"I will try not to." Although other than Turley and Exeter and their ladies, Nate didn't know who would bother to give him assistance. Rather the opposite. And he was extremely attracted to Miss Stern. He'd never met a lady quite like her. Or at all like her. Yet he had a feeling courting her would not be easy.

They reached his house and Turley bade him farewell.

As Nate climbed the steps, he wondered if any more of his clothing had been delivered. It hadn't mattered before, but he did not wish to wear what he had on when it would only end up smelling like horse. And he didn't want to wear an older suit.

Hulatt opened the door and bowed.

"Have Styles attend me," Nate said as he passed by.

"I believe he is already in your dressing room, my lord. A package arrived, and he took it upstairs."

"Excellent." Or he hoped it was. Then again, she had already seen him in his country-made kit and hadn't seemed to mind. In any event, how busy could the Park be? It was still two weeks until Easter.

CHAPTER FIFTEEN

Henrietta waited with Georgie while Dorie went to the nursery to tend to her baby. "I am very happy you arrived so early."

"As am I. We would have been here sooner"—Georgie got a strange sort of smile on her face—"We were not far from London, but I was tired, and Turley insisted we stop for the night." She gave a happy sigh and took Henrietta's hands. "I have never been happier. He is all I could have dreamed of in a husband and more."

"I am glad for you." And for all her friends. "I will not be content until I find a gentleman who treats me as well as your husbands treat you, Adeline, Dorie, and Augusta." It had surprised all of them that Augusta found marriage so much fun. Then again, she had wed a gentleman who was interested in the same things she was.

"You must think it might be Lord Fotherby." A small line formed between Georgie's brows. "I mean"—she bit down on her lower lip—"he appears to be a very nice man."

"Yes." And that was the crux of the problem. He was an extremely kind gentleman, and a responsible and caring one. "But he must also deal with his past. I spoke with

Grace Worthington, and she told me how Merton had changed. Apparently none of the Vivers liked him at all. And I do believe Fotherby has changed from what he was before."

"But?"

"But when my sister decided to marry Merton she was not going against *her* family." Henrietta wondered what Dotty would have done if Mama and Papa had not liked Merton. "If he does not make peace with my sister and Merton, not to mention my parents, what would I do? I refuse to allow myself to grow fonder of him if it means breaking with my family." They were too important to her. She could not imagine never being on good terms with them.

Georgie wrinkled her nose. "That is a point, and a good one. The only thing you can do is let him work it out." She took up her cup, swirled the now-cold tea, and set it back down again. "If you decide you want to know him better, we will give you all the assistance we can." She looked Henrietta in her eyes. "You know we will."

She patted her friend's hands. "I do know that. I would dearly love to be able to let this take its course, but I"—she what? Was afraid? She had never been fearful of anything before—"I must give it more thought."

Georgie gave Henrietta a small smile. "It will all work out the way it is meant to. I firmly believe that. It has with the rest of us, even Augusta."

Augusta, who had vowed not to wed until she had finished her studies, but had married Lord Phineas after all. "Then I suppose I must too." The problem was, Henrietta did not like not being able to control a situation. "I think I hear Dorie." She placed her bonnet on her head and attached it with a long hat-pin. "I cannot wait to see this new carriage."

"Neither can I." Georgie drew on her gloves. "Exeter has a talent for designing them."

A moment later Dorie swept into the room smiling brightly. "My carriage is waiting for us."

Exchanging a humorous glance, Henrietta and Georgie followed their friend out of the morning room and to the hall, where they retrieved their mantels, then strolled out of the house.

The barouche was almost a work of art. The body was Pompeian red, but flowers painted in multiple colors and gold piping decorated the body. The wheels and lines of the vehicle were also picked out in gold. The interior bench was black, but the squabs were the same red as the body and embroidered with flowers. The effect was stunning.

"I do not believe I have ever seen such an elaborately designed barouche." Henrietta walked around the carriage. She looked for a door on the other side, but there was none. "What is inside?"

"Exeter had tables that fold out added." Dorie was almost giddy. "Do you like it?"

Henrietta did. "I do. How did he come up with the idea?"

Her friend's cheeks turned an interesting color red. "We were talking one night, and he asked me to describe the type of barouche I would like. I told him my fantasy of a carriage, but I never thought he would actually have one made to my specifications."

"It seems he did." Georgie reached for the handle, but a footman opened the door. "You will be the envy of every lady in Town."

Henrietta agreed. "I predict flowers painted on carriages

will become the newest rage." Turley and Exeter trotted up on their horses. "It is time to test the cushions."

The footman assisted her into the carriage, but the gentlemen dismounted and handed their wives in. Unexpectedly, the seat was long enough that the three of them could easily fit on one bench. Even being in the middle she did not feel crowded. It struck her forcefully that she truly did wish to wed. It was no fun at all being the sole unmarried female in a group of married couples. An image of Fotherby unhelpfully entered her mind. She was surprised he had not been invited to accompany them.

The carriage started forward, jerking her thoughts back to the luxury of the barouche. "The seat is extremely comfortable. I could almost take a nap."

Dorie wiggled around a bit, then settled in. "They are, but you dare not fall asleep. I have heard Lady Jersey is in Town, as well as some of the other patronesses."

"You need not fear. I will be on my best behavior." As Henrietta always was when she was in Polite Society. She knew full well that her behavior reflected on her sister Dotty and their younger sister.

"I was not concerned." Dorie's lips tipped up. "I would merely have poked you."

"No doubt." Henrietta glanced at the sky. "But you must admit this is the most comfortable barouche in which you have ridden."

"I do." Dorie glanced at her husband. "Exeter did an amazing job with it."

He rode closer to the carriage. "I am glad you enjoy it, my love."

Turley rode up next to Georgie. "Would you like a carriage? I am more than happy to have one made for you."

"Thank you, perhaps next Season." Georgie grinned at

him. "We must make sure that this one is made use of. And I have my phaeton if I wish to drive."

"As you wish." The way he smiled at her almost made Henrietta jealous. But only of their closeness. "Tell me if you change your mind."

"I shall."

"You might want one for summer when you are in the country," Dorie suggested.

"Oh!" Georgie frowned slightly. "I had not thought of that." She glanced at her husband. "I shall require one after all."

Turley and Exeter exchanged grins. "I shall have some drawings done for you to review."

Now Henrietta knew why she was seated in the middle. Apparently, it would not do for her friends to talk to their husbands over her. She settled back and enjoyed the ride. At the rate this was going, she would be able to concentrate on her difficulties and not have to speak with anyone. Perhaps she should sit on the backward-facing seat.

A few minutes later they drove through one of the gates into the Park. They had just reached the carriage way when two gentlemen rode up.

"Who are they?" Henrietta whispered.

Dorie glanced at her husband, but he shrugged.

"Turley, well met," the taller of the two men said. When he smiled Henrietta could see that his bottom teeth were slightly crooked, but other than that they were in good condition. His blond hair curled under a beaver top hat. His light blue eyes reminded her of the tales of Vikings she had heard when she was a child.

"Bolingbroke, glad to see you made it to Town," Turley responded. "How have you been?"

"Well. I have been well." The gentleman raised one brow and stared at him, clearly expecting an introduction.

"Yes, of course." Turley waved his hand in the general direction of the carriage. "You already know my wife. Lady Exeter, Miss Stern, may I make the Earl of Bolingbroke known to you?"

Dorie regally inclined her head. "My lord, it is nice to meet you."

Henrietta decided to copy her friend and inclined her head as well. "It is a pleasure to make your acquaintance, my lord."

He doffed his hat and bowed. "Ladies, it is my privilege to meet you."

"And on the other side of the landau is Exeter." Turley looked at the other man and back at them. "I would also like to present the Earl of St. Albans."

Unlike his friend, Lord St. Albans had a head of curly, reddish-brown hair and the most interesting amber eyes over an aquiline nose. Both of the gentlemen were tall with broad shoulders, and quite handsome. Henrietta judged them to be in their late twenties.

Once again greetings were exchanged. The coachman had stopped when the gentlemen had ridden up, but, at a signal from Dorie, he started the horses.

"Bolingbroke and St. Albans were at the house party Georgie and I attended last autumn." Turley's attention turned back to the men. "Have any of the others arrived in Town yet?"

"Montagu will be in Town soon," St. Albans said. "I think Barfleur has decided to eschew the Season this year."

"That sounds like an excellent idea," Georgie muttered.

The gentlemen had started talking about what was

pending in the Lords, giving Henrietta a chance to ask, "Why is that?"

"I will have to tell you later," her friend whispered as the gentlemen's conversation died down.

"St. Albans is the Duke of Cleveland's eldest," Dorie whispered.

Henrietta was about to ask how Dorie knew, then remembered she had memorized *Debrett's*.

"Good afternoon." Fotherby addressed his greeting to the group, but then caught Henrietta's gaze with his own.

"Ah, Fotherby, are you acquainted with Bolingbroke and St. Albans?"

"No, I have not had the honor." Fotherby nodded to the other gentlemen.

Introductions were made in short order, and it appeared that all three gentlemen had decided to ride alongside the carriage.

Georgie nudged Henrietta. "Lords Bolingbroke and St. Albans are very good-looking."

"They are." But after having admired both gentlemen Henrietta found she wanted more than mere good looks and wondered if she could have it. Her friends had, and her family had as well. She would have to discover if either of the other two gentlemen were interested in the same things she was. She already knew Lord Fotherby and she thought along the same lines.

"Miss Stern," St. Albans's low tone caught her attention. He was riding very close to the coach. And she was very sure only she and Dorie could hear him.

Henrietta glanced up at him. "Yes, my lord."

"Please say you will allow me to take you for a carriage ride tomorrow afternoon."

Henrietta ignored her friend's intent gaze heating her cheek. "I would be delighted."

He smiled, clearly pleased with himself, and rode apart from the carriage.

Next to her, Georgie worried her bottom lip. "We should have had you sit on the outside."

"Nonsense," Henrietta said. "You could not have known the other gentlemen would join us." She was actually pleased that she was in the middle. It stopped gentlemen from hovering too long. Still, she was happy that Lord St. Albans had asked her to ride with him. She would use the time to get to know him better.

Lord Fotherby gazed at her but made no attempt to engage her in conversation. Then again, they had spoken quite a bit earlier.

Nate had not expected that there would be other gentlemen riding with Exeter's carriage and engaging Miss Stern in conversation. But he should not have been astonished. She was beautiful and very eligible. He wasn't quite sure what to do. If he left, he'd clear the field for the other two gentlemen, and St. Albans had a smug expression on his mien. Nate wondered if he should depart. If he stayed, he'd be seen as openly vying for her attention. Not only that, but contrary to his earlier thoughts, there were many more people in the Park than he'd thought there would be, increasing the chance he'd be recognized. Nate would rather be in control of that narrative.

He considered riding closer to the carriage, but his polite conversation was rusty. He used to know how to make small talk, but it had been so long, he wasn't sure he had the skill any longer.

"I think it's turned into a fine day," Bolingbroke remarked. "What think you, Miss Stern?"

"Yes, indeed." She opened a frilly parasol, tilting it to shade her face. "I hope that this weather will continue."

"I just arrived in Town late yesterday," St. Albans said. "Do you know if any entertainments have been planned?"

"Not anything large," Dorie responded. "Easter is a few weeks away. Although, judging by the number of people here today, there are sure to be smaller entertainments."

"Please keep me in mind if you plan anything." St. Albans smiled, and even though he spoke to Lady Exeter, Nate was certain his smile was for Miss Stern, who, as an unmarried lady, could not hold an entertainment.

"I, as well, would appreciate an invitation." Bolingbroke directed his smile at her too.

She glanced at Nate, and it felt as if a vice had suddenly gripped his heart. A small smile played around the corners of her lips. "Lord Fotherby, would you also like invitations?"

"Naturally, I would be honored to attend any event at which you will be present." That came out better than he'd thought it would. "My mother is in Town and planning to host a few small entertainments before the Season begins. May I ask her to invite all of you?"

Miss Stern's smile froze on her luscious red lips, but both the other ladies nodded.

"That would be delightful," Lady Exeter said approvingly.

"I agree." The look Lady Turley gave him made him feel like a boy who had done something right.

Still, he wanted to hear from Miss Stern. He held his breath until she nodded. "I would be happy to receive an invitation."

"I say," Lord St. Albans broke in. "I believe m'mother

is due to arrive within the next week or so. I'll have to speak with her about her plans for the Season."

"Mine as well. I'm certain she'll be here soon," Lord Bolingbroke said.

Nate kept his grin to himself. If the ladies did not have plans to travel to the metropolis, they would as soon as their sons wrote to them.

He was about to make his excuses when the boy he'd seen at the Phoenix Society ran up to him. "Sir, the butler told me I'd find you 'ere. Can you come? We need some 'elp."

Someone had clearly been working on the lad's diction, even if he did still drop his *H*s. "Yes. I will go with you now." He bowed to the ladies and inclined his head to the gentlemen. "If you will excuse me. I hope to see you another time."

Henrietta's shapely black brows slammed together, and her head tilted as if she was trying to work out a problem. If he hadn't been on horseback, he would have offered to take her with him. Yet, as it was . . .

"Sir, please hurry," the youth urged.

He turned his horse toward the far gate and reached his hand down. "Shall I meet you there, or do you wish to ride behind me?"

"I'll ride with you." The lad grabbed Nate's hand and swung himself onto the back of his horse.

CHAPTER SIXTEEN

Henrietta watched Lord Fotherby ride off with Toby. Mrs. Perriman must be short-handed again. Had the boy gone to Merton House and been informed she was out?

"I wonder who that young lad was?" Georgie mused.

"It must be someone who works for him." Lord St. Albans seemed to easily dismiss it all as he turned his smile back to Henrietta.

"That must be it." Lord Bolingbroke started his horse as the coach rolled forward, and their uninvited escort moved with it.

Dorie poked Henrietta in the side, but she shook her head. This was not a subject she would discuss now. Still, it was unexpected that Lord Fotherby had been summoned by Mrs. Perriman. That was the only reason she would send Toby to Fotherby. For some reason she had needed assistance. But what impressed Henrietta was that he had not hesitated in the least to answer the call for help. She wondered if her sister knew. Well, there was only one way to find out. She would have to ask.

The rest of the ride around the carriage way and home was filled with what passed for fashionable talk, when she would much rather have been assisting in the rescue. By the time they reached her house, she was heartily sick of polite chatter. It was one thing to put up with it in snatches during a dance, but it was quite another thing to be fed a steady stream of it without respite. Goodness, what was wrong with her? Polite conversation had never irritated her before.

Lords Bolingbroke and St. Albans quibbled good naturedly about which one of them should be allowed to hand her down from the barouche. It was rather childish behavior, but when she slid a glance to Dorie and Georgie, they were laughing lightly, clearly entertained. Perhaps Henrietta should consider their behavior as lighthearted flirting. Bolingbroke won the honor of handing her down to the pavement. But he could not stop St. Albans from following them to her door.

"I hope, Miss Stern," Lord Bolingbroke said, "that I may be allowed to call on you."

"Yes, of course." He bowed over her hand and kissed the air above her fingers. Despite her earlier irritation, she began to be amused. This might be a more interesting Season than she thought it would be.

"Miss Stern." Lord St. Albans bowed as well. "I am looking forward to our ride tomorrow."

"As am I." Once again the air over her fingers was kissed. *Much more interesting*. She should not have been so out of sorts earlier.

The door had opened at some point during their farewells, and Parkin gave the gentlemen a wry look as they took themselves down the steps to their horses. "I see it is going to be a lively Season, Miss Henrietta."

She tried not to laugh. "Apparently it is." Poor Parkin. He was obviously not looking forward to it. "Is my sister in?"

"Yes. She is in her parlor. The weekly report from the Phoenix Society arrived not long ago."

If Fotherby had gone to help Mrs. Perriman, Henrietta wondered who had been left to bring it around. "Thank you."

She made her way to Dotty's parlor, where she found her sister staring at a pile of banknotes. Had Dotty made a large withdrawal? No. If that was the case, she wouldn't be staring at the money as if she had never seen it before.

"Good afternoon." Henrietta strolled into the room. "Where did that come from?"

"Mrs. Perriman sent it over with the report." Her sister raised her head, revealing a perplexed look. "It is a donation."

Henrietta gazed down at the banknotes. "How much is it?"

Dotty took a breath. "One thousand pounds. Mrs. Perriman hired a constable to bring it over."

"One thousand pounds?" Henrietta's heart almost stopped, and she dropped into the chair next to the desk. They had never received such a large donation before. "Who is it from?"

Dotty shook her head. "That's just it. I have no idea. The person wished to remain anonymous." She smoothed out a letter that had been partially folded and picked it up. "She said a youngish gentleman brought it by on the instruction of his employer." She glanced at Henrietta. "She also said that the gentleman who helped you came to speak to her as well. He wanted to know how the baby was doing. His name is Mr. Meadows, and he offered to be of assistance should she need help in the future."

"That was kind of him." She knew Fotherby would not give his true name. He was not ready for her sister or

Merton to know he had met her. And she agreed with that sentiment. But she had not thought he would tell an outright lie. Then Henrietta remembered that he had been Mr. Meadows for much longer than he'd been Lord Fotherby. Therefore, not a complete falsehood, and it was for a good cause. And now she knew why he had been summoned. Could he also be the unknown benefactor? Based on what he told Mrs. Perriman, it stood to reason that he would want to help the society continue.

"Yes, it was." Dotty placed the letter back on the desk. "I must say, I am looking forward to meeting this Mr. Meadows. He sounds like an excellent man."

Henrietta wanted to test her hypothesis. "I believe that the money came from him as well. What do you think?"

"It very possibly could have." Dotty's brows drew together. "It makes sense." She paused for a moment, making the neat pile of bills even straighter. "He must be quite well off to give such a large bestowment."

That was something Henrietta had not considered. He had not showed off his wealth in the way she had seen other gentlemen do. In fact, even with the new garments he had acquired, he dressed rather simply. Henrietta wondered what her sister would do when she discovered Mr. Meadows was Lord Fotherby, and that Henrietta had known who he was. Well, that was a bridge she would cross when she came to it. In any event, Merton was bound to be the first member of the family to "discover" who Mr. Meadows was. From what she had heard, they had known each other since Eton, when Lord Fotherby would have been Mr. Meadows.

Dotty took out a key and unlocked one of the three drawers along the upper part of her desk. Once open, she placed the money and letter into the drawer, locked it again, and tugged the bell-pull. "I must have Merton's secretary take this to the bank."

Parkin arrived. "Please tell Mr. Hanwell I have an errand for him in the morning."

"As you wish, my lady." The butler bowed and left the parlor.

When he'd left she smiled at Henrietta. "I apologize for being so preoccupied. How did your day go?"

"Well. Very well." Thinking back on today, she was amazed at how much had occurred. "After tea at Exeter House Dorie, Georgie, and I went for a ride in Dorie's new barouche. Exeter and Turley accompanied us. I met two gentlemen I had not known before, Lord St. Albans and Lord Bolingbroke. Lord St. Albans asked me to ride in the Park with him tomorrow, and Lord Bolingbroke asked if he could call on me. I agreed to both propositions." Henrietta grinned to herself. "They also would like to be invited to any entertainments my friends host."

Her sister's eyes sparkled with humor. "Did someone tell them that not much would go on between now and Easter?"

"Yes, but that did not seem to deter them at all. In fact, that was when they asked to be invited to our events." Her sister nodded thoughtfully. "There should really be more to do before the Season begins. I do not think a ball would be appropriate, but there would be nothing wrong in having an informal dancing evening."

Henrietta would like to know both Lord St. Albans and Lord Bolingbrook better. As much as she was drawn to Fotherby, she was afraid her family would never accept him. What a pickle this was.

* * *

It wasn't long before Nate and the boy were threading their way toward Covent Garden and Phoenix Street. "Tell me what's happened, and it would be helpful if I knew your name."

"Name's Toby. Mrs. Perriman and Tim had a rescue today, and then he went off to send a letter about placing the babe. The new man Gregory went with the other lady that started working with us to place a young girl with a family and they aren't back yet. After Tim left, another note came about another child, and Mrs. Perriman can't go by herself. Even now it ain't . . . isn't safe."

"I understand." The Phoenix Society was having a busy time. Nate urged Darragh to a quick trot. A few minutes later he was in front of the charity's building, where a shabby-looking town coach stood. It reminded him of any of the numerous hackney coaches he'd seen around London.

"I can take your horse around back," Toby said as he slid off the side of the horse. "We have a small stable. I'll look after him good."

"Thank you." He threw the reins to the lad. "Darragh, go with Toby. I'll be back soon."

The big chestnut nodded his head, as if he understood. Well, he did in a way. He knew that Nate wanted him to go with the boy, otherwise the horse wouldn't have gone. He took the four shallow steps by twos and knocked on the door.

"I cannot tell you how glad I am you came." Mrs. Perriman stuck two hat-pins in a shabby bonnet that went along with the rest of her garments. If he didn't know better, he'd have thought she was from Seven Dials. She glanced at Nate and frowned. "It's a shame we don't have anything to fit you. Ah, but I do have an old coat that will hide your garments." She left him for a few minutes. When she returned she was carrying a large, well-worn caped coat and a battered hat. "Do you have a pistol?"

"Er, no. I wasn't at home when Toby found me."

"Let me get you one. I do not expect trouble, but it is better to be prepared." She went through what had probably been the green baize door to the kitchens at one time, and returned a few moments later, handing him a coaching gun. "I loaded it."

"Thank you." Nate slipped the weapon into the greatcoat pocket. He now knew why she had been chosen to run the charity. Although the weather was nice, it wasn't warm enough to make the coat uncomfortably hot. "Where are we going?"

"To the edge of Seven Dials." She made the statement like another lady would have said Piccadilly or some other safe environment.

"I take it the coachman will be armed as well?" The man had damn well better be.

"Yes. I only wish we had a third person with us. Even if we do not go far into the area, it can be dangerous."

And it would be dark soon. He held his arm out to Mrs. Perriman. "Let's be off."

She blushed as she took it, but disregarded his assistance into the carriage. No sooner had he closed the door than the coach lurched forward. He'd expected the springs to be as old as the vehicle looked, but their ride was amazingly smooth. It was also clear that what he'd taken as job horses were actually quite sprightly. The disguise was well done. Only someone with very sharp eyes would recognize the carriage or the horses. Even the coachman looked like any other hackney driver.

Before he knew it, the carriage slowed and shadows

seemed to block what was left of the sun. The vehicle stopped.

"We're here." Mrs. Perriman motioned for him to open the door. "Do not worry about helping me down. We do not want to cause anymore notice than need be. Keep your back to the carriage."

Nate nodded his agreement. In this he was an absolute novice.

"Hank"—Mrs. Perriman's tone was so soft only the coachman and he could hear her—"do you see anyone who looks like they are waiting to meet us?"

"Just down the street and under a baker's sign a young woman is holding a small 'un's hand. She's looking around her like she's waiting for someone."

"That must be her." She glanced at Nate. "I will go first. You try to keep your back to Hank. He'll watch to make sure no one comes in behind you. I will approach the woman."

"I understand." He did as he was told, moving slowly, as if he was merely ambling around and always with his back to the coach. He glanced over his shoulder and saw the coachman slowly turning the carriage so that it pointed toward the way out. Then Hank positioned himself on top of the vehicle to keep watch.

No sooner had Nate looked back around than Mrs. Perriman came running toward him with the woman and child in tow. "We need to go. Now!"

He dashed to the door and jerked it open, then picked up the child and got it inside the coach. The woman, actually more of a girl, dove in, and Mrs. Perriman followed. Nate barely had the door shut when something thumped the back of the vehicle and a man started swearing loudly.

"Ye won't get far. I'll find ye and make ye sorry ye ever lived. Ye've cost me ten quid, ye have."

The only color in the young woman's pale face was bruising around her eyes and on her left cheek. If it hadn't been so important to get her away, he'd go back and show the blackguard how it felt to be beaten by someone stronger.

Fear widened her bright-blue eyes. "Meebe I should go back."

"Don't you even think about it." Mrs. Perriman put an arm around the woman's shoulders. "You and your child will be safe from now on. We'll make sure of it."

It wasn't until then that he took a good look at the child as she sucked her thumb. She had her mother's big blue eyes, and blond curls surrounding her chubby face. She was a beautiful little girl and couldn't be more than three or four years old. Nate's spine felt as if cold fingers were pressing down on it. He did not wish to know what was being sold for ten pounds.

Hank drove the coach east for several streets before heading north and back toward the west. It was probably a good idea not to go directly to Phoenix Society. He pulled up on a side street near the Phoenix Society, and Mrs. Perriman opened the coach door. "Mr. Meadows, you may retrieve your horse. I am going to take these two to safety."

"If you're certain you do not need my assistance any longer." He really did not like to abandon them.

"I am sure. We are going out of London. Please tell Toby I will be back tomorrow."

Not able to do anything else, Nate bowed. "As you wish."

He closed the door and strode down what looked like an old mews until he found Toby with Darragh. "Thank you for taking such good care of him." Nate removed the hat and coat, placing them on a chair, then handed the boy a shilling.

A broad smile appeared on the boy's face. "I woulda done it for noth'en. Thank you."

He ruffled Toby's hair. This was one child who was safe from harm. "But it's worth it to me, and you did a good job." Nate swung onto his horse. "Mrs. Perriman said she'll be back tomorrow." He didn't like leaving the lad by himself. "You could come to my house until she returns."

"No, thank ye. Tim will be back soon. I'll tell him what Mrs. Perriman said." Toby ran off toward a gate, opened it, and slipped through. Once the gate closed, Nate could hear a lock slide shut.

He had forgotten about the older boy. He wanted to take his time riding home, but the lamplighters were already at work, and he'd have to bathe and change before dinner. The many church bells of the London area rang the time, and he urged his horse into a trot. The rescue had gone quickly, but it was later than he'd thought. It wasn't until he reached home that he had the opportunity to consider what Miss Stern had thought of him going off to assist the Phoenix Society. She had to have known Toby. Nate might not be skilled at small talk anymore, but he hoped she would think what he'd done more important.

CHAPTER SEVENTEEN

The following day Nate joined Exeter and Turley for lunch at Brooks's. A bill in which Nate was interested was coming up for a vote the following day, and he planned to be present for it. Tomorrow would be the first time he'd set foot in the Lords in four long years.

Later that afternoon he accompanied Mama to Lady Thornhill's salon. And he was once again struck by how his mother had changed in the past few years. Lord and Lady Thornhill were famously liberal, and eccentric, and not at all the type of people Mama had counted as her friends in the past. Nate remembered being alarmed that Merton had visited the salon; now Nate was strolling up the steps with his mother about to enter what he had once termed a "den of subversives." He grinned to himself. Finally, he would be able to see what all the fuss was about.

A very proper butler answered the door and guided them to a large drawing room where a tall lady—dressed in what appeared to be long pieces of embroidered silk wrapped around her—stood chatting to new arrivals.

He bent his head so his mother would be the only one who could hear him. "What is she wearing?"

"I believe it is called a *sari*. It is from India." Mama smiled and held out her hands to Lady Thornhill. "What a pleasure to see you in Town so early."

Her ladyship returned the smile. "We did not go abroad this year. Both my daughters and one of my daughters-in-law decided to add to their families. Because of that, we have traveled the length and breadth of England." She briefly closed her eyes as she shook her head, then smiled broadly. "However, they all did an excellent job of it. I have two new grandsons and an adorable new granddaughter. Of course, they are all endearing at that age, but we have been waiting for a girl."

"Excellent." His mother drew him forward. "I would like to make my son known to you."

Lady Thornhill lifted a quizzing glass that hung on a chain around her neck and focused it on Nate. "I must say I approve." She dropped the quizzer. "I'm glad you have finally decided to come to Town."

Nate bowed. "It is a pleasure to finally meet you, my lady, and to attend one of your salons."

She waved her arm in a sweeping motion to indicate the rest of her guests, who were gathered in groups. "No matter your interests, I'm sure you will find those whose conversation you will find stimulating."

"Thank you, my lady." He backed away as her ladyship turned to his mother and started talking.

He surveyed the room, and didn't recognize anyone present. Therefore, the only way to find conversation that interested him was to go from group to group. Footmen circulated with drinks and food. Nate supposed that was Lady Thornhill's way of encouraging her guests to continue talking. He approached several men who were heatedly discussing something and listened.

"I tell you, his painting of the shipwreck has been accepted by the Paris Salon." The speaker, a man with a heavy French accent, tossed off a glass of wine.

"I don't believe it." A second man sneered. "Géricault has studied with no one important."

"Nevertheless," the third member of the circle was clearly part of the gentry, "it is a fact. I received a letter about it just the other day. I plan to travel back to Paris for the Salon."

Nate ambled past the men. Although he enjoyed viewing good art, he was neither an artist nor a connoisseur, and he had no idea who the artist in question was. A few steps away five gentlemen and four ladies were discussing philosophy. He heard Wollstonecraft's name mentioned and listened for a few minutes as one of the ladies argued that the property of a female should rightfully belong to her even after marriage. Considering the gathering, he was surprised at the vociferous argument made against the idea. Nate took a pastry from one footman and a glass of claret from another as he listened. He almost missed the one lady's sharp retort when he bit into the pastry and found it was filled with meat instead of being a sweet. It was like a pasty, but with puff pastry instead of a piecrust.

"And that is the very reason I will never wed a gentleman who does not agree that I may keep my own property," a second lady proclaimed. "Especially now that I have my own wealth."

As he strolled on, Miss Stern came to mind. She would no doubt agree with the ladies when it came to property. He'd never considered the matter before, but now that he did, why should a female, especially one with wealth, become a beggar to her husband after marriage? In the past he would have said because that was the way it had always been. Yet now, he wasn't at all certain he believed that. He had seen how women could well handle the purse strings. His own mother was an excellent example. How many other things had he taken for granted as some custom or practice that should be accepted simply due to the fact that it had always been that way? He remembered visiting an experimental farm in Norfolk and returning with new ideas, and having to prove to his tenants that the new way was better that what they had been doing. How strange that he'd been changing how he thought about the old ways and never even knew it before.

After finishing the pastry, he began to go by another group when a lady's hand stopped him. "Fotherby"—he'd completely forgotten his mother was here—"would you come with me, please? There are two people I would like you to meet."

"Yes, of course." He felt his brows draw together on their own accord. "Mama, do we have a copy of *A Vindication of the Rights of Women* in our library?"

Her eyes widened. "Um, yes. Yes, we do. What do you intend to do with it?"

"What?" What did she think he'd do? "Read it. I just heard an argument regarding a woman's property and I wish to read her arguments on the matter."

"I see." She patted his arm. "I will fetch it for you when we return home. Here we are. Duchess, may I present my son?"

Ah, Lady Fitzwilliam, better known as the Duchess of Bristol. He should not be surprised she was here. Seeing her next to Miss Stern intensified the resemblance between her, her grandmother, and her sister. The duchess's eyes twinkled as she inclined her head. "Fotherby. I can see why your mother is so pleased with you."

"Your grace." He bowed, but was perplexed by her statement. He had made a mull of their last meeting. Next to her, Miss Stern gazed at him, but her expression told him nothing.

"Henrietta," the duchess said. "Shall I introduce Lord Fotherby to you, or have you previously made his acquaintance?"

"We have met." Miss Stern held out her hand. He took it and bowed.

"Excellent. I believe you might have a great deal in common." The duchess smiled like a cat with a bowl of cream.

The problem was now that he held Miss Stern's fingers in his palm, he did not want to give them back. "It is a pleasure to see you again, Miss Stern."

"I am glad you are here." She glanced around. "It is a little thin of company. Are you having an entertaining time?"

"I am." He realized that his polite answer was the truth. "I've been listening to some interesting discussions."

The corners of her lips tipped up, and her eyes reflected the smile. "But you have not joined any of them."

"No. I fear I don't yet have the requisite knowledge." He was still holding her hand, and Nate decided to keep it unless she let him know she wanted it back. "However, I intend to remedy my lack of understanding." He grinned. "Now, if you can show me a circle that is discussing agriculture, I am more than able to hold my own."

Her smile widened. "Probably not this time, but as the Season draws closer, there will be one."

"I'm glad to hear it." He looked around. "Would you like to stroll around the room with me?"

"Go on, dear," her grandmother said. "I wish to chat with my friends, and you would be in the way."

That could only mean they intended to gossip about topics Henrietta was not supposed to know about. She almost rolled her eyes, but the laughter in Fotherby's eyes let her know he understood. Her lips started to twitch as she held back her laughter.

At first Henrietta was surprised that her grandmother knew Fotherby's mother. Then she was shocked that Grandmamma was willing to present him. But allowing—nay, encouraging—Henrietta to stroll with him was almost unbelievable good luck. The question was, should she? Would her sister view it as a betrayal? Before she could talk herself out of it, she said, "Yes, I would love to."

He released her hand, but put it on his arm. She was not certain how she felt about that. She had liked the sensation of his strong fingers around hers. For some reason, his touch made her feel safe. Or maybe that was not the right word. "Effervescent" was more how he made her feel. No other gentleman's touch made her skin tingle. Whatever that sensation was, she enjoyed it. So much so that she wished they were not wearing gloves.

Fotherby bent his head, and his warm breath caressed her ear. Henrietta stifled the sudden urge to take a sharp breath. "Perhaps you'll be able to introduce me to some of the other guests. I don't know any of them."

"If there is anyone here I know." She saw there was an addition to the usual group of artists who came to argue, eat, and drink. The gentleman dressed much better than did the others.

"I stopped to listen to them," Fotherby said. "But they were discussing a French artist of whom I had no knowledge."

"We shall pass them by. They can be entertaining at times, but mostly when they flirt." Henrietta grinned up at him. "I don't think you would be interested in that."

"Not at all." His tone was dry, but he did not seem to take it amiss that artists would flirt with young ladies.

Still, she did not particularly wish to be pulled into the artists' conversation. "I must assume you began your last circuit on this side of the room. Rather than retrace your steps, let us start on the other side."

"I like that idea." He turned them around and they passed by her grandmother, his mother, and their friends.

They found one group discussing music, another debating poets, and four older men comparing their Grand Tours to their recent travel. Most of those present were her parents and grandmother's age. "I do not see anyone I know."

"I'm surprised there is no one discussing politics."

"That is because the Lords is in session, and the other interested parties are not yet in Town." She glanced up at him, once again struck by his blue-green eyes. They had to be the most beautiful eyes she had ever seen. Henrietta led him to a window seat. If they were not interested in any of the other conversations, they could have their own. "Why did Toby come to fetch you yesterday?"

If he was startled by her question, he did not show it. "I went to see Mrs. Perriman to find out how the babe was doing and ended up offering to help when she needed it." He gave Henrietta a rueful smile. "I did not, though, give her my current name. I told her I was Mr. Meadows. The name I had before I became a peer."

"I assume you did that to avoid my sister and brother-in-law discovering you are in Town."

"Yes. You might not think it was well done of me"—he paused and stared out the window for a few moments—"but I believe Merton will remember when I was Mr. Meadows. In any event I am attending a vote in the Lords tomorrow and shall probably see him then."

Fotherby was a perfectly nice gentleman, and eligible if her family could forgive him. Then again, her grandmother apparently had pardoned him. "If he still doesn't recognize you, will you make yourself known?"

"I don't know. On one hand, he would not make a scene in public." He grimaced. "On the other hand, he could give me the cut direct."

That was very true, and it would cause a great deal of difficulty for Lord Fotherby. "I wonder what the best way to approach him would be." Unfortunately, she had no idea. Even if he was not the gentleman for her, he did not deserve to be pilloried for the rest of his life for even extremely stupid behavior.

"Perhaps my mother or your grandmother will know."

"Perhaps." Henrietta's curiosity about yesterday prodded her. "Who did you rescue?"

"A small child and her mother. A man, probably the one who had beaten the young woman, chased after us, shouting threats. The coachman took a roundabout route back to the house, and Mrs. Perriman had the coach pass by the mews, where I got out. She continued on. She wanted to get them out of London."

"She most likely took them to the house in Richmond. It is far enough away they will be safe, but not so far that she could not travel back that evening."

"That house has never done so much good. It sat empty for years before I was made to lease it to Merton."

"That is your property?" Henrietta was shocked. She had never even thought about to whom it belonged. Yet, if she had, she would have believed either Merton or the Phoenix Society owned it.

Fotherby nodded. "Yes." He gave a quick smile. "For my sins, I was to lease it to Merton for use as a home for widows, orphans, and who knows who else, for a period of ten years. But now, after seeing the good it is doing, I might just give it to the Phoenix Society."

That was generous indeed. "You will not miss it?"

"How could I when I never truly used it? It was left to me by a relative." He shrugged. "Houses shouldn't sit vacant, and that's what was happening."

"I am certain the gift will be appreciated." He smiled down at her, and she wanted to discover what, other than saving people, riding, and politics they had in common. "Are you looking forward to the Season?"

He took a breath and blew it out. "I don't know. My only plan was to take things one day at a time and see what happened." He flashed a grin, and Henrietta was again struck by how handsome he was, and how he did not appear to hide himself behind a polite mask. "My mother has put herself in charge of seeing that I am invited to the right entertainments and that I receive vouchers for Almack's."

Henrietta couldn't stop from laughing. "You sound like any young lady making her come out."

"I suppose I do." He had a chagrined look on his face. "But I'm not young enough to fritter my time away while I'm here, and it is time I find a wife."

"I had not thought of it that way for a gentleman. Exeter is the only gentleman of my acquaintance who was in dire need of a wife the moment he returned home." She told Fotherby about Exeter being shocked that his two younger sisters had been left in his care because his mother had remarried and not taken the girls with her. "Even though Dorie did not originally wish to marry him, she came around. I always thought it would be a good match."

"It sounds like it made the Season interesting."

"You have no idea. Littleton and Adeline had their difficulties as well . . . and then we had Turley and Georgie dancing around each other until the autumn Season." By the time she had relayed everyone's stories, Fotherby was laughing.

"I had no idea a Season could be so entertaining. We must see what this one brings."

"Yes, we should." Except this time perhaps Henrietta would be the one who married. The only question was to which gentleman. After all, she had three prospects.

CHAPTER EIGHTEEN

As Nate listened to Miss Stern, he acquired a growing appreciation for the possible complications involved in finding a mate. Compared to her friends, Merton's courtship and marriage to his wife seemed relatively straightforward. Or it would have been if it hadn't been for Nate. He wondered if he could ever truly forgive himself for what he'd done. He thought he had, but it had become clear that he really hadn't. If he could only bring himself to approach his former friend. He still had to summon the courage to do so. If he continued to court Miss Stern, the matter must be resolved sooner rather than later.

"I am surprised you are not at the Lords." Miss Stern's sudden question took him by surprise.

"I would have gone today, but I was already promised to my mother. I will attend tomorrow."

She gave him a look of approval. "Yes, you did mention you would be there for the vote. It is important for all peers to do their duty, even if they do not like politics."

He remembered part of the conversation he'd had with Exeter and Turley. "Are you thinking of Lord Littleton?"

Miss Stern let out a light sigh. "Yes. He will come to

Town for an important vote. But he will not participate in discussions."

Nate couldn't see her married to a man who was not politically involved. Although he was sure she'd give her husband a push. "Cannot his wife convince him?"

"Oh, no. Not Adeline." Miss Stern's lips flattened, giving her a disgusted look. "She does not care for politics at all."

He couldn't help chuckling. "In that case, it's a good thing they are married to each other."

"They *are* very well suited. It is just that we all wish they would take more of an interest." She tilted her head and gazed at him. "If tomorrow's vote is important, you might meet him. Littlewood is only about two hours away."

Nate would like to meet Littleton, but that wouldn't happen on the morrow. "I'm sorry to disappoint you, but Turley mentioned having Littleton's proxy."

"Why . . . oh, the babies. Of course he would not wish to leave so soon." She must have seen the confusion in his expression. "They had twins a few weeks ago." She shook her head. "How could I have forgotten?"

Nate thought he knew exactly the reason she forgot. Miss Stern was a lady who could focus her attention on something to the exclusion of all else. He'd like to have her attention on him, but he had a feeling that he'd have to convince her he was worth it.

He glanced at his mother, who was speaking with the duchess. Both of them gave him clear signals they would like to depart. "I believe we are being called by our respective chaperones."

Miss Stern glanced at the brooch watch pinned to her spencer. "We have been here quite a while." Nate was pleased when she tucked her hand in the crook of his arm. They started strolling to the door. "It has been lovely speaking with you. I cannot tell you how glad I am that you assisted Mrs. Perriman."

He bent his head so that only Miss Stern could hear him. "I like being useful. Although I have my correspondence sent to me, at home I also spend time visiting tenants and attending to various other duties. Therefore, I have time on my hands in Town."

"Enjoy the quiet." She raised one finely shaped brow. "You will have more than enough to do soon."

"That sounds daunting." He'd been on the Town before, but had not really participated in the Season when it came to young ladies.

"It can be." Her tone was dry, but her eyes twinkled. Was she still comparing him to a young lady making her come out? "At least you will not have to be approved to be able to waltz at Almack's."

He thought she would have said more, but they'd reached his mother and her grandmother. Lady Thornhill was with the older ladies, and they bade her farewell.

When they gained the pavement Nate bowed to the duchess. "Your grace, it was a pleasure meeting you."

"And I was happy to meet you." She inclined her head.

Miss Stern held out her hand and he took it. "I hope we will see each other again soon."

"I am certain we will." She smiled. "After all, you ride in the mornings."

"I do." Even though he wanted to continue to stand there with her, duty and good manners demanded he assist the duchess into her town coach. Once she was settled, he handed in Miss Stern. "Until the next time."

"Yes." She gave a barely perceptible nod. "Until then."

He backed up, closed the door, and watched as the vehicle started forward.

His mother touched his arm. "Did you enjoy yourself?"

"I did, but I don't understand why the duchess allowed me to be alone with her granddaughter."

Mama lifted one shoulder in a shrug. "You made a good impression on her when she joined us for dinner."

Obviously he was going to be told no more. He helped his mother into the carriage, then jumped in, settling on the rear-facing bench. "Thank you."

Mama shook her head. "I will not deny I had something to do with it, but it was you who made the difference."

Remembering how unnerved he'd been that evening, he didn't understand how that could be. "I wish I knew how."

"By being the man you have become." She leaned forward slightly. "You must have faith that everything will work itself out. I would not have encouraged you to take part in the Season if I did not believe you were ready."

Nate knew his mother well enough to believe that. She wanted to see him married and taking his place in Polite Society, but she would not have been in favor of this year if she hadn't thought he was now thoroughly prepared. "Thank you. I will do my best."

His first test had been being introduced to Miss Stern. Tomorrow was the second test, meeting his old friend again. The third? That would be convincing Miss Stern that he was the right gentleman for her.

"Henrietta." Grandmamma had settled back against the velvet squabs of her elegant town coach. "I must say I was impressed by Lord Fotherby."

All she did was greet him, and Henrietta wondered why. Surely she had been at least as angry about him abducting Dotty as the rest of the family. "How so, ma'am?"

Grandmamma touched the quizzing glass she wore pinned to her gown, and Henrietta wondered if she was going to be the recipient of "the eye," as she and her brothers and sisters called it. "You probably do not know that his mother has been a dear friend for many years. And I have been privy to what her son has been doing. How he has been meeting his new challenges and maturing."

Now that Henrietta thought of it, she would wager her pearls that this was not a chance meeting. "Indeed?"

Her grandmother's chin rose. That was interesting. She had never seen the duchess so defensive. "Catherine recently invited me to dinner. I went in disguise."

This was becoming more interesting. "Disguised as what?"

"We told him I was Lady Fitzwilliam." Grandmamma finished the sentence as if it was a pronouncement.

Considering the way she habitually carried herself, Henrietta had trouble believing that Lord Fotherby did not think something was smoky. "Your masquerade was calling yourself by one of your lesser titles?"

"Yes." Grandmamma fidgeted, as if she was not sitting quite comfortably enough. "Although I think he became a bit suspicious at times."

He was not at all stupid. If she had questioned him—the duchess was incapable of using anything other than interrogatory questions—he would have wondered what was going on. "I understand."

"I knew you would." She gave a decisive nod. When Henrietta did not respond her grandmother widened her eyes. "Are you not interested in what I discovered?"

As tempted as she was to say no, that would not make her grandmother happy. Not only that, but she really did want to know what she could tell him about Lord Fotherby.

"I am, a little. I will not be rushed into making a decision. There are two other gentlemen who have also caught my eye."

"My dear child, you must do as you wish, but I can tell you that Lord Fotherby is looking for a love match. And he wishes a helpmate."

She was glad she hadn't been drinking anything. As it was, she almost choked, and quickly covered it as a cough. "You asked him if he wanted a love match?"

Grandmamma stared out the window for a few moments, as if considering how to answer, before fixing her gaze on Henrietta. "Do you know, I might have done just that? But he volunteered that he wanted a helpmate and would value his wife's opinion."

Her mouth had dropped open, and she shut it so quickly her teeth clicked together. Good Lord. Poor Lord Fotherby! She could not imagine him having to have *that* conversation with her grandmother. "I see." Her words were a little shakier than she would have liked. Poor, poor Fotherby. But what was amazing was that he had not indicated at all that he had met her grandmother before. That was true discretion. Well, she certainly was not going to mention the conversation with him. He had suffered enough embarrassment.

"Thank you." Henrietta only uttered the words because that was what her grandmother would expect to hear. "However, under the circumstances, I am hesitant to encourage him."

"I expected you to say that." Grandmamma gave an exasperated huff. "Oh, very well. I see it is up to me to put him on the same footing as your other suitors."

"How are you going to do that?" Henrietta had been attempting to think of something for almost a week now, as had her friends, and none of them had come up with any ideas at all. One could not simply tell one's family to forget all about the abduction. If her sister had not decided to allow Lady Fotherby to school her son, Henrietta was absolutely certain Merton and Worthington would have found a way for him to be sent to the Antipodes.

"I am not yet certain." Grandmamma frowned. "I believe I will be able to talk your parents around. It is your sister and Merton who will be harder to convince."

As far as Henrietta was concerned, they would all be difficult. She would like to say she would choose the gentleman with whom she fell in love. But Dorie had tried that, and it had not worked at all. It had been, in fact, a Grand Failure.

When Henrietta arrived home she was greeted by two lovely bouquets of hot house flowers set on the table in the hall.

"Where would you like them put, Miss Henrietta?" Parkin asked.

"Hmm. I think in the morning room." Her sister entered the hall from the corridor leading to the morning room. "Do you mind if we take them there?"

"No." Dotty shook her head. "They are from Lords Bolingbroke and St. Albans."

The cards had been placed against each vase. Henrietta opened the first card and read it out loud.

Dear Miss Stern,

It was a delight meeting you. I look forward to our ride this afternoon.

Yr. servant,
St. Albans

"Unexceptional." Her sister nodded. "He said all that was proper. You, however, forgot to tell me you were going riding with him." Dotty glanced at her watch brooch. "You do not have much time to change."

Henrietta distinctly remembered telling her sister she was going riding with him today. "I can wear what I have on." She placed the card on the table, opened the second one, and read it to her sister.

Dear Miss Stern,

I was honored to meet you today. Please tell me you will accompany me on a carriage ride tomorrow.

> *Yr. servant,*
> *Bolingbroke*

"This was nicely done as well." Both messages were much better than the poetry she had received from many of the younger gentlemen last Season. "I shall send a messenger with my acceptance to his request."

"Yes," her sister agreed. "I will ask Merton about the gentlemen. It is always good to be forewarned if there are any problems."

"Is that necessary?" Surely Dotty must be overreacting. "He did not do that last year."

"Indeed it is." Her brows rose, reminding Henrietta of their grandmother. "Worthington did the same for Charlotte, Louisa, and me. Merton did not do it last Season because you showed very little interest in any of the gentlemen you met." Dotty glanced at the flowers again. "This reminds me of Lord Harrington and Lord Bentley. They too were beforehand with Charlotte and Louisa."

Harrington and Bentley? "But neither of them married those gentlemen."

"No. They did not." Dotty gave a droll smile. "The early bird does not always catch the worm." Her hand slipped to her stomach.

Henrietta had not been around when her sister was pregnant the first time, but she had not heard Dotty suffered a great deal of fatigue or suffered memory loss. Henrietta was starting to worry. "How are you feeling?"

"A little tired. This baby is much more active than Vivi was." Dotty covered her mouth and yawned. "That reminds me. Lady Merton cannot come to Town. She slipped and broke her leg."

"Broke her leg?" That was horrible news, but more for her ladyship than for Henrietta. "I hope she is all right."

"According to the short note she sent, she seems to be. She is more concerned about you than herself." Dotty yawned yet again. "The problem is that now I need to find someone to help chaperone you."

"Dorie would be happy to chaperone me. Perhaps Grandmamma will assist as well." Henrietta studied her sister. Fine lines had formed in Dotty's forehead. "You should take a nap. You look tired. I will write a letter to Grandmamma, asking her if she would be willing to take me to some of the events." Henrietta would tell Dorie. She would be thrilled.

"Just what every pregnant lady wishes to hear." Dotty gave a rueful smile. "I wonder if Grandmamma will. But we will never know unless you ask her."

Henrietta thought about her grandmother taking her to Lady Thornhill's house today. "We shall know soon enough." Dotty yawned a third time, and Henrietta felt like yawning too. "You really do need to take a nap. You are making me tired."

"We can't have that." She smiled. "I shall, but first, how was your luncheon with Grandmamma?"

"Lovely. Afterward we went to Lady Thornhill's salon, but there was no one there I knew." The words were out of Henrietta's lips before she had thought about them. Although, other than Lord Fotherby, there *was* no one she knew. And she was not ready to discuss him with her sister. But she could mention his mother. "She met a friend of hers there, Lady Fotherby."

"Yes, I believe she has known our grandmother for many years. She is usually in Town for the Season." Dotty's tone had become brittle. "As long as she does not bring her son, I am perfectly content."

Henrietta barely avoided frowning. She should not be surprised. After all, she had expected that her sister would not be pleased he was in Town. Well, there was nothing she could do about it now.

She kissed her sister's cheek. "If I do not have a chance to speak to Dorie in the Park, I will go to see her when I return."

"Very well. I shall see you in an hour or so." Dotty made a wan smile, and Henrietta watched as her sister made her way slowly up the stairs before going to the morning room.

She should probably try to pay more attention to Lord Bolingbroke or Lord St. Albans.

CHAPTER NINETEEN

Henrietta was staring out at the garden. The early flowers dotted the lawn and flower beds.

A knock came on the door. "Miss, Lord St. Albans is here. Should I put him in the front parlor?"

"No, that will not be necessary." She rose. "I will be there shortly." She picked up her bonnet and put it on her head, fixing it with hat-pins.

When she reached the hall he was standing there.

"Good day, my lord." He was handsome, but not in the same way as Lord Fotherby. Lord St. Albans was not quite as tall, nor were his shoulders quite as broad. He also seemed more carefree. Then again, he could be. He did not yet hold the title. "Thank you for the lovely flowers."

"Good afternoon." He held out his arm, and she placed her hand on it. "They are but my poor offering. They cannot compare with you. Still, I'm delighted you like them." His amber eyes sparkled with good humor as he smiled.

She returned his smile. "They are very pretty." As were his words. "Thank you."

He led her to a curricle painted in blue the color of a

bright summer sky and picked out in red and gold. Light-gray leather covered the seats. The carriage was pulled by two matched grays. The effect was beautiful. "What a lovely carriage. Did you select the horses to go along with the blue?"

"No." He grinned as he handed her up. "I found the horses and had the carriage painted to coordinate with them."

"I think that actually makes more sense than having to search for horses to match the color of a carriage."

"It does." He climbed up on the other side, and the boy who had been holding the horses scrambled onto the back of the curricle. "Not that I haven't done it the other way before." Lord St. Albans threaded the ribbons through his fingers and started the horses. "I bought these fellows from a friend who had to sell them. And as I had admired the beasts for some time, I took them off his hands."

"I can see why." Henrietta was by no means horse mad, but she did appreciate the action of the pair. They had been very well trained. "What are your plans for the Season?"

He slid a glance at her. "I have not yet decided. I returned from my Grand Tour late last summer and have been at loose ends since then."

"You do nothing?" For some reason she could not imagine having no occupation.

"Not that." He grinned. "I was taught how to run our estates and dabble in that. However, my father is not ready to allow me to take over. I am attempting to convince him I should be allowed to have full control of the estate that is reserved for the heir."

"But he will not allow it?" She wondered why not.

His lips thinned. "Not yet." They had passed through

the gate into the Park. "What are your plans? I assume you will take part in Almack's and other forms of entertainments."

That was probably as close as he felt comfortable coming to asking her if she was searching for a husband. "Yes. I suppose I will." This Season she would not be solely attending entertainment for young ladies. "This is my second Season and I refuse to be run ragged." This might be a good time to query him about charitable work. "I also have my charitable work with abandoned children."

He raised one imperious blond brow. "Are there not enough homes for foundlings?"

That did not sound promising. Henrietta smiled sweetly. "If there were, we would not be so busy." For some reason Lord St. Albans seemed a bit disconcerted by her answer. Before he could recover, she was hailed by Mary Turner. "Good afternoon." She gave a little wave. "I had no idea you would be in Town this early."

"Nor I you. Is Mrs. Fitzwalter here as well?"

"No." Mary frowned. "She is too close to her time. I am fortunate that I was able to come."

"Ah, yes." Amanda must be almost ready to give birth. She had forgotten that the Fitzwalters were expecting their first child. Actually, the child should have already made an appearance. "I hope you are doing well."

"I am." She smiled broadly. "We have a little boy. His name is Robert. I just came out to see who is here." She turned her attention to Lord St. Albans. "My lord, how nice to see you as well."

"My lady, you glow." Henrietta wondered if he had always spoken to ladies in such a fashion—in other words a consummate flirt—or if it was something he'd learned on the Continent.

"Thank you, my lord." Mary glanced at Henrietta. "I hope to see you again soon." As she finished her sentence, the coachman started the carriage forward.

Why did it seem as if everyone she knew was married? *Probably because they are.*

She must stop thinking about being the last of their group to wed, but it was like a bur that kept sticking in her mind.

"Fitzwalter must be a happy man," Lord St. Albans commented.

It took her a second to understand to what he was referring. Of course, it was the child. An heir. "I imagine he is."

"I have begun to notice how many of my friends have married and started filling their nurseries," he said in a thoughtful tone.

"I have been thinking the same." More and more Henrietta wanted to marry and have a family.

"I wish them all well, but it makes it hard to spend time with them." St. Albans's tone was rather petulant, and there was more than a hint of disgust in it.

"Really? How sad for you, my lord." She was not so innocent that she did not have a good idea of what kind of things he and his friends had got up to. "I have not found it difficult at all to spend time with my married friends."

He opened his mouth and shut it again, and after a moment he said, "Indeed. I should make more of an effort to broaden my activities, as you have clearly done."

Henrietta was not quite sure what he meant by that. Unless it was liking to spend time with children, which she rarely did. Then again, the activities in which she and her friends engaged had not changed very much, whereas his friends' activities probably had.

They were stopped by several more people as they made their way around the carriage way. One of whom was Lady Bellamny, who inclined her head. "I am happy to see you, Miss Stern." She raised her quizzing glass and one black eye stared at Lord St. Albans. "Is that you, St. Albans?"

His hand came up, as if he was about to tug on his cravat. "Yes, my lady. As you see."

"Well, I certainly hope Europe has improved you. But I doubt it. It rarely does."

Trying not to laugh out loud, Henrietta pressed her lips together as he searched for a way to answer her ladyship's question without giving offense. What had he been up to before?

"My mother arrives tomorrow," he said, neatly sidestepping an answer that could not go well for him.

"I will be pleased to see her." Lady Bellamny turned to Henrietta. "I received a letter informing me that the duchess is in Town."

"Yes, my lady." There was no one her grandmother did not know. "I hope to convince her to remain for the Season."

"Good luck with that." Lady Bellamny's tone was dubious. "I have known her since we were girls. She was always restless."

"Nevertheless, I am quite hopeful that she will." In fact, Henrietta sent up a prayer that her grandmother would agree to remain. "Merton's mama was to have chaperoned me this Season, but she is unable to."

Lady Bellamny made what sounded like a grunt. "Expect to receive an invitation for my soirée." She poked the back of her coachman's seat with her cane, and spared another dubious look at Lord St. Albans. "I look forward to seeing you again."

"Thank you." A bubble of laughter tried to escape, but Henrietta refused to let it out.

"I'm glad that's over." Lord St. Albans sounded more than relieved. "I've known her all my life, and for most of it she's scared me to death."

"Almost every gentleman I know has that same reaction," she mused, more to herself than to him.

"She won't be happy until every single gentleman she knows is leg—wed."

Henrietta glanced at him, but he was minding his pair. *Is he not interested in marriage?*

She must ask Georgie what she knew of his lordship. If he was not interested in finding a wife, Henrietta was not going to waste her time with him.

His brows furrowed as he looked at Henrietta. "To which duchess was she referring?"

"My grandmother." She gave him a bright smile. "The Dowager Duchess of Bristol."

He made what sounded like a groan. "Would you like to go around again?"

She looked around and saw the gate coming just ahead of them. "No, thank you."

They soon pulled up to Merton House. But before Lord St. Albans could come around to her side of the carriage, a footman, who had been stationed in front of the house, put down the steps for her. "Thank you for a lovely ride, my lord."

He escorted her to the open door. "It was my pleasure. I would like to take you again some time."

Henrietta pasted a polite smile on her lips. "I would enjoy that."

The moment he was out of sight she turned to Parkin. "I need a footman."

"Yes, miss." He glanced over her shoulder. "Clauson will accompany you."

The servant was tall, as were almost all their footmen, with blond hair and blue-gray eyes. He bowed. "It would be my honor, Miss Henrietta."

She had yet to be assigned a footman for the Season. The one she'd had last year had married one of Charlotte's maids and had gone to her household. "Thank you. It is not far."

"Yes, miss."

He held the door for her and followed after she stepped out. It was not long before she was shown into her friend's private parlor.

"Henrietta." Dorie bussed her cheek. "I did not expect you today. Did you not visit your grandmother?"

"I did. We had luncheon together, then visited Lady Thornhill's salon." As Henrietta spoke, she removed her bonnet. "You will never guess who was there."

"I have not a clue." Dorie poured a cup of tea and handed it to Henrietta. "It is fresh. Who was there? Not a famous artist?"

"No, Lady Fotherby and Lord Fotherby. Grandmamma knew they would be there. It seems that she has been in close contact with Lady Fotherby and is now convinced that Lord Fotherby has redeemed himself."

Dorie clapped her hands together. "That is wonderful news!"

"It would be if my sister agreed. She is still harboring

a grudge." And rightly so. After all, Dotty had no idea what Fotherby was like now.

"But you knew she was." Dorie patted the seat next to her on a pink-and-cream-striped sofa. "I must say, he cuts a fine figure, and Exeter likes him a great deal."

"Still, I might be better off looking at either St. Albans or Bolingbroke. It would be easier."

Dorie sipped her tea, then set it down. "Sometimes what appears easier is not always."

"I have watched you, Adeline, and Georgie." Henrietta sighed. "I do not suppose I will have a better time of it." If only she knew what to do or which gentleman she liked the most. So far, it was Lord Fotherby, but she had only just met the other two. "I do not have to make a decision soon."

"No, you do not. Take your time." She heard someone walk into the room, and Dorie smiled. "After all, marriage is for life, and you want to wed a gentleman with whom you will be happy."

"I concur with my wife," Exeter said, grinning as he strolled into the room straight to Dorie.

She smiled at him, before turning back to Henrietta. "How was your carriage ride with Lord St. Albans?"

"It was nice. He was nice." Henrietta might as well tell her friend the other impression she got. "I am not sure he is interested in changing his single status."

"I wouldn't let that concern you," Exeter said. "Not every gentleman who comes to Town intending not to wed leaves single."

"I suppose you are right." She could think of at least two gentlemen who had sworn they were not going to marry and did. She glanced from Dorie to Exeter. "I have something I must ask you." She was certain she knew what the answer would be, but it seemed a strange thing to ask her friend. "The Dowager Lady Merton has injured herself and cannot come to Town. I will write to my grandmother, asking if she is willing to chaperone me, but I cannot depend on her for every entertainment. In fact, I imagine she will agree to attend only the most important ones. Would you be willing to act as my chaperone?"

"Of course I would." Dorie grinned. "I would be delighted. I would wager that Georgie will help as well."

Henrietta knew Georgie would be willing, but she was getting bigger every day. "Thank you. I must write to my grandmother. I can see myself out."

"Henrietta," Dorie said.

"Yes?"

"I assume your sister will wish to approve the events to which you have been invited. Please send me the details."

How could she have forgotten that would be needed? "I will. Oh, I saw Lady Bellamny in the Park today. She said she would be sending an invitation to her soirée. I will see you soon."

Clauson appeared as Henrietta reached the hall. "Let us go home."

On the short walk back to Merton House she decided not to decide about the gentlemen. Dorie was a case in point that one should follow one's instincts and not try to plan which gentleman one wanted. As for chaperoning, Henrietta should probably decide which entertainments would interest her grandmother. Dorie could chaperone her to anything else.

Henrietta went to her desk and pulled out a piece of

pressed paper, dipped her sharpened pen into the standish, and began to write.

> *Dearest Grandmother,*
>
> *Poor Lady Merton has broken her leg and cannot act as my chaperone. Would you be willing to accompany me to some of my entertainments?*
>
> > *Your loving granddaughter,*
> > *Henrietta*

She wondered if she should be more voluble, but her grandmother generally liked directness. This would have to do. She sanded the letter, sealed it, and took it to be delivered by a footman to the Pulteney.

As she was getting ready to dress for dinner, a knock came on the door. Spyer answered it. "Her grace sent a verbal message. She said that she will accompany you to those of your entertainments you choose. You are to keep her informed."

"Thank God for that." When she went down to dinner she could tell her sister all was arranged. She had to ensure that the events Grandmamma attended with her were ones where she would not become bored. That meant some of her friends would be present as well. Almack's was one choice, as was Lady Bellamny's soirée. Neither of them would be for another few weeks. Henrietta would have to wait to receive invitations before she could make any other decisions.

CHAPTER TWENTY

The next morning Nate rose early, as was his habit, and donned the suit of clothing his valet had laid out for him. With Padraig at his side, he strode down the stairs and out the door, where a groom stood with Darragh. "Good morning."

"A fine day for a ride, my lord," the groom answered.

Nate's timing couldn't have been better. As he passed the far entrance into Grosvenor Square, Lady Exeter and Miss Stern, riding on either side of a phaeton driven by Lady Turley had turned onto Upper Grosvenor Street. When he came alongside of them, he tipped his hat. "Good morning, ladies."

"Good morning," they all answered at once, but the only voice he heard was Miss Stern's. To his ears, her tone was lower and more musical than the others. "May I accompany you?"

"Of course." She smiled at him, and his heart skipped a beat. The other ladies moved ahead, and she fell back and rode beside him. "I admire how your dog paces alongside you."

"Yes"—he glanced at the wolfhound—"this is one of

his favorite things to do, and he knows he must be very well behaved around Darragh." As if he knew he was being talked about, Padraig looked up and lolled out his tongue.

Her head tilted slightly to one side, and Nate knew he had her attention. "You have Irish names for both horse and dog?"

"They're both from Ireland. I went there looking for a horse. Darragh is a Trakehner Chestnut. I found him and a litter of puppies. They were probably the last or one of the Irish Wolfhounds left."

She glanced at the horse and again at the dog, as if trying to decide which one to talk about first. "Is that not a horse breed originally from Prussia?"

"It is." Her knowledge surprised him. "You must know your horses."

Miss Stern's laugh sounded like the tinkling of chimes. "My brother knows his horses. The youngest son of one of our neighbors was in the cavalry. When he came home in between assignments, he brought his favorite horse with him. My brother could talk of nothing else for at least a week."

They rode through the gate into the Park. "I suppose he wanted one of his own?"

"He did indeed." She smiled and shook her head. "My father said he would have to give up his horse if he wanted another one. That was something my brother was not prepared to do."

"Not even for such a magnificent animal?"

"No." The twinkle Nate look forward to seeing entered her lovely green eyes. "No one could take Perseus's place."

"I'm glad I didn't have to make that decision." He thought his first horse. "I didn't truly have a choice. I'd had Midnight since I was ten or eleven. He let me know most forcefully that he was ready to retire."

Her smile widened. "How so?"

"He would stop in the middle of a road, or field, or anywhere else that was inconvenient, and refuse to go farther until he'd had a rest." He grinned at her. "It got to the point that it took two days to visit my tenants. Finally my head groom told me about a breeder in Ireland who had a Trakehner for sale and convinced me to go take a look."

Miss Stern gazed at her horse's neck. "I hope that when Lilly is ready to go to pasture I will know it without being told."

"You probably will." There wasn't much he imagined Miss Stern had to be told. In the distance Lady Exeter was galloping, and Lady Turley followed behind in her carriage. "Would you like to gallop?"

"I would." The smile Miss Stern had on her face was luminous. For a moment he couldn't breathe. My God, she was beautiful. "That is the most important reason to ride so early in the day." She glanced around and must have seen her friends. "I am glad Georgie decided to come with us."

And kind. "I imagine not being able to ride is one of the hard parts about being in a delicate condition."

"Yes." Her tone was different and her expression dimmed.

He hoped it was because she too wanted a husband and children. "Let's go."

They urged their horses into a gallop and rode next to each other until they reached a tree where the other ladies were talking.

"I have decided to have a dinner followed by an informal dance in two weeks," Lady Turley announced. "That will give me sufficient time to discover who is in Town and send out the cards." She glanced at him. "You will be invited."

"I'm honored." He bowed, and they all started to laugh. Nate hadn't had so much fun in ages. He not only found himself being drawn to Miss Stern more and more, he liked her friends as well.

"And I shall have an al fresco luncheon next week," Lady Exeter said. "You are also invited my lord."

"Excellent." Nate bowed again. "I am sure to have a grand time."

"Henrietta, do you want to race?" Lady Exeter asked.

Miss Stern glanced at him.

"No, please go ahead. I shall keep Lady Turley company."

She smiled that brilliant smile again. "On the count of three. One. Two. Three."

Just like that, the ladies were off, cantering down the path.

"I wish I could. . . ." Lady Turley blew out a breath.

"Do you miss riding?" From what Miss Stern had said, her friend probably did, but it gave them some sort of conversation.

"I do." A frown formed on her ladyship's countenance. "I love that I will have a child, but I do miss riding."

"It's not forever," Nate ventured.

"No, it is not. My husband frequently reminds me of that." When she mentioned her husband her frown dissolved. "He was the one who suggested I drive the phaeton this morning."

"An intelligent man." And one who cared about his wife a great deal.

"He is." She started the carriage forward. "Thus far we

have all been fortunate in our marriages." Lady Turley glanced speculatively at him. "We hope Henrietta will find the right gentleman this Season."

That was his hope as well, but he wanted the man to be him. "As do I."

Nate arrived home in time to change and make his way to Exeter House, where he broke his fast, then accompanied Exeter and Turley to the Lords. Even when Nate had been in Town before, he'd only gone for votes, and voted as he'd been told to. That was something he planned to change. It was past time he stepped forward and became involved in drafting bills and making speeches to urge their passing.

The entrance to Westminster brought back faint memories. The only thing he actually remembered was that peers sat by rank. They met with some other gentlemen to whom Exeter introduced Nate. After the introductions, they stood talking as the members entered the chambers.

"I'm going in now," Exeter said. "You'll be fine with Turley."

"Thank you. It is a little strange being here again." Just then Nate saw Merton pass by with three gentlemen. Two of them Nate didn't know. The third was the Earl of Worthington. This wasn't happening as Nate thought it would. For some reason he had imagined fewer people, and Merton looking at him as he had from his carriage. Instead Nate was simply part of the crowd of peers taking their seats, indistinguishable from the other gentlemen.

"Are you ready?" Turley asked.

"Yes. Lead the way." At this point Nate didn't know if Merton would see him at all. Unless he made an effort to be seen. If Nate wanted to try to attach Miss Stern's affection, he had to resolve his relations with her sister and brother-in-law.

He started in to the side on which he'd taken his seat before, and Turley took Nate's elbow. "This way."

"Ah, yes." He was no longer a Tory. He took a seat on the padded bench next to Turley. It was a good day for him to begin attending the Lords again. The only item on the agenda was the approval of the Convention of 1818, a treaty between England and the United States that established the forty-ninth parallel as the northern boundary between British North America and England's former colonies.

"Good morning," Lord Bolingbroke said as he passed them.

"Good morning." Nate saw the man take his place among the earls. "I don't see St. Albans."

"You won't," Turley responded. "He's the Duke of Cleveland's eldest."

Nate nodded. "I think my father knew Cleveland."

"He most likely did." Turley shrugged. "They were both Tories."

"They were." Nate's father would have had apoplexy seeing him here. But he was convinced it had been the right move, along with all the other changes he'd made. He didn't know how long they'd be here, but he had to get Merton's attention before he left. One way or the other, this situation had to be resolved.

Once Georgie made the turn toward Green Street, where Turley House was located, Dorie rode closer to Henrietta. "I hope you did not mind that both Georgie and I promised to invite Lord Fotherby to our entertainments."

Henrietta slid her friend a look. "No, I did not mind at

all. You know that I have not yet made any decisions." Dorie raised a brow. "Well, I have decided not to make a decision. Unfortunately, falling in love with him would be very complicated."

"I can assure you that the falling in love part is not complicated at all. It is the dealing with the family that is sometimes difficult." Dorie furrowed her brows. "Did you not think your grandmother liked him?"

"Yes." Grandmamma would never have introduced him if she had not. "I suppose you are correct about the falling in love part. Still, I was not even interested in any of the gentlemen last Season or in the autumn Season, and now three men have caught my attention." That in itself was amazing. "But you are correct. Thus far, Fotherby is the most interesting of the three." Henrietta recalled how Lords St. Albans and Bolingbroke flipped a coin over who would escort her to the front door. At first she'd thought it was silly, but upon second thought it seemed as if they were playing a game. And she did not intend to be an object of their sport, or whatever they were doing. Still . . . "I suppose you should invite Lord Bolingbroke and Lord St. Albans as well."

Dorie's brow puckered. "I shall have to discover which young ladies are in Town." A delighted smile appeared on her face. "Did you hear that we will have another set of Tice and Martindale?"

"No." There couldn't be. "Do you mean to say their mothers each managed to have three daughters each with like ages?"

"Four." Dorie nodded. "I wonder if they will wish to wed gentlemen who live near each other, the same as their sisters did."

"We will know shortly." Henrietta also hoped that the

two young ladies did not decide to use the same antics their sisters had last Season. Tricking a gentleman into marriage was a horrible thing to do.

"I do hope they are more mature than their sisters," Dorie commented.

Yet was that fair? The sisters had acted like complete featherheads during the Season, but, once married, suddenly had become responsible matrons. But this was the Season they were discussing. "I do as well." Henrietta halted Lilly in front of her sister's house. "We will meet all the young ladies at Lady Bellamny's party in a few weeks."

"Perhaps I shall have my al fresco luncheon after her ladyship's event," Dorie said. "It will be nice to invite some of the ladies making their come out."

"I agree. I remember how wary I was until I met you, Georgie, Adeline, and Augusta. It is hard to believe we have only known each other for a year."

"It seems as if we have been friends forever," Dorie agreed.

A groom came forward, and Henrietta unhooked her leg, then slid down from her mare. "Do you have plans for today?"

"I am going to take the girls shopping. Would you like to join us?"

When Dorie had married Exeter, he'd come with two much younger sisters. Well, much younger than he was. The oldest, Penelope, was only two years younger than Dorie. Penelope would make her come out next year. "Yes. I'd like that."

Henrietta climbed the steps and the door opened. "Good morning, Parkin."

He bowed. "Good morning, Miss Henrietta. Did you have a pleasant ride?"

"I did. Lady Turley decided to join us in her phaeton."

His eyes widened into a horrified look. "Not one of those high-perch ones?"

"No, no." Henrietta strove not to laugh. "The normal one. It was very safe."

"Thank the good Lord for that."

She almost expected him to make some sign.

"I must hurry. I know I smell like a horse, and I am starving." She forced herself not to run up the stairs.

Less than an hour later she entered the breakfast room to find her sister already there. "Good morning."

"Good morning," Dotty replied from behind a newssheet. "How was your ride?"

"It was wonderful. I love riding in the morning." Henrietta picked up a plate and began to fill it.

Once she'd taken her seat and poured tea, her sister said, "I received a message from Mrs. Perriman. Mr. Meadows assisted her yesterday in rescuing a young woman and her daughter." Dotty lowered her paper and frowned. "For some reason that name sounds familiar. I wonder if he was the one who gave the one-thousand-pound donation?"

"That is what we surmised before." Henrietta used her brightest tone. Her sister was definitely becoming forgetful. She was glad she had not yet taken a sip of tea. She would have spit it out. She took a sip now. It was odd to keep information from her sister, and a spear of guilt struck her.

"Yes." Dotty picked up a piece of toast, glanced at the marmalade, and shook her head. "She praised his ability to take instruction from her. Apparently, the husband, or whoever he was, came after them. She thought he might attempt to fight the man, which would have caused a delay, but he went to the carriage when she told him to."

"That was good of him." She needed to change the subject. "Where did she take the woman and child?"

"Richmond. As you might suppose, the woman was terrified the man would find her. But I think she will be safe there." Dotty bit into the toast.

"I agree." Henrietta wished she could tell her sister that Fotherby planned to sign the house over to them. "Did she say anything else about Mr. Meadows?"

"Only that he was very well dressed." Dotty took a sip of tea. "He must have gone to a tailor, but he did not hesitate to wear the old coat she gave him, and a hat."

"He sounds like an extremely helpful man." Henrietta almost cringed. What would her sister do when she found out the truth? "Has Merton left already?"

"He has. There is a vote in the Lords today."

Applying herself to her breakfast, she wondered if he and Lord Fotherby would meet.

Dotty glanced at Henrietta. "Mr. Meadows has been helpful. He clearly likes to aid others." Her sister's brows rose slightly as she gave a light shrug. "Perhaps I should tell Mrs. Perriman that I would like to meet him."

This time she had been in mid-sip and quickly brought the serviette to her lips.

"Is something wrong?" Her sister gave her a searching look.

"No, not at all." Her voice croaked like a frog's. Henrietta cleared her throat. "That is a wonderful idea." This whole situation was going to come crashing down on them. Then what would happen? But she was not in love with him. She hardly knew him. Still, she did not want him harmed. "I simply wonder if he runs in our circles. It is possible he might not be comfortable with us." Oooh, God was going to strike her dead.

"My dear sister"—this time Dotty's disapproving look reminded Henrietta of their mother—"when did you become such a snob?"

"Me? A snob? I am not. I simply do not wish him to be uncomfortable." Henrietta was out on a shaky limb and she knew it. Their father, a vicar before he inherited the baronetcy from his brother, had been extremely clear that they should never treat others differently, no matter their social status.

Dotty's glare made Henrietta feel like a worm. "I've never heard such rot from you."

Neither had she. "Perhaps I am wrong."

"Perhaps?"

Drat, she'd done it now. "I'm sure you are correct that he would not be at all disconcerted." She made a point of glancing at the clock and rose. "I must go. I am meeting Dorie."

"This conversation is not over," her sister called after her.

No one knew better than she that it was not over. The only question was how it would end. What would happen when Merton saw Fotherby today?

CHAPTER TWENTY-ONE

Nate blew out a frustrated breath. After several speeches the bill had finally passed, but he'd really not been in doubt about that. Still, if it took that long for a piece of legislation to succeed when almost everyone agreed, he had a hard time seeing how they could pass a bill when there was opposition. After the act passed, there were still a few pieces of business that were discussed before an adjournment was called.

Again he saw Merton pass by, but by the time Nate entered the corridor, his former friend was gone. At this rate he was never going to be able to attempt to clear things up between them, and if he wanted to marry Miss Stern . . .

Marry Miss Stern.

That was exactly what he wished to do. Henrietta Stern was the only woman he'd ever met who made him want to marry. He could envision himself sitting across a breakfast table with her, discussing politics, or the estate, or other matters. He could also see her in his bed. The image was so real he groaned with need. Yet he could not cause a rift between her and her family.

Exeter met Nate and Turley as they reached the doors leading outside.

"It's almost time for luncheon," Exeter said. "Would you like to join me?"

"I would. Brooks's?" Nate might be able to catch Merton there.

"Our meeting at Brooks's is tomorrow," Turley replied.

"No, my house," Exeter said. "My wife will want to hear how the session went." They reached the pavement.

"I cannot." Turley shook his head. "I promised Georgie I would review her plans for the nursery when I finished today."

"Fotherby?" Exeter raised a questioning brow.

"I'd be delighted." Nate hoped Miss Stern would be present. He knew she spent a great deal of time with her friends.

"Excellent." Exeter gave a pleased smile.

They strolled past several town coaches before entering St James's Park, then onto Green Park. Turley left them when they reached Grosvenor Square. They arrived at Exeter House as an empty carriage was being driven away.

"It appears as if my wife just arrived." Exeter strode through the still-open door.

At first it looked as if someone had come for a visit. Boxes and packages were placed in groups on the floor. Lady Exeter, two girls wreathed in smiles, and Miss Stern were removing their bonnets.

"Alex, you should see what we bought." The smaller of the young girls hugged him.

"Are you certain I want to?" He took out his quizzer and made a point of surveying the bundles.

The taller girl shook her head. "You are being silly. This

is nothing compared to what it will be like when I come out next year."

Nate was hard put not to laugh when Exeter gave a dramatic shudder.

"Those are his sisters," Miss Stern's low, musical voice whispered.

"I thought they must be some sort of relation, but the girls don't look at all like him."

"No. They favor their mother."

"Lady Penelope and Lady Phillida," Exeter said. "I'd like to present Viscount Fotherby. Fotherby, m'sisters."

He bowed as they performed graceful curtseys. "It is a pleasure to meet you, ladies."

Penelope held out her hand, and he took it. "It is very nice to meet you as well, my lord."

Not to be outdone, Phillida extended her hand as well. He took her fingers in his hand too. "I am delighted to meet you, my lord."

He glanced up as Exeter was wiping a hand down his face. Nate was happy he wouldn't have a daughter or sister coming out next Season. For the first time he was relieved that his sisters were all older than he.

Just then a lady dressed neatly, but not in the latest fashion, came down the stairs. "Come along, girls."

"Oh, Holly, you will never believe all the things we bought!" Lady Phillida exclaimed, losing her veneer of dignity.

"In that case I am looking forward to seeing it all." The governess shooed the girls up the stairs as a maid and two footmen followed carrying the packages.

Lady Exeter took her husband's arm. "I am looking

forward to hearing how the day went. Was there anything exciting?"

Nate held his arm out to Miss Stern and was pleased when she slipped her small hand in the crook of his arm. "I'm positive you had more excitement shopping than we did in the Lords."

"I understand the only important order of business was to vote on a treaty." She nodded.

"Yes." He took a breath. "I saw Merton before the session, but he didn't see me. By the time I was out of the room, he was gone."

"Mrs. Perriman sent word about you assisting with the latest rescue." Miss Stern grimaced, and he braced himself for bad news. "My sister voiced a desire to meet Mr. Meadows, and mentioned that Meadows sounded familiar."

It wouldn't be long before Merton worked out who Nate was. Truth be told, he welcomed it. But Lady Merton was the greater problem. Her wanting to meet him was an unexpected complication. "I see."

Miss Stern—Henrietta—didn't say anything, but her expressive eyes indicated that she agreed with him. "I tried to tell her that you might not be in our circle and she called me a snob."

When Nate barked a laugh, she glared at him. "I apologize. I didn't mean to laugh. Nothing could be further from the truth. You are not a snob."

Her nose scrunched up. "No, I am merely hiding you from her."

"I will make things right with them. I swear to you, I will." He had spoken with more fervor than he intended.

Henrietta stopped walking and met his gaze. "I know you will."

She trusted him. And, perhaps, she was interested in him. Nate let out the breath he'd been holding.

They had followed Lord and Lady Exeter into a small dining room where the footmen were laying out two more places and a cold collation had been set out on the table. He was pleased to see her ladyship sit next to her husband. Miss Stern was on Exeter's other side and Nate took the chair next to hers. The talk soon turned to an act concerning children working long hours in factories that had first been proposed when he was last in London.

"I would have thought, because it was a Tory bill, it would have passed by now." At least it should have. They *were* in charge of the government.

Exeter swallowed. "Not yet. We will try again this session."

"Forgive me." Miss Stern—Henrietta,—placed her fork on her plate. Her lips were pressed together, reminding him of his mother when she was extremely angry. "But it is almost as if the factory owners want free labor. Very much like the plantation owners do."

He hadn't thought of it quite like that. "That's an interesting point."

"It is," Lady Exeter concurred as her husband nodded.

"I agree that everyone must have enough money to live, but they pay the workers a pittance for dangerous conditions. It is wrong." He wasn't at all surprised at her vehemence, even though he'd never heard her speak this way before. He had expected that to be her view. "The system must be changed. The only question is how one does it."

"By chipping away at it one piece at a time." The others

stared at him for a moment. "If a large piece of legislation is introduced, there will be too much opposition."

"But taken a little bit at a time, the bills will have more of a chance of passing."

Miss Stern's intelligent green gaze met his and he sucked in a breath. There was nothing he couldn't do with her by his side. "That is a brilliant idea."

Henrietta had known he was kind. Now she knew he could be an excellent politician. He was everything she had been searching for in a husband. Yet . . . there was still the difficulty with her family. But if they were supposed to be together, perhaps that would work itself out as well.

She felt a little better about her attraction to him. Surely fate would not be so unkind as to show her a gentleman who was perfect for her and snatch him away. And he had said that he would reconcile with her sister and brother-in-law.

"Thank you." His eyes caught hers, and for a second neither of them could break their gazes away.

"Well, then," Dorie said brightly, "now we know our way forward. I am sorry to end our luncheon, but we must spend time with our son. Henrietta, I will send a footman to walk you home if that is acceptable."

"Of course." She placed her serviette on the table and rose.

Fotherby offered her his arm again, and she tucked her hand in the crook of his arm, marveling at how right it seemed. "May I escort you home?"

"Do you think that is wise?" Lord only knew what would happen if her sister or brother-in-law saw him.

The lean lines of his face hardened as he raised a brow. "I am not in hiding."

"Of course you are not." Henrietta had not meant to

insult or anger him. "It is just that . . ." That she might not be able to see him if he was discovered, and she didn't like that thought at all. "Very well." They strolled to the hall, and Dorie assigned a footman to follow Henrietta and Fotherby. She bussed her friend's cheek. "Give the baby a kiss for me."

Dorie grinned. "I shall." She turned to Fotherby. "My lord, would you like to join us this afternoon in the Park? It will be as before. We ladies shall ride in my carriage, and the gentlemen will be on horseback."

"Yes." He inclined his head. "I would enjoy very much joining you."

Drat! Henrietta almost wished she had not made prior plans. "I am riding with Lord Bolingbroke this afternoon."

"Lord Fotherby, you are still welcome to accompany *our* carriage," Dorie said.

"Thank you." He inclined his head. "I still accept."

"Meet us here shortly before five. We look forward to seeing you." She shot Henrietta a grin. "We shall no doubt see you in the Park."

"No doubt." Henrietta slid a look at Fotherby. He had said he was not hiding, but this might be tempting fate too far. At least for her. Then it occurred to her that he did not seem the least bit put out that she was going riding with another man. Yet he had spoken passionately about their problem.

One of Dorie's footmen followed as they left the house and started down the street in the opposite direction from which she usually went. Merton House was diagonal to Exeter House. This way would enable them to stroll together longer.

"I would like to ask you to ride with me"—he pulled a face—"but my carriage needs repairs from sitting so long.

I hope to have it in working order within the next week or so."

Henrietta was not going to mention her sister and brother-in-law. He knew that was his fence to take. Until then there were morning rides. "I suppose that was to be expected. Are you glad to be involving yourself in politics?"

"I am." He smiled at her, and her breathing quickened. Goodness. That was another reaction she had not had for a man before. "I have found that I enjoy being useful."

"I feel the same. It is gratifying to be able to help others." She found herself walking closer to him and wondered how that happened.

They crossed to the other side of the square, and he stopped on the corner, just one house down from her home. Raising her hand, he kissed it. "It goes against the grain, but I must leave you here."

"I know." He bowed and strolled toward Grosvenor Street. As she continued to Merton House, she sent up a prayer that his difficulties with her family would resolve themselves soon.

Parkin opened the door, and Henrietta entered the hall and removed her bonnet. "Where is my sister?"

"Still resting. His lordship has gone to luncheon at his club and then to the boxing salon."

Well, then. She could occupy her time writing a few letters until her ride this afternoon. "I shall be in my rooms."

Henrietta sighed. Despite liking Fotherby the best, she would give the other gentlemen a fair chance. She thought back to what St. Albans had said about his friends marrying. If they were looking to wed, that was. Lord Bolingbroke was a peer and would, therefore, need to marry. She tried to concentrate on what little she knew of him from reading *Debrett's*, but her thoughts kept returning to Lord

Fotherby. Shaking her head, she picked up one of the letters on her desk. With any luck at all, she would be able to concentrate on her correspondence.

She knew from the writing, it was from her mother. After relaying all the news of the neighborhood and their family, she reminded Henrietta that she did not have to wed this Season if she did not wish to. Mama had said the same thing to Dotty when she'd come out, and to Henrietta last Season. The next sentences caused a hard lump to form in her throat.

> *You must always follow your heart. When you find love and it is returned, do not allow anyone to convince you to let it go. I do not want to know what would have happened to me if I had not refused the matches my father tried to arrange and insisted on your papa. I do know I would never have been happy.*
>
> *Your loving mother*

Tears pricked Henrietta's eyes, and when she lifted her hand to her face her cheek was damp. If Mama only knew what the ramifications of her advice might be, would she have still given it? Henrietta recalled what she had been told of her parents' marriage. Her uncle and her father had been friends, but when Papa refused to give her up, her uncle broke with him. Grandmamma had stood with Mama and Papa against her husband and her eldest son until the marriage was allowed. Yes, she would probably still give the same advice, and her grandmother would stand with Henrietta if need be. But she did not want a rift in her family. She did not yet know if she was falling in love with Fotherby.

Henrietta rubbed her temples to stop a headache from forming. She was riding with Lord Bolingbroke today. She would give him her full attention.

CHAPTER TWENTY-TWO

Nate scowled to himself.

Damn Bolingbroke.

Damn every gentleman in Town who wished to ride or dance with Miss Stern. He hastened his steps as his frustration rose. He had been very careful not to show his ire when she had said she was riding with the man. He was not yet in a position to show her how he truly felt about her engagement this afternoon.

Entering his house, he headed to his study. He'd see what work had to be done and then he'd go to Jackson's Boxing Salon. His technique would be rusty—it had been years since he'd boxed there—but it was the only way to defeat the disappointment he was feeling. It didn't matter if he was any good; he'd still be able to hit someone. With any luck, it would be Bolingbroke. Unlike Merton, Nate had never been skilled enough to box with the great Jackson himself, outside of having taken a few lessons, that was. Nate had been much more interested in fashion than boxing. He'd gone to Jackson's only because it was the fashionable thing to do. Now he badly needed to hit something or someone.

An hour later he walked into Jackson's and looked around. Nothing had changed since he'd been there the last time. Jackson was teaching a young man the finer points of the sport. Nate watched, remembering the stance and the boxer's advice to always keep one's fists up. After a few minutes he was approached by one of the trainers. The man was about his age, but had the look of someone who'd spent time in fighting competitively. "May I help you, sir?"

"Yes. I'd like to spar a few rounds with someone. It's been a long time since I've boxed."

The man glanced at two men fighting in the center of the room. "Mr. Jackson don't have any appointments left, but I'd be happy to give you some practice. The name's Jim Johnson."

"Thank you, Mr. Johnson. I'm Fotherby." Nate motioned with his head toward the other end of the long room. "I assume the changing room is in the same place?"

"Yes, sir." The man grinned. "Nothing here's changed."

Nate went into a room with wooden pegs on the wall and began to strip down to his trousers and stockings, then joined the trainer. He donned a pair of boxing gloves, and they spent a few minutes on Nate's form, slightly bent, shoulders forward, knees bent and relaxed, and fists up.

He surprised himself by performing better than he had in the past. He'd even got a hit on Johnson. "You didn't let me do that, did you?"

"No, sir." The man grinned. "Doing that don't teach a man to box. You earned that one."

They were about to go another round when Nate heard the voice he'd been waiting to hear since he'd got to Town. "You're much better than you used to be." Nate turned to see Merton, already stripped down and looking like he'd be happy to do serious damage. "Why don't you try fighting me?"

"If you wish." Nate nodded to the trainer. "Thank you for your help."

"Good luck. His lordship's a damn good fighter. Watch his left," the man muttered.

Nate nodded. "Thank you." He moved toward the wall as Merton took Johnson's place. "When you're ready."

Merton lashed out with his right fist, and Nate blocked it, but before he could hit back Merton landed a hit with his left fist on Nate's jaw, and his head snapped back as he staggered. That's what the trainer had meant. He could feel the anger radiating from Merton as they circled each other. Nate feinted with his left and struck with his right, hitting his old friend's cheek. Merton stuck at him again, and this time Nate didn't hesitate to hit back, landing a blow to Merton's stomach. He came back with a punch to Nate's stomach, and the fight was truly on. Sweat ran down into his eyes as he stumbled from a blow. The only good thing was that Merton wasn't looking any better. Nate had a vague knowledge of the other men in the room placing bets.

He was breathing heavily when someone called out, "Gentlemen, that is enough." Merton went in for another hit when he was grabbed by one of the trainers. "My lord," Jackson's commanding tone rang out. "I said to stop."

Nate bent over, placing his hands on his knees and took several long breaths, wondering how bruised he'd be later. He glanced at Merton and saw he was doing the same thing.

Johnson removed Nate's gloves and slapped him on the back. "Well done, sir."

Merton nodded at Jackson, then approached Nate. "Are you ready for a drink or two of beer?"

THE MOST ELIGIBLE BRIDE IN LONDON   221

It was all Nate could do to keep his jaw from dropping, but he nodded. "Yes."

Neither of them spoke as they grabbed cloths to wipe their faces and upper bodies. They donned their clothing and strolled out of the boxing salon to a small inn with mullioned windows across the front. They both had to duck to get through the entrance. The interior had an old brick fireplace with a wooden beam for a mantel decorated with pewter plates. Merton led Nate to a small table in the far corner of the common room.

Once the mugs of beer had been set down, Merton took a long drink. "That was you I saw walking the Irish Wolfhound."

"It was. I've had him for three years." Nate picked up his mug and drank.

"You've changed." His former friend leaned back in the chair.

He nodded. "I needed to."

Merton took another drink and set down the mug on the table. "Why?"

Nate didn't even have to ask what Merton was asking about. It could only be one thing. "Rank stupidity. A lady told me you'd been trapped by Miss Stern, but you really wished to wed her cousin. You wouldn't talk to me about your betrothal, and I wanted to believe it was true." Nate shrugged. "I thought you'd be happy if she left. It never occurred to me you had feelings for her." He took a long draw from the mug. "I'm sorry I did it, but I can't regret the consequences. If I hadn't been sent home, I might still be prancing around without a thought for anything but my own pleasure."

Merton grimaced. "If I hadn't fallen in love with Thea, I'd be doing the same. I thought I could change her to fit what I wanted in a wife." He smiled wryly. "Instead, she changed me." He took another drink. "I could feel what was happening to me and couldn't bring myself to talk about it." He leaned his head back and chuckled softly. "I was preparing to have my mother instruct her how to go on as my marchioness when I discovered her grandmother was a duchess." He shook his head. "No. I couldn't discuss it with anyone." Merton took a drink of beer. "I suppose you must be Mr. Meadows?"

"Yes." Nate inclined his head. "I decided I could do more good if no one knew I was a peer." He wiped a hand down his face. "That, and I was certain that my help would not be wanted if you or your wife knew it was me."

"You were right." Nate felt as if he'd been punched in the gut again. He'd hoped the fight would set things right between him and Merton. "What have you been doing for the last four years?"

Perhaps this was his chance to resolve their problem. At least with Merton, if not his wife. "After I finished having a good sulk I took up the reins of my estates and learned my duties."

Merton gazed steadily at Nate. "My sister-in-law mentioned you were in Town to help a neighbor retrieve his daughter."

It was strange that Nate had no problem maintaining eye contact with Merton. "As I said, I like to be of use. I've learned a lot about that."

Merton finished his beer. "It appears that my sister-in-law is interested in you."

Answered honestly, Nate's response would reveal a wealth of information. There was nothing to be gained by lying. "I am interested in her as well."

"How did you meet her, formally?" Merton signaled the serving maid to bring him another beer.

Nate was not going to tell him about Lady Exeter planning the meeting. There might be repercussions that would upset Henrietta. "My mother and the Dowager Duchess of Bristol are old friends. She introduced us at Lady Thornhill's salon." Nate shrugged. "There was no one there either of us knew, so we spent the time talking." Nate took a sip of his beer. He didn't drink much anymore and he needed to keep his wits about him. "She is an interesting lady."

Merton muttered something that Nate couldn't hear, then said, "Bolingbroke and St. Albans are interested in her."

"I am aware." But neither of those gentlemen knew Henrietta Stern the way Nate did. Merton was still trying to stare him down, but it wasn't going to work. "I would like to get to know her better. I think we have many things in common."

Merton's lips thinned. "I doubt my wife is willing to forgive and forget."

"I'd like to apologize to her for my behavior." If there was any way possible, Nate wanted to get past this. He wanted to be able to take Miss Stern riding during the Grand Strut, to court her in pubic.

"There is also the matter of her parents." Merton's eyes bore into Nate's, almost as if he was trying to catch Nate lying.

He nodded. "If she can forgive me, would not her family listen to her?"

"Most likely. However, I am not at all certain she *will* forgive you." Merton picked up his mug and drank again.

"I'll ask her if she will allow you to try to excuse your past behavior."

"Not excuse." Never that. "I was wrong, and I callously failed to heed her protests." Nate wished he hadn't been so weak before.

"I'll ask her. That is all I can do."

"Thank you." He rose from the table and put down several coins, enough to pay for his and Merton's drinks.

Before he could leave, Merton said, "The one thousand pounds came from you, did it not?"

"It did." Would Lady Merton try to return it if she knew Nate had made the donation? He didn't want that to happen. "I beg you not to tell your wife. I made the donation because saving children and women is a just cause."

"Did you tell my sister-in-law?" The hardness still had not left Merton's face.

Nate was starting to feel insulted. "No, and I don't plan to."

"I shall ask my wife if she will meet with you." He donned his hat. "I wouldn't hold my breath."

That was what Nate was afraid of. There had to be a way. He just hadn't found it yet. "Thank you."

"Have you decided to attend Parliament while you're in Town?" Merton asked.

"I already have. I was there for the recent vote."

"Odd." Merton lips flattened downward, as if he was thinking. "I don't recall seeing you there."

Nate lifted one shoulder and let it drop. "I saw you. You were with Worthington and two other gentlemen."

"Yes, Kenilworth and Rothwell. They're the husbands of my wife's closest friends." Merton stared at Nate for a few seconds. "Where did you sit?"

"I decided to change parties. I sat with the Whigs."

Rubbing his chin, Merton nodded. "I'll probably see you soon, then."

"Probably."

Nate left the inn after Merton and squinted in the bright sunlight. Even if Lady Merton refused to allow Nate to make amends, he still wanted to see Henrietta. But had letting Merton know of his interest in the lady killed his chances with her? He hoped not. The more time he spent with her, the more he wanted her in his life. Still, this problem with Lady Merton did not seem as if it would go away. He couldn't simply trust to fate. Somehow he had to find some way for her to if not forgive him, at least accept it was up to Henrietta to decide who she would have. Naturally, he would do everything possible to make sure it was him. Perhaps it was time to seek his mother's advice.

Walking slowly, he made his way home. "Hulatt, where is her ladyship?"

Nate's butler bowed. "In the morning room, my lord."

"Thank you." He handed the man his hat and cane. "That's where I'll be."

"Very good, my lord. Shall I send a tea tray?"

"Yes, please." Boxing had given him an appetite.

He ambled slowly to the morning room with thoughts of Henrietta Stern filling his mind. He wanted her family to accept him, but failing that, he wanted her to choose him over her family. Yet did he really want that? Her insistence that he reconcile with her sister and brother-in-law did her great credit. If they married, he'd want that same kind of loyalty from her for their family. Nate leaned his head back and sighed. He'd just put himself squarely back to the beginning when she discovered who he was. He was not sure even his mother could help him. He rubbed a hand down the side of his face. There had to be a way to have her as his wife, and have the support of her family.

He entered the morning room, one of his favorite parlors in the house. The pale yellow silk wallpaper was covered with paintings done by family members over the years. The furniture was comfortable rather than fashionable, and situated to make conversation easy. Long windows were spread across the back and one side of the room. Miniature portraits decorated one large, round table in a corner. In the other corner was a cabinet where any number of games could be found. His mother was on the chaise reading a letter.

"Good afternoon," Nate said as he entered the parlor.

"Ah, Fotherby." Mama put down the letter and glanced at him. "What happened to you?"

"Merton." Nate grinned. "I went to Jackson's Boxing Salon, and he came in while I was there. He doesn't look any better than I do." He gingerly touched his jaw. "I'd hoped that indulging him would help him forgive me."

Mama gave him a dubious look. "Did it?"

"I'm not sure." Hulatt brought in the tea, including biscuits and several small sandwiches. Nate waited until the butler left before taking a seat on a leather chair next to the chaise. "We went to an inn and had a drink and talked. His wife still thinks badly of me. He said he'd ask her if she would listen to my apology. But I have the feeling he did not hold out much hope of her agreeing."

His mother poured them cups of tea, and he took two sandwiches and several lemon biscuits. After she had a sip of tea she set down the cup on a low table between his chair and the chaise. "How do you plan to go forward if she will not speak to you?"

"I am not certain." He sipped his tea. It tasted like a new blend. "I haven't tasted this before."

Mama fluttered her fingers. "I decided to try something different. Do you like it?"

"I do like it." He finished his cup, poured another, then ate a sandwich.

"Back to your problem." She let the sentence hang.

"I believe we are becoming closer. However, I don't wish to cause Miss Stern problems with her family. I am positive that neither of us wishes to go behind her family's collective back to see each other."

"Does Lord Merton know you have met?" she asked thoughtfully.

"He does." Nate hadn't thought about his former friend's reaction to that news. He'd been more concerned about Lady Merton's feelings toward him. "I told him the duchess introduced us."

His mother tapped a finger against her cheek. "Did he warn you away from Miss Stern?"

"No." Nate mentally reviewed the conversation. "No, he did not." That, in and of itself, was interesting. "After I told him that I would like to know her better, we discussed his wife's feelings about me." He'd not thought of what that might mean. There was no overt approval, but Merton said nothing about Nate not seeing her. "He was more concerned about his wife."

"I must say, that does not surprise me at all," Mama said. "I understand that she is in a delicate condition and is not able to chaperone her sister."

No wonder Merton was so concerned about her. If it was Henrietta, Nate would be very worried. An image of her large with his child invaded his thoughts. "Perhaps I should visit Miss Stern's father."

Mama's brows rose. "That might not be a bad idea. Although I believe it is a bit too soon."

"But if I had his permission—"

"She is still quite close to her sister," Mama said.

Nate slumped back in the chair. He had to find a way forward that would, if not satisfy everyone, at least be acceptable.

CHAPTER TWENTY-THREE

Henrietta paused before knocking on the door to her sister's parlor as Dotty barked a sharp "no" to someone. "I will not allow him to make excuses for his behavior."

They must be talking about Lord Fotherby. Had he managed to have a meeting with Merton? Henrietta leaned closer to the door.

"I do not care if he has changed." Her sister's tone was harder than she had ever heard it, and considerably louder. Dotty must be much more affected by what had happened than she had let on.

Merton said something in a soft voice that Henrietta could not hear, to which her sister did not respond. Footsteps started toward the door, and she hurriedly knocked. She was not going to be caught like the twins and Madeline, eavesdropping.

"Come," Dotty called.

Henrietta took one step into the room. "I just wanted to tell you I will be going for my carriage ride with Lord Bolingbroke soon."

A weak smile that did not match her still-angry eyes appeared on her sister's face. "Have a good time."

"I hope to. I will see you later." Turning, Henrietta strode back down the corridor. She did not think her sister would tell her what Merton said, but *he* might. Perhaps before dinner this evening she would find him alone. The only thing she knew was that it had to do with Fotherby, and she needed to know what it was.

Lord Bolingbroke arrived as Henrietta was making her way to the hall. It would be easier if she could fall in love with either him or Lord St. Albans. Yet she knew from Dorie's experience that the heart wanted what the heart wanted, and there was no way to get the stupid thing to change its mind. The only course left to Henrietta was to try to like one of the other two men more than she liked Fotherby.

She smiled at his lordship as he waited for her, and he bowed. "It is a beautiful day today."

"I must agree." He took her mantle from Parkin and helped her don the garment. "However, if you feel a chill, I have brought a blanket with me."

That was well done of him. "How thoughtful. Thank you."

She placed her fingers on his arm, hoping to feel the strength she experienced with Fotherby. It was hard enough, but there was no feeling of excitement. Yet she had felt it the first time she had touched Lord Fotherby's arm. Perhaps that type of thing could develop. Then again, that was not a simple ride in the Park. Time would tell.

She smiled up at him. "Shall we depart?"

He returned her smile. "Naturally."

His carriage was much less colorful than Lord St. Albans's curricle. Lord Bolingbroke's was painted a deep brown with gold edging. The seats were covered with lighter brown leather. The matched pair of bays with white stockings was hitched to the carriage.

"Your horses are lovely." Henrietta wished she had a high-perch phaeton so she could tool herself around.

"Thank you." He handed her up to the well-padded bench. "They are sweet-goers." He went around to the other side, climbed in, and clicked to start the horses. "Do you drive?"

"Only at home. I do not have a carriage in Town." She watched the horses' action and agreed with his assessment. "Although I suppose my sister would allow me to use hers. The issue has never come up." Dotty was not using it this Season, and last Season Henrietta frequently rode with Dorie in her high-perch phaeton.

"My oldest sister told me that many ladies enjoy being able to take their own carriages out in the afternoon." He slid Henrietta a glance, then looked toward his horses again.

"When did she make her come out?" If she was interested in Lord Bolingbroke, it would behoove her to discover more about him and his ideas.

"Several years ago. I was still at Eton." They had reached the Park and joined the others on the carriage way. "She married a gentleman who is a diplomat. They are currently in Spain."

"That must be interesting. Are there just the two of you?"

"No." He grinned. "I have four sisters and three brothers. All the girls are older and married. One of my brothers is still at Eton. My other two brothers are at Oxford and Cambridge. You must be looking forward to your Season."

"Not as much as I was last year, but I also have charitable work that takes some of my time." She watched him for a reaction.

"Of course you do." He gave her an almost indulgent smile. "My mother always has some charity project she is working on."

That sounded promising. "What types of charities?"

"I'm not sure." His brows slid together as he seemed to think about it. "But every year she holds events to raise funds for them."

"Does she spend much time visiting them?" If Henrietta could discover more, his lordship might be a good prospect.

"Heaven forefend." His eyes had widened, and he appeared appalled. "No lady would go into the areas of the metropolis that would require."

Fortunately, she was saved from answering by Dorie hailing them. Lord Bolingbroke pulled his curricle up beside them. Georgie sat next to her, and they were accompanied by their husbands and Fotherby. It never ceased to impress Henrietta what a good seat he had. As they all exchanged greetings, she noticed a light bruise on Fotherby's chin. How had he come by that? She supposed she would have to wait until tomorrow to hear about it.

"There are definitely more people here than there were just yesterday." Dorie glanced back. "You will have to move along soon. Lady Bellamny is behind you."

Exeter and Turley groaned.

Lord Bolingbroke seemed bewildered. "Who is Lady Bellamny?"

"That's right," Turley said. "You haven't spent much time on the Town."

"I have had a lot to keep me busy in the past few years."

Henrietta wondered how often he came to Town. Was he interested in politics?

"She is a lady with very strong opinions," Exeter said. "Most of which revolve around gentlemen marrying."

Lord Bolingbroke laughed. "I imagine that might be a problem for some gentlemen."

"But not you?" Dorie asked

"No." His eyes warmed when he glanced at Henrietta. "Not for me."

At least she knew he wished to wed. But was he the right gentleman for her? She glanced over the landau at Fotherby and stifled a sigh, then gave herself an inner shake. The Season had not even begun yet. Perhaps she was in too much of a hurry for the rest of her life to be decided. She should be happy she had at least one, possibly two good prospects her family would accept. And there might be more.

"My mother is set to arrive before Sunday," Lord Bolingbroke said.

She glanced up as he smiled at her. "How nice."

"Yes, it is. She has indicated that she would like to host some entertainments."

"Excellent." Georgie grinned. "I have decided to hold my small dinner early next week. I shall include her in your invitation."

Henrietta stared at her friend. She had changed her mind again about the date of her dinner.

Despite Dorie's prophecy that Lady Bellamny would soon be upon them, the next carriage to reach them was a landau holding Lady Fotherby and Henrietta's grandmother.

Henrietta had to lean forward in order to speak to them. "Good afternoon, Grandmamma, my lady."

Lord Bolingbroke raised a brow, and she introduced her two friends and the gentlemen.

Grandmamma's eyes narrowed as she stared at Fotherby. "What did you do to yourself?"

Henrietta had been looking at her grandmother, but now turned her attention to Fotherby.

He had a chagrined look on his handsome face. "I went to Jackson's and got into a conversation with an old friend."

Merton. It had to be Merton.

"Men." Her grandmother looked disgusted. "Well, I hope he looks the same as you."

Fotherby eyes lit up and his lips curved. "I daresay he might very well."

He sounded proud of himself. Yet before Henrietta could verify his opponent was her brother-in-law, Lady Bellamny's barouche stopped and the older ladies greeted one another. Dorie wiggled her fingers and quietly directed her coachman to move ahead. Lord Bolingbroke followed her lead, and they were all on their way.

Henrietta was glad when he brought her home. She wanted to speak with Merton and hoped he was there. She wanted the whole story. Mainly she wanted to know if he was going to try to stop her from seeing Fotherby. Drat! She should not think of him in such a familiar manner.

Lord Bolingbroke drew up to Merton House and got to Henrietta's side of the curricle before the footman. Taking her hand, he helped her down the steps. The only problem was that it was just a hand. No warmth accompanied the touch. No sparks made her skin tingle through her glove. There was no heat to warm her blood. And that was an essential part of attraction. Everyone she had spoken with about it agreed.

When they reached the door she curtseyed. "Thank you for the lovely ride."

He bowed. "It was my pleasure. I do not think I have spent a more enjoyable afternoon."

He must live a very dull life. "Yes it was enjoyable." Fortunately the door opened before this leave-taking became awkward. She gave him a polite smile. "Until the next time."

Nate caught the look Miss Stern gave him when he'd said his opponent had been an old friend. She probably suspected it was her brother-in-law. The next thing he knew, Lady Exeter's carriage started forward and Boling-broke followed. Nate didn't like the warm look in the other man's eyes when he glanced at Miss Stern. He didn't like having to watch her with another gentleman. He wished he could ask her to ride with him in the Park. Then it occurred to him that there was no privacy during these carriage rides. All of them were required to stop frequently to speak to one person or another as they made their way forward. His morning rides with her gave him more of an opportunity to get to know her better. Yet even knowing that, he was still discontented. He wanted more time with her. Alone.

"And this is Lord Fotherby." Nate shook himself out of his own thoughts to pay attention to what was going on. Another carriage carrying a matron who looked much too young to have given birth to the three young ladies accompanying her had come beside them. Two of the girls, obviously twins, but distinguishable from each other, sat on either side of a girl with dark hair. The young ladies stared at him as if he were some type of exotic animal.

Nate bowed. "Good afternoon."

They broke into smiles and returned his greeting. The matron grinned at the young ladies before turning to him. "Good day, my lord."

"Lady Worthington, this is Lord Fotherby,"—the older woman inclined her head—"Lady Alice Carpenter"—the girl on the far side of the carriage nodded—"Lady Madeline Vivers"—the one in the middle inclined her head—"and Lady Eleanor Carpenter"—she nodded as well.

"It is a pleasure to meet you. Are you making your come out this Season?"

They looked at one another and giggled.

"They are not," Lady Worthington said firmly. "They have another two years before they come out."

"Ah, I understand. You are being shown the way of things." He wished someone had done that for him before he was on the Town.

Still smiling, the girls nodded again.

Lady Worthington raised an amused brow. "Dorie, Georgie, we shall see you later."

"Send us a message when you will hold your first at-home." Georgie said. "We will come by."

Lady Worthington's carriage started forward, and the Exeter landau followed suit.

"That was very nice of you to ask the twins and Madeline if they were making their come out," Lady Exeter said. "They will talk about that for a week."

"Thank you." It had actually been the only thing he could think of to say at the moment. He really *had* lost his skill at making small talk. The name Vivers nagged at his mind. Then he remembered. "Merton's cousins are Vivers."

"Yes," Lady Turley said. "Lord Worthington is his cousin."

For some reason he remembered the event. "He married Lady Grace Carpenter."

"Indeed he did." Lady Exeter grinned. "He added Grace's seven brothers and sisters to his four sisters when he did that."

Aha. He'd been right. "I thought she appeared too young to be their mother."

The two other ladies who had come out with Lady Merton were part of that family.

"Lady Augusta Vivers came out at the same time I did," Lady Turley said. "She is now traveling with her husband, Lord Phineas Carter-Woods."

He shook his head. "I cannot imagine being part of such a large family."

"It can be a bit manic at times." Lady Exeter smiled. "Lord and Lady Worthington now have two children of their own, as well as another one on the way."

"It is only fair." Lady Turley laughed. "They got the three older sisters married off."

"There were two ladies with Lady Merton when she came out. Are those the ones who wed?"

"Yes." Lady Exeter smiled. "They are now the Marchioness of Kenilworth and the Duchess of Rothwell."

Merton had mentioned Kenilworth and Rothwell as being married to his wife's friends. Nate had not known how right he'd been in thinking there was turning out to be a number of highly placed people who could stand between him and Henrietta Stern. But Lady Worthington and her younger sisters had seemed more interested in him than angry at him. Could her ladyship be an ally? He already had his mother and Miss Stern's grandmother, but one more couldn't hurt, especially when she was the sister of both of Lady Merton's friends.

"I thought of getting together a party to attend the theater," Lady Exeter said. "Unfortunately, until Lent is over the only thing on offer is a lecture on Mondays, Wednesdays, and Fridays."

No wonder his mother had not yet arranged the theater party he had asked her to.

Lady Turley glanced at her husband. "Gavin, has our stable master said what the weather will be?"

"He expects relatively warm and sunny days for the rest of the week." Lord Turley's brows furrowed as he regarded his wife. "Why?"

"Well, as there is nothing particular going on tomorrow evening, I thought a ride out to Richmond and an al fresco luncheon might be fun. If you gentlemen can take a day from the Lords, that is." Nate joined Turley and Exeter in nodding their agreement to the plan. Then she pressed her lips together and shook her head. "It won't do. I forgot Dorie was planning a party in her garden."

Lady Exeter waved her hand as if to say it was no matter. "I have not seen any young ladies to invite. As I said before, I must wait until after Lady Bellamny's soirée."

"Very well." Lady Turley smiled at them all. "Let us agree to meet tomorrow at eleven for a trip to Richmond. I shall send a note to Henrietta when I get home."

Nate thought that was an excellent idea. It would give him even more time with Henrietta. Hopefully tomorrow he'd find time to be alone with her.

Henrietta.

He'd been calling her that to himself, and he should not.

What if it slipped out? She had not, after all, given him permission to address her by her first name.

The other four chatted amiably the rest of the way around the carriage way, until Lady Turley turned her attention to him. "Lord Fotherby, you are being very quiet."

A flush of warmth rose from his neck. "I suppose I am." He shrugged. "I was thinking how long it had been since I'd visited Richmond Park." He hadn't done it when he'd been on the Town. "I believe the last time was when I was a child."

"Now that I think of it, it was the same for me," Lady Exeter said.

"I as well." Lady Turley tilted her head. "How strange that we did not go last year."

"I recall last Season being extremely busy." Lady Exeter moved the angle of her parasol as they swung toward the gate.

"In that event we should all enjoy ourselves," he said to himself. Henrietta had probably not been there at all. He wondered if there was a map of the park at home. Then it occurred to him that with riding with her in the morning and the visit to Richmond Park, he would spend most of the day with her tomorrow. Thank God for that. He'd felt at a disadvantage with Bolingbroke and St. Albans. Nate had honestly believed that once he had it out with Merton, his problems would be over. Yet that did not appear to be the case. Perhaps he had been going about this the wrong way. If he was able to attach Henrietta's attentions, that might go a long way to being accepted by her sister and brother-in-law. He sighed softly. Even if her grandmother accepted him, and possibly her parents, he suspected her relationship with her sister was strong enough to present difficulties. Then again, what sort of man was he if he gave up before he was even challenged? Yes, he had made a serious error in judgment, but he was still an eligible gentleman. Merton hadn't let anyone or anything get in the way of marrying the woman he wanted. It was time for Nate to stop wallowing in self-castigation.

He parted from the group when they continued to Turley House on Green Street and went home. Tomorrow, he'd change his tactics.

CHAPTER TWENTY-FOUR

Henrietta grinned at Parkin as she stepped into the hall. He closed the door behind her. "Thank you for being so prompt."

"Only doing my duty, Miss Henrietta. I thought you might need a little assistance."

"You were right." She removed the hat-pins in her bonnet. "Is Merton here?"

"No. He returned from the boxing salon and left again."

At this rate she would never find out if he and Fotherby had fought and settled their differences. "My sister?"

"Her ladyship is resting."

It seemed that was all Dotty did these days. Not for the first time, Henrietta sent up a prayer for her sister and the baby. Her sister probably would not be in Town if it was not for her requiring a second Season. She wondered if Dorie or Georgie had returned from the Park. They must have. Their carriage was before Lord Bolingbroke's leaving the Park.

A knock came at the door, and Henrietta turned to see

who it was, but Parkin blocked her view. When he turned back around he handed her a missive. "From Lady Turley."

"Thank you." She took the letter. "I shall be in my parlor. Please have tea sent up."

"At once, Miss Henrietta." The butler bowed and spoke to a young footman standing off to the side.

The note seemed to burn through her gloves to her hand, and she wanted to open it before she got to her apartments, but she made herself wait. Spyer took Henrietta's spencer, bonnet, and gloves. The tea came, and the second the door was shut she popped open the seal.

My dearest Henrietta,

I have decided to get up a small party for an al fresco luncheon at Richmond Park. It will be just the six of us. I hope that is acceptable. Six? Who is the sixth person? Fotherby. That must be it.

We will depart at eleven o'clock and fetch you shortly thereafter.

I look forward to seeing you in the morning for our ride.

> *Your friend,*
> *G. T.*

Henrietta took out a piece of pressed paper and wrote her acceptance. Once she had sealed the letter she strolled into her dressing room and found her maid putting away new gowns.

"They turned out well," Spyer commented.

For the first time Henrietta noticed that her gowns were of slightly deeper colors than last year. At least she had more choices. "They did."

Her maid looked up from what she was doing. "Did you need something?"

"A footman to take this note to Lady Turley. But I will do it. You are already occupied." Henrietta walked out of the dressing room, stepped into the corridor, and found a footman. "Please take this to Parkin. It must be sent straightaway to Turley House."

"Yes, miss."

She had just settled down with a cup of tea when a rap sounded on the door. Rather than letting her maid take it, Henrietta opened the door to find the same footman.

"This just came for you, miss."

"Thank you." She could tell from the paper that this missive was from her grandmother. As long as the duchess did not want her tomorrow, all would be well.

Once again she sat down at her desk and opened the message.

My dearest Henrietta,

I am pleased to invite you to dine with me. I will see you tomorrow evening at eight o'clock.

B.

Henrietta frowned at the brief missive. As always, her grandmother simply assumed she had no other plans. And at this time of year she did not. She only hoped that once the Season began Grandmamma would take a busier schedule into consideration. Actually, she would have to considering she was helping to chaperone Henrietta.

She pulled out a piece of her finest paper. There was no response needed, but it was only polite to confirm that she'd received the summons.

Dearest Grandmother,

  I look forward to seeing you tomorrow at eight.

        With much love,
        H. S.

A few minutes later she went back to the corridor, where the same footman waited, and handed him the letter. "The Duchess of Bristol is at the Pulteney Hotel. Tell Parkin I will require a town coach tomorrow evening at twenty minutes to eight."

The young footman dipped his head. "You can count on me, Miss Henrietta."

"Thank you." She really must ask someone who her personal footman would be this Season.

Tomorrow was going to be a busy day, but Henrietta looked forward to it. She especially looked forward to spending more time with Fotherby.

Nate had no sooner walked through the front door when he was handed a folded note.

"From her ladyship," his butler said.

"Thank you. I'll be in my study." Strolling to the back of the house, he opened the missive.

Fotherby,

  We have been invited to dine with the Duchess of Bristol tomorrow evening. I have accepted for both of us. Miss Stern will be present as well.
        Mama

But not Lord and Lady Merton. Nate wondered if he was going to be tested again. After the last time he distrusted the duchess. This time he'd be prepared.

Nate reached his desk just as Chetwin, his secretary, placed a stack of letters on it. "All of these came today?"

"Most of them are invitations for the early entertainments." Nate raised one brow. "They are all for after Easter."

"Good. Send them to my mother. She is a much better person to work out which ones I should attend."

"As you wish." Chetwin removed well over half the stack and grimaced. "Better you than me."

Nate leaned back in his chair. His secretary came from a good family. His older sisters had married well, but, as usual in the *ton*, the younger sons had to seek employment. "If any of your family is in the metropolis this Season, you know I will not keep you from attending their entertainments."

"I do know that." Chetwin gave a small smile. "Although it will be nice to see them, the truth of the matter is that I prefer quiet to balls and all those other things."

"I can understand." Truth to tell, Nate had not attended many large events when he'd been here before. Other than seeing Henrietta, he didn't expect to find much enjoyment in them this year. That reminded him that his mother would select the events Henrietta was most likely to attend, and there would be dancing. He would not look forward to seeing her dance with anyone else. Yet if he failed to become betrothed to her, that was the only thing to which he could look forward.

His secretary took the cards and returned to his office. Nate glanced at his mother's note. Was the duchess meddling? If so, he was glad of it. Whether she knew it or not, she had succeeded in insuring that he'd be able to spend most of tomorrow with Henrietta. He turned to the correspondence that had been forwarded to him. If he kept coming to Town, he'd have to engage a steward. Until then, he'd try to manage from here. He opened the first letter that turned out to be from the tutor he had hired in an attempt to start a dame school.

> *Dear Lord Fotherby,*
>
> *I regret to inform you that for the past week none of the children have attended classes . . .*

Bloody hellhounds! He'd been afraid of that.

> *I did go around to some of the families, but they all claimed they needed the children at home.*
> *It is a waste of my time and your money to keep me on. Therefore, I herewith tender my resignation.*
>
> > *Yr. Servant,*
> > *K. Kimble.*

Nate resisted the urge to crumple up the damn thing and throw the letter into the fireplace. How in God's name was he to educate his tenants' children when he met with such resistance? On the other hand, he'd had to personally take—it had really been more like dragging—two of his tenants to Coke's experimental farm in Norfolk. The only thing Nate could do was try again when he returned home. But he needed ideas to make it work. His new friends might know how to start a school and make it work. They were all very forward thinking. Yet the person he should probably ask first was Henrietta. He'd be surprised if she did not have an opinion, and an excellent one at that. He set the letter aside. It was a shame he had to wait until morning to see her.

The next day he opened the window and stared up at a grayish-blue, cloudless sky. In the east, streaks of pink and yellow painted the horizon. The sun was making its first appearance. If he wanted to meet up with Henrietta and the other ladies, he had to hurry. Nate opened the door to the corridor just in time to see one of the maids. "Please tell Hulatt that I need my horse in ten minutes."

Putting down her bucket and cloths, she bobbed a curtsey and dashed toward the hall. He cleaned his teeth, dressed, and called for Padraig, who was still sleeping at the foot of Nate's bed. "Come, boy. We're going out." Never an early riser, the Wolfhound stretched before standing on the bed on his hind legs and putting his front paws on the floor to stretch again. "I'm going to have to start waking you earlier."

The dog yawned when he opened the door. For a second he thought the Wolfhound would go back to bed, but Padraig wagged his tail and followed Nate out the door. They reached the pavement as Darragh was brought around. Unlike his dog, the horse was ready for exercise. He passed Grosvenor Square but didn't see the ladies. Looking toward the Park, he spied them a street away. Keeping his horse to a trot, he reached the small group just before they went through the gate.

"Good morning." He lifted his hat to them.

"Good morning," Lady Turley said from her carriage.

"Good morning." Lady Exeter tilted her face up toward the sky. "It promises to be a lovely day."

He glanced at Henrietta, and her smile made him slightly dizzy. "Good morning. I wondered if you would join us."

Little did she know he always wanted to be where she

was. She looked particularly beautiful this morning in a deep, rose-colored habit. Nate glanced at Padraig. "Some of us are harder to awaken than others."

The Wolfhound yawned again, and she laughed. "I can see that."

They'd reached the Park, and the three of them who were riding gave their horses their heads as they raced down the carriage way. They slowed as they reached Lady Turley.

Nate was only a little surprised when she and Lady Exeter dropped back, giving him a chance to speak with Henrietta alone.

Now was a good time to ask for her help. He took a breath. "I wondered if you could assist me with a problem I'm having at my main estate."

Letting her mare amble, she kept her gaze on him. What would it be like to have him be her focus all the time? "Of course, if I am able to."

"I decided last year to start a school for the children of my tenants and the village. I had imagined something like a dame school. Unfortunately, the teacher I hired wrote to inform me that the children stopped attending and that he was resigning. Apparently, their parents don't see the value in the school."

Her rosy lips curved into a small smile. "That has been a problem for other landowners. But there are solutions." She tilted her head. "However, are you certain you want to have a dame school? Their goal is to teach only very basic reading, writing, and arithmetic."

He hadn't actually thought about it. "Is that not sufficient?"

She shrugged. "It depends on what you wish to accomplish in the long term. Many of my father's tenants have large families, and it is not feasible for all the boys to remain at home. Of course, they expect the girls will marry. Yet, even so, they can still benefit from a better education."

"You're right. If the boys can't remain, they will need apprenticeships or something else. And not all girls wed. They too could benefit from apprenticeships."

"That is certainly part of it." Henrietta gave him a look of approval. And for some reason he wanted to puff out his chest. "We have discovered that very intelligent people can be found at all levels of society. Giving them the opportunity to study more advanced subjects separates the cream, so to speak. My father has sponsored several boys and some girls by sending them to other schools or universities. One of the girls became a teacher. Another opened her own business. As for the boys, there are solicitors, doctors, accountants." She gave him a rueful grin. "I could go on, but I am sure you understand."

She had told Nate her father was a Radical, and here was the proof. "I do understand, and I agree. No one should be held back by their status in society." His father was probably rolling over in his grave. "However, I still have to get them to school."

"What have you tried thus far?"

Not much at all. "I naively thought that offering the school would be enough."

Her lips twitched. "I think everyone's first attempt is the same." Henrietta chuckled lightly. "Unfortunately, it can be difficult to convince people to change their way of thinking."

That was the truth. "I've found that out. What do you suggest I try next?"

Her lips formed a moue, making him want to kiss her. "Well, if their parents are very recalcitrant, you might have to be more high-handed, but in a way that gives the parents a clear benefit." Her black brows furrowed. "Lord Littleton not only pays a stipend to the parents equal to what the child's benefit to the family is for the time the child is in school, he has a wagon that picks them up in the morning."

"I assume merely offering to pay the families didn't work." Nate had a hard time understanding why it would not, but he had to simply accept that it did not.

"Unfortunately, no. Sending the wagon around did work. It seems to have provided the incentive that offering the school and money did not."

"I understand." No tenant would want to put himself up against the landowner. "I'll try that method. Now, I just have to find another teacher."

"I am certain I or one of my friends can help you." Her brows furrowed again, causing a line between her eyes that he wanted to smooth away. "You might want to hold off lessons until the spring planting is finished."

"Another good idea." He'd started the school in January, thinking that it would be a good time to begin. And it probably was. But now was not a good time. "I can still start searching for a teacher. If I am to expand what the students are taught it will take time to put the plan in place."

"Indeed." Her green eyes met his. "I am happy to be of help. If you require it, that is."

Yes, yes, yes! That would give him more time with her. "I am quite sure I will."

CHAPTER TWENTY-FIVE

Henrietta wanted to laugh out loud with joy. This was exactly the type of conversation she wanted to have with whomever she married. The same type of give-and-take her parents, sister, and friends had. Something inside her had told her it would be like this with Fotherby. She would have to find out if it was the same with Lords Bolingbroke and St. Albans. Just to be fair. She had promised herself she would give them a chance. Although it might be just Lord Bolingbroke who was interested in marriage this year. Remembering what he had said about visiting charities, she grimaced to herself. On the other hand, he might not be worth considering after all.

She glanced at Fotherby, and his beautiful, blue eyes were sparkling with happiness as he gazed back at her. Henrietta dragged her gaze from his. "We should catch up with the others."

Looking around, he shook his head slightly. "I had no idea they were so far ahead of us. But it will give us an opportunity to gallop again."

She had just thought the same thing. "It will."

They brought their horses to a canter, glanced at each

other and laughed. She did not think she had ever been so happy. Not only that, but they would have the whole day together. It was what she wanted. Although it might not be the wisest thing she had ever done. In fact, she was sure it was not. She shrugged to herself. For now she was going to enjoy herself.

They reached Dorie and Georgie in a few minutes and pulled up. Dorie gave Henrietta an inquiring look and Georgie just smiled smugly. If Henrietta did not know better, she would believe they were matchmaking. But they had encouraged the other two gentlemen as well. Ergo, if they were trying to make a match for Henrietta, they had not settled on anyone in particular. It was lovely to have friends who not only cared about one, but would assist when needed.

"It is going to be wonderful weather for our jaunt to Richmond," Georgie said.

"Indeed it is," Dorie agreed.

Henrietta had already told them she was engaged to dine with her grandmother this evening, and they promised they would be back in good time. "I am so looking forward to our outing."

"I am too." Fotherby glanced at her at the same time she looked at him.

Warmth infused her cheeks, the sound of wheels made her look away, and they all stopped for a dray carrying milk.

He broke away from them when they reached Park Avenue, where she and her friends continued on to Turley House on Green Street. As she and Dorie rode to Grosvenor Square, her friend said, "You seemed to be having an interesting conversation with Lord Fotherby."

"I was." Henrietta grinned. "We were discussing a school he wants to start for his tenants' and the village children."

"It is always telling when a gentleman asks a lady for assistance," Dorie commented with a smile.

"It is certainly a good indication of what kind of man he is." Henrietta thought it said more about him than flowers and poems and polite conversation ever could.

"Did Lord Bolingbroke or Lord St. Albans talk about anything of substance?" Dorie asked.

"No." Henrietta shook her head. "The only part of the conversations I remember was when I admired their carriages and horses. To be fair, I have spent more time with Fotherby."

Dorie's brows rose. "Fotherby?"

Drat. Henrietta knew she would make a slip. "I have recently started thinking of him in that way."

"Yet not the other two gentlemen," her friend said archly.

"No." She felt herself slump and straightened her back. "To be honest, if it was not for my sister, I wouldn't bother with them at all. Fotherby seems to be everything I want in a husband."

Dorie gave Henrietta a sympathetic look. "If it makes you feel better, Georgie and I agree it would be a good match." They turned into Grosvenor Square. "Our husbands like him as well. Apparently, Lord Bolingbroke has no interest in politics, and Lord St. Albans is not yet a peer."

"One does not have to be a peer to be interested in what can make a difference in people's lives." Henrietta could think of a few examples when gentlemen with courtesy titles were involved in politics. "Look at Georgie's older sister's husband. He is not yet a peer, but they hold soirées for the purpose of recommending legislation or gathering support for bills."

"You are correct." Her friend nodded decisively. "There is no excuse."

They had reached Merton House. "I shall see you at eleven."

"We will bring the barouche around to fetch you." Dorie grinned as she rode off.

Henrietta slid off her horse and rubbed her forehead before handing the reins to a waiting groom. This thing with Fotherby seemed so impossible. It was almost as if she had fallen in love with a merchant.

She stopped.

In love?

This was even worse than she'd thought. Why did it have to be *him*?

She strolled through the door. "Good morning, Miss Henrietta," Parkin said cheerfully. "Did you have a good ride?"

She pasted a smile on her face. "I did, Parkin. Thank you."

A half hour later she entered the breakfast room and was pleased to find Merton there reading a newssheet, alone. "Good morning."

He raised a brow. "Is it?"

"Yes. The sun is shining, the birds are singing, and it's fairly warm." Henrietta went to the sideboard. "I take it Dotty is not feeling well."

"She is not." He put down the paper. "I thought to have a doctor look in on her, but I'm afraid he would try to bleed her, and I won't stand for that. I wish I knew why this child is so much more active than Vivi was."

"What about a midwife?" Henrietta took two baked eggs and a slice of beef.

"They are difficult to find in London." He pressed his lips together as if he was angry. "The medical profession has made it almost impossible for them to become licensed to practice here."

She sat at her usual place and poured a cup of tea. "Grace Worthington is expecting a baby about the same time Dotty is due. She might be able to at least advise Dotty. It will be her third."

Merton stared at Henrietta for several seconds. "That is an excellent idea. Grace is also old enough to remember many of her mother's pregnancies." He drained his cup. "I will suggest she do that."

"Please do not go," Henrietta said as he started to stand. "I have something I must speak with you about."

Merton lowered himself back onto the chair, and she poured him a fresh cup of tea. He looked wary, and she decided to confront him directly. "It's about Lord Fotherby."

Her brother-in-law dragged a hand down his face. "I wish I could say I am surprised, but I know that your grandmother introduced him to you."

Merton *had* spoken with Fotherby. "Did you and he engage in fisticuffs?"

She had meant to ask Fotherby about it, but the issue with his school had pushed it out of her mind. "Yes. At Jackson's."

She studied Merton's face. "You do not have any bruises."

"I would have, but I know how to treat them. You wish to know what we discussed." A statement, not a question.

"I do." She tapped her fingers on the table, and decided

to make the question more roundabout. "He doesn't seem at all like the man with whom you were friends."

"I agree with you." Merton sipped his tea for a few moments. "Apparently, your grandmother has the same opinion. I tried to speak with Thea"—the name he always called Dotty—"but she wouldn't listen. I've never seen her so upset about something like this."

Henrietta took her time spreading marmalade on a piece of toast. "She has seen other people change for the better, and she insisted on marrying you."

Merton barked a laugh. "And I am very glad she did. I wish I knew what to say to you about Fotherby. She will not listen to anything I say about him."

"I wonder if the baby is affecting her brain," Henrietta muttered to herself. "I shall think of another way."

"I take it you mean to have him, even with what you know?"

She met her brother-in-law's gaze. Even though it had not been a conscious decision, she *had* made up her mind. It must have happened when she realized she loved him. He was everything she wanted in a husband. To continue denying her feelings or desires would have her run the risk of sneaking around during the Season and actually having to lie to her sister. That Henrietta would not do. And now that she thought about it, she knew when her feelings for him had begun. "He saved me that day. If he hadn't caught little Meggie, she would have died from the fall. I could not have lived with that."

After a long moment he nodded, as if he too had made a decision. "I'll help you if I am able."

"No." She shook her head. "I do not want you and Dotty to be at odds. I will think of something."

One imperious brow rose. "As long as it's not a trip to Gretna Green, I'll support your endeavor."

"That's all I can ask. Thank you."

"You're welcome." Grinning, he stood. "I can't imagine how Thea thinks to keep you and Fotherby apart. You are at least as single-minded as she is." He patted her hand. "Now, I must be leaving."

Henrietta ate absently, not even tasting most of what she consumed. Her mother was right to tell her not to give up when she fell in love. Perhaps the first thing she should do was convince her parents Fotherby had changed. For that she would need her grandmother's help. This evening she would start her campaign. There must be a way to bring Dotty around. To have her accept Fotherby as Henrietta's husband. What was the quote from Virgil? Love conquers all. It had better. She was not giving up either her sister or Fotherby. But first she must make sure he wanted to marry her. With any luck, that would be the easy part. Once that was decided, she would fight for her sister's acceptance.

When Nate strolled into the breakfast room he was surprised not to find his mother already there. He hoped she wasn't ill. "Hulatt, do you know where her ladyship is?"

"Yes, my lord." The butler took a fresh pot of tea from a footman and placed it on the table. "She broke her fast and left. She said to tell you she would see you this evening."

That was unusual. "Did she tell you where she had gone?"

"This is her day to visit the charity school of which she is a sponsor."

His mother was involved with a charity school? She

really had changed. Yet, he was glad for it. "Thank you. I will depart shortly before eleven. Please have Darragh brought around before then."

"Will you be taking Padraig as well?"

Nate glanced at the dog lying before the fireplace. He couldn't put the dog in the carriage with the ladies, and he did not like the idea of him being on the road during the ride to Richmond. Then there was the matter of having to mind him while he was there, and the only thing he wanted to concentrate on today was Henrietta. "No. I'll leave him here."

"Very good, my lord. We will be happy to care for him."

"Thank you." Although Padraig would most likely sleep most of the day away.

A plate was set before Nate. They did not have a side-board with selections as they had in both his father's and brother's time; both he and his mother ate the same thing every day. Some form of eggs, toast, and some kind of meat, so there was no need for it. He picked up the news-paper that had been folded and set next to his plate. As he suspected, there was not much going on until the Season began. He read over the list of new arrivals to Town, but knew only a few of them, who had been friends with his father. Nate would cultivate his own set of friends, as he had started doing. He turned the page. Even the court schedule was thin of events.

At eleven he rode to the entrance of Grosvenor Square and met Henrietta and her—no, their—friends. It was good to be able to say that, even if only to himself.

A chorus of "good mornings" rang out when they saw him.

"Good morning," he called out. Nate didn't think he'd ever been happier. When he glanced at the carriage, he saw Lady Exeter was holding her baby, and a maid sat on the backward-facing seat. Four footmen rode behind the landau.

"I could not leave her for so long," she said.

"She's beautiful."

"We think so." She beamed with pride.

They made slow progress until they reached the city's outskirts and the countryside opened up. There was still some traffic, but the gentlemen were more easily able to converse with the ladies. Although it was harder for Nate, as Henrietta was seated in the middle again.

"I see you decided to leave Padraig at home," she said.

"I was concerned about the London traffic." Nate grinned at her. "And I could not very well beg a seat for him in the carriage."

Her eyes sparkled with laughter. "No, we have enough passengers. Perhaps you can design a carriage with a box for him on the back."

He had an image of her in an open carriage and a place for his dog in a seat behind the main part of the vehicle. "Hmm, you've given me something to consider."

Both Lady Exeter and Lady Turley flashed him looks of approval. He wondered if they were promoting Boling-broke and St. Albans as well, then decided not to think about the other men. Nate was in too good a mood to spoil it by thinking of his rivals.

"Does anyone know where the best place to set up our luncheon will be?" Henrietta asked.

"I did some research yesterday," Turley said. "I think Pen Ponds will be a nice area."

"That is what Exeter decided as well," his wife opined.

When they arrived Nate helped the other two men lay out large blankets and take the baskets of food and drink to the blankets where the ladies unpacked them. Large chunks of cheese, bread so fresh you could still smell it, roasted chickens, salad, fruit, wine, and cider made up the meal. Henrietta made up plates for both of them.

"I just gave you a little of everything."

"That's perfect." He took the porcelain plates as she sat on an area of the blanket he had chosen. "What type of cheese is that?"

"I do not know, but I am positive it comes from their main estate." She glanced at the other two ladies. "Some of us are becoming competitive over cheese."

"I hope it doesn't cause a falling out." He spread some of the soft cheese on a piece of bread.

"I do not think it will. Thus far, everyone has different cheeses. As you see, the Exeter cheese is soft. Whereas the Littleton cheese is crumbly and very sharp. I have not had an opportunity to taste the Turley cheese, but I have been told it is much like Stilton cheese." She spread a large serviette on her lap. "Do you make cheese?"

"I do." She munched on a chicken leg and waited for him to continue. "It is yellow and semi-hard. I don't know quite how to describe the taste, but I think you will like it a great deal."

"We could have a tasting someday."

"That would be interesting." Did that mean she wanted him? Sometimes he thought she did, but at other times he wasn't sure. A footman came around with white wine that looked as if it had been chilled and more cider. "Would you like a glass of wine?"

"Yes, please." The base of the wine glass was as large as the cup, making it more stable on the ground. She set it down next to her.

"You look as if you have a deal of experience dining al fresco."

"I do. My family and the Carpenter family, Grace Worthington's relations, are close neighbors. It was a way we could all come together easily. Did you not have neighbors with whom you socialized?"

"Not in that way." He wished he had. "The gatherings were much more formal. My father was a high-stickler."

"Ah." Henrietta gave him a pitying look. "The sort of person who would not allow you to play with others of inferior status or rank?"

"Yes. I was sent away to school at eight years." Even now he recalled how distraught he'd been at leaving home at that age.

Her lips pressed into a straight, disapproving line. "My brother did not go to Eton until he was twelve."

Nate swallowed the last of his bread and cheese. "When I have a son that is what I'll do too. Eight is too young."

"Much too young," she agreed.

He could see them with a son, loving him and teaching him all he needed to know before going off to school. He glanced at her and their eyes met. Had she been thinking the same thing?

CHAPTER TWENTY-SIX

Henrietta fell into Fotherby's blue-green gaze. It was almost as if they were planning their lives together. A footman came around, breaking the spell she seemed to be under.

"May I take the plates?" the servant asked.

"Yes." She handed the plates, silver, and glasses to the footman, then rose, shook out her skirts, and glanced around. All of their friends had fallen asleep. "My lord, would you care to take a walk?"

"I would." Fotherby had already scrambled to his feet when she stood. "There appear to be a good many paths. Which way would you like to go?"

Somewhere she could be alone with him. After her discussion with Merton this morning and the decision she had come to, it was time she made Fotherby understand that she had made her choice. He was the only gentleman she wished to wed. One way or another, they would find a way to deal with the consequences. For a scant second Henrietta wondered if he had decided on her as well, but he had never given her reason to believe he had not. She took a breath. "It is a little warm. The woods look refreshing."

"We'll see if your supposition is correct." He grinned as he held out his arm, and she tucked her hand in the crook.

The path to the wood was fairly short and they reached it within a few minutes. It was like stepping into another world. Not only was it cooler, but small spring flowers dotted the ground, and the songbirds were a little louder. She could still see the pond on the right.

"Look over there." Fotherby pointed to the right. "The deer."

There was a stag and a hind with a rounded belly. They stood quietly and watched the animals graze before ambling on.

The sound of ducks made Henrietta glance toward the pond. "It is so peaceful here."

"It is." He laughed lightly. "Even though it is not quiet, with the birds singing and the ducks flapping around and quacking. It's like a place out of time."

Henrietta knew what he meant. "I almost expect to see woodland fairies or pixies hidden among the flowers."

"I hope you don't see them. Neither of the beings is particularly helpful."

"You have a point." They absolutely did not need any more trouble than they already had.

She glanced up at him as he looked down at her. Before she had always been fascinated by his eyes, but now she noticed how well shaped his lips were. His bottom lip was slightly larger than his top lip, but not so much that he appeared as if he was pouting. What she really wanted to know was how his lips would feel on her lips. If only she could bring herself to stand on tiptoe and press her mouth to his. But even she was not that bold. There were some things she must leave to him. She felt herself move closer to him, and his arm went around her waist. Then his head bent, and his lips touched hers as if they were a feather brushing gently.

Henrietta placed her hand on his jacket and slid them over his shoulders and around his neck. Fotherby pulled her closer, tilted his head, and deepened the kiss. Frissons of pleasure speared through her body, and she pressed closer, flattening her breasts against his hard chest. His tongue gently probed the seam of her lips, and she opened to him. She had heard about this form of kissing, but it never occurred to her she could actually like it. Yet with him she did.

He stroked and caressed her with one hand while the other held her tightly to him. Each stroke, each caress built the fire inside her higher. An ache formed between her legs. If only he would touch her *there*. As if he knew what she needed, his leg pressed her thighs apart and moved against the place that ached. His hand covered her breast, and even through her stays she could feel his heat. The tension between her legs increased, and she rubbed against him, needing to somehow relieve the ache that only grew stronger and more insistent. Then her body quaked and quivered and shattered. This was what she'd been told was so intense it could not truly be described. This was what occurred between a man and a woman who were in love. But that could not be. She was certain it was supposed to happen when they were joined. She hadn't noticed his hand on her bottom, holding her until it moved in a light caress. She felt stirrings of passion again, but he moved his hand to her waist before she begged him for more of what he had done. Yet there was a hollow space that had not been filled.

"Henrietta." His breath was soft and warm against her ear. "I love you." He feathered kisses along her jaw. "I have from almost the second I saw you. When I discovered who you were, I tried to step back, but I couldn't. I wanted you so much."

Fotherby's words sank deep into her heart. Tears pricked her eyes. She was filled with so much joy it almost paralyzed her. She forced herself to lean back and gaze into his eyes. "I love you too." She lowered her eyes, then lifted them to his once more. "When I found out who you were I still wanted to meet you. I should not have, but I did. I even attempted to form an interest in other gentlemen, but there was nothing there, and I could not do it. It was not until then that I knew I loved you."

"We will work out our problems. I won't allow you to be estranged from your family. I couldn't be that selfish."

"Well." Henrietta cupped his cheek. "We have one, possibly two of my family on my side."

His eyes widened in surprise. "Your grandmother, and who is the other person?"

"Merton. He told me his main concern was my sister, but he would not stand in our way. It might be because he knows what it is like to want to marry against a woman's guardian's wishes."

"Worthington didn't want him to marry your sister?"

"No." She shook her head. "I did not know about that until recently."

Nate drew Henrietta close to him again. "I hope someday Merton and I can be friends once more. But right now I have three questions to ask you." Regretfully, he loosened his hold on her. "I made free with your name without your permission. May I call you Henrietta, and will you call me Nate?"

Her brilliant green eyes looked as if they were swimming

in water, but she was smiling, so it couldn't be bad. "Yes and yes."

He dropped to one knee and took her hands. "Will you do me the honor of being my wife and helpmate, the mother of my children, and my love for the rest of our lives?"

Tears trembled on the rim of her eyes and tumbled over. "I will, gladly."

Nate rose to his feet, took out his handkerchief, and dabbed the tears from her cheeks. "Who do I ask for permission to marry you?"

The tears stopped, and a calculating look entered her eyes. "That is a bit harder. The understanding Merton has with my father is that my father will go along with his decision." She tapped one finger against Nate's chest. "In our case, I believe we must get my grandmother involved to speak to my parents."

"My mother and I are dining with her this evening. I will speak with her then."

"I am dining with her as well." Although Henrietta was looking at him, he knew she wasn't seeing him; then her eyes refocused. "I should not be surprised. I think she has been promoting a match between us. Although"—her finger started tapping against him again—"she might have a good idea as to how we go about gaining permission to wed."

Knowing what he did of the formidable older lady, he had no doubt. "Shall we allow ourselves to be guided by her?"

"I think we must. She was the one who made it possible for my mother and father to marry."

"In that case she must know what she is doing." At least, Nate hoped she did. "Once we do have permission, how soon do you wish to wait before we wed?"

Henrietta slowly shook her head. "Not long at all. Before the Season begins."

He took her in his arms again, then heard a baby cry. "We should be going."

"If we must." She shook out her rumpled skirts. "Shall we tell everyone and swear them to secrecy?"

"Unless you think we can keep the secret." The full knowledge that they were actually going to marry hit him like one of Merton's punches. Nate almost staggered. "I confess, I'm so happy, I have to tell someone."

Her smile was at least as wide as his. "I feel the same way." She took his hand in her much smaller one. "Let us see what they have to say."

Their happiness and intentions must have shown on their faces. Lady Turley saw them first and motioned to the other three.

She was fairly bouncing on her toes, and he couldn't leave her in suspense. "Henrietta has agreed to marry me."

The ladies gathered around Henrietta, and the gentlemen around him.

After they were well hugged and he was slapped on the back in congratulations, Lady Exeter held up her hand for silence and glanced at him. "We are all on a first-name basis in private. As you are going to be joining our little group, we would like you to use our first names as well."

"Thank you." He gave a short bow. "Please call me Nate."

Lady Exeter touched her chest. "I am Dorie. My husband is Alexander. Although for some reason the gentlemen never seem to use first names for other gentlemen." She indicated Lady Turley next to her. "This is Georgie, and her husband is Gavin." Dorie glanced around. "We must go back to Town."

"There is just one thing," Henrietta said. "You cannot tell anyone that we are betrothed. Nate must speak with my father or someone before it is official."

"Merton?" Dorie asked.

"He knows how I feel about Nate, and he said he will not stand in our way. However, I cannot put him in a position that would set him against my sister."

"That is one obstacle taken care of," Georgie said. "I have faith it will all work out." She rubbed her stomach. "Do you have any cheese and bread left? I'm a bit hungry."

Her husband went toward the footmen, and Nate wondered what it would be like when Henrietta was breeding. He hoped it wouldn't be long before he found out.

He escorted Henrietta to the barouche and helped her up. Now that she was his, he'd never let her go. The ride home seemed much shorter than the one to Richmond. Dark clouds were on the horizon, but if they did bring rain, they wouldn't be here until sometime that night.

The carriage reached the Grosvenor Street entrance to Grosvenor Square, and he bade adieu to the rest of the party, before turning to Henrietta. He wished he could fetch her from Merton House. "I'll see you this evening."

She smiled at him, and he thought he saw the same wish in her eyes. "I will see you then."

Nate rode the rest of the short way to his stable in the mews behind his house and handed the horse to a groom. He was almost halfway to the door when he heard a loud, mournful howl. *Padraig.* What the devil was wrong with him? He strode through the garden door and up the servants' stairs. The howling faded slightly. *Damn.* He'd gone the wrong way. The dog had to be in his study. Retracing his way, he crossed the hall and down the other corridor.

All the servants appeared to be standing at his study

door. "What's going on?" The second he spoke, the noise stopped, and Padraig scattered the crowd of servants to get to him. The dog pushed his head under Nate's hand "Are you all right, boy?"

"See, it's just what I telled ye," a small lad Nate had never seen before said. He crossed his arms over his thin chest. "All he wanted was to be stroked. I coulda done it." Some of the younger servants rolled their eyes. "How long has this been going on?"

"About two hours, my lord." Hulatt gave him a worried look. "I've never seen him act like that before. He wouldn't allow anyone near him."

"That doesn't sound like him." Nate continued to rub the dog's head. Then again, he had been gone longer than usual today. Before coming to Town, he'd spent almost every minute with the dog.

"No, my lord. One of the grooms said he might have rabies and we shouldn't try to get near him."

"*I* didn't think it, my lord." The little boy's chin inched defiantly higher.

"Sammy," Hulatt said. "Go back to your duties."

Nate put a hand on the lad's shoulder, staying him. "What exactly are his duties?"

"He's the shoe boy."

There would be more times when he'd be away from Padraig for hours at a time. If it hadn't been Styles's half day off, he could have kept the poor Wolfhound with him. But he needed a more permanent solution. He looked at the boy. "How old are you, Sammy?"

"I'm eight years old. Old enough to have a position."

What was it about the age of eight that some parents wanted to send children away? "I have an idea." Hulatt had a look of long suffering on his stern face. "Am I right that you like dogs?"

"I like *that* dog." Sammy stared at Padraig longingly. Much in the same way Nate probably looked at Henrietta. "He's let me stroke him before."

"Very well, then. You are to spend at least an hour a day with Padraig when I'm away." Nate glanced at his butler. "I assume he will still be able to perform his duties?"

"Yes, my lord. It shall be as you wish."

"Thank you. Sammy, you will start this evening. I must go out again."

"Yes, my lord." He was nodding his head so hard, Nate thought he'd dislocate it. "I'll make sure he knows he is not alone."

"Well, then, that's settled. I must change. Hulatt, I require a bath. Padraig, come."

Nate entered his chamber and had visions of Henrietta in his bed. He'd been harder than granite when he'd pleasured her earlier. It had been all he could do to keep from spilling. Even riding had been painful for the first mile or so. He wished they could be married tomorrow, but he'd be lucky if they were wed by the start of the Season. Even though their feelings had been resolved there were still hurdles to jump before they could wed.

Styles entered the room and pulled out the bathtub from a cabinet next to the fireplace. "The water will be here soon, my lord."

His valet began laying out his kit for the evening. When Styles took out Nate's jewelry box, it reminded him that he would have to select a ring for Henrietta.

Bloody hell-hounds!

He couldn't give her anything until they could make their betrothal pubic. He undressed, placing the clothes he'd been wearing over the screen. What had him so fussed? He sank into the tub and, for some reason, thought of the way Merton had behaved after he'd become betrothed. "Drat it all. I'm doing the same thing. I just want to get married. I want her with me."

"Did you say something, my lord?" Styles asked from the dressing room.

"No." *I'm just talking to myself.*

No wonder Merton hadn't wanted to talk to Nate. His friend had found the right woman for him and was not going to listen to anyone else. Not to mention having difficulties with Worthington, who was acting as Dotty Stern's guardian. And Nate had taken it as anger because Merton had to marry her. "I was an idiot."

Padraig padded over to the bathtub and put his head on Nate's shoulder, prompting him to pet the dog. "I'm glad I brought you home with me." Padraig licked Nate's cheek. "I'm happy you're glad as well. I suppose I can tell you that you are about to get a new mistress. I'm going to wed the lady with the mare. But it's a secret. Not that I think you'll tell anyone."

The Wolfhound sighed and went to lie by the fireplace. Nate stood, poured a now-tepid bucket of water over himself, and grabbed the drying towel from a rack in front of the fire. His secondary valet arrived and gathered the clothing he'd wear that evening.

Nate made his way to the drawing room to wait for his mother. He glanced at the walnut-encased clock on the fireplace mantel. There was time for a glass of wine before he and his mother left for the Pultney. Someone plied the door knocker to the front door. Who could be visiting now? A few seconds later Hulatt opened the door to the drawing room. "Miss Stern is here, my lord."

"Show her in, and tell my mother."

Hulatt bowed and brought Henrietta to him. The butler left the door partly open.

"Henrietta." She was stunning in a turquoise evening gown with very little adornment on it. Her hair was done in a complicated combination of braids, with curls framing her face. Her only jewelry was a pair of gold earrings and a gold chain with an oval locket. Nate had never seen her in an evening gown before. He held out his hands, then took her into his arms. "What brings you here?"

"I decided that you could either ride with me, or I could ride with you and your mother. It was ridiculous to take two coaches."

"I would like to know what you are both doing, embracing in the drawing room where anyone could see you."

CHAPTER TWENTY-SEVEN

Henrietta pressed her forehead against his chest for a moment before nodding to him and turning to face his mother.

He bowed slightly. "Mama, Henrietta and I are betrothed."

"Mostly," she added, and curtseyed. "We still must decide who Nate must ask to make it official."

He didn't think he had ever seen his mother stunned before. She opened her mouth and closed it. Then did it again.

Henrietta had met Lady Fotherby several times last Season, but she had never seen the woman speechless. "Nate," Henrietta whispered to her betrothed. "Three glasses of wine."

"Yes, of course."

She went to her ladyship, took her hand, and led her to a sofa. "I know it must seem sudden, but we love each other and want to wed."

Lady Fotherby took a glass of wine from Nate and drank half of it down at once. Henrietta glanced at him, and he shook his head.

"Mama, will you say something." His brows furrowed, and he moved a chair closer to the sofa next to Henrietta. "You knew I wanted to marry Henrietta. We thought you would be happy."

Her ladyship placed a hand on her bosom and took a few deep breaths, then looked first at her, then him. "I am delighted, of course. But neither of you seem to realize that you, Miss Stern, are a minor, and you, my son, must ask her parent or guardian for permission to address her before you may properly ask her. What possessed the two of you to enter into a betrothal in a way that would cause a scandal were it to get out?"

She did have a point, but Henrietta did not think it was *that* scandalous. It was merely a matter of who should give the final approval. "I spoke with Merton, and he said that he would support me if I wanted to marry Nate."

"Miss Stern, be that as it may, it is for my son to speak to him." Lady Fotherby drained her glass and held it out to be refilled.

Henrietta noticed that he had not touched his wine. "The problem is that would cause him difficulties with my sister. She will not even discuss the matter, or allow Nate to apologize to her."

"We plan to ask the duchess if I should travel to Henrietta's home and speak with her father," he added.

"That is an excellent idea. However, you may not go around as if you are indeed betrothed. Fortunately, there is another two weeks before the start of the Season." Her ladyship rubbed her forehead, then put the glass of wine on a small, round side table, and rose. "Let us go to the duchess. I agree, this is a matter that must be put before her."

Henrietta stood and put her hand on his arm. "The coach?"

"I'd prefer to take mine. Yours can either remain here or you can send it back."

Now that she had made her point that one way or the other she would ride with him to her grandmother's hotel suite, it did not matter which vehicle they rode in. "I will send it back. There is no reason to have the pair unhitched, then hitched up again to take me home."

He gazed at her and smiled as if she had made the most brilliant of decisions. He held out his other arm to his mother. "May I escort you as well?"

"Yes, my dear." She placed her hand on his arm, and he led them to the hall and out the door to the waiting coach. She glanced at her coachman. "Take them back, please. I will ride with Lady Fotherby."

"Yes, miss."

Nate assisted Henrietta and her future mother-in-law into the carriage, then got in himself. As soon as the steps were up, the coach moved forward. She sat next to her ladyship and across from Nate. Lady Fotherby's mouth was set into a thin line, and there was no attempt by any of them to make conversation. Fortunately, less than ten minutes later, they drew up to the hotel, and made their way to her grandmother's suite. The butler showed them into a parlor and announced them. If Grandmamma was surprised to see them enter together, she did not show it.

"Welcome." She bussed Lady Fotherby's and Henrietta's cheeks.

Nate elegantly bowed over Grandmamma's hand. "Thank you for inviting us. We"—he held out his hand to

Henrietta, and she took it—"have something about which we need your advice."

Grandmamma's sharp green eyes flicked from him to Henrietta, then to Lady Fotherby, who still looked disapprovingly at Nate. "Come, we shall have a glass of sherry."

Once they were seated—Henrietta and Nate on one small sofa, her grandmother and his mother on the sofa facing them—Henrietta said, "Lord Fotherby and I wish to wed. Merton said he would not stand in my way, but he does not appear to want to be involved."

Lady Fotherby heaved a sigh. "My son has acted precipitously by already proposing."

Henrietta was certain she saw her grandmother's lips twitch, as if she was trying not to laugh. Grandmamma took a sip of sherry before piercing them with a look that would have had Henrietta trembling, if not for the humor in her eyes. "Once I saw you two together, I knew how it would be." She set her glass on a square, marble-topped table at her elbow. "You are very like your mother. She did not take the easy way either." Grandmamma glanced at Nate. "My son-in-law defied my late husband and asked for my daughter's hand despite being rejected. I must say that in a worldly way, you are much more eligible than he was."

"Will there not be problems with your daughter and son-in-law?" Lady Fotherby asked.

"I do not believe so." Grandmamma had a smug expression on her face. "Acting on my feeling it would come to this, I wrote to my daughter and related the changes Fotherby has made, how he and Henrietta met, and what my impression of him is. I also said I would be surprised if the two of them did not decide they would suit."

Henrietta wanted to jump up and hug her grandmother,

but such exuberant behavior was never encouraged. "Thank you. Did Mama answer you?"

Her grandmother's brows rose. "She said she would write to you."

Henrietta had to blink back tears of joy. "She did write to me, and told me to follow my heart. But Papa?" Her thought was that her father might not have forgiven Nate. But that was not at all like Papa. He firmly believed in redemption, and it was clear to anyone with eyes that Nate had redeemed himself.

"If there is a problem," Grandmamma said, "I am certain your mother will talk him around."

Nate had listened to the conversation with interest. It seemed that there was tacit approval for them to marry, but it did not answer his most pressing question. "Your grace, who do I approach about marrying Henrie—Miss Stern? There are also the marriage settlements to consider."

Grandmamma's forehead furrowed slightly, then she gave a sharp nod. "Since I promoted the match, I shall take responsibility for approving it. Therefore, my lord, you have permission to marry Henrietta. I will, however, demand Merton's solicitor draw up the marriage contract. That is the least he can do, considering he abrogated his duty in this instance."

Nate reached over and squeezed Henrietta's hand. "Shall I leave my solicitor's name with you?"

"Yes. I shall send it along with my letter to Merton." The duchess rose. "Shall we go into dinner? Fotherby, you may escort me."

He would rather have had Henrietta on his arm, but he was not going to argue with the one person who had said he could wed her. "With pleasure, ma'am."

The table was square, allowing them to speak easily. He

sat on the duchess's left and his mother was across from him, allowing Henrietta to sit on Nate's left. Instead of the dishes placed on the table, the butler and a footman handed them around. Nate had forgotten how hungry he was and was determined to do justice to all the dishes. He was happy to see Henrietta did not stint herself. There was white soup, followed by sole in a delicate lemon sauce, and buttered lobster. Capons were served with sautéed mushrooms removed by broccoli in a butter sauce, cabbage pudding, and carrots. After which a salad was served. Dessert consisted of fruit, a selection of cheeses, and pears in red wine sauce. It was accompanied by a very fine champagne.

The duchess held up a glass. "To Henrietta and Fotherby. I wish you happy."

"I too wish you happy." Lady Fotherby raised her glass. "I admit I was a bit concerned at the way you went about it, but everything has worked out for the best."

"Thank you," Nate and Henrietta said at the same time, then glanced at her at the same time she looked at him, and they both laughed. He leaned close to her and in a low voice said, "We are officially betrothed."

"I know. I wonder how we will arrange the wedding." Her smile faded a bit. "I will have to tell my sister."

"If you like, I will join you when you do." He had a wry look on his face. "But I doubt my presence would help."

"It would not help at all." Henrietta bit her bottom lip, and he was reminded of their kisses earlier.

He wished they could marry quietly, by special license. That, though, was an air castle. "If worse comes to worse, we will have the wedding breakfast at my house. It is not unusual to have it at the bridegroom's residence."

"If she does not change her mind, I think I would like

to have a small event. Perhaps only our families and our friends."

He liked how "our friends" sounded. Nate had really never had many friends. He was acquainted with the other gentlemen in the area near his home, but none of them were in the same situation as he. They were either older, with daughters they were trying to marry off, or married with young families, or younger and ripe for trouble. It occurred to him that when he and Henrietta wed, he'd have more in common with some of them. Merton had been Nate's only real friend.

"You look solemn. Are you thinking about the wedding?" Henrietta appeared concerned.

"Actually, I was not. I was thinking about my neighbors. There are a few with young children." He looked forward to her meeting the people where he lived. He couldn't wait to have her with him every day, and in his bed every night. Even now his fingers itched to slide through her silky hair, kiss her, make her his.

She smiled up at him. "I will enjoy meeting them. Our children will have others to play with."

"Fotherby." The duchess's formidable tone interrupted them. "Do you have a desire to sit in solitary splendor with a bottle of port?"

He hadn't seen her rise and quickly got to his feet. "No, your grace. I am more than happy to join you."

"Come along, then." She swept out of the dining room, followed by his mother.

Henrietta tucked her hand in the crook of his arm. "Will you want to have port alone after we marry?"

"I think we can make a new tradition. We can simply spend time together." He arched a brow. "Unless you would like to join me when I drink port."

She gave an exaggerated shiver. "I do not like port at all. You may, however, join me in whichever room we decide to occupy after dinner and bring the bottle with you."

"That sounds like an excellent plan." He'd had fantasies about having her in his bed and making love to her, but he knew now that he was going to enjoy being married to her, living their lives together. They entered the parlor, and the duchess and his mother were engaged in close conversation. "Do you want to go on a wedding trip?"

"I would like to." Her voice was a little wishful. She sat on the sofa they'd sat on before dinner. "Perhaps we can visit Paris for a few weeks. Both the Turleys and the Exeters went there after their weddings."

Nate took his place next to her. Paris was an excellent idea. They could finally be alone. "In that case, they will be able to tell us where to stay and what to see."

She had a beatific smile on her beautiful countenance. "I cannot believe how easy this was, our becoming betrothed."

Almost too easy, but he wasn't going to ruin her mood, or his for that matter. He grinned to himself. Bolingbroke and St. Albans were going to have to find another lady to squire around.

"You look like a cat in the cream."

He took her hand and brought it to his lips. "I was thinking of all the things I could not do before that I can now."

His beloved Henrietta appeared confused. "Such as?"

"Give you flowers. Take you for carriage rides, unless you'd rather have your own sporting carriage."

She tilted her head, obviously giving it some thought. "Perhaps later. What else?"

"I will be able to take you to the theater, and balls, and other entertainments. Do you realize that we will probably not dance together until we are married?" And make love to her all night and day if they wanted.

"I had not thought of it, but you are right." She glanced quickly at the older ladies. "Is there not anything else?"

"Minx. Finish what we began this afternoon." Nate wished he could take her in his arms.

"That sounds like a fine idea." Henrietta grinned. She was more than willing to continue what they had started. In many ways, marriage to Nate was going to be a new adventure. "Tell me about your home."

"My main estate is called Ouse Tower. It's in Bedford-shire, not far from the town of Bedford. It was originally just a tower castle, but over the years it grew. Fortunately, my ancestors did it in a way that didn't make it a mishmash of styles."

She had never heard of a tower castle in England. "I thought all the tower castles were on the border with Scotland?"

"I think it might be the only one left in England. It was built as a defense for Bedford in the tenth century. But according to our records, two wings were quickly added, making the tower the hall of the castle."

"It sounds fascinating." Henrietta could not wait to see it. There was also an important aspect to its location. "I take it your estate is on the west side of Bedford." Nate nodded. "My family's home is on the east side. It is probably only a half-day's journey."

Just then, tea was brought in and set on the table between the sofas. Her grandmother glanced at her and inclined her head. "Henrietta, you may pour."

"Thank you, Grandmamma." She moved to the edge of the sofa, and poured her grandmother's cup first. "My lady, how do you like your tea?"

"One lump and a little milk, thank you."

She made Nate's cup next, then hers. Henrietta had not yet swallowed the sip she took when her grandmother said, "You have had tea together before."

She brought the serviette up to her mouth before she spewed the tea all over her gown.

Nate took her cup from her and in a bland tone said, "Lady Exeter invited me to her house for tea, and Henrietta was there."

"Ah, yes," Grandmamma said. "Your mother told me you were particular friends with her."

Henrietta picked up her cup and took another sip of tea. "Five of us started last Season together. Although it was Dorie's second Season. We have all remained close."

"I hope that continues. I still have friendships from my first Season." She inclined her head toward Lady Fotherby. "Catherine's mother was one of my closest friends."

"Yes, the duchess is my godmother." Lady Fotherby's eyes became a little misty. "After my mother died she was a great source of solace to me, and our friendship started to grow." The ladies went back to their conversation.

"A lot of things make a great deal more sense now," Nate murmured.

"What do you mean?" Henrietta kept her voice low.

"It was the duchess who approached my mother with the punishment your sister had decided."

"Interesting." Henrietta wondered if the ladies had planned to get them together all along. "Do you think they planned our match?"

"The duchess said she wanted it."

"No. I mean before you came to Town this Season."

He shook his head. "I don't see how she could have.

Even I didn't know I was coming to Town until the last minute."

"I suppose you are right." Henrietta finished her tea. "It is just strange how everything seemed to fall into place."

He took both her hands in his large, warm ones. "Would it matter to you if they had planned it?"

She only had to think about it for a second. "No. No, it would not matter at all. I love you and I'm thrilled we will marry."

"I feel the same way you do."

And that was the best feeling in the world. That he loved her as much as she loved him.

CHAPTER TWENTY-EIGHT

It was still fairly early when Henrietta almost floated through the front door and into the hall.

Parkin bowed. "I trust you had a good evening with the duchess?"

"I had a splendid evening, Parkin." She had not stopped smiling since her grandmother had wished Nate and her happy. "Is his lordship still up?"

"I believe he is in his study. Her ladyship has retired for the evening."

"Thank you." She headed down the corridor toward Merton's study. There was no reason not to tell him what Grandmamma had done.

Henrietta reached the room and knocked. "It is Henrietta."

"Come in."

Merton was standing behind his desk when she entered, and he waved her to one of the two leather chairs in front of his desk. "I didn't expect to see you this evening." He went to a side table. "Would you like a glass of claret?"

"Yes, please." Having something to hold would keep her from fidgeting. He had, after all, acted as her guardian since she came out. She took the goblet. "Thank you."

He lowered himself onto the other chair. "I must assume you have something you wish to discuss."

"I do." She nodded. "Lord and Lady Fotherby had also been invited to dine with Grandmamma." Henrietta waited for him to digest the information. She tried to think of a way to soften the next part but could not. As her father said, plain speaking was often the best way. "Because you did not wish to make a decision about Fotherby and myself, she decided she would give her consent to our marriage." Merton's mouth opened, but Henrietta held up her hand. "She has already written to my parents. I received a letter from Mama the other day. In it she told me to follow my heart. At the time I did *not* know that she knew." Merton stared at another part of the room. Henrietta did not know if he could not bear to look at her, or if he was simply thinking. "Grandmamma has left the settlement agreements to you to negotiate. Fotherby gave her his solicitor's direction, and she will send it to you tomorrow."

At this, Merton seemed to perk up. "Indeed." He nodded, more to himself than to Henrietta. "Indeed, I will be happy to negotiate the contract. You must, of course, be part of the discussions."

She knew that was not how things were usually done, but she was happy to be involved. "I appreciate that."

He took a sip of wine. "Have you set a date yet?"

"I wish to be wed before the Season begins. Fotherby has agreed."

Merton muttered something like, "I'll wager he does." But she could not be certain. Leaning over his desk, he took a cut piece of foolscap and a pencil and made a note. Then he focused his considerable attention on her, and she was glad she had the glass of wine. She took a drink, careful not to make it too large. "Who is going to tell Thea?"

"I will. Marrying him is my choice. It is only fair that it be me."

"I agree." Merton blew out a breath. "She will not be happy."

That was an understatement. Henrietta expected her sister to be furious. "I shall do it tomorrow."

"I will notify you when the first draft of the settlement agreement is ready."

"Thank you."

He moved to his large leather chair behind the desk. "Once you're wed I'm taking Thea back home. I'm concerned about her health."

"That is a good idea." Henrietta prayed there was nothing seriously wrong with either her sister or the baby. She rose. "If there is nothing more, I will probably see you at breakfast."

"I'll see you then."

"Good night."

She got to her bedchamber as quickly as she could without running. Once she had closed the door, she twirled around and fell onto her bed. She was going to be married to a gentleman she loved. And the only hurdle was her sister. Not that Dotty could stop the wedding, but she could try to make Henrietta feel guilty. It would be horrible if this caused a permanent break between the two of them, but Mama was right. Henrietta had to follow her heart. And, she thought, her head. Of all the gentlemen she'd met, Nate was the one who fit her the best.

Styles came in to help Henrietta get ready for bed.

"You must have had a very good dinner with her grace," Styles commented as she took down Henrietta's hair.

"I had a wonderful time." She wanted to tell her maid,

but would wait until after her sister knew. That was only right. Yet she was so happy she still could not stop smiling!

Once her hair was braided, she crawled under the covers. She did not think she would be able to sleep, but Morpheus must have had his way, because the next morning she woke fully refreshed. Henrietta threw her legs over the bed and rushed to the window. The sun was barely coloring the antelucan sky.

Just as she'd finished splashing water on her face and brushing her teeth, Styles entered with a cup of tea and a piece of toast. Henrietta hurried through her food and drink as her maid put up her hair and affixed a small hat with a feather on it.

"It looks like a fine day for a ride, Miss Henrietta."

"It does, doesn't it?" The smile was back on her face. In a few minutes she would see Nate again. And she must speak with her sister. "Can you find out what my sister's schedule is today?"

"Of course," Styles said.

Dorie and Georgie were almost to Merton House as Henrietta mounted her horse. She would be glad when Nate could meet her here. No. She would be happy when she was leaving from his—their—house.

"You are very cheerful this morning," Georgie commented. She threw a glance at Dorie. "More so than poor Dorie."

Now that Henrietta's attention was drawn to her friend, she noticed the dark smudges under her eyes. "Did the baby keep you up?"

"He did. It would not have been so bad, but every time I put him down, he cried. No one else could comfort him. He is finally sleeping."

"What was the problem?" Henrietta supposed she would

also go through the same thing someday. In fact she knew she would. She was old enough to remember her younger sister's birth and infancy.

"Flatulence." Dorie wrinkled her nose as Georgie and Henrietta tried not to laugh. "When it finally expelled it was quite smelly. Nurse says it happens sometimes."

"Oh, dear. Poor David." Henrietta remembered something like that happening with either her younger brother or sister.

"Good morning." Nate greeted them with a smile that matched her own. Even Padraig appeared happy.

"Good morning to you." She moved to ride next to him. "It looks to be a glorious day."

"I take it that the matter of whom to ask was solved?" Georgie asked.

"It was." Henrietta and Nate answered at the same time. "I wonder how often we will do that in the future."

"A great deal, I expect," he responded.

"We want the whole story," Dorie said. "It will take my mind off my sleepless night."

They were through the gate to the Park by the time Henrietta finished the tale. "I spoke with Merton last night." She turned to look at Nate. "He is happy to do the settlement agreements." Then she glanced back at her friends. "I will speak with my sister today."

They moved their horses into a trot, the dog keeping pace with them. "We will meet you at the elm tree." Dorie and Georgie waved, and Henrietta and Nate galloped down their regular path.

When they pulled up he sidled his horse closer to hers, put his arm around her shoulders, and kissed her quickly, before the horses pulled apart. "I love you. This morning I thought that soon we will both leave from our house."

"I thought that as well." She was positive she had never been happier, and prayed nothing would ruin it. Then she remembered her sister. For some reason that made her think of his mother. "Will your mother live with us?"

"No. She has stated often enough that she will move to the Dower House when I marry. She has always maintained that a house can only have one mistress. I believe she has already changed it to her liking." He chuckled. "No wonder she wanted me to come to Town this year."

"I'm glad you did." What would have happened if she had not met him?

"I am too. I'm even happier that we met when neither of us knew who the other was." His voice had dipped lower at that last part.

"Indeed. I had already formed a good opinion of you." She could not seem to stop looking at him.

"And I you." He was keeping all his attention on her as well.

"The two of you look besotted." Georgie laughed. "I am so happy for both of you."

"As am I." Dorie rubbed her eyes. "Unfortunately, I should go home and try to rest. I really am too tired."

"There will be tomorrow." Henrietta was ready to go home and think about what she would say to her sister.

"I gather little David kept you awake last night." Nate gave her a sympathetic look. "My sisters have complained about the same thing."

"I hope it does not happen on a regular basis," Dorie muttered acerbically. "I have discovered I like my sleep."

"You should have Exeter speak with him about keeping his mother up." Nate sounded serious, but his turquoise eyes were alight with laughter.

Georgie started to laugh. "Henrietta, you were not there

when Littleton spoke to the babies before they were born, chastising them for keeping Adeline up."

"That must have been funny." Henrietta did remember thinking that Adeline was quite large to have only been a few months pregnant at the time. Now that she thought about it, Grace Worthington was large as well. Could Dotty be carrying twins? Perhaps she should mention it.

Dorie and Georgie turned on to Park Street. Henrietta would have asked for a groom, or gone with them, if Nate had not started accompanying them. But it was only another street up to Grosvenor Square, and now that they were betrothed, she did not need a groom with them. The thought stopped her. If Dotty or Merton had known, they would have insisted she bring a groom. There was no point saying it was only one street. They would both point out that anything could happen even in that short distance.

"Henrietta, you're deep in thought. Is there something on your mind?" Nate looked as serious as he sounded.

"Not really." Should she tell him? She did not want to keep secrets. "It just occurred to me that when I did not accompany my friends to Green Street, I suppose I should have had a groom."

"You should have." Only because they could not yet make their betrothal known, Nate thought. "I didn't even consider the matter." He'd have to bring a groom tomorrow morning, and for the next day or two, until news of their betrothal got around. "I plan to send my secretary back to Ouse Tower to fetch the collection of wedding rings." There was one in particular he thought she would like. "Unless you wish to select a new one, that is."

Her frown disappeared and her lips tipped up. "I would love to look at the family rings first."

"Excellent. I'll send Chetwin today." Perhaps by the

time the secretary returned, Henrietta could dine with Nate and his mother after she selected her ring.

She had captured his gaze, and he couldn't have looked away if he'd wanted to. "I am looking forward to not only that, but us being married, and our wedding trip."

"No more so than I." He couldn't believe that he had found the perfect lady for him. Henrietta was everything he wanted in a wife. He just wished her conversation with the sister was over. He didn't think she would change her mind, but it had to put a pall over what was a happy event. They were at the entrance to Grosvenor Square. "I shall wait here until I see you are safely inside."

Henrietta laughed. "My knight gallant."

Nate bowed. "As you see."

"I will send word after I have spoken with my sister." She looked so concerned he wanted to take her into his arms. Then again, he always wanted to hold her.

Next to them, his dog whined.

"You are right, Padraig. I need to go home." She glanced at Nate again. "I look forward to seeing the rings."

As she rode away, he wished again he could kiss her, or draw her close to him, or make that meeting not be so fraught. He sent up prayers to the deities that it would be good news. Or rather, that her sister didn't talk Henrietta out of marrying him. Yet that was an unlikely outcome. His betrothed was a strong-minded woman. And she had the support of her grandmother and mother. All would be well. It had to be.

Nate reached his stables, dismounted, handed Darragh's reins to a groom, and strolled into the stables, where he found his coachman, a man in his middle years with sandy hair who had started as a groom when Nate was a boy. "Good day."

"Good day, my lord. Is something awry?"

"Not at all. I'm sending my secretary to Ouse Tower on an errand as soon as he can be ready to depart. He'll come straight back. Will there be any difficulty in returning by tomorrow early evening?"

The coachman rubbed his chin. They had made the same journey not long ago, but he liked to consult with the man. "As long as we don't run into weather, it will be fine. I'll take one of the grooms along with me to spare me with the driving."

"Very well. Be ready in about an hour."

"Easily done, my lord."

"I'll have Cook make a basket for you unless you prefer to stop and eat at an inn along the way. Naturally, I'll also send the funds if you must spend the night."

"This time of year, it will be just as well to drive straight through. I don't doubt the inns will be full with folks coming to London."

"You have a good point." Nate hadn't even thought of that. "I wish you a trouble-free trip."

"Thank you, my lord."

Nate gained the town house via the garden gate, making sure to lock it behind him, then braved the domain of his cook.

"Goodness, my lord. What brings you down here?" Cook was a tall, broadly built woman whose skill in the kitchen rivaled any French *chef de cuisine*. Before coming to them, she had worked for an English family in France after the war.

"I'm sending Mr. Chetwin back home to fetch something and I want the journey to be as quick as may be. He'll leave in about an hour. Can you have a basket prepared by then?"

"Of course, my lord. Nothing easier."

"Thank you." Nate gave her a short bow that made two of the kitchen maids giggle, took himself to his bedchamber, and sent for his secretary to attend him.

Once he'd told his secretary what he wanted, Chetwin grinned. "Would I be too precipitous to wish you happy?"

"Not at all. The matter was settled last night." Nate donned his jacket. "Your good wishes are appreciated."

His mother was already in the breakfast room buried in a newssheet when Nate arrived. He'd have to remember to ask Henrietta what her morning habits were. He took his place at the table. "I've sent for the wedding rings."

"I believe we have some in the safe here as well." Mama lowered the paper. "The duchess and I discussed the matter of your wedding last evening. If Lady Merton will not plan it, we will. I understand that her mother might help as well."

He hadn't expected that, but he was glad for it. Henrietta had been a bit concerned. "Thank you."

His mother picked up the newspaper again, and his butler brought his breakfast. It was amazing how everything seemed to be going on as normally when his whole life was about to change so drastically.

CHAPTER TWENTY-NINE

When Henrietta reached her chamber, Spyer said, "Her ladyship has not been waking until after ten o'clock. After which she breaks her fast and starts on her correspondence."

"Thank you." Henrietta glanced at the clock. There was at least another three hours before she could even attempt to see her sister. She would speak with Dotty after she ate and before she started answering letters. At least Henrietta had no reason to rush her meal. In fact, she might have trouble waiting for her sister to finishing eating.

Surprisingly, the time went fairly quickly. Of course she had read every newssheet on the breakfast table. She had even perused the personal advertisements. She had no idea how many people were searching for other people. The clock struck eleven, and she rose from the table, then made her way to Dotty's chambers.

Pausing before the door, Henrietta wiped her suddenly damp palms down her skirt. She had decided that no matter what her sister said, she would maintain a calm countenance. Unfortunately, no one had told her hands.. Or her stomach, which felt a little sick.

The footman standing beside the door bowed, and she nodded. He knocked on the door and waited. Dotty's maid opened the door, bobbing a curtsey to Henrietta. "Come in, Miss Henrietta."

Her sister sat behind her desk, a lovely walnut with a burl top, in the shape of a kidney. Dotty came out from behind it. "Henrietta, I feel as if I have not seen you for days."

"It does seem that way." She embraced her sister and bussed her cheek. Goodness, even she could feel the baby moving. "It's very active."

Dotty sighed. "I have decided it must be a boy."

Henrietta took her sister's hands and led her to a sofa. "I have something about which I wish to speak to you."

"Well, if it is about either Bolingbroke or St. Albans, I do not think you would be happy with either of those gentlemen. Bolingbroke is very conservative, and St. Albans only wishes to wed in order to receive the property he has been promised."

That was interesting. She was very glad she had not been smitten by either gentleman. "No. It is not about them." This was much more difficult than she thought it would be.

Dotty tilted her head in the exact way Henrietta and their mother did when attempting to understand something. "Do you require more gowns?"

"Well, I might, but that is not what I wish to say. I think you should sit."

Her sister raised one brow. "I am sitting. You are standing."

She had not even noticed. Instead of sitting, she began pacing. "The thing is, I have found a gentleman I wish to marry." Henrietta stopped and faced her sister. "Do you remember the gentleman we discussed, a Mr. Meadows?"

"Oh, famous." Dotty clapped her hands in front of her chest. "You have been introduced to him?"

"I have." She purposefully spoke slowly. "He has become friends with Lords Turley and Exeter as well." Perhaps if she told her sister about all Nate's good points, Dotty would not be too upset. "And you already know that he involves himself in charitable endeavors."

"Yes, yes, of course. But that is wonderful that he is getting on with the other two gentlemen!" She looked so happy that Henrietta hated to ruin her mood. "It is always good when the husbands of your friends like the gentleman you like."

"It is." She nodded. "He has also met Grandmamma, and she approves of him as well."

Dotty's brows drew slightly together, forming a line above the bridge of her nose. "And has he spoken to Merton?"

"After a fashion. They met at Jackson's"

"Jackson's?" She seemed slightly confused. "He said nothing about meeting a Mr. Meadows."

"Er. Yes." Henrietta bit down on her lip. This was it, then. "Mr. Meadows is Lord Fotherby."

Dotty's expression turned from slightly confused to hard anger. "*Fotherby!*" Dotty's voice was full of loathing, as if he was the lowest creature on the earth. "No. I will not allow it. How dare he court you when he must know how I feel about him." Her glare turned on Henrietta. "How dare you accept an introduction to him?"

This was exactly the reaction Henrietta had been dreading. "I only know what you told me about what he was like four years ago." She kept her tone as steady as she could. "If you remember, I knew him before we were introduced." Her sister's expression had not softened. "Please understand. He is not the same man at all. If only you would meet with him, you would know that."

"I said no. I will not even consider the match." Dotty's face flushed and her breathing quickened.

"I love him." Henrietta never thought she would plead, but she was. "He truly is different, and he is very sorry that he abducted you. If you would just speak with him . . ."

"No. Never." Dotty shook her head. "If you insisted on meeting with him, I shall send you home."

There had to be some way to get through to her. "You married the man you loved when Worthington and his family disapproved. Mama married the man she loved." Henrietta stared at her sister's hard mien. Could she do this? Could she live without her sister in her life? But could she live without Nate? She straightened her shoulders. "I shall marry the man I love. And he loves me. As much as I love you, I will not allow you to stand in the way of my happiness. You have no right to do so."

"No right?" Dotty slammed her hand down on the writing desk, causing the inkpot to rattle in its stand, and Henrietta almost jumped. She willed herself not to react. Not to change her mind. "He abducted me the day before my betrothal ball! He did not even care about my reputation. He is a scoundrel, a blackguard, a snake. Can you not see how he is tricking you?"

Dotty's anguish rolled off in waves so real, Henrietta felt it. Tears pricked her eyes. For a moment she considered telling Nate that they would have to wait. But wait for what? She was not sure her sister would ever change her mind. Could she really give him up? She took her sister's hands in hers, hoping to calm Dotty. This could not be good for the baby.

"I will tell Merton to forbid you from marrying," Dotty spat the words.

Henrietta dropped Dotty's hands. "Even if it means destroying my happiness?"

"You are beautiful and intelligent. You will find someone else."

"How can you even say that?" Finding someone to love wasn't a matter of going to a store and ordering one. Nate was the first gentleman she had ever been interested in. He was the only man who fit her. "Do you not care that we love each other?"

Her sister seemed to hesitate; then her face was like marble again. "I will do whatever it takes to stop you from being with him."

She blinked back the tears threatening to fall. Nothing was going to change Dotty's mind. "You can try." Henrietta swiped at her eyes. "Grandmamma has already given her permission, as has Mama."

Dotty's eyes flew open. "No! She did not."

"Yes." Henrietta nodded. "I did not want to upset you, but I have made up my mind. He is the only gentleman I wish to wed." She walked to the door and turned to face her sister again. "I am truly sorry you cannot bring yourself to find it in you to even give him a chance to ask for your forgiveness."

"I will never see him." Tears welled in Dotty's eyes. "I will not see you if you wed him."

"I am sorry it has come to this. I thought our love for

each other would make you want to try to understand what I see in him."

"Never."

"I realize that now. I will ask Dorie if I can stay with her until the wedding." Henrietta blinked back her own tears, opened the door, and ran to her room.

She threw herself down on her bed and let the tears flow. This was every bit as bad as she feared it would be and worse. Everyone else had come around. Why could her sister not at least try?

"Oh, there you are," Styles said. "The boy from the Phoenix Society is asking for you."

Henrietta grabbed her handkerchief and wiped her eyes. "Send him to my parlor."

Her maid gave her a dubious look. "Yes, miss."

She went through the door to her parlor, and a few seconds later a footman brought Toby in. "What is it?"

"Mrs. Perriman said as we're gonna need help today, and if you'd come. We got a mess of babies to pick up. She thought it 'ud be fine 'cause it's full day."

"Yes, of course." This, at least, would give her something to do. "I'll change and be right down. You can ask Cook for something to eat in the kitchen."

"Ain't got time. I got another place ta go."

"Very well. I'll go straight to Phoenix House."

The lad gave two sharp nods and dashed out of the room.

Henrietta rushed back into her bedchamber. "I must change. The dark blue wool serge gown."

She got out her pistol and loaded it. "Tell Parkin I will need two men to accompany me."

In less than a half hour, one of the servants was up

with the coachman and the other was on the back of the carriage.

Nate saw Henrietta in her brother-in-law's unmarked town coach turning onto Grosvenor Street. He'd wager she was going to Phoenix House as well. He was about to hail her when she turned her head in his direction and saw him.

She signaled to the coachman to stop. "Are you going to Phoenix House?"

He rode over to her. "I am. I take it you're going there as well."

"Yes. Take Darragh back and you can ride with me." Her lovely lips were set in a thin line. "We are betrothed. No one will think anything of it."

"Very well." Nate was glad they were still betrothed, and he wondered if she had had her conversation with Lady Merton. "Do you want to tell me what happened?"

"Not at the moment." She gave him a watery smile. "I'll tell you on the way back."

The coach followed him to the mews and turned around as he gave his horse to a groom.

He signaled to the footman in plain clothes to remain where he was and jumped into the coach sitting next to his betrothed. "Did Toby visit you?"

"He did." Nate finally had a good look at Henrietta. Her eyes were a bit red and puffy, as if she had been crying. What had her sister said to her?

No matter what it was, now would be a good time to take her mind off it. "Do you have any idea how many children compose a mess?"

"I have no idea at all." Henrietta's lips curved into a crooked smile. He wished he could take her into his arms and tell her everything would be fine. "I suppose we will find out when we get there."

When they turned onto Oxford Street the traffic became a heavy mix of coaches, carriages, drays, and other wagons. "I hope Mrs. Perriman does not expect us there immediately."

"She must know how busy the streets are this time of day." Henrietta reached out and took his hand. He closed his over her fingers.

If her sister had upset her, perhaps he'd be better off letting her tell him about the confrontation. She shouldn't be distracted during a rescue. He tried again. "Did you speak with your sister?"

She bit down on her lower lip and nodded.

"I won't pry, but if you tell me about it, you might feel better."

She nodded again. "I told her that we loved each other and were going to marry. She became very angry. I had never seen her like that before." Henrietta took a breath, and he handed her his handkerchief. "Thank you," she said with a small smile. "It ended by me telling her that I would move to Exeter House until the wedding."

He squeezed her hand. If she stayed with Dorie, it would cause talk. Merton wouldn't like that. She could reasonably reside with her grandmother, but Nate didn't know how the duchess would like the arrangement. Or he could invite her parents to stay with him. He had to write to her father in any event. He could broach the subject then. Nate glanced out the window. They would be there soon. "There are other options you can consider. I will support you whatever you decide. We can both leave Town and plan a country wedding."

She squeezed his hand and smiled at him. "I knew I could depend upon you to understand."

He'd understand anything that didn't take her away from him. "Always. For the rest of our lives."

They drove into the mews behind Phoenix House, and he got out, then lifted Henrietta down. It wasn't until then that he noticed she wore the same gown she had when they first met. He was also in the same kit. He'd have to borrow the greatcoat and hat from Mrs. Perriman again.

Toby was there to unlock the garden gate, and the footman and another servant who'd sat with the coachman followed them to the house.

Mrs. Perriman came out of a parlor off the hall. "Miss Stern, Mr. Meadows, thank you for coming. I don't know what I would do without you today."

Henrietta waved her hand toward the footmen. "We brought reinforcements as well."

"I'm afraid I'll have to borrow the greatcoat and hat, if I may," Nate said. Mrs. Perriman almost rolled her eyes and he smiled. If he continued to do this, he'd have to find a suitably shabby coat and hat. "I did bring my own pistol."

"Well, that's something. I have the greatcoat, but not the hat. Wait here and I will get the garment."

Henrietta was finally smiling. "What will we do with you?"

He gave her his I-am-a-peer look. "I don't know about anyone else, but you, miss, are going to marry me."

"Yes, I am."

Mrs. Perriman was back in a matter of seconds. As he donned the coat, she told them what was going on. "I received five requests, and all the children are to be fetched today."

Henrietta's forehead creased. "Are they from the same person?"

Mrs. Perriman appeared a bit worried. "That is just it.

I'm not certain. There is a lad by the name of Jack who keeps his ear to the ground about children who need help, or mothers who want to give their children up. I was not here when he told Tim about four of them. However, Jack came back yesterday and said there was another one." She donned her coat and a plain bonnet. "Quite honestly, I was more concerned to have enough people to carry the children." She glanced at Henrietta. "I have notified the house in Richmond."

Henrietta nodded. "You will take them straight there?"

"Yes. All of you might have to come with me."

"That is not a problem," Henrietta assured the woman. "I have nothing planned this evening."

Mrs. Perriman glanced at Nate.

"Neither do I. We are at your disposal."

"Thank you." She moved toward the door to the garden. "I thought about asking your sister for more employees, but it is feast or famine. We wouldn't want to pay for people to do nothing but wait."

"I understand," Henrietta responded. "It would be hard to have people working on an ad hoc basis, especially when there are so many secrets one must keep."

Nate hadn't thought about it quite like that, but she was right. Anyone who worked here could not talk about what they did or, more importantly, where the women and children went after they were rescued. "Where are we going?"

"To the outskirts of Seven Dials." Mrs. Perriman pulled on her gloves. "Close to where we were the last time you helped us. We always change the meeting sites."

Tim, the former soldier Nate had met when he was looking for Henrietta, joined them.

He hadn't thought about having to do that. But it was

an excellent idea. She strode down the corridor to the garden, and they followed.

When they reached the mews, a traveling coach was waiting. "This is handy to have."

"It is for longer journeys," Mrs. Perriman said. "We have houses outside the London area."

As with the other carriage, the coach appeared shabby on the outside, but it was well-sprung and in good working condition.

When they reached Neal Street, the coachman turned the vehicle around before stopping. This area actually looked worse than the last place. Nate watched as Henrietta moved her pistol to a pocket in her cloak. "Do you think there could be trouble?"

Her brows rose slightly. "Even on the edge of Seven Dials, one should always be prepared for difficulties."

Once again he was surprised at his ignorance of the two major slums in London. "I must depend on your deeper knowledge."

He was glad to see a small smile on her lips.

"Miss Stern, I would like you to stay back a little with one of your footmen," Mrs. Perriman said. "Mr. Meadows, please come with Tim and me."

That left the coachman and the other footman to watch them from behind.

They arrived at the meeting place to see two men carrying two infants, accompanied by two other children who couldn't be more than two years old. Behind him, Henrietta sucked in a breath, and he looked closer at the men. They were the same ones from the first time they had met. Nate moved to block either of the men from seeing her, but it was too late.

"You!" One of the blackguards started toward her, but Nate and the others drew their weapons.

"Don't be stupid. You can make good coin or you can die." Nate heard the low growl in his voice. "Give the infants to that man and woman and tell the children to come to us."

The man who'd approached them stayed where he was until his companion said, "Bart, we can't help Gran if we ain't got the money. Don't do no good to get yerself killt." He glanced at Henrietta, who had drawn her pistol. "If he don't kill ye, she will."

The man growled but pushed the older children forward, and Henrietta took one by the hand.

Once they had the children, Mrs. Perriman tossed a sack of coins toward the villain who'd spoken. Suddenly, Bart pulled a knife and lunged at Henrietta. Before she could react, Nate shot the blackguard.

"Telled ye I'd find ye," a man carrying a stout cudgel shouted. "Jest took longer than I thought. What'd ye do with my woman and the kid?"

Bloody hell-hounds!

"Back off now or I'll shoot you," she said, her tone as cold as ice.

The rogue's eyes bulged, and she nodded. "In that case, we will leave."

Henrietta took his arm, but as Nate turned, a searing pain hit his head. A shot sounded, and all hell broke loose. Someone half dragged, half carried him to the carriage and shoved him in.

"Oh my God! He's bleeding," Henrietta said from somewhere above him.

That must be the warm liquid he felt dripping down his face. Damn, his head hurt.

"We need something to bind the wound," Mrs. Perriman said, and a cloth was pressed to his head.

The coachman took a corner and Nate heard a groan from somewhere. He'd never been in this much pain before.

"He's passed out, miss," one of the footmen said.

No, I haven't.

"That's for the best," Henrietta said. "We need to get him home and fetch the doctor. Why is there so much blood?"

"Head wounds bleed a lot," Mrs. Perriman responded tightly.

"Where's he live, miss?"

"Grosvenor Street. We will have to move him to my town coach. Once we arrive I'll send for Dr. Daintree."

CHAPTER THIRTY

Before the door had closed on Henrietta, tears were leaving trails down Dotty's cheeks. From the door to the dressing room, she heard a sniff, indicating that her maid disapproved of something or someone. "What is it?"

"Not my place to say, is it?" Polly commented.

"That never stopped you before," Dotty said under her breath. The maid had been with her since before she was old enough to put up her hair.

"Seems to me I know exactly what your papa would say about you not giving a man a chance at redemption." Polly had stopped talking. Just when Dotty thought the maid had finished, she started up again. "And what he'd say about you trying to make Miss Henrietta choose between you and the gentleman she wants to marry." Polly shook her head mournfully. "He'd be that disappointed in you, he would, my lady."

No. Dotty did not believe her father would blame her for her stance. Papa would understand. He had been furious about what Fotherby had done to her. It was hard to even think of the man without feeling like a snake was crawling up her leg. She had never had such a visceral dislike of anyone but him.

"And if your mother and *grandmother*—"

"You have made your point. I will think about it." The look on her sister's face had been as hard as stone. Why could Henrietta not understand how Dotty felt about him? How could she have allowed herself to fall in love with the blackguard?

She wanted to talk with someone. Someone who would agree with her. Someone who would help her stop this wedding. Dotty rubbed her forehead. She supposed she could discuss it with Dom, but would he want to get in the middle of this contretemps with her sister? Then again, he was her husband. Even if he had made his peace with Fotherby, he knew she had not.

She glanced at the clock. It was past time she visited with her daughter. *Visit*. That was all she had been doing lately. It was time to spend more time with Vivi. "Send word to Nurse that I wish to take my daughter for a walk, then help me change into my blue walking gown."

"Yes, my lady." Polly stepped into the corridor, then came back and went into the dressing room.

Several minutes later Dotty climbed the stairs to the nursery and was glad to see Nurse already had Vivi ready. "Will you come with us?"

"Only if you are certain you need me." She held up a tiny gown with a tear in it. "There are several things I need to get done."

"We will be fine."

Vivi lifted up her arms, and Dotty picked up the little girl and hugged. "Come, sweetheart, let us go to the park in the square. You are going to have to walk until we get downstairs to your chariot. Mama cannot carry you." Dom had had a large, leather basket attached to wheels with a bar that could be pushed or pulled. A mattress covered the bottom and cushions were fixed on the sides and back. Lacking another word for it, they called it a chariot.

Vivi gave Dotty a wet kiss and scrambled down. "I walk, Mama."

"Thank you." She took her daughter's hand. Whatever happened, she had to spend more time with Vivi.

When they reached the hall the chariot was at the bottom of the steps, and Smith and Conners, Dotty's two personal footmen, stood beside it. She fixed a smile on her face. "Good morning."

"Good morning, my lady," the men said in unison.

"We will just go around the square a few times."

"Very good, my lady." Jones took the bar that had been swiveled to the back so that he could pull the device, and Smith dropped behind them as they set off with Dotty walking beside the chariot.

Vivi chattered and pointed to flowers, birds, other people, and everything else she saw. They were on their way back to the house when Merton's unmarked town coach flew by the entrance to the square. What in the name of God was going on?

Dotty increased her pace and reached the front door a second before it opened. "Parkin, do you know where the town coach is going?"

"Miss Henrietta took it a while ago to go rescue a child."

There must be an injured child in the house. "Where is the child?"

"There is no child." Parkin shook his head, as if he did not understand. "Miss Henrietta has not returned."

None of this was making any sense at all. "But where was the town coach going in such a hurry?"

"I have no idea, my lady. Would you like me to send a messenger to Phoenix House?"

"Yes. That would be the best thing to do." Dotty hoped nothing had happened to her sister. But if it had, surely she would have been brought here. "Thank you for thinking of it."

Parkin bowed. "You are welcome, my lady."

Dotty was finishing the luncheon tray she had had brought to her in the parlor when Dom strolled in and fixed her with a hard look. "You have been weeping."

"I did for a while. However, I will be fine." She wondered what he knew about the contretemps. "Henrietta and I spoke."

"Loudly, from what I hear." He lifted a blond brow.

"I believe we became quite loud at times." Dotty bit her lip. "After that Henrietta left to rescue a child, but she has not returned home."

"The messenger was reporting to Parkin when I arrived," Dom commented calmly.

She hated when she had to pull information from him. It was always when he did not wish to upset her. "What is wrong? Where is Henrietta?"

"She is at Fotherby House with him," Dom said.

Dotty could not believe what he had said. "She would not go there. It is not proper." Pushing herself back from the table, she rose. "I am going to get her. She must come home now."

"Thea, please sit down. There is something you should know." Dom rarely spoke to her in such a firm tone.

"What?" She found herself sitting again. "What has happened?"

He sat in the chair across from her, planting his elbows on the table. "First, tell me what was said in your conversation with her."

Dotty twisted the glass of porter she still had not finished. "The long and short of it was that when I forbade her to marry Fotherby, she informed me that she already had permission to wed him. I told her if she did, I would not have anything to do with her. That was when she announced she would move to Exeter House and left the parlor. I did not know she went to rescue a child until I returned from taking Vivi for a walk."

"Fotherby was called upon to assist as well. He suffered an injury to his head. Henrietta is nursing him."

"You went to Fotherby House?"

Dom nodded. "I did."

"Have you forgiven him?" Dotty forced herself to breathe.

He leaned back in the chair and touched his fingertips together. "When he abducted you I was furious. If you had wanted it, I would gladly have sent him to India or the Antipodes. But you did not wish me to do that. By giving him to his mother to discipline, you gave him a second chance." Dotty shifted in her chair, suddenly uncomfortable with the conversation. "You know I spoke with him." She nodded. "I also fought with him at Jackson's."

"Men." She closed her eyes. "Why is it that men can have a fight and all is well?"

Dom shrugged one shoulder. "I have no idea. But back to the matter at hand." He sat up again and leaned his arms on the table. "You were the one who gave him a second chance. An opportunity to better himself. You should know that your actions succeeded beyond what I ever thought could happen. I've known the man most of my life and never thought he could change as he has." He caught her eyes with his. "My love, you should be proud of the results. What I do not understand is why you are angrier now than after the event occurred."

"I do not know." Dom was right. Ever since she learned he might be in Town, she had become angrier with Fotherby than she ever had been before. "I am going to see Grace."

"I'll be here when you return." Dom came around the table and drew her into his arms. "I love you. If you still want me to try to stop Henrietta from marrying Fotherby, I will find a way to do it."

"I am not sure you could accomplish more than delaying the marriage." Dotty kissed her husband. "I must send Grace a note."

Dotty took a sip of porter, then took out a piece of pressed paper, ink, and a pen. Her best friends were not yet in Town, but Grace was. Dotty had known Grace Worthington all her life. It was because Grace had agreed to sponsor her when her younger sister, Dotty's closest friend, Charlotte, came out that Dotty had met Dom. If anyone knew what she should do, it was Grace.

Dear Grace,

I need to speak with you as soon as you have time. Please give your answer to the messenger."

Your friend,
D. M.

Less than fifteen minutes had passed when her butler knocked on the open door. "Lady Worthington said she is available now if you would like to visit her."

"Thank you. Please bring the town coach around."

"Yes, my lady."

It did not take long to reach Worthington House in Berkeley Square. Dotty had strolled up the steps to Worthington House and raised her hand to knock on the door when it opened and Royston bowed.

"Her ladyship is waiting for you."

"Thank you. Is she in her study?"

"Yes, my lady. She is."

"Please do not announce me." Dotty forced herself to give him a smile. "I know the way."

"As you wish, my lady." Royston bowed again.

She walked slowly, trying to organize her thoughts. She had acted on a sudden need to talk to Grace, but Dotty had not considered what she would say once she arrived. Words, arguments, jumbled around in her head, but when she stepped through the open door, instead of greeting her friend like the calm person she always prided herself in being, she burst into tears. "I'm go-go-going to lose my sister."

The next thing she knew she was sobbing in Grace's comforting arms. "Shush, now. Everything will be fine. Come and sit with me. We'll have a nice cup of tea and a talk, and you will feel better."

Putting her arm around Dotty's shoulders, Grace led her to a sofa facing the fireplace, which had been lit, and Dotty let herself be gently guided to sit on the sofa.

"Now," Grace said as she poured two cups of tea, fixing one cup exactly the way Dotty liked it. "I suppose this is about Henrietta and Lord Fotherby."

Dotty blew her nose and, not yet trusting her voice, nodded, then picked up the cup of tea and drank, letting the warmth of the liquid soothe her. Everyone seemed to know about them long before she did. "Yes. She is determined to have him. He says he loves her. Even Merton has grudgingly given his approval, as have my mother and grandmother." She drained her cup and set it down. "But I cannot think of him without being reminded of his callous disregard for me when he abducted me. I do not want my sister to marry him. I never want to see him again! But she says she loves him, and that the man she knows is nothing like I have described him. Grandmamma gave them permission to marry, and I don't know what to do." That last part ended on a wail Dotty never thought could come from her. She thought of what she had said to Henrietta, and the stern set of her face. "I behaved badly when Henrietta told me." Tears clogged Dotty's throat and Daisy, Grace's Great Dane, shoved her head under one of Dotty's hands. For a few moments she stroked the dog. "I do not want to be estranged from her."

Grace poured another cup of tea and handed it to Dotty. "I have a fair idea of what you are going through." Grace gave a wry smile. "After all, I was also abducted. Even though I knew Matt would rescue me, it was terrifying."

Dotty remembered hearing the story. If Matt had not been there almost immediately, Grace would have suffered much more than she had. At least after Dotty had discovered her kidnapper was Fotherby, she knew she would not be physically harmed. Although her reputation would have been in tatters if anyone found out. "You were fortunate to be rescued so soon."

"Indeed I was. However, what you suffered was not unimportant," Grace said gently.

"No. It was not." Ever since then, she had carried sufficient funds at all times to enable her to get home from as far away as France if need be.

Grace set down her cup and raised a questioning brow. "But despite everything, Henrietta loves him?"

"Yes." Another lump had formed in Dotty's throat and getting the word out hurt.

"I had a feeling that might be the case." Grace made up a plate of ginger biscuits and a lemon tart and handed it to Dotty. "She came to speak to me when she discovered who he was. She also said the same thing she said to you, that he was nothing like the man you and Merton told her about."

"When was that?" The query came out sharper than Dotty had wanted it to.

"A few weeks ago." Grace gave Dotty a sympathetic smile. "She was concerned that if she liked him it would cause problems with you." She opened her mouth, but Grace held up a hand. "You, of all people, must know that hearts are difficult if not impossible to control."

Dotty snapped her mouth shut. "Merton."

"Indeed. No one liked the idea that you would marry him." Grace took a sip of tea. "But you saw or felt something about him that Matt and the others did not."

"Yes. But he never abducted anyone." He had been the perfect gentleman, most of the time. "He never harmed anyone."

"Did he not?" This time when Grace raised her brows, she stared directly at Dotty, daring her to say her nay. "He might not have kidnapped a lady, but his votes in the Lords did harm to a great number of people."

"But that is in the past." Grace knew that. "He has changed and has done many good things since then." Grace's steady gaze made Dotty want to fidget. She did not want to admit that the situations might be the same. But she could not lie, not even to herself. She took a breath and let it out, then closed her eyes. "As Fotherby has done."

"Yes." Grace rose, went to a small sideboard, and poured two glasses of claret, then handed one to Dotty. "Tea is excellent to calm one down, but hard revelations call for wine. I met him in the Park when I took the twins and Madeline out. There is nothing of the Dandy about him now. He was very kind to the girls."

Dotty took a sip of wine. "Thank you."

"You are welcome. I thought it might help." Grace set down her glass while Dotty turned hers nervously. "Merton came to talk with Matt. He said that—using his family name—Fotherby had donated a great deal of money to the charity and assisted in at least one rescue after he had helped Henrietta. Merton had to ask Fotherby about the donation. He did not reveal it, and he did not wish Henrietta to know about it. Under his own name, naturally, he has gifted the house in Richmond to the charity."

Dotty nodded. At first she had thought he had done those things in order to increase his chances with her sister. But it had become clear that he had done it because he cared about the women and children in need. "I agree." Lord, how she hated to say that. "He does appear to be a different person."

"My dear, can you not accept that he has changed and allow Henrietta the happiness she deserves?" Grace's gaze was steady, and Dotty almost felt as if she was in the schoolroom again.

"It does not seem as if I have much of a choice." She knew she sounded churlish. "She already told me she would marry him. She even said she would live with Dorie Exeter until her wedding."

"You could continue to object." Grace shrugged. "I imagine you might have some sway with your parents."

Dotty shook her head, knowing that was a lost cause. "My grandmother has already spoken to them. She is on Henrietta's side."

Grace put her glass of wine on the table and took one of Dotty's hands. "You have a choice to make. You can be the smaller person and hold on to your anger, or you can be forgiving and accept the apology he seems to desperately want to make."

She always thought of herself as a kind person. A fair person. One who believed in giving people another chance. The thought that she could be acting in a way she would condemn in another made her feel like a hypocrite. "I suppose I should act the way I expect others to do." She drained the rest of the wine. "Thank you for listening to me."

Grace smiled. "That is what friends are for."

Dotty leaned over and bussed her friend's cheek. "I had better go home and tell Henrietta that she has my blessing."

"You will make her very happy." Grace returned Dotty's kiss. "Let us know when the wedding is to be."

"I expect it will take place within the next two weeks." She shook her head, but this time she was able to smile. "None of us like long betrothals."

That made Grace laugh. "Very true."

"I do not know why things are bothering me so much." Dotty had to blink back tears. "I've become a watering pot. I do not know how Merton stands it."

Grace's brow puckered. "How far along are you?"

"Five months. This baby is so different from Vivi. He is constantly kicking me. And he is so much larger."

Grace's brows furrowed. "Have you never thought you might be carrying twins?"

Dotty could not stop her jaw from dropping. "No, it never even occurred to me."

"I will give birth about the same time as you. To twins." Grace paused, as if she was letting her words soak in. "I remember when my mother was pregnant with Alice and Eleanor. She was normally a very calm woman, but at that time she was easily upset."

"You are not." Dotty's hand went unconsciously to her stomach. Twins!

"No, but I am not going about as much, and I do not have a young lady to watch over. I also know the symptoms and rest accordingly."

Suddenly, the aforementioned twins and Madeline rushed into the room. Grace looked at them and sighed. "You knew I had someone with me."

"We did," Alice said, and the other two nodded.

"It was better than falling into the room," Madeline muttered.

"We have an idea that might help Dotty," Eleanor added.

"Yes," Alice agreed. "Do you remember when you had Gabe, and we were so upset?" Gabe was Grace's eldest.

"I do," Grace said, looking intrigued.

"Mrs. Winters talked with us," Eleanor said. "And we decided it might be because Mama was giving birth when she died. And we were afraid it would happen to you."

Madeline directed her direct, dark blue gaze at Dotty. "Do you think you might have been more afraid than you admitted, and knowing Lord Fotherby is here again made you afraid?"

Dotty and Grace exchanged a glance.

"It is true that you were extremely calm about the whole incident," Grace said thoughtfully.

Dotty knew that type of thing occurred. Why had she not thought of it herself? She looked at the three girls. "You might have a point. Thank you."

"That was all we wanted to say." Alice and, after picking up a ginger biscuit each, the other two girls left the room as quickly as they had entered it.

"When are they coming out?" Dotty glanced at Grace.

"Two more years." She sighed. "We expect everyone to be on hand. Augusta has promised to be back by then."

Dotty selected a biscuit from her plate. "What did Madeline mean about falling through the door?"

"They have taken to listening at the door in the side corner of this parlor." Grace pointed toward it. "The latch is not secure, and if the two in the back push to be able to hear better, the door opens—"

"And they fall into the room." Dotty laughed. It felt good to laugh again. "I do have a question." Grace inclined her head. "How can I be sure that I am carrying twins?"

"My midwife is coming to Town in a few days. She can examine you." She pursed her lips as if she had eaten something sour. "I trust her far more than I trust a doctor."

"I had an excellent midwife when Vivi was born. Unfortunately, I did not think to have her examine me before we came to Town."

"You really had no reason to." Grace picked up a lemon tart. "I, on the other hand, had a strong feeling it was just a matter of time before I would have twins."

"I had better go." Dotty rose. "I would not be surprised if Henrietta has not already begun to move to Exeter House."

Grace held out her hands to Dotty and she took them. "And you. Are you feeling better?"

"Yes, much better." The dratted tears pricked her eyes again. "Thank you." At least she felt better knowing why she was so tired all the time. Yet she could still not find it in her heart to forgive Fotherby.

"I shall walk you to the hall." Grace stood and linked arms with Dotty.

Royston sent a running footman to find her coach, and in a few minutes she was on her way home.

CHAPTER THIRTY-ONE

Henrietta wiped her bloody hands on her skirt as she followed the footmen carrying Nate through the door of Fotherby House. The pad she'd applied to Nate's head was already soaked. As she stepped into the hall, the butler bowed. "I am Miss Stern. I've sent for a doctor. In the meantime I will need hot water and bandages." The butler sent a footman running. "Is her ladyship here? Your name, please."

"Hulatt, miss. Her ladyship is out. However, I shall apprise her of his lordship's injury when she returns."

"Thank you, Hulatt." Henrietta gazed up the stairs, wondering where Nate's chamber was.

"If you will follow me?" the Hulatt said.

"Thank you." She was relieved he was not going to argue with her.

Hulatt left and an older woman came scurrying into Nate's bedroom, followed by a maid carrying what she needed. Henrietta pointed to the bedside table. "Please place the bowl and bandages there."

The maid nodded, and the older woman joined Henrietta at his bedside. "I'm Mrs. Garford, the housekeeper."

Henrietta gave the housekeeper a quick smile. "I am sorry to meet you under these circumstances, Mrs. Garford. I am Henrietta Stern."

The housekeeper nodded to herself, as if a question had been answered. "His lordship's betrothed. I'm glad to meet you too, miss. George, the footman sent to get me, said your coachman had gone to fetch a doctor."

She had not known if Nate had told her staff, but it was clear that he had. "Yes." She glanced at him. "I must clean the wound and change the bandage."

Mrs. Garford replaced the cravat Henrietta had placed under Nate's head to protect the bed-linens with a larger cloth. "Tell me what you want me to do."

"If you turn his head to the side, that would help." As Henrietta washed her hands, the housekeeper did as she asked and, also, placed another large piece of linen around the front of his neck, tucking one side in. Henrietta dipped one of the pieces of cloth into the water, rubbed a bit of soap on it, and gently started cleaning the side of his head. Once most of the blood was gone, she could see the jagged wound. It was still bleeding, albeit more sluggishly now. She took a breath, forcing herself to remain calm. Henrietta had seen bad cuts and broken bones, but she had never before seen so much blood on someone she loved. "The doctor is someone my family uses in emergencies. He'll know what to do."

"Do you want to put some brandy on the injury?" Mrs. Garford asked.

"That's a good idea." The cudgel had been filthy. The blood had helped clean some of the debris, and Henrietta was sure she had got the rest of it. The housekeeper handed her a cloth soaked with spirits, and she pressed it carefully to the ragged cut on his head. The housekeeper handed her two clean cloths folded into pads. "Thank you. Can you hold these to the wound while I wind the bandage around his head?"

"Yes, miss." The woman pressed down on the pads, and Henrietta quickly tied a strip of linen around his head. "That should keep him until your doctor gets here."

She nodded. Nate still hadn't moved, and she was becoming even more worried than she had been. His eyes had not fluttered even when she applied the brandy. "We will need more water and cloths when Dr. Daintree arrives."

"I'll have it fetched." Mrs. Garford glanced at the maid. "Millie?"

"I'll get it ready and bring it up when he gets here, ma'am." She picked up the bowl of blood-tinged water and the cloths. "Miss, you have blood on your skirts."

Henrietta glanced down at her dark blue gown. Aside from where she had wiped her hands, blood from Nate's head had stained the skirts. "I suppose I do. Thank you for telling me."

The maid smiled, and she turned back to Nate.

"I'll send someone over to get you a fresh gown," the housekeeper said.

"I will see to that."

Henrietta glanced over her shoulder. A man dressed like a valet bowed. "I am Styles, his lordship's valet. Shall I bring your dresser as well?"

At this point there would be no need to formally meet the senior staff. The only one she had not met was the cook. "Yes, please. Tell her to bring enough clothing for two days."

"It shall be done." He turned to go.

"Her name is Spyer," Henrietta called after him.

She sank onto a wooden chair someone had set by the

bed and watched Nate. He was so quiet. It occurred to her that she had never seen him not in motion. Whether it was riding his horse, walking his dog, or moving his hands when he spoke, he always gave the impression of energy. Blinking back unhelpful tears, Henrietta sent up a prayer that he was not injured too badly and would soon be conscious again. She told herself not to worry. His breathing was regular, and even though he was paler than normal, he was not a deathly shade of white. She did not know how long she had been staring at him, hoping for some sort of change, when she heard voices filtering from the hall and steps on the stairs.

"Miss Stern."

Rising, she faced the gentleman entering the room. "Dr. Daintree, I am so glad you have arrived."

"Tell me what happened." He set his bag on the bed and opened it as she related how Nate had been injured and what she had done to treat the wound.

"He has lost a great deal of blood." She moved the chair out of the way. "Or that is how it seems to me."

"We can't tell much from that. Head injuries do bleed a great deal." The doctor removed the bandage. "You did an excellent job tending to the wound."

"Thank you. I have some experience, and the house-keeper helped." Henrietta frowned as the doctor pressed his fingers around the injury. "Will he require stitches?"

"No. But, I do want the swelling brought down." He straightened. "Cold rags, or ice if it is available, will help."

"I'll fetch them, miss," Millie offered.

"Thank you." Henrietta had not even noticed that the maid had returned. For that matter, the number of people in the chamber had grown. She glanced at Dr. Daintree. "He has been unconscious since it occurred."

"He is probably concussed. It will be a while before he wakes up, and when he does, he's liable to have quite a headache." He reached into his bag. "I'll leave this willow bark powder with you. Do not give him laudanum. It can only harm his recovery. He should remain quiet, preferably in bed for the next few days, until he can stand up without pain or dizziness." She took the package. "Apply the cold compresses once every two hours for the rest of the day. Not on the wound, but around it. If it looks worse tomorrow, send for me. You know to change the bandages."

"I do."

"In that event, I will see you in two days." He grinned. "Unless you have need of me sooner."

Henrietta grimaced. "We have been sending for you a great deal recently."

"I'd much rather attend to the patients you bring me than people who only think they are ill." Dr. Daintree smiled. "Don't forget to get some rest yourself."

"I will remember." She would rest when Nate was better.

"I will see that she does, sir." Spyer entered the room carrying a small travel bag, followed by a footman carrying one of Henrietta's smaller trunks. "Miss is just like the rest of her family. Always tending to others first."

She closed her eyes and shook her head. Spyer had only been with Henrietta for a little over a year, but she had obviously been with her long enough to take the measure of her family.

Her maid glanced around the room and focused on Mrs. Garford. "I am Spyer, Miss Stern's dresser. Where would you like me to put these?"

"I am Mrs. Garford, the housekeeper. If you follow me, I'll show you to a room."

Millie came in as the other two women left. "Here's your ice, miss."

"Thank you, Millie." The maid must be the housekeeper's second in command.

She put a bowl on the bedside table. "Is there anything else I can do for you? Some tea?"

"Not right now. Perhaps in a little while. Thank you for asking."

The maid bobbed a curtsey and left the room, but Styles entered the bedchamber in her wake "Thank you for fetching Spyer."

"It was my pleasure, Miss Stern. If his lordship was awake, I am certain he would want me to lend you any assistance I am able. I am happy to sit with his lordship while you change. I will also make myself available to take care of any errands you have."

In other words, he would have footmen and maids running around fetching Henrietta anything she needed or wanted. "I appreciate your offer, Styles."

"Of course, miss." He bowed again. "May I say that it will be a pleasure to serve you?"

Tears pricked Henrietta's eyes again. "I look forward to joining the family."

When he left through a side door she hadn't noticed before, she finally sank back onto the chair and began applying the ice to Nate's injured head, praying that he would soon wake up. If only she could do something more.

Dotty entered Dom's study and he came out from around his desk. "Let us sit in front of the fire."

She allowed him to guide her to the small leather sofa and sank down on it, then rubbed her forehead.

He poured two glasses of wine, handed her one of them, grabbed a plate from his desk, and sat next to her. "How did your talk with Grace go?"

Dotty took a sip of wine. "I have no idea why I thought she would give him up once she had made up her mind. I am not usually so stupid." A smile tugged at Dom's lips, and she wanted to roll her eyes. "You are thinking that she is much like I am."

"That, my love, is because she is." His smile grew. "And your mother, and your grandmother." He looked at the plate, selected a piece of cheese, and ate it. "I take it you have changed your stance on the marriage."

Dotty did not even try to stifle her sigh. "That is where Grace comes in. She has a way of making one see when one is being difficult, or has not taken everything into account."

"She does have a way of doing that," Dom agreed.

"Alice Carpenter thinks I could be having some sort of delayed reaction to the abduction."

"Alice?" His brows rose.

"For a sixteen-year-old, she can be very perceptive." Dotty grimaced.

"What do you think of her opinion?" He had turned so that his knee was on the sofa and he was facing her.

"I think she might be right. As you and Grace both pointed out, I do believe in second chances. I really did not believe I had been afraid. I was never in any danger. I always thought I was more irritated that he was trying to make me miss my betrothal ball and make you doubt me."

"But?"

Dotty took a larger sip of wine. "I have decided to let him talk to me."

Dom inclined his head. "I think that is a good idea. When he can talk, that is."

"What do you mean by that?"

"I told you he had a head injury." She nodded. "He is unconscious. Apparently he bled a great deal. While you were gone, Henrietta sent for another gown because hers was bloody."

"Oh no!" Dotty covered her mouth. As angry as she still was with him, she had not wanted him harmed. "Will he live?"

"I saw Daintree, and he thinks Fotherby will be all right, but we must wait and see."

She had thought her sister was there simply to lend moral support. "Henrietta must be frantic with worry."

"Not she." Dom barked a laugh. "Apparently she entered the house, introduced herself, and started giving orders to the staff, as well as cleaning and bandaging the wound. They are all quite impressed." He gazed steadily at Dotty. "The footman who accompanied them said Fotherby saved Henrietta from being stabbed with a knife."

And she still took things in hand. Dom had not exaggerated when he compared Henrietta to Mama, Grandmamma, and Dotty. How had she not seen the strength in her own sister? "When will she be home?"

Her husband raised a brow. "That will depend on you. I know you are still not happy about the wedding."

"No, I am not." Even after everything Dotty had been told, she still could not bring herself to forgive him. She decided to tell him the other piece of information she had learned while at Worthington House. "There is something else that might interest you."

"What is that?"

"Grace thinks I might very well be carrying twins."

He jumped up and stared at Dotty. "Twins?"

She nodded. "We are due within a month of each other,

and we are about the same size around. She said that would explain my moodiness and why I am not sleeping well."

He dragged a hand down his face. "I am definitely taking you home as soon as possible."

"Yes, well." She grimaced. "First we have a wedding to get through."

"Not to mention your family coming to Town." He reached down and took her hands as he sat again. "I suggest letting your mother and Lady Fotherby plan the wedding breakfast."

"That is exactly what I shall do." Dotty would smile and pretend to be happy for her sister, but, at this point, that was all she could manage.

"I, on the other hand, must negotiate the settlement agreements." An evil grin appeared on her husband's face.

"You are going to do to him what Worthington did to you." It was not even a question. She did not know all the details, but she knew that he had held Dom's feet over the fire.

"That is my intent. As soon as he is well enough to engage in a mental battle." He unfolded himself from the chair and stalked around the table. "Now, though, you are going to take a rest. You've had a tiring day."

She could not disagree with that. Dotty had no sooner risen when she was swept up into his strong arms. "I can walk."

"I am quite sure you are able to drag yourself to your bed, but I am more than capable of carrying my wife and children."

"We will not know for certain until next week, when Grace's mid-wife arrives."

"For some reason I have a feeling Grace will be proven correct." He gave Dotty a chagrined look. "Yet again."

Dotty couldn't stop a burble of laughter from escaping her. Before meeting Grace, he had not been impressed with the thought processes of females. But all that had changed. He had realized that women were quite capable of reasoning as well as men.

Thank God he had.

CHAPTER THIRTY-TWO

Nate's head pounded like someone was beating on it. His mouth tasted like he'd eaten barn hay and he wasn't sure where he was. Wherever he was, he was not alone. The sound of another person breathing, someone very close by, made him turn his head. The scant warmth of a candle touched his cheek and he knew he'd be better off not looking at it. But he needed to see who was here. Raising his hand, he blocked the light and squinted down at the head, shoulders, and arms of a female sleeping as she leaned over from a hard, wooden chair to the side of his bed. Her hair was in a long black braid. Curls escaping from it framed the side of her face where she slept on her arms.

Henrietta. What is she doing here?

He slowly lowered his hand and reached out, brushing back the locks covering her face. She was so beautiful, he ached to kiss her.

"Nate?" Her green eyes lifted to his, and he could see the fatigue in her face. "You are awake. Thank God! You are awake."

Opening his lips, he tried to talk, but nothing came out.

"Let me get you some barley water."

Nate started to shake his head. He didn't want her to leave, but a stab of pain took his breath away and stopped him from moving again.

"Do not move." She leaned over and poured a glass of what he could only assume was barley water. "The doctor said you would have a headache when you woke. I will help you."

How the hell he was going to drink without sitting up he didn't know.

Henrietta braced herself against the headboard and, using his pillow to support his head, lifted him slightly. His temple still throbbed, but that was all. "Slowly, now." She lifted a wide-rimmed glass to his lips. "If I have to, I'll spoon it into you."

He drank, swishing the liquid in his mouth until it no longer felt so dry. "How long?"

"Four days. You have given us quite a scare." She wiped his chin and set the glass to his lips again. "We were afraid." Tears filled her eyes. "I was afraid you might never awaken."

Four days?

No wonder she was upset. Nate wanted to hold her in his arms and tell her he was fine. "Never leave you," he managed to croak.

"I know." She brushed a tear away. "Drink some more of this. I added the willow bark powder the doctor left to help with your headache."

How did she know his head hurt? Instead of asking, he did as he was told. He'd seen enough about head injuries to know he would be in bed at least another day or two. "Tired."

"I imagine you are." Setting down the glass, she took his hands, and he squeezed them.

He closed his eyes and closed his fingers more tightly around hers. "Don't leave."

"I will remain with you."

Her other hand caressed the unhurt side of his head, and he leaned into her touch. She kissed him lightly, and he moved his lips against hers, then sighed. He was in no condition to even kiss her properly.

When Nate woke again weak light filtered into the room. His head was not throbbing as much, but he was still unwilling to move it on his own. He opened his eyes, testing the light, but there was no pain.

Henrietta was still there. Or there again. Her hair was up and her gown was fresh. If only he could wrap his arms around her.

She studied him and frowned.

"What's wrong?"

"I must change your bandage, but Dr. Daintree will be here soon. He might wish to do it himself." Apparently having made up her mind, she rose. "Mrs. Garford brought something to keep the broth warm. Would you like some?"

His stomach growled. He wanted more than broth, but that was all he was going to get until he could talk this Daintree into real food. Nate was definitely not going to be a difficult patient for his betrothed. "Yes, please."

"Good." Henrietta placed another pillow behind him, easing him up high enough for him to drink the broth before going to the fireplace.

Slowly he turned his head and enjoyed watching her derrière sway under the skirts of her gown. This damned injury had better not delay their wedding.

"Here we are." She placed a serviette over her gown and balanced the bowl on it, then scooped the first spoonful and fed it to him. When he finished the pot-liquor she smiled. "I hope for your sake the doctor will allow you to have real food soon."

"I hope it's soon." It was satisfying to be able to speak in whole sentences.

"I am sure you do." She took away the bowl and poured a glass of something. "You are a much better patient than my father or brothers."

"I'm trying." When she turned her eyes were twinkling like emeralds in candlelight. "Come here."

Henrietta stepped over to the bed and sat on it. "Can you drink more barley water?"

"In a minute." The problem was that he did not think he could get up and use the chamber pot. Just the thought of it made his head ache more.

He wrapped his hand around her much smaller one. "How did you come to be here?"

"I brought you home." As she tilted her head, her forehead creased. "Do you remember what happened?"

"I was hit on the side of the head. I remember being lifted into the coach." When had he lost consciousness? "I heard you say I must be moved to the town coach, but I don't remember anything after that." Except a gunshot.

"When we got here Mrs. Garford helped me clean your wound and bandage it. My sister sent over my maid and clothes"—Henrietta grinned at him—"and I have been here ever since."

She slid past the part of her sister so quickly he almost didn't notice it. "Your sister?"

"Yes." Her face scrunched up adorably. "We had a horrible row, but something must have happened between the time I left and she appeared here." She shook her head. "Merton has come by to see how you are doing, as have the Exeters and the Turleys. Your mother looked in on you, but she really is *not* good at nursing."

That made Nate chuckle. "It's not one of her strong points."

"She kept talking to you and telling you to wake up, as if you could hear her," Henrietta said in a bemused tone.

"No doubt she thought I was just being difficult." He would have chuckled, but it might make his head hurt more.

"Yes, well." Henrietta smiled cheerfully. "She quickly lost patience, and Styles and I took over again."

He glanced at the door when it opened, and a gentleman a bit taller than medium height with light brown hair and a worried look on his countenance entered the room.

"Dr. Daintree." Henrietta stood. "Our patient has awakened. Once a few hours before dawn and then again about an hour ago. I gave him the powder last night. He's had a glass of barley water and just finished a bowl of broth."

"Excellent." The concern on the doctor's face was replaced by a smile. "I'm glad to hear you are mending, my lord."

She glanced from Nate to the doctor. "Allow me to introduce you. Fotherby, this is Dr. Lord Robert Daintree. Dr. Daintree, Lord Fotherby."

"My lord," Nate said.

"None of that." The doctor scowled at Henrietta. "Doctor is good enough." Millie, the head maid, came in with a bowl and linens. Once she'd set them down, Daintree moved to the bed. "Miss Stern, I will require your assistance."

"Of course." Henrietta joined him at the head of the bed and began removing the bandages.

Once she had finished, Daintree took out his quizzer

and inspected Nate's injury. "It's healing well. You will still require a loose bandage for another several days, but after that we can dispense with it."

Nate's stomach growled. "Can I eat food?"

The doctor laughed. "Yes. Just a little at first. You haven't had much of anything in the last four days, and you don't want to get sick."

"I promise to be careful." That wouldn't be hard. He had been almost full from the pot-liquor.

The doctor opened his bag and handed Henrietta several packets. "One every four to six hours for his pain."

"I will make sure he takes them." Henrietta glanced at Nate. Thank the Lord he was healing. She poured out a half glass of barley water and mixed a packet in it. "I will give him a dose now, and we shall see how he does."

"Very well." Daintree snapped his bag shut. "I'll stop by tomorrow."

"Thank you." She walked him to the door. When she turned back around Styles was there. "I am going to give him something for the pain now. But he will need you to attend to him soon enough. When he does have to get up, be very careful of his head."

"I will, miss." The valet glanced at the bed. "You have taken better care of him than anyone else could have."

A feeling of joy filled her. It was not just that Nate was awake and seemed to be healing, but that all the servants had been so welcoming to her and her maid. Henrietta had finally found her home. "Thank you. I appreciate you telling me. And thank you for helping me take care of him." Nate stirred restlessly, and she hurried back to the bed. "It is time for your medicine."

"If you insist." He sighed, but his tone was teasing.

"I do." She raised her brow and gave him a stern look. "Unless, of course, you wish to put off the wedding."

"Absolutely not." He helped her guide the glass to his mouth and drank. "We are not going to have much time to prepare for the wedding."

"The preparations are already being made." She took away the glass. "When you did not awaken the day after you were attacked, we were concerned. But my grandmother and your mother decided you would probably not die and began planning the wedding breakfast. Grandmamma also contacted the rector at St George's and set a date for the ceremony. I sent a note to my mantua-maker with a list of what I required, and she was kind enough to come here to discuss the details with me." Henrietta should probably tell him about the invitation his mother made. "Your mother wrote to my parents and invited them and the children to stay here before the wedding. They will arrive in a few days' time."

Nate's eyes widened. "Your parents are going to stay here?"

She did not understand it either. "It appears so. I have had enough to keep me busy and left it to them." She grinned at him. "I suppose they are of an age to make the decisions they think proper."

He let out a laugh and immediately clutched the side of his head. "I must not do that again for a while."

Henrietta could not imagine how much pain he was in. She should not have made the joke. "I am so sorry."

"It's not your fault." He dropped his hand from his head and took her fingers in his. "How could you have known?"

Just then a large, shaggy head bumped her arm and pushed under it. "Padraig stayed with you the whole time."

She removed her fingers from Nate's hand and he

stroked the dog. "I'll be up and about in no time." He glanced at her. "I trust he's been going for walks."

"Yes." Oh, dear, how was she to tell him that his small shoe-boy had been walking the dog? She would wait. "Yes. He is being exercised."

Nate yawned. "I think I am going back to sleep."

Henrietta straightened the covers. "That is the best thing for you. I shall have Cook prepare something for when you awaken."

"Thank you." His hands covered hers. "For everything."

She brought his fingers to her lips and kissed them. "I love you."

"I love you too." He kissed her knuckles. "And I cannot wait to be your husband."

"Neither can I." Henrietta brushed a hand over his forehead. "Sleep now."

Nate closed his eyes and was soon asleep. She wished she could crawl into bed with him. Instead, she glanced at Padraig. "Keep him safe while I get someone to sit with him. I am about to fall asleep on my feet."

She walked to the dressing room door, and Styles opened it. "I'll stay with him, miss."

Henrietta nodded. "He would most likely be fine, but until he can get up on his own, it is better to have one of us with him."

She stifled her yawn until she was in the corridor. Lord, she was tired. It was as if the energy that had sustained her over the past four days had vanished. But before she slept she had to send Merton a note that Nate had woken and would be fine.

Sitting at the desk in her bedchamber she pulled out a piece of paper and dipped the pen in the standish.

My dear Merton,

Fotherby awoke today. Dr. Daintree has been to see him and expects him to make a full recovery. He still has quite a bit of pain where he was hit, but that should lessen soon.

> *Your friend and sister,*
> *Henrietta*

She sanded and folded the note, then sealed it.

Spyer entered the room, and Henrietta moved to the dressing table. "I have a message for Merton."

She sighed with relief when her maid took apart her plait and began to brush her hair before braiding it again. "I'll get it sent out as soon as you're in bed."

"Thank you." She barely noticed her gown slipping down and her stays being removed. Once she had her nightgown on she slipped between the soft linen sheets.

Her maid closed the bed hangings, and Henrietta's thoughts went to her brother-in-law and Nate.

At first she had been surprised at the concern Merton had shown for his old friend. But it became clear that the changes Nate had made in himself had allowed Merton to forgive him. Now if only her sister could be brought around.

CHAPTER THIRTY-THREE

Nate was allowed out of bed two days after he'd woken up. Thereafter, his healing rapidly improved. Now, a few days later, he had only a slight soreness where he'd been hit. The only problem was that his mother seemed intent on keeping them apart. They had not been left alone for more than a minute at a time. He'd argue with her that he and Henrietta were betrothed, but it wouldn't do any good. He had been pleased that Henrietta had decided to remain here. Although, considering her parents would arrive tomorrow, it was not as unusual as one might think. He still couldn't work out exactly why they were staying at his house instead of Merton's.

Merton had come by every day after Nate had opened his eyes. At first the visits were not long, mostly due to him being unable to remain awake for more than a half hour at a time if that. Today, Merton was bringing the settlement agreements he'd had drafted. Nate was looking forward to signing them. It would make his and Henrietta's marriage so much more real. Thus far, he had not been consulted on anything. It appeared that his only duty was to make the short trip to the Archbishop of Canterbury's offices at Doctors' Commons for the special license.

A light tap came on the door, and Hulatt ushered Merton in to the room, followed by two footmen carrying tea and large plates of biscuits, tarts, spice cake, and sandwiches. Nate smiled to himself. Cook was on a mission to put more flesh on him again.

He rose and held out his hand. "Merton."

"You still look a little shaky on your pins." He shook Nate's hand, then took a seat in front of the desk. "Are you certain you're ready for this?"

"Quite sure." Nate sat back down. "The days in bed seem to have weakened me some, but I am well on the mend." He grinned. "Tomorrow, I am being allowed to ride again."

Merton barked a laugh. "Thank God I have never had to go through that. Is it because it is a head injury that Daintree is being so careful?"

"It is as you suppose." Nate pointed to the tea and his friend nodded. "He wants to ensure that I am steady on my feet and do not injure that area again."

Merton took the cup of tea. "What happened to the scoundrel who attacked you?"

After pouring a cup Nate shook his head. "I don't know. I heard shouting and a shot. But no one has said anything about it." He shrugged. "I could ask Henrietta, but, to be honest, I don't care what happened to him. There might be a way to find him and have him arrested, but I haven't decided whether I want to do that or not."

He and Merton drank their tea and sampled the offerings.

Nate bit into a piece of spice cake. It wasn't Cook's usual cake. It must be the one Henrietta told him about. He was glad she was already starting to take over as the mistress. He poured another cup and reached out for the documents Merton had set on the desk. "Try the spice cake while I read this."

The contract was much more modern than Nate had thought it would be. All Henrietta's property was to remain with her in a trust. Perhaps he wasn't the only one who had read Wollstonecraft. Not that he agreed with everything the woman wrote, but once he'd thought about it, there was no reason a woman had to lose all her property simply because she wed. He also agreed that if he predeceased her, she would have a choice of living in the Dower House or another house of her choosing. That made sense. His mother had never wanted to live with his grandmother. The only thing that truly surprised him was the amount of her dowry. Even knowing her grandmother was a duchess, he had not thought it would be so much. The rest were provisions about children and property given to her by him. If anything did happen to Nate and they had not had a son, she would have nothing about which to be concerned.

Nate reached out and picked a pen, then pulled the stopper out of the inkwell, and began signing the documents.

"Wait!" Merton's hand shot out a second after Nate had finished. "Is there nothing you wish to change?"

"No." He poured sand on his signatures. "Nothing at all. I find it extremely fair."

Merton leaned back in the chair and stared at Nate. "You have had a serious head injury. Perhaps you should have your lawyer look at it."

He fought the laughter wanting to escape. "There is nothing wrong with my cognitive abilities. I read the document, and I agree with all the provisions." Nate frowned.

He should have shown them to Henrietta before he signed them. "Perhaps I should have Henrietta read them."

"She already has," Merton said as he pulled the documents toward him. "She found nothing to change." He took the pen Nate handed him and signed the contract.

There was one thing he wanted to ask his friend. "Do you have any idea why Sir Henry and Lady Stern have decided to stay here instead of with you?"

Merton leaned back in his chair again, placing one leg across the other. "If you're allowed, you might want a glass of wine for this."

No one had told Nate he couldn't have wine. In fact, he'd had a glass at dinner last night. Rising, he went to the sideboard and poured two goblets of claret. He handed one to Merton. "Go on."

"When I decided I would wed Thea, Worthington was furious about it. But there was nothing he could do—"

"Because she had been compromised?" Nate asked.

"Because she had agreed to marry me." Merton took a sip of wine. "That's excellent. You'll have to let me know where you buy it." He took another drink. "She had enough people helping her that if we'd had a long betrothal, another scandal would have come along and ours forgotten, allowing her to jilt me. I was determined that was not going to happen. My mother and I came up with the idea of inviting Thea's parents to stay with us. Thus enabling her to stay with me as well."

Nate drank some of the wine. "I still don't understand."

"Sir Henry enjoyed seeing how I treated my betrothed and how the servants treated her. He later told me that he was glad he had seen me in my own home. He had been prepared to take her back with them if he had not liked what he saw."

"I am to be inspected." Nate wasn't sure if he liked the idea or not. But he was positive he wanted Henrietta to remain in his—their house.

"You are." Merton smirked. "And do not expect him to respect your rank. He called me 'boy' and 'son.'"

At that Nate did laugh. His friend had never been treated like that in his life. "Your future father-in-law might be a baronet, but he's a Radical."

"That explains a lot about how Henrietta thinks and acts." It also meant that she fit perfectly into his new life.

"And my wife as well." Merton tossed off the rest of his wine and stood. "I will get these to my lawyer to be copied."

Nate rose as well. "Is there any chance your wife will speak with me? I know it is hurting Henrietta that her sister is against our marriage."

Merton rubbed his forehead. "Unfortunately she has not yet softened toward you. It will take time."

"Thank you for telling me." Nate didn't know what he could do to change her mind if she wouldn't speak to him. "Let me walk you out. I will go buy the special license while I am thinking about it."

If he could bring Lady Merton around, that would be the best present he could give his betrothed.

Once Merton had gone Nate called for his carriage. It shouldn't take that long to get to Doctors' Commons and back. "Come, Padraig. You can go with me." The dog rose slowly and wagged his tail as he nuzzled Nate's hand. "After I've finished my business we will walk part of the way back.

Just over two hours later, he had the special license. The coach turned on to Berkeley Street, and Nate knocked on the roof of the coach. "Stop here. Padraig and I will walk the rest of the way."

"Yes, my lord."

He opened the door and Padraig bounded out, then waited for Nate. They were almost at Berkeley Square when a young maid, pulling a child in some sort of contraption on wheels and holding another young child's hand, screamed and fell. Nate hurried toward her when a ball rolled into the street, and the boy dashed after it.

"Master James!" the maid shrieked.

Blast me. A carriage!

Nate ran into the street and grabbed the child.

Master James wiggled to be free and Nate tightened his grip. "Ball. I want my ball."

"You shall have it soon." He took the boy to his maid, who had managed to stand. "Are you injured?"

"No, sir. I tripped over something, but I'm fine." As if just remembering, she bobbed a curtsey. "Thank you for saving Master James. I—I couldn't have stood it if he'd been hurt."

"You're welcome. I was glad to be of help." Nate glanced across the street and saw the ball. "If you'll hold on to him, I'll fetch the ball."

She took her charge's hand. "Thank you again."

Looking for any traffic before he crossed, he saw a carriage carrying a woman who seemed to be staring at him, although, she was pressed back against the squabs, and he couldn't see her well at all. Shrugging, he got the ball, returned it to the boy, and glanced at the carriage again. It had started moving forward. As it passed, he noticed Merton's crest.

Lady Merton. It had to be her.

* * *

Henrietta had spent the last several days attending to things that had been put to the side during Nate's illness. One of those items was a visit to Hatchards, and other shopping, and fittings. As usual, Dorie and Georgie accompanied her.

"I love the new gowns you ordered," Dorie said. "Especially the emerald-green walking gown. It is the same color as your eyes."

"I am partial to that one as well." In fact, she so loved the color that she had decided to use it in her soon-to-be bedchamber and parlor for some of the pillows and other things. "Did I tell you that Lady Fotherby is encouraging me to redecorate my new apartments?"

"How nice of her." Georgie held a bonnet trimmed in flowers and ribbons over Henrietta's head. "I think this would be lovely on you, and it would go with at least three of your new gowns."

She took the hat and placed it on her head. The brim stood up in a circle and was lined in pale yellow silk. A white ruffle completed the lining. The crown was fairly shallow but trimmed in blues and deep pink flowers. A narrow ribbon the same color of the lining tied under her chin. She peered into the mirror. "You have a good eye. This will look well with the gowns."

"When will Fotherby be allowed to ride again?" Dorie asked.

"Tomorrow. If he is awake, I will ask him if he would like to join us." Henrietta handed the bonnet to a clerk. "However, I do not wish to wake him."

"No, absolutely not," Dorie stated, then grinned wickedly. "He must be in good health for your wedding."

"And the wedding trip," Georgie added with her own grin.

And thank the deities they were going on a honeymoon. Henrietta had thought that she would be able to be alone with Nate, but once he started getting better, they had been seriously chaperoned. "My grandmother has arranged for a suite for us at the Pultney for our wedding night." She paid for the bonnet, and they turned toward Hatchards. "At least then we will be alone."

Dorie grasped Henrietta's arm. "Do you mean to tell me that you have not had *any* time to be together?"

"Not since he awakened." She sighed. "I had hoped. But I was no longer allowed in his chamber alone. And his mother's room is between his bedchamber and mine. I thought that was odd, and I was correct. Apparently her apartments are on the opposite side of the house, but she moved into those rooms after I brought Nate back."

"That is not helpful," Georgie muttered.

"I do not think it was meant to be," Henrietta retorted. "My parents and brothers and sister arrive the day after tomorrow. Mama and Papa will be given the rooms in which Lady Fotherby is now sleeping."

Dorie patted Henrietta's arm reassuringly. "You only have a few more days until the wedding."

"That is true." She just wished she and Nate could be together before then. She was not nervous about the ceremony but was concerned about the wedding night. It seemed as if there was so much pressure for everything to go right. If they could just make love before then, everything would be so much more enjoyable.

The next morning Henrietta woke as the sky was just lightening. Her red riding habit was already laid across a chair. She jumped out of bed and began her ablutions.

Before she was finished Spyer entered with toast and tea. "I explained to the kitchen that you like to ride early but needed some sort of sustenance before going out."

"Thank you." Henrietta cradled the tea cup in her hands before taking a sip and dressing. "Do you know if Lord Fotherby is awake?"

Her maid shook her head. "Sorry, miss. He is not."

It had been too much to expect. And they had arranged to go for a ride later in the day. "In that case, he should sleep."

"Padraig is up and waiting to go out." Spyer brushed out Henrietta's braid and twisted her hair into a knot. "If you want to take him, that is."

She and the dog had become good friends over the past week or so. The question was whether or not he would stay with her. Well, there was only one way to find out.

When she reached the hall one of the footmen she had not seen before sat by the door. "Can you tell me where Padraig is?"

The servant jumped to his feet and bowed. "Sammy's already left with him, miss."

That was that. "I will not be too long."

"Yes, miss. I was told you'd be riding this morning." He turned his head and tried to stifle a yawn.

She hoped the man would be able to go to sleep soon. Not all households had servants attend to the front door all night, but apparently this one did. She reached Lilly and the groom came around to assist her. As she walked the mare to Grosvenor Square, she reviewed the things she had to accomplish before her parents arrived the next day. High on her list of things to do was to go over the fabric samples that had been sent to her and meet with the decorator. Nate had decided he would like his rooms refurbished as well. . . . That was it! She could spirit him to the adjoining chambers. The only problem might be Lady Fotherby. Henrietta tried to recall what her future mother-in-law's schedule was for today and could not for the life of her remember. Perhaps she had not been told. She would have to ask when she returned.

Dorie and Georgie waved as they approached the turn on to Grosvenor Street, and Henrietta joined them.

Dorie rode up next to Henrietta. "You seem distracted."

She was not going to tell even her best friend what she was planning. "It is just that my parents arrive tomorrow, and I have a great deal to accomplish before then." Such as convince her soon-to-be-husband to make love to her. "I keep going over the list in my head."

"I understand," Georgie said. "My parents were in the North when Turley and I decided to wed. My grandmother and her friend arranged everything."

"I remember," Henrietta mused. "I'm glad you had Adeline to help you." Henrietta wondered if Adeline would be able to come to Town for the wedding. Henrietta had written to her but had not received an answer.

"We are here to help you," Dorie said stoutly. "Do you still plan to go to Paris for your wedding trip?"

"We do." Henrietta glanced at Georgie. "Turley said he would give us a list of places to visit."

A delighted smile dawned on Georgie's face. "He has done better than that. He has made arrangements for your stops on the way to Paris, and to stay at the same beautiful hotel we did."

Henrietta started to clap her hands together and remembered she was holding the reins. "How good of him. I'm sure Fotherby will be as thrilled as I am."

Georgie screwed up her face. "Actually, I think Fotherby asked him to do it."

"Even if he did, it was still very nice for your husband to make the plans." Henrietta was happy that he had made such good friends with her friends' husbands.

They crossed Park Street and entered the Park, with Georgie taking the lead. "What are your plans for the day?"

"I must decide on the rest of the fabric and furnishings for my apartments. They will be redone while we are gone."

"If you want any assistance, I am happy to help," Dorie said. "I had to refurbish practically all of Exeter House."

"I remember." Henrietta grinned. "I will certainly call upon you if I have difficulties."

"Go have a gallop, you two." Georgie made a shooing motion. I shall meet you by the tree."

They gave their horses their heads and flew down the carriage way onto the lawn, pulling up their mares beneath the large branches of the tree to which they always rode.

Dorie looked at Henrietta again. "I always found that Alex was extremely helpful in selecting furniture and fabrics."

She slid a glance at her friend. "Indeed? Perhaps I should ask Nate if he would like to help me."

And Henrietta had thought she was being so original in her scheme. The only thing to do now was to find a way to evade Lady Fotherby.

CHAPTER THIRTY-FOUR

Nate pushed back the bed hangings only to see the sun streaming through his window. "Bloody hell-hounds. I missed the ride."

"Did you say something, my lord?" Styles asked.

"I thought I would wake in time to join Miss Stern this morning." Nate threw his legs over the bed. At least he'd see her at breakfast, but that wasn't for another two hours. "Has she returned yet?"

"No, my lord."

He might catch her if he hurried. "I wish to dress."

"I'll call for your horse as well." Styles disappeared into the dressing room.

From the corner of his eye, Nate thought he saw his valet's lips twitch. He brushed his teeth and splashed water on his face. By the time he was done dressing, Padraig lifted his head. "You can come with me."

The Wolfhound stretched and joined him as he made his way to the hall and out the door. As he reached the Park, he saw Dorie Exeter and Henrietta with Georgie Turley on the far side of the carriage way and rode toward them.

"Nate!" Henrietta's eyes lit up like emeralds.

Reining in next to her, he greeted the other two ladies. "I was afraid I had missed you entirely."

"I am glad you did not." She smiled at him. "Although we are not here much longer."

"I thought as much." It was enough that he was with her now.

"I understand Sir Henry and Lady Stern arrive tomorrow," Dorie commented.

"So we've been told," he replied. "After that there are only a few more days until the wedding." Nate still had not asked anyone to stand up with him. He wanted to ask Merton, but considering his wife's feelings, that might not be a good idea. Perhaps he would ask Exeter or Turley.

"Henrietta told us that she is redecorating the viscountess's rooms," Georgie said.

"Are you?" Nate wondered why he had not known that.

"Yes." Henrietta nodded as they started moving again. "Your mother suggested it. The work will be accomplished while we are away." Her friends each gave her the same look, as if they wanted her to do something. "Would you like to help me choose some of the fabrics or furnishings?"

"If you wish." He didn't know how much help he could be. He barely noticed his bedchamber. But now that he thought about it, why not make a few changes? "You could help me with my room as well."

She let out a breath, and her friends had satisfied smiles on their faces. He must be missing something. They were nearing the gate when it finally hit him that if he helped her and had her help him, they might actually be alone. Nate had given up trying to be with her until after the wedding. He was getting hard just thinking about her in his bedchamber. They'd only really kissed once. He'd have to go very slowly. The other question was whether he should try to seduce her before the ceremony. That had not worked out well for John Odell and Emily. On the other hand, Nate had a special license, and a clergyman could be summoned quickly if something were to happen to him within the next few days. He glanced at Henrietta, taking in her firm jaw, slender neck, and bountiful breasts. Knowing she was beneath his roof, he'd been trying not to think about how desirable she was. His body tightened with the need to hold her and make her his.

Their little group reached the gate, and Dorie and Georgie turned left, while he and Henrietta rode straight on.

Her green eyes speared him with a searching look. "You have been quiet. Are you feeling all right?"

"Yes." God, yes. "I've just been thinking about"—this had to be believable—"your parents' arrival."

Her deep pink lips rose at the ends. "I do not think you have anything to worry about. Papa will treat you the same way he treats Merton or my older brother."

"That's what Merton said." Nate didn't think he'd mind that at all. In fact, he was looking forward to it.

But right now he wanted to be alone with Henrietta. They stopped in front of his house, and he hurried around to lift her from her horse. She breathed in sharply when his hands circled her waist. Then her eyes widened when he slowly lowered her feet to the pavement. "Do you think this would be a good time for me to see the samples?"

The pulse at the base of her throat quickened, and he hoped her thoughts were the same as his. "I think it would be an excellent time."

Holding hands, they strolled into the house and up the staircase. The corridor was quiet. The only movement was from the upstairs maid heading back downstairs. It occurred to him that he had rarely been in the vicountess's rooms. Nate couldn't even remember what they looked like. Opening the door, he waved Henrietta through to the parlor.

Drawing out a wicked-looking hat-pin, she removed the small hat from her head. "The fire has been lit. I did not think they would do that until later."

He hoped the fire in the bedroom had been lit as well. "Why later?"

"I will be selecting the fabrics and colors for the rooms." She took off the lacy cravat she wore around her neck.

"Ah." He tossed his gloves on a table and noticed fabric swatches covered the sofa and all the chairs. He'd never actually seduced a woman before. Should he look at the material first? He glanced at her for some sort of hint, but she was staring at him, her still-gloved hands clutched tightly at her waist. Henrietta was nervous. Why had he not thought of that before? Naturally this would be her first time.

Reaching out, he took her hand. "Let me help you." Slowly, he pulled off the first glove, then kissed each of her fingers, and did the same with the second hand. Henrietta came willingly into his arms and slid her hands up his chest and around his neck. "I have waited so long to do this."

Henrietta sighed as Nate's lips touched hers, and she opened for him. She had been nervous at first; then she'd seen the heat and love in his eyes and knew this was the right time. His large hands cradled her face as he slanted his head, deepening the kiss. She clung to him, absorbed in the feel of him. Threading her fingers through the soft waves of his hair, she pressed her body as close to his as possible. God, how she loved this man. Heat pooled between her legs, and she noticed she was pressed against a hard ridge. One of Nate's hands lowered, caressing her neck, her décolletage, and finally the side of her breast. Fissions of pleasure shot through her, and the place between her legs began to throb. Her breathing was so shallow, she had trouble drawing a breath.

Nothing had ever felt so good or so frustrating. "More."

"My pleasure." Nate's voice seemed deeper, almost rusty. He released the buttons on her jacket and slowly peeled it off her shoulders.

She should do her part as well. Once her spencer was off, she started to untie his cravat. "Your jacket—" He dipped his head and claimed her lips again as he shrugged off his jacket. The waistcoat was the next garment to go. He started unmooring the buttons down her back, caressing her skin as he did. Desire for him surged through her veins.

"We should move to the bedchamber," he murmured against her neck. Before she could answer, her gown dropped to the floor, and he swept her up into his arms. Seconds later he gently placed her on the ornate, multi-colored counterpane covering the bed. "That's better."

Henrietta's jaw dropped, and she shut it quickly as he pulled his shirt over his head, revealing taut skin stretched over the muscles of his chest and flat stomach. No wonder he had felt so strong. The light covering of chestnut curls seemed to exist merely to tempt her to touch him.

The ridge she had felt looked larger, and she reached for the buttons of his breeches, but he stopped her. "Let's save that for later."

Nate removed his boots and stockings before gazing at her again. She touched the laces of her short stays, but he placed his hands over hers. "Allow me. Please." The stays went the way of all clothing, and he drew her into his arms. "Tell me if you want me to stop."

Henrietta did not think she would ever want him to stop. "I will." She moved farther back onto the bed, bringing him with her. "Should I remove my shift?"

"Not yet." Nate's eyes seemed to take in every inch of her body, and heat rose from her neck to the cheeks. "You are beautiful. I can't believe how lucky I am that you're going to be with me forever."

"You are beautiful as well." She reached out, stroking his chest. "Much better than the marbles."

"A compliment indeed." His lips tilted up, but his eyes devoured her as he lowered her chemise and stroked her breasts, feathering his thumbs over her nipples. She had not known her breasts could be so sensitive. Could respond to him so easily. "I want you to enjoy this."

Henrietta shivered as he took one tightly rolled bud into his mouth, and her hips lifted as if they knew what they wanted to do. As he ministered to her other breast, the throbbing in her mons increased until it was almost painful. She was going to expire before he finished. "I don't think I can take much more."

Suddenly he cupped the place between her legs, and his fingers caressed her, one entered her sheath, and her hips rose frantically to meet him. "Let it take you, my love."

Tremors shook her body, and his mouth covered hers as she cried out. Nothing had ever felt so good, so right. But it wasn't all. She knew it wasn't all. He pulled her shift down over her hips, stood, and removed his breeches. The hard ridge sprang free. As large as it looked, Henrietta knew it would fit. But it would also hurt. Her body started to tense, as if fearing an invasion.

Nate kissed her again and concern grew in his eyes. "I will try to make this as painless as possible."

He moved over her, caressing her as he had before. Slowly her body relaxed, and the now-familiar throbbing started again. This time when her hips rose, she felt his member at her opening, rubbing that sensitive spot.

"Are you ready?" Nate groaned.

"Yes." She bit her lip to keep from crying out as he tore through her maidenhead and gasped at the pain of him stretching her. He slowly moved back and forth, giving her time to get used to him. Again her hips rose to greet him, and soon tension coiled deep within her.

"Wrap your legs around me if you can."

Henrietta did as he instructed, and he plunged into her, until she was tumbling through waves of pleasure.

Calling her name, Nate surged into her once more. For a moment she thought he would collapse on top of her, but he rolled onto his back, bringing her with him. "Are you all right?"

"I am perfect. You were perfect." She had never felt this way before, as if she could not be more in love with him. She now understood why her friends could never explain how it felt to make love to the man one loved. "It hurt a little, but that went away." She wished they could stay here for hours more, but nearby a door opened and closed. "I believe your valet is up and about."

He groaned. "We have to get you back to your chamber."

That meant she would have to dress again. Not perhaps all the way dressed. If she pulled on her gown and spencer, she could carry her hat and gloves, and her maid could get her other clothing later. "As much as I hate to move from this lovely position, I had better go now. I will need help with my gown."

358

Ella Quinn

"You're right." He lifted her from him, kissing her as he did. "If we remain here any longer, someone will find us. Stay here for a moment." He rose and went behind a screen. "Drat. I should have expected there'd be no water."

That confused her. "Why do you need water?"

"To clean both of us." He walked out from behind the screen, and she saw blood on his member.

"Oh. I had not thought about that. I will be glad when we are married." She climbed out of the bed and gathered her stays and chemise. "I'll send Spyer in to collect the other items while I bathe."

Nate took his handkerchief out of a pocket in his breeches and gently cleaned her before using it himself.

"Thank you." She had noticed she was wetter down there than before. It was his seed.

He pulled on his breeches. "It might be better if Styles gathered your garments and brought them to your maid."

That way no one would see Spyer in the corridor with the clothes. "That is a good idea."

A few minutes later Henrietta was dressed. She poked her head out of the door and, seeing no one about, rushed down the corridor to her rooms. The first thing she saw was the bathtub full of water.

The second she closed the door behind her, her maid entered the room. "Miss Henrietta, what happened to you?"

A quick glance in the mirror and she saw exactly what Spyer did. If it was not for the fact that Henrietta had no shoes and stockings, and her hair was not falling down in places, she might be able to get away with saying she fell, but that lie was not going to work now. Then again, she was going to be wed in just a few days. "I would prefer not to discuss it. It is private."

"As you wish." Spyer nodded sharply. Henrietta sat at

the toilet table and her dresser put her hair back up for her bath. "Mr. Styles said that you and his lordship had returned, so I had the water brought up."

Well, that was one person who appeared to know what had happened. He had probably heard Henrietta and Nate when he was in the other bedchamber. Henrietta fought the rising heat in her face. "Thank you." She decided it was time to change the subject. "Lord Fotherby and I have decided to go to Paris for our wedding trip. We will leave the day following our marriage."

"Oh, my lady!" Her dresser smiled broadly. "That is excellent. If you like, I will show you the best places to shop." Spyer tapped her cheek. "I had better look at what you will need."

That would take her mind off Henrietta's appearance. The next time. If there was a next time before her wedding, she would take down her hair.

Nate held his breath as Henrietta rushed to her rooms. He'd hated to let her go. All he had wanted to do was hold her forever. It hadn't occurred to him that being with her would be so unlike anything else he had ever experienced. Seeing her respond to him, feeling her body accept him, knowing she was his forever. The difference had to be that he loved her, and she loved him. Nate had never had a woman love him before.

He went back into the bedchamber, took out his handkerchief again, and dabbed at the spot of blood. Fortunately, the counterpane contained myriad dark colors, including red, and the spot didn't show very much. He might have to have his valet clean it. He looked at the crumpled cloth in his hand. At least Styles wouldn't make a fuss about it.

Using the door between the rooms, Nate entered his bedchamber. The full bath was already in front of the fireplace, and his valet was laying out his clothing. "Some of my betrothed's garments are in the viscountess's chamber. They will need to be given to her dresser."

"I shall see to it, my lord. Is there anything else?"

He opened his hand. "This must be taken care of."

Styles's expression didn't change at all. "Indeed, my lord. I shall take care of that as well."

Nate glanced at the clock. It was still early, but he was hungry, and he knew Henrietta would be as well. "Send a message to Cook that I will be down within the hour to break my fast."

"Do you wish to have breakfast served earlier from now on?" Styles asked

Nate stepped into the tub. That would be a good idea, except for Henrietta's family arriving. His beloved rose early enough. "Tomorrow I do. After that Miss Stern's parents arrive. I do not know if they are early risers or not."

His valet nodded. "I have it ordered for tomorrow for you and Miss Stern."

"Thank you." It would be nice to have breakfast with only his betrothed.

Just under an hour later, Nate knocked softly on her door. Her dresser opened it and stood aside. "Miss, his lordship is here."

She placed the book she was reading on the table next to her. When she rose he caught his breath. The pale pink gown she wore matched the color in her cheeks. How was it that every time he saw her she was more beautiful? "Has something happened?"

"Not at all." He held out his hand to her. "I ordered

breakfast for us. I am hungry, and I thought you might be as well."

Her smile almost brought him to his knees. "That was an excellent idea. Let us go break our fast."

As if by mutual consent, they refrained from speaking until they had reached the first landing. "I sent instructions for Cook to have breakfast ready tomorrow morning at about this time as well. What I do not know is whether your family are early risers."

Henrietta patted his arm consolingly. "They are. But we have today and tomorrow."

And, after they wed, the rest of their lives.

CHAPTER THIRTY-FIVE

The next morning, Henrietta and Nate had been able to sneak into her future rooms and make love again. What she had not expected was that her dresser and his valet would be ready to attend to them as soon as they were finished.

Her parents arrived shortly before luncheon. After greeting them she motioned to Nate, who was standing by the stairs as if he was unsure about coming forward.

"Mama, Papa, I would like to introduce Viscount Fotherby to you. Nate, my parents, Sir Henry and Lady Stern."

Nate stepped over to them and bowed to Mama before offering his hand to Papa. Henrietta held her breath until her father not only clasped Nate's hand, but drew him into a hug. "So you're to be my new son."

"Yes, sir."

"Welcome to the family." Her father beamed. "We trust you will make Henrietta happy."

"I shall do my very best." She thought she saw a shine in his eyes as he put his arms around her father.

Mama took out a handkerchief and blew her nose. "Yes, indeed. Welcome."

"Thank you, sir, ma'am." Nate's voice seemed to catch. "I am honored to be a part of the Stern family."

"Is someone going to introduce us?" Stephen, her younger brother, who was fifteen, said.

Martha, their nine-year-old younger sister, tugged Henrietta's hand and pulled her down. "He is very handsome."

"I think so too. Let me introduce you." She turned to Nate, who directed his attention to the children. "Martha, may I present my betrothed, Lord Fotherby. Nate, my youngest sister, Miss Martha Stern."

Her sister performed a very creditable curtsey and held out her hand. "It is very nice to meet you, my lord."

He took her hand and bowed. "It is my great pleasure to meet you. Please call me Nate."

When her sister smiled and looked up to her, she nodded. "You may call me Martha."

"Well done," Henrietta whispered to her sister. "Now we have Mr. Stephen Stern, my youngest brother. Stephen, Lord Fotherby."

Nate held out his hand and grasped the one Stephen offered. "Very pleased to meet you."

"I'm glad to meet you too, sir. I understand you live not far from us."

"About a half a day's travel," Nate confirmed.

"Good, good," Papa said. "We'll be able to see you and Henrietta more often."

The only one who was not here was her older brother. "When will Henry arrive?"

"We expect him this afternoon," her father said. He glanced at Nate. "Henry is a barrister in Bristol. I suspect he will decide to run for the Commons within the next few years."

Just then, Nate's mother and her grandmother entered the hall, prompting more greetings and introductions.

"Well, then," Lady Fotherby said. "Mrs. Garford will show you to your rooms, and we will meet in the breakfast room for luncheon."

When everyone else had gone upstairs Henrietta took Nate's hand, led him to the morning room, and wrapped her arms around him. "I would like a kiss."

He dipped his head and drew her closer to him. At first he feathered kisses across her lips, then his mouth claimed hers. Stroking her tongue with hers, she rose on her tiptoes to deepen the kiss as he stroked her breasts, sending flames through her body.

He moved them back toward the daybed, when suddenly Martha said, "I wonder if they are in here."

"We may as well have a look. They aren't anywhere else," Stephen retorted.

Nate dropped his hands and Henrietta stepped over to the large windows overlooking the garden. "Are you ready for luncheon?"

Pushing through the door together, her brother and sister both nodded.

"In that case." Nate reached for her. "Let's go to the breakfast room. We are informal today."

Martha took Henrietta's hand while Stephen walked with Nate.

"I heard you have a Trakehner," her brother said.

"I do indeed. His name is Darragh." She could hear the smile in his voice. "Would you like to see him after luncheon?"

"Wouldn't I just," Stephen said eagerly. "My older brother wanted one but didn't want to give up his first horse."

"Understandable."

They reached the breakfast room to find the rest of their families were coming down the corridor.

Once they had finished eating Lady Fotherby cleared her throat. "As this is Lent and there will be no betrothal ball, the duchess and I decided a dinner would be in order. It will be small, only family and close friends." She smiled at Henrietta. "I am pleased to say that everyone has accepted their invitations. It will be here tomorrow evening."

She exchanged a glance with Nate, who imperceptibly shook his head. Neither Dorie nor Georgie had mentioned it this morning. Was it to have been a surprise?

"That reminds me of something." Nate stood. "Stephen, I'll have a groom take you to see Darragh. There is something I must show Henrietta before this goes any farther."

What in God's name did that mean? She had already seen everything in the house. Placing her serviette on the table, she rose. "Lead away."

"Henrietta," Mama said. "Perhaps after you and Nate have finished you will show me the colors you have selected for your apartments."

"Yes, of course. I'll send for you." She clasped Nate's hand. "Will I like it?"

"I hope so. It's too late to have anything else made."

Nate had had one ring sized for her. It had come back yesterday, but with everything else going on, he'd forgotten about it. They entered his study, and he motioned for her to sit on the sofa in front of the fireplace. "I'll be just a moment." Going to his desk, he pulled out a key and opened the second drawer. His valet would put the other rings back in the safe when he was done. The rings had been set in a tray lined with velvet that he took to the low table between the sofa and two chairs. He picked up one. It was set in a plain white gold band with a ruby in the middle and diamonds on either side of it. "This is the ring I thought you would like the best." He held his breath as he slipped it on her finger. "Well?"

Henrietta briefly looked over the other rings, then back to the one on her hand. "I do like this one the best."

He took her into his arms. "Thank you."

Her smile was everything he could have asked for. "Thank you for knowing me so well."

"Perhaps we should come back later?" Nate looked toward the door to see Merton and his wife standing there. "I do apologize. I told your butler not to announce us."

"No, it's fine. I was just showing Henrietta her wedding ring." He glanced at his betrothed, frozen at his side. "Please come in. I'm sure Hulatt will have tea brought in shortly." He waved them to the two chairs opposite the sofa. Once they were seated he and Henrietta sat as well. She reached the short distance across the cushion and wound her fingers through his. When the tea tray was brought she poured, and he handed the cups around. He took a sip. "This is an unexpected visit."

"Yes," Lady Merton said tightly. She took a drink of tea.

Henrietta's hand gipped his with a strength he didn't know she had. "Dotty, why have you come?"

Lady Merton stared directly at her sister. "To ask you to forgive me and to make my peace with your soon-to-be-husband." She glanced at Nate. "I saw you rescue a child the other day. Dom was right. I would not have recognized you if it had not been for your dog. It was not until then that *I* knew you had changed."

He was right. It had been her.

"And to give you some interesting news," Merton added, as if he would change the subject.

She spoke again. "I was wrong to attempt to make you

do something I refused to do. Give up the gentleman you love." Lady Merton bit her lip and looked at Nate. "I had what I can only call a delayed reaction to the abduction." He started to apologize, but she waved her hand, cutting him off. "Please allow me to speak. As I have been reminded more than once, I wholeheartedly believe that a person can change, I made the decision to allow you the opportunity."

"Without being sent to the Antipodes," Merton commented dryly."

"I was wrong to dismiss your change out of hand. I must ask your forgiveness for that."

A lump formed in Nate's throat, but he had to speak. "I am so very glad you did give me a chance to redeem myself. To discover how gratifying it is to help others without expecting anything in return." He took a breath. "I hope someday you find it in your heart to forgive me for being such an abject scoundrel."

The corners of Lady Merton's lips tipped up. "I already have." She turned toward Henrietta. "It finally dawned on me that you are a woman with a great deal of sense, and that you could never love a man who was in any way cruel. I hope you can forgive me."

She almost flew to her sister and, taking Lady Merton's hands, knelt next to her. "I will always love you. You are my sister. We are Sterns."

Tears filled her ladyship's eyes and spilled over. "And Sterns stick together."

Henrietta nodded. "Like glue."

He'd never heard that saying before, but he liked it. He glanced at Merton, who mouthed, *Their father*.

"I don't know about the rest of you," Merton drawled. "But I believe this calls for champagne."

Nate grinned at his old friend. "I agree." He walked over to the bell-pull and tugged, and the door immediately opened. How the devil had Hulatt made it there so quickly?

"My lord." He bowed.

"Champagne."

"At once, my lord. I thought you might wish some." He clapped his hands, and three footmen entered with champagne, glasses, and small tarts.

Henrietta raised one black brow and he shrugged.

"I wish my butler was as well trained as yours," Merton grumbled.

The rest of them laughed. "I believe"—Lady Merton accepted a glass of champagne from Hulatt—"that Worthington had it right when he said we get the butlers we need."

Once they each had a glass of champagne, Hulatt bowed to her. "Thank you, my lady."

Henrietta moved her sister to the sofa, and dark heads together, they spoke in hushed tones. Nate found Merton at his side. "I would like to ask you to stand up with me."

He raised his glass. "I hoped you would ask."

"You said you have news." Nate took a sip of the wine. "I trust it is good."

"Thea, can you come here, my love?"

"Of course." She stood next to her husband and Henrietta stood next to him.

"It was confirmed earlier today." Merton raised his wife's fingers to his lips. "We are having twins."

Nate caught Henrietta's glass before it fell. "Is that why you are—"

"So big?" Her ladyship laughed. "It is. However, it is also the reason I have been so short-tempered and difficult.

I visited Grace. She was the one who first thought of it. I saw her mid-wife today."

"We will depart for the country a day or two after your wedding," Merton added.

"I am so happy for you." Henrietta hugged her sister. "Twins. I cannot believe it. I have never heard that we have twins in our family."

"It was a shock to hear it." Her ladyship's eyes widened as she shook her head. "Apparently twins can happen at any time to anyone. I had no idea."

"That is good to know." Henrietta's hand went to her stomach, then she quickly snatched her glass of champagne out of Nate's hand and took a drink.

Merton coughed. "There is something to be said for short engagements, is that not right, my love?"

His wife grinned up at him. "Indeed there is."

Henrietta glanced between the two of them and tilted her head slightly. "When will you tell the rest of the family?"

"This evening at dinner. Our grandmother requested we be there." Lady Merton glanced at Nate. "I suppose you should call me Dotty. Everyone but by husband does."

He inclined his head. "Thank you. Please call me Nate." His friend looked at him in surprise and he grinned. "I have grown used to it."

"If you have time," Henrietta said to her sister, "I shall show you the colors I have selected for my rooms."

"I would love to see them."

He kissed her cheek. "We'll come back down later."

Linking arms, they went out of his study, chatting.

Merton raised his glass. "Welcome to the family."

* * *

"I think we should all congratulate ourselves on a successful match." Catherine Fotherby said as she raised a glass of champagne.

"I agree," the duchess and Cordelia Stern said at the same time, raising their glasses as well.

"I do not mind telling you, I was a little concerned for Henrietta," Cordelia took a drink of wine. "It was not that we would have pushed her into marriage; she was just not interested in any of the gentlemen she had met." She sighed. "She had a list of requirements a future husband must meet."

"And none of them did," the duchess agreed. "That was when I thought of Fotherby. The problem was getting them together."

"Yes, that worked out more fortuitously than I ever could have imagined," Cordelia agreed.

Catherine had been sipping her wine. "It was pure serendipity. Although I do wish you would have included me in your scheme. When he told me of meeting a lady, and I worked out that it was probably Henrietta"—Catherine took another drink of wine—"It was a bad moment."

"Fate." The duchess nodded. "We could not have done a better job ourselves."

"As I recall"—Cordelia glanced at her mother—"you had rejected one idea after another. Yet the way it happened, they both knew almost instantly the other's best points."

"Yes." Catherine had been so worried it would come to nothing, and her son's heart would be broken. "I was scared to death that their chance meeting would not work out."

"She wrote to me immediately, asking me to come directly to Town." The duchess chuckled. "I thought something had gone horribly wrong."

"It would have been more helpful if you had told me when you first got your idea about the two of them," Catherine repeated.

"I am sorry about that." Her old friend gave her a regretful look. "I should have done so. If I had had any idea they would meet accidently, I would have. I had been sharing your letters with Cordelia, and she agreed Fotherby had turned into the perfect gentleman for Harriett."

Cordelia glanced at Catherine. "What will you do now? Is there a Dower House? Where will you stay when you come to Town, or will you?"

This was always the problem when one's eldest son, the heir married. "Your mother and I have decided to go traveling. I have never been to the Continent. I'll make more decisions when we return."

"Yes." The duchess reached over and patted Catherine's arm. "We will not go too far afield for a while. You will want to be there for the birth of your first grandchild."

"I will indeed. I hope they get around to it soon."

Cordelia laughed. "If they have not already."

Catherine's jaw dropped. "They would not have. They cannot have. I have been very careful."

The other woman just grinned. "Where there is a will, there is a way. I have a feeling there was a lot of will on both their sides."

She sat back in her chair and poured another glass of champagne. "Well, I am certainly not going to ask."

Cordelia and her mother went into peals of laughter.

CHAPTER THIRTY-SIX

The three days after Henrietta's parents had arrived were frantic. Final fittings had to be done, they had borrowed luggage from Dorie and Alex because it was too late to order their own. Fortunately Henrietta had been correct that Alex and Nate had worked out the details of the wedding trip. As far as she was concerned, the dinner with family and friends was better than any ball could have been. Best of all was that Nate had been accepted by everyone.

Now, today, she was to marry the gentleman of her dreams.

She was awake before Spyer had entered the room with tea, toast, and a baked egg. "I thought you might need something more substantial this morning." She hummed as she brought out the gown Henrietta would wear for her wedding.

She held up her teacup. "You are happy this morning."

"Of course I am, miss." Her dresser blushed. "You will soon be Lady Fotherby and we will be on our way to Paris."

Hmm. Somehow she did not think that was all of it. "I do hope you and Styles are getting along well. After all, you will be in fairly close quarters for the next month or more."

Her dresser turned away, but not before she saw the color in the woman's cheeks deepen. "That will be no problem at all. He is a very nice man."

So that was the way the wind was blowing. "I'm so glad you think so. I agree. He is a very nice man."

Spyer was dressing Henrietta's hair when her mother, grandmother, Lady Fotherby, Dorie, Georgie, and Adeline strolled in, followed by Martha.

"Adeline! You did not even tell me you were coming." Henrietta tried to jump up, but her maid's hand was firmly on her shoulder, holding her down.

"I would not have missed it." Her friend came over and pecked her cheek. "I finally told Fritz that I was going even if he was not."

He did not want to see her wed? "Why didn't he want to come?"

"Do you remember Gertrude, the cow I told you about?" Henrietta nodded. "She is getting ready to give birth. Ergo, we are here for your wedding and traveling directly back."

Dorie clapped her hands. "Henrietta, we had to coordinate how we would do this." Her friend smiled at Martha. "We will begin with you."

Martha stepped up to Henrietta and handed her a light-blue handkerchief embroidered with bluebells. "I made this for you. It is blue."

Tears started pricking her eyes. How she was to get through this without crying, she had no idea. "Thank you, sweetie."

Dorie, Adeline, and Georgie took Martha's place. Dorie

held out a long box. "Unfortunately, the something old cannot be *your* combs. This is new."

Henrietta gave a watery chuckle and took the box. "I suppose not." In the box lay three combs made of white gold and pearls. "Thank you so very much."

Her mother was next. "Your friends could not give you something old. Therefore, your grandmother and I decided we would do that part." Mama put a large rectangular box on the toilet table. "This has been in our family for years."

Henrietta knew it was some sort of necklace, but what would it look like? She opened the box. A plain chain of white gold held one large ruby at the end of it. Below the necklace were matching earrings. "This is so much like my ring."

"That is what we thought," her grandmother said. "I knew at once it should be yours."

"This is not part of any tradition," Lady Fotherby said. "However, this bracelet belongs to the parure that matches your ring. Fortunately none of the jewels are part of the estate. It was waiting for you." Henrietta's grandmother cleared her throat. "You may borrow it for now," Lady Fotherby said hastily."

Chuckling, Henrietta dabbed her eyes. "Thank you."

"No need." Dotty hurried into the room. "I am sorry I am late. She handed Henrietta a pearl bracelet. "This is something borrowed."

She hugged her sister. "Thank you."

"Come along now or we will be late," Dorie said. "And Henrietta, no crying." Mimicking what she used to say.

"Yes, ma'am."

They arrived in the hall to her father, waiting patiently. "Which one of these ladies is standing up for you?"

"I am, sir." Dorie moved beside Henrietta.

He held out both of his arms and grinned. "It's time to go to church. Your young man is probably on tenterhooks."

"There is no reason for him to be. I am not late."

"Neither was your sister." Her father's eyes sparkled with mirth. "But Merton was fit to be tied."

"Nate will be fine." He knew she would soon be his wife.

Nate reached up to grab his cravat, and for the third time Merton slapped his hand away. "Leave it alone. You'll mangle the thing, and we don't have time to get you another one."

"I'm more nervous than I thought I'd be." Nate rubbed a hand down his trousers. "I don't understand why we just couldn't come here together."

"I understand the feeling, but this is what her family wants." Merton stilled, as if remembering something. "It will all be worth it when you see your bride at the door."

Henrietta's brothers, sisters, mother, grandmother, and his mother arrived. That was progress. He'd known the ladies had something to give his betrothed before coming here. "It won't be long now."

The next to enter were Georgie and Turley, and a couple he hadn't met. He glanced around the chapel. "Where is she?"

"There." His friend pointed toward the side door.

Lord, she was beautiful. Her deep pink gown was covered by silver netting and sparkled as she walked toward him. The ruby she wore on a silver chain stopped just above her breasts. Damn! He was going to fantasize about tasting her breasts until they could be alone. Silver slippers adorned her small feet and she carried a posy of red and white roses with greenery. "She is exquisite."

"She is," Merton murmured, but he was looking at his wife.

Finally, she was next to Nate, and he took her hand.

"Not yet, my boy." Sir Henry laughed. "I'll give her to you when the vicar says it's time."

That was when Nate saw the young-looking vicar standing in front of them. "If you are ready, we will begin."

"Yes, please," he and Henrietta said at the same time.

His almost-father-in-law handed her to him when the vicar asked who would give her to him. Gazing into each other's eyes, they said their vows in strong, firm tones. Finally they were pronounced man and wife and signed the register. After that, pandemonium broke loose. Everyone had to hug both of them. He was introduced to Adeline and Fritz Littleton, a pair Nate had heard a great deal about.

When he led her outside his carriage had been decorated with pots and pans and flowers and ribbons. So much for sneaking back to his—their house. "Who did this?"

His three newest friends looked over his shoulder and grinned.

Henrietta—his wife—pulled him toward the gaudy coach. "If we do not go, my grandmother will lecture us."

"I suppose we don't want that."

"No. We do not."

"In that case, come, wife."

"Husband." She smiled up at him. "I am so happy we are married."

Ouse Tower
Nine months later

"Push now, my lady." The mid-wife looked beneath Henrietta's shift again. "I can see a head."

She squeezed Nate's hand and pushed as hard as she could. After talking with Turley, Littleton, Exeter, and Merton, Nate had planted himself in her room and refused to move. When his old nurse asked what he thought he could do, he said he'd be there for Henrietta. "Did that do it?"

An indignant squall was her answer. "Boy or girl?"

"It's a boy." The mid-wife handed her baby to Nurse. "Once more. We need to get the afterbirth out."

Again Henrietta pushed with all her might. She knew how dangerous even a piece of the afterbirth could be.

"Excellent, my lady." The mid-wife beamed. "I don't think I'll have any trouble making sure it's all there."

Her dresser wiped her forehead and cleaned the rest of her. Nate lifted her up, and new linens were put on the bed. As soon as she was in a new chemise, she held out her arms. "I want my son."

Taking the babe from Nurse, Nate handed him to her. "Have we decided on a name?"

They had both thought the baby would be a girl. "Henry after my father, Robert after yours, and Edward for your mother's father?"

"That makes three Henrys when we're with your family, and when your brother marries and has a son he is likely to be Henry as well. What about Edward Henry Robert?"

She scrunched her face. "I know you were not close to your father, but Robert Edward Henry sounds better."

"Perhaps it will remind me not to treat my sons differently because of their birth order." He leaned over and kissed her before stroking the baby's head. "Very well, Robert Edward Henry Meadows it is." He got to his feet. "I'd better go tell your father, our mothers, and your grandmother."

"He's still sleepy." She handed him little Robert. "Show them the baby, but bring him back right away. He'll want to nurse."

"I'll give them just a quick look." Nate grinned. "I love you."

"I love you too."

AUTHOR'S NOTES

Formal adoption did not exist until much later. But people did talk about adopting children or minors, bringing them into their homes and changing their names. It happened to one of Jane Austen's brothers. If an estate was not encumbered and could pass to anyone the testator wished, the adoptee could inherit. Naturally they could not inherit titles or any encumbered property.

Géricault was a real French painter whose major work was of a shipwreck and was indeed shown at the Paris Salon.

Slavery became illegal in England in 1807 and any slave who landed on the island was automatically free. Yet it was not until 1833, with the Slave Abolition Act that slavery was abolished in all of Britain's colonies. Under the act, the government agreed to pay slave owners the sum of twenty thousand pounds. That's the equivalent to approximately sixteen billion pounds today. At the time it was fully 40 percent of the treasury's annual income. The last payment was made in 2019.

It is true that it was rare to find a medical-school-trained physician in the country. When someone was ill or injured most people called on a surgeon, who also acted as the local barber or apothecary. Many households had handwritten journals of remedies for different maladies.

Richmond Park was a day trip for Londoners. Even

though it was not that far from Town, it was too far for a nice ride there. Additionally, one had to take a main road, and it was not proper for ladies to ride horses on main roads.

The baby carriage as we know it was an American invention that dates to 1825. The first mention of one in England was in 1887. By 1903 the baby carriage was jokingly referred to as a perambulator, or pram.

Porter was an English drink much like stout. It was considered a health drink for pregnant women.

I hope you enjoyed Henrietta and Nate's story! The next three books will be about Alice, Eleanor, and Madeline.

If you haven't already, please meet up with me on The Worthingtons Facebook group, on Instagram @ellaquinn-author, on my Facebook page EllaQuinnAuthor, and sign up for my newsletter at www.ellaquinnauthor.com.

I look forward to hearing from you!

Ella